Maya Banks has loved romance novels from a very (very) early age and, almost from the start, she dreamed of writing them as well. In her teens, she filled countless notebooks with over-dramatic stories of love and passion. Today her stories are only slightly less dramatic, but no less romantic.

She lives in Texas with her husband and three children and wouldn't contemplate living anywhere other than the South. When she's not writing, she's usually hunting, fishing or playing poker. She loves to hear from readers and she can be found online at either www.mayabanks. com or www.writemindedblog.com, or you can e-mail her at maya@mayabanks.com.

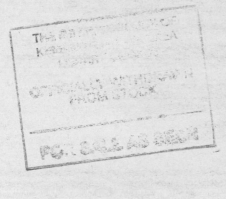

THE TYCOON'S PREGNANT MISTRESS

BY
MAYA BANKS

To Marty Matthews and Shara Cooper. That bar conversation at RT 2007 was the first kick in the behind to do something about my long-standing dream of writing for Desire™. I still remember that gush-fest fondly.

To Roberta, for saying, "Let's do it" when I outlined my career goals in the summer of 2007. Hey, we did it!

To Amy: You of all people know how much I love category and just how excited I was to be given a chance to write it. Thanks for being just as thrilled as I was.

To Dee, who I think wanted this for me as much as I did and was with me every step of the way. Thank you!

And finally to Steph, who started it all for me. Without you, I wouldn't have written *The Tycoon's Pregnant Mistress* and I wouldn't have submitted. It was that phone call that started everything in motion. I'll always love you for that.

One

Pregnant.

Despite the warmth of the summer day, an uncomfortable chill settled over Marley Jameson's skin as she settled on the bench in the small garden just a few blocks from the apartment she shared with Chrysander Anetakis.

She shivered even as the sun's rays found her tightly clenched fingers, the heat not yet chasing away the goose bumps. Stavros wouldn't be happy over her brief disappearance. Neither would Chrysander when Stavros reported that she hadn't taken proper security measures. But dragging along the imposing guard to her doctor's appointment hadn't been an option. Chrysander would have known of her pregnancy before she could even return home to tell him herself.

How would he react to the news? Despite the fact they'd taken precautions, she was eight weeks pregnant. The best she could surmise, it had happened when he'd returned from an extended business trip overseas. Chrysander had been insatiable. But then so had she.

A bright blush chased the chill from her cheeks as she remembered the night in question. He had made love to her countless times, murmuring to her in Greek—warm, soft words that had made her heart twist.

She checked her watch and grimaced. He was due home in a few short hours, and yet here she sat like a coward, avoiding the confrontation. She still had to change out of the faded jeans and T-shirt, clothes she wore only when he was away.

With reluctance born of uncertainty, she forced herself to her feet and began the short walk to the luxurious building that housed Chrysander's apartment.

"You're being silly," she muttered under her breath as she neared the entry. If the doorman was surprised to see her on foot, he didn't show it, though he did hasten to usher her inside.

She stepped onto the lift and smoothed a hand over her still-flat stomach. Nervousness scuttled through her chest as she rode higher. When it halted smoothly and the doors opened into the spacious foyer of the penthouse, Marley nibbled on her lip and left the elevator.

She walked into the living room, shedding her shoes as she made her way to the couch, where she tossed her bag down. Fatigue niggled at her muscles, and all she really wanted to do was lie down. But she had to determine how to broach the subject of their relationship with Chrysander.

A few days ago, she would have said she was perfectly content, but the results of today's blood tests had her shaken. Had her reflecting on the last six months with Chrysander.

She loved him wholeheartedly, but she wasn't entirely sure where she stood with him. He seemed devoted when he was with her. The sex was fantastic. But now she had a baby to think about. She needed more from the man she loved than hot sex every few weeks as his schedule permitted.

She trudged into the large master suite and started when Chrysander walked from the bathroom, just a towel wrapped around his waist.

A slow smile carved his handsome face. Every time she laid

eyes on him, it was like the first time all over again. Goose bumps raced across her skin, lighting fire to her every nerve-ending.

"Y-you're early," she managed to get out.

"I've been waiting for you, *pedhaki mou,*" he said huskily.

He let the towel drop, and she swallowed as her eyes tracked downward to his straining erection. He paced forward predatorily, closing rapidly in on her. His hands curved over her shoulders, and he bent to ravage her mouth.

A soft moan escaped her as her knees buckled. He was an addiction. One she could never get enough of. He had only to touch her, and she went up in flames.

His mouth traveled down her jawline to her neck, his fingers tugging impatiently at her shirt. Of their own accord, her fingers twisted in his dark hair, pulling him closer.

Hard, lean, muscled. A gleaming predator. He moved gracefully, masterfully playing her body like a finely tuned instrument.

She clutched at his neck as he lowered her to the bed.

"You have entirely too many clothes on," he murmured as he shoved her shirt up and over her head.

She knew they should stop. They needed to talk, but she'd missed him. Ached for him. And maybe a part of her wanted this moment before things changed irrevocably.

He released her bra, and she gasped when his fingers found her highly sensitized nipples. They were darker now, and she wondered if he'd notice.

"Did you miss me?"

"You know I did," she said breathlessly.

"I like to hear you say it."

"I missed you," she said, a smile curving her lips.

It shouldn't have surprised her that he made quick work of her clothing. He tossed her jeans across the room. Her bra went one way, her underwear the other. Then he was over her, on her, deep inside her.

She arched into him as he possessed her, clinging to him as he made love to her, their passion hot and aching. It was always like this. One step from desperation, their need for each other all consuming.

As he gathered her in his arms, he whispered to her in Greek. The words fell against her skin like a caress as they both reached their peaks. She snuggled into his body, content and sated.

She must have slept then, because when she opened her eyes, Chrysander was lying beside her, his arm thrown possessively over her hip. He regarded her lazily, his golden eyes burning with sated contentment.

Now was the time. She needed to broach the subject. There would never be a better occasion. Why did the thought of asking him about their relationship strike terror in her heart?

"Chrysander," she began softly.

"What is it?" he asked, his eyes narrowing. Had he heard the worry in her voice?

"I wanted to talk to you."

He stretched his big body and pulled slightly away so he could see her better. The sheet slid down to his hip and gathered there. She felt vulnerable and exposed and trembled when he slid his hand over the peak of one breast.

"What is it you want to talk about?"

"Us," she said simply.

His eyes grew wary and then became shuttered. His face locked into a mask of indifference, one that frightened her. She could feel him pulling away, mentally withdrawing from her.

A buzz sounded, startling her. Chrysander cursed under his breath and reached over to push the intercom.

"What," he demanded tersely.

"It's Roslyn. Can I come up?"

Marley stiffened at the sound of his personal assistant's voice. It was late in the evening and yet here she was, popping into the apartment she knew he shared with Marley.

"I'm very busy at the moment, Roslyn. Surely it can wait until I come into the office tomorrow."

"I'm sorry, sir, but it can't. I need your signature on a contract that's due by 7:00 a.m."

Again Chrysander swore. "Come then."

He swung his legs over the side of the bed and stood. He strode toward the polished mahogany wardrobe and pulled out slacks and a shirt.

"Why does she show up here so often?" Marley asked quietly.

Chrysander shot her a look of surprise. "She's my assistant. It's her job to keep up with me."

"At your personal residence?"

He shook his head as he buttoned up his shirt. "I'll return in a moment, and we can have our talk."

Marley watched him go, her chest aching all the more. She was tempted to save the discussion for another night, but she had to tell him of her pregnancy, and she couldn't tell him of the baby before she knew how he felt about her. What he thought of their future. So it had to be done tonight.

As the moments grew longer, her anxiety heightened. Not wanting the disadvantage of being nude, she rose from the bed and dragged on her jeans and shirt. So much for looking composed and beautiful. She shook her head ruefully.

Finally she heard his footsteps outside the bedroom suite. He walked in with a distracted frown on his face. His gaze flickered over her, and his lips twitched.

"I much prefer you naked, *pedhaki mou.*"

She gave a shaky smile and moved back to the bed. "Is everything all right with work?"

He waved his hand dismissively. "Nothing that shouldn't have already been taken care of. A missing signature." He stalked toward the bed, a lean, hungry glint in his eyes. As he came to a stop a foot away from where she sat, he reached for the buttons on his shirt.

"Chrysander…we must talk."

Annoyance flickered across his face, but then he gave a resigned sigh. He sank down on the bed next to her. "Then speak, Marley. What is it that's bothering you?"

His closeness nearly unhinged her. She scooted down the bed in an effort to put distance between them. "I want to know how you feel about me, how you feel about us," she began nervously. "And if we have a future."

She glanced up to check his reaction. His lips came together in a firm line as he stared back at her. "So it's come to this," he said grimly.

He stood and turned his back to her before finally rotating around to face her.

"Come to w-what? I just need to know how you feel about me. If we have a future. You never speak of us in anything but the present," she finished lamely.

He leaned in close to her and cupped her chin. "We don't have a relationship. I don't do relationships, and you know this. You're my mistress."

Why did she feel as though he'd just slapped her? Her mouth fell open against his hand, and she stared up at him with wide, shocked eyes.

"Mistress?" she croaked. Live-in lover. Girlfriend. Woman he was seeing. These were all terms she might have used. But mistress? A woman he bought? A woman he paid to have sex with?

Nausea welled in her stomach.

She pushed his hand away and stumbled up, backpedaling away from him. Confusion shone on Chrysander's face.

"Is that truly all I am to you?" she choked out, still unable to comprehend his declaration. "A m-mistress?"

He sighed impatiently. "You're distraught. Sit down and let me get you something to drink. I've had a trying week, and you are obviously unwell. It benefits neither of us to have this discussion right now."

Chrysander urged her back to the bed then strode out of the suite toward the kitchen. After a long week of laying traps for the person attempting to sell his company out from under him, the last thing he wanted was a hysterical confrontation with his mistress.

He poured a glass of Marley's favorite juice then prepared himself a liberal dose of brandy. The beginnings of a headache were already plaguing him.

He smiled when he saw Marley's shoes in the middle of the

floor where she'd left them as soon as she'd come off the elevator. He followed the trail of her things to the couch where her bag was thrown haphazardly.

She was a creature of comfort. Never fussy. So this emotional outburst had caught him off guard. It was completely out of character for her. She wasn't clingy, which is why their relationship had lasted so long. Relationship? He'd just denied to her that they had one. She was his mistress.

He should have softened his response. She probably wasn't feeling well and needed tenderness from him. He winced at the idea, but she'd always been there ready to soothe him after weeks of business trips or tedious meetings. It was only fair that he offer something more than sex. Though sex with her was high on his list of priorities.

He turned to go back into the bedroom and try to make amends when the piece of paper sticking out of Marley's bag caught his eye. He stopped and frowned then set the drinks down on the coffee table.

Dread tightened his chest. It couldn't be.

He reached out to snag the papers, yanked them open as anger, hot and volatile, surged in his veins. Marley, *his* Marley, was the traitor within his company?

He wanted to deny it. Wanted to crumple the evidence and throw it away. But it was there, staring him in the face. The false information he'd planted just this morning in hopes of finding the person selling his secrets to his competitor had been taken by Marley. She hadn't wasted any time.

Suddenly everything became clear. His building plans had started disappearing about the time that Marley had moved in to the penthouse. She'd worked for his company, and even after he'd convinced her to quit so that her time would be his alone, she still had unimpeded access to his offices. What a fool he'd been.

Stavros's call to him hours earlier stuck in his mind like a dagger. At the time, it had only registered a mild annoyance with him, a matter he'd planned to take up with Marley when he saw her. He'd lecture her about being careless, about being safe, when in fact, it was him who wasn't safe with her. She'd gone to his office then disappeared for several hours. And now documents from his office had appeared in her purse.

The papers fisted in his hand, he stalked back to the bedroom to see Marley still sitting on the bed. She turned her tear-stained face up to him, and all he could see was how deftly she'd manipulated him.

"I want you out in thirty minutes," he said flatly.

Marley stared at him in shock. Had she heard him correctly? "I don't understand," she choked out.

"You have thirty minutes in which to collect your things before I call security to escort you out."

She shot to her feet. How could things have gone so wrong? She hadn't even told him about her pregnancy yet. "Chrysander, what's wrong? Why are you so angry with me? Is it because I reacted so badly to you calling me your mistress? It came as a great shock to me. I thought somehow I meant more to you than that."

"You now have twenty-eight minutes," he said coldly. He held up a hand with several crumpled sheets of paper in them. "How did you think you'd get away with it, Marley? Do you honestly think I would tolerate you betraying me? I have no tolerance for cheats or liars, and you, my dear, are both."

All the blood left her face. She wavered precariously, but he made no move to aid her. "I don't know what you're talking about. What are those papers?"

His lips curled into a contemptuous sneer. "You stole from me. You're lucky that I'm not phoning the authorities. As it is, if I ever see you again, I'll do just that. Your attempts could have crippled my company. But the joke is on you. These are fakes planted by me in an attempt to ferret out the culprit."

"Stole?" Her voice rose in agitation. She reached out and yanked the papers from his hand. The words, schematics, blurred before her eyes. An internal e-mail, printed out, obviously from his company ISP address, stared back at her. Sensitive information. Detailed building plans for an upcoming bid in a major international city. Photocopies of the drawings. None of it made sense.

She raised her head and stared him in the eye as her world crumbled and shattered around her. "You think I stole these?"

"They were in your bag. Don't insult us both by denying it now. I want you out of here." He made a show of checking his watch. "You now have twenty-five minutes remaining."

The knot in her throat swelled and stuck, rendering her incapable of drawing a breath. She couldn't think, couldn't react. Numbly, she headed for the door with no thought of collecting her things. She only wanted to be away. She paused and put her hand on the frame to steady herself before turning around to look back at Chrysander. His face remained implacable. The lines around his mouth and eyes were hard and unforgiving.

"How could you think I'd do something like that?" she whispered before she turned and walked away.

She stumbled blindly into the elevator, quiet sobs ripping from her throat as she rode it down to the lobby level. The doorman looked at her in concern and offered to get her into a cab. She waved him off and walked unsteadily down the sidewalk and into the night.

The warm evening air blew over her face. The tears on her cheeks chilled her skin, but she paid them no heed. He would listen to her. She would make him. She'd give him the night to calm down, but she would be heard. It was all such a dreadful mistake. There had to be some way to make him see reason.

In her distress, she took no notice of the man following her. When she reached the curb, a hand shot out and grasped her arm. Her cry of alarm was muffled as a cloth sack was yanked over her head.

She struggled wildly, but just as quickly, she found herself stuffed into the backseat of a vehicle. She heard the door slam and the rumble of low voices, and then the vehicle drove away.

Two

Three months later

Chrysander sat in his apartment brooding in silence. He should have some peace of mind now that there was no longer any danger to his company, but the knowledge of why was hardly comforting. He stared at the pile of documents in front of him as the evening news droned in the background.

His stopover in New York was going to be short. Tomorrow he'd fly to London to meet with his brother Theron and have the groundbreaking ceremony for their luxury hotel—a hotel that wouldn't have happened if Marley had gotten her way. A derisive snort nearly rolled from his throat. He, the CEO of Anetakis International, had been manipulated and stolen from by a woman. Because of her, he and his brothers had lost two of their designs to their closest competitor before he'd discovered her betrayal. He should have turned her over to the authorities, but he'd been too stunned, too *weak* to do such a thing.

He hadn't even ridded his apartment of her belongings. He'd assumed she'd return to collect them, and maybe a small part of him had hoped she would so he could confront her again and ask her why. On his next trip back, he'd see to the task. It was time to have her out of his mind completely.

When he heard her name amidst the jumble of his thoughts, he thought he'd merely conjured it from his dark musings, but when he heard Marley Jameson's name yet again, he focused his angry attention on the television.

A news reporter stood outside a local hospital, and it took a few moments for the buzzing in Chrysander's ears to stop long enough for him to comprehend what was being said. The scene changed as they rolled footage taken earlier of a woman being taken out of a rundown apartment building on a stretcher. He leaned forward, his face twisted in disbelief. It was Marley.

He bolted from his desk and fumbled for the remote to turn the volume up. So stunned was he that he only comprehended every fourth word or so, but he heard enough.

Marley had been abducted and now rescued. The details on the who and why were still sketchy, but she'd endured a long period of captivity. He tensed in expectation that somehow his name would be linked to hers, but then why should it? Their relationship had been a highly guarded secret, a necessary one in his world. His wish for privacy was one born of desire and necessity. Only after her betrayal had he been even more relieved by the circumspection he utilized in all his relationships. She'd made a fool of him, and only the knowledge that the rest of the world didn't know soothed him.

As the camera zoomed in on her pale, frightened face, he felt something inside him twist painfully. She looked the same as she had the night he'd confronted her with her deception. Pale, shocked and vulnerable.

But what the reporter said next stopped him cold, even as an uneasy sensation rippled up his spine. He reported mother *and* child being listed in stable condition and that Marley's apparent captivity had not harmed her pregnancy. The reporter offered only the guess that she appeared to be four or five months along. Other details were sketchy. No arrests had been made, as her captors had escaped.

"Theos mou," he murmured even as he struggled to grasp the implications.

He stood and reached for his cellular phone as he strode from his apartment. When he broke from the entrance of the well-secured apartment high-rise, his driver had just pulled around.

Once inside the vehicle, he again flipped open his phone and called the hospital where Marley had been taken.

"Her physical condition is satisfactory," the doctor informed Chrysander. "However, it is her emotional state that concerns me."

He simmered impatiently as he waited for the physician to complete his report. Chrysander had burst into the hospital, demanding answers as soon as he'd walked onto the floor where Marley was being treated. Only the statement that he was her fiancé had finally netted him any results. Then he'd immediately had her transferred to a private room and had insisted that a specialist be called in to see her. Now he had to wade through the doctor's assessment of her condition before he could see her.

"But she hasn't been harmed," Chrysander said.

"I didn't say that," the doctor murmured. "I merely said her physical condition is not serious."

"Then quit beating around the bush and tell me what I need to know."

The doctor studied him for a moment before laying the clipboard down on his desk. "Miss Jameson has endured a great trauma. I cannot know exactly how great, because she cannot remember anything of her captivity."

"What?" Chrysander stared at the doctor in stunned disbelief.

"Worse, she remembers nothing before. She knows her name and little else, I'm afraid. Even her pregnancy has come as a shock to her."

Chrysander ran a hand through his hair and swore in three languages. "She remembers nothing? Nothing at all?"

The doctor shook his head. "I'm afraid not. She's extremely vulnerable. Fragile. Which is why it's so important that you do not upset her. She has a baby to carry for four more months and an ordeal from which to recover."

Chrysander made a sound of impatience. "Of course I would do nothing to upset her. I just find it hard to believe that she remembers nothing."

The doctor shook his head. "The experience has obviously been very traumatic for her. I suspect it's her mind's way of protecting her. It's merely shut down until she can better cope with all that has happened."

"Did they…" Chrysander couldn't even bring himself to complete the question, and yet he had to know. "Did they hurt her?"

The doctor's expression softened. "I found no evidence that she had been mistreated in any way. Physically. There is no way to find out all she has endured until she is able to tell us. And we must be patient and not press her before she is ready. As I said, she is extremely fragile, and if pressed too hard, too fast, the results could be devastating."

Chrysander cursed softly. "I understand. I will see to it that she has the best possible care. Now can I see her?"

The doctor hesitated. "You can see her. However, I would caution you not to be too forthcoming with the details of her abduction."

A frown creased Chrysander's brow as he stared darkly at the physician. "You want me to lie to her?"

"I merely don't want you to upset her. You can give her details of her life. Her day-to-day activities. How you met. The mundane things. It is my suggestion, however, and I've conferred with the hospital psychiatrist on this matter, that you not rush to give her the details of her captivity and how she came to lose her memory. In fact, we know very little, so it would be unwise to speculate or offer her information that could be untrue. She must be kept calm. I don't like to think of what another upset could cause her in her current state."

Chrysander nodded reluctantly. What the doctor said made sense, but his own need to know what had happened to Marley was pressing. But he wouldn't push her if it would cause her or the baby any harm. He checked his watch. He still had to meet with the authorities, but first he wanted to see Marley and said as much to the doctor.

The physician nodded. "I'll have the nurse take you up now."

Marley struggled underneath the layers of fog surrounding her head. She murmured a low protest when she opened her eyes. Awareness was not what she sought. The blanket of dark, of oblivion, was what she wanted.

There was nothing for her in wakefulness. Her life was one black hole of nothingness. Her name was all that lingered in the confusing layers of her mind. Marley.

She searched for more. Answers she needed to questions that swarmed her every time she wakened. Her past lay like a great barren landscape before her. The answers dangled beyond her, taunting her and escaping before she could reach out and take hold.

She turned her head on the thin pillow, fully intending to slip back into the void of sleep when a firm hand grasped hers. Fear scurried up her spine until she remembered that she was safe and in a hospital. Still, she yanked her hand away as her chest rose and fell with her quick breaths.

"You must not go back to sleep, *pedhaki mou*. Not yet."

The man's voice slid across her skin, leaving warmth in its wake. Carefully, she turned to face this stranger—or was he? Was he someone she knew? Who knew her? Could he be the father of the child nestled below her heart?

Her hand automatically felt for her rounded belly as her gaze lighted on the man who'd spoken to her.

He was a dominating presence. Tall, lithe, dangerously intent as his amber eyes stared back at her. He wasn't American. She nearly laughed at the absurdity of her thoughts. She should be demanding to know who he was and why he was here, and yet all she could muster was the knowledge that he wasn't American?

"Our baby is fine," he said as his gaze dropped to the hand she had cupped protectively over her abdomen.

She tensed as she realized that he was indeed staking a claim. Shouldn't she know him? She reached for something, some semblance of recognition, but unease and fear were all she found.

"Who are you?" she finally managed to whisper.

Something flickered in those golden eyes, but he kept his expression neutral. Had she hurt him with the knowledge she didn't know him? She tried to put herself in his position. Tried to imagine how she'd feel if the father of her baby suddenly couldn't remember her.

He pulled a chair to the side of the bed and settled his large frame into it. He reached for her hand, and this time, despite her instinct to do so, she didn't retract it.

"I am Chrysander Anetakis. Your fiancé."

She searched his face for the truth of his words, but he looked back at her calmly, with no hint of emotion.

"I'm sorry," she said and swallowed when her voice cracked. "I don't remember...."

"I know. I've spoken to the doctor. What you remember isn't important right now. What is important is that you rest and recover so that I can take you home."

She licked her lips, panic threatening to overtake her. "Home?"

He nodded. "Yes, home."

"Where is that?" She hated having to ask. Hated that she was lying here conversing with a complete stranger. Only apparently he wasn't. He was someone she had been intimate with. Obviously in love with. They were engaged, and she was pregnant with his child. Shouldn't that stir something inside her?

"You're trying too hard, *pedhaki mou*," he said softly. "I can see the strain on your face. You mustn't rush things. The doctor said that it will all come back in time."

She clutched his hand then looked down at their linked fingers. "Will it? What if it doesn't?" Fear rose in her chest, tightening her throat uncomfortably. She struggled to breathe.

Chrysander reached out a hand to touch her face. "Calm yourself, Marley. Your distress does you and the baby no good."

Hearing her name on his lips did odd things. It felt as

though he was speaking of a stranger even though she did remember her name. But maybe in the madness of her memory loss, she'd been afraid that she'd gotten that part wrong, and that along with everything else, her name was a forgotten piece of her life.

"Can you tell me something about me? Anything?"

She was precariously close to begging, and tears knotted her throat and stung her eyes.

"There will be plenty of time for us to talk later," Chrysander soothed. He stroked her forehead, pushing back her hair. "For now, rest. I'm making preparations to take you home."

It was the second time he'd mentioned home, and she realized that he still hadn't told her where that was.

"Where is home?" she asked again.

His lips thinned for just a moment, and then his expression eased. "Home for us has been here in the city. My business takes me away often, but we had an apartment together here. My plan is to take you to my island as soon as you are well enough to travel."

Her brows furrowed as she sought to comprehend the oddity of his statement. It sounded so…impersonal. There was no emotion, no hint of joy, just a sterile recitation of fact.

As if sensing she was about to ask more questions, he bent over and pressed his lips to her forehead. "Rest, *pedhaki mou*. I have arrangements to make. The doctor says you can be released in a few days' time if all goes well."

She closed her eyes wearily and nodded. He stood there a moment, and then she heard his footsteps retreating. When her door closed, she opened her eyes again, only to feel the damp trail of tears against her cheeks.

She should feel relief that she wasn't alone. Somehow, though, Chrysander Anetakis's presence hadn't reassured her as it should. She felt more apprehensive than ever, and she couldn't say why.

She pulled the thin sheet higher around her body and closed her eyes, willing the peaceful numbness of sleep to take over once more.

When she woke again, a nurse was standing by her bedside placing a cuff around her arm to take her blood pressure.

"Oh, good, you're awake," she said cheerfully as she removed the cuff. "I have your dinner tray. Do you feel up to eating?"

Marley shook her head. The thought of food made her faintly nauseous.

"Leave the tray. I'll see to it she eats."

Marley looked up in surprise to see Chrysander looming behind the nurse, a determined look on his face. The nurse turned and smiled at him then reached back and patted Marley's arm.

"You're very lucky to have such a devoted fiancé," she said as she turned to go.

"Yes, lucky," Marley murmured, and she wondered why she suddenly felt the urge to weep.

When the door shut behind the nurse, Chrysander pulled the chair closer to her bed again. Then he settled the tray in front of her.

"You should eat."

She eyed him nervously. "I don't feel much like eating."

"Do you find my presence unsettling?" he queried as his gaze slid over her rumpled form.

"I—" She opened her mouth to say no, but found she couldn't entirely deny it. How to tell this man she found him intimidating? This was supposed to be someone she loved. Had made love with. Just the thought sent a blush up her neck and over her cheeks.

"What are you thinking?" His fingers found her hand and stroked absently.

She turned her face away, hoping to find relief from his scrutiny. "N-nothing."

"You are frightened. That's understandable."

She turned back to look at him. "It doesn't make you angry that I'm frightened of you? Quite frankly, I'm terrified. I don't remember you or anything else in my life. I'm pregnant with your child and cannot for the life of me remember how I got this way!" Her fists gripped the sheet and held it protectively against her.

His lips pressed to a firm line. *Was* he angry? Was he putting on a front so as not to upset her further?

"It is as you said. You don't remember me, therefore I am a stranger to you. It will be up to me to earn your...trust." He said the last word as if he found it distasteful, and yet his expression remained controlled.

"Chrysander..." She said his name experimentally, letting it roll off her tongue. It didn't feel foreign, but neither did it spark any remembrance. Frustration took firm hold when her mind remained frightfully blank.

"Yes, *pedhaki mou?*"

She blinked as she realized he was waiting for her to continue.

"What happened to me?" she asked. "How did I get here? How did I lose my memory?"

Once again he took her hand in his, and she found the gesture comforting. He leaned forward and touched his other hand to her cheek. "You shouldn't rush things. The doctor is quite adamant in this. Right now the most important thing for you and our child is to take things slowly. Everything will come back in its own time."

She sighed, realizing he wasn't going to budge.

"Get some rest." He stood and leaned over to brush his lips across her forehead. "Soon we will leave this place."

Marley wished the words gave her more reassurance than they did. Instead of comfort, confusion and uncertainty rose sharply in her chest until she feared smothering with the anxiety.

Sweat broke out on her forehead, and the food she'd picked at just moments ago rolled in her stomach. Chrysander looked sharply at her, and without saying a word, he rang for the nurse.

Moments later, the nurse bustled in. At the sight of her, sympathy crowded her features. She placed a cool hand on Marley's forehead even as she administered an injection with the other.

"You mustn't panic," the nurse soothed. "You're safe now."

But her words failed to ease the tightness in Marley's chest. How could they when soon she was going to be thrust into an unknown world with a man who was a complete stranger to her?

Chrysander stood by her bed, staring down at her, his hand covering hers. The medication dulled her senses, and she could feel herself floating away, the fear evaporating like mist. His words were the last thing she heard.

"Sleep, *pedhaki mou*. I will watch over you."

Oddly, she did find comfort in the quiet vow.

Chrysander stood in the darkened room and watched as Marley slept. The strain of the frown he was wearing inserted a dull ache in his temples.

Her chest rose and fell with her slight breaths, and even in sleep, tension furrowed her brow. He moved closer and touched his fingers to her forehead, smoothing them across the pale skin.

She was as lovely as ever, even in her weakened state. Raven curls lay haphazardly against the pillow. He took one between his fingers and moved it from her forehead. It was longer now, no longer the shorter cap of curls that had flown about her head as she laughed or smiled.

Her skin had lost its previous glow, but he knew restoring her health would bring it back. Her eyes had been dull, frightened, but he remembered well the brilliant blue sparkle, how enchanting she looked when she was happy.

He cursed and moved away from the bed. It had all been a ruse. She hadn't ever been happy. Truly happy. It seemed he'd been incapable of making her so. All the time they were together, she'd plotted against him, stolen from him and his brothers.

Though he'd considered her his mistress, he'd never placed her in the same category as his others. What he'd shared with her hadn't been mercenary, or so he'd thought. In the end, it had boiled down to money and betrayal. Something he was well used to with women.

Yet he still wanted her. She still burned in his veins, an addiction he wasn't equipped to fight. He shook his head grimly. She was pregnant with his child, and that must take precedence above all else. They would be forced together by the child, their futures irrevocably intertwined. But he didn't have to like it, and he didn't have to surrender anything more than his protection and his body.

If she would once again be placed under his protection, then he'd do all he could to ensure she had the best care, her and their baby, but he'd never trust her. She would warm his bed, and he wouldn't lie and say that prospect wasn't appealing. But she would get nothing more from him.

Three

Two days later, Marley sat nervously in a wheelchair, her fingers clutched tightly around the blanket the nurse had draped over her lap. Chrysander stood to the side, listening intently as the nurse gave him the aftercare instructions. Marley fingered the maternity top that one of the nurses had kindly provided for her and smoothed the wrinkles over the bump of her abdomen. They'd all been exceedingly kind to her, and she feared leaving their kindness to venture into the unknown.

When the nurse was finished, Chrysander grasped the handles of the wheelchair and began pushing Marley down the hallway toward the entrance. She blinked as the bright sunshine speared her vision. A sleek limousine was parked a few feet away, and Chrysander walked briskly toward it. The driver stepped around to open the door just as Chrysander effortlessly plucked her from the wheelchair and ushered her inside the heated interior. In a matter of seconds, they were gliding away from the hospital.

Marley stared out the window as they navigated the busy New

York streets. The city itself was familiar. She could remember certain shops and landmarks. She possessed a knowledge of the city, but what was missing was the idea that this was home, that she belonged here. Hadn't Chrysander said they'd lived here? She felt like an artist staring at an empty canvas without the skills to paint the portrait.

When they pulled to a stop in front of a stylish, modern building, Chrysander bolted from the limousine while the doorman opened the door on her side. Chrysander reached inside and carefully drew her from the vehicle. She stepped to the sidewalk on shaky feet, and he tucked her to his side, a strong arm around her waist as they walked through the entrance.

A wave of déjà vu swept over her as the lift opened and he helped her inside. For the briefest of moments, her memory stirred, and she struggled to part the veils of darkness.

"What is it?" Chrysander demanded.

"I've done this before," she murmured.

"You remember?"

She shook her head. "No. It just feels…familiar. I know I've been here."

His fingers curled tighter around her arm. "This is where we lived…for many months. It's only natural that it should register something."

The lift opened, and she cocked her head as he started forward. His phrasing had been odd. Had they not lived here just a short time ago? Before whatever accident had befallen her?

He stopped and held out his hand to her. "Come, Marley. We're home."

She slid her fingers into his as he pulled her forward into the lavish foyer. To her surprise, a woman met them as they started for the large living room. Marley faltered as the tall blond young woman put a hand on Chrysander's arm and smiled.

"Welcome home, Mr. Anetakis. I've laid out all contracts requiring your signature on your desk as well as ordered your phone messages by priority. I also took the liberty of having dinner delivered." She swept an assessing look over Marley, one that had Marley feeling obscure and insignificant. "I didn't imagine you'd be up for going out after a trying few days."

Marley frowned as she realized the woman was implying that Chrysander had been through the ordeal and not Marley.

"Thank you, Roslyn," Chrysander said. "You shouldn't have gone to the trouble." He turned to Marley and pulled her closer to him. "Marley, this is Roslyn Chambers, my personal assistant."

Marley gave a faltering smile.

"Delighted to see you again, Miss Jameson," Roslyn said sweetly. "It's been ages since I last saw you. Months, I believe."

"Roslyn," Chrysander said in a warning voice. Her smile never slipped as she looked innocently at Chrysander.

Marley glanced warily between them, her confusion mounting. The ease with which the woman moved around the apartment that Chrysander called home to both of them was clear, and yet Roslyn hadn't seen Marley in months? The proprietary way his assistant looked at him was the only thing currently clear to Marley.

"I'll leave you two," Roslyn said with a gracious smile. "I'm sure you have a lot of catching up to do." She turned to Chrysander and put a delicate hand on his arm once more. "Call me if you need anything. I'll come straight over."

"Thank you," Chrysander murmured.

The tall blonde clicked across the polished Italian marble in her elegant heels and entered the lift. She smiled at Chrysander as the doors closed.

Marley licked her suddenly dry lips and looked away. Chrysander was stiff at her side as though he expected Marley to react in some way. She wasn't stupid enough to do so now. Not when he was so on guard. Later, she would ask him the million questions whirling around her tired mind.

"Come, you should be in bed," Chrysander said as he curled an arm around her.

"I've had quite enough of bed," she said firmly.

"Then you should at least get comfortable on the sofa. I'll bring you a tray so you can eat."

Eat. Rest. Eat some more. Those dictates seemed to compose Chrysander's sole aim when it came to her. She sighed and allowed him to lead her into the living area. He settled her on the soft leather couch and retrieved a blanket to cover her with.

There was a stiffness about him that puzzled her, but then she supposed if the roles were reversed and he'd forgotten her, she wouldn't be very sure of herself, either. He left the room, and several minutes later returned with a tray that he set before her on the coffee table. Steam rose from the bowl of soup, but she wasn't tempted by the offering. She was too unsettled.

He sat in a chair diagonally to her, but after a few moments, he rose and paced the room like a restless predator. His fingers tugged at his tie as he loosened it and then unbuttoned the cuffs of his silk shirt.

"Your assistant…Roslyn…said she left work for you?"

He turned to face her, his eyebrows wrinkling as he frowned. "Work can wait."

She sighed. "Do you plan to watch me nap then? I'll be fine, Chrysander. You can't hover over me every moment of the day. If there are things that require your attention, then by all means see to them."

Indecision flickered across his handsome face. "I do have things to do before we leave New York."

A surge of panic hit her unaware. She swallowed and worked to keep her expression bland. "We'll be leaving soon then?"

He nodded. "I thought to give you a few days to rest and more fully recover before we go. I've arranged for my jet to fly us to Greece, and then we'll take a helicopter out to the island. My staff is preparing for our arrival as we speak."

She stared uneasily at him. "Just how wealthy are you?"

He looked surprised by the question. "My family owns a chain of hotels."

The Anetakis name floated in her memory, what little of it there was. Images of the opulent hotel in the heart of the city came to mind. Celebrities, royalty, some of the world's wealthiest people stayed at Imperial Park. But he couldn't be *that* Anetakis, could he?

She paled and clenched her fingers to control the shaking. They were only the richest hotel family in the world. "How… how on earth did you and I…" She couldn't even bring herself to complete the thought. Then she frowned. Had she come from such a family?

Fatigue swamped her, and she dug her fingers into her temples as she fought the tiredness. Chrysander was beside her in an instant. He picked her up as though she weighed nothing and carried her into the bedroom. He carefully laid her on the bed, his eyes bright with concern. "Rest now, *pedhaki mou.*"

She nodded and curled into the comfortable bed, her eyes already closing with exhaustion. Thinking hurt. Trying to remember sapped every ounce of her strength.

Chrysander slumped in his chair and ran a hand through his hair. He fingered the list of phone messages as his gaze lighted on the one from his brother Theron. There was a message from his other brother, Piers, as well.

He shifted uncomfortably and knew he wouldn't be able to put them off for long. They would have gotten his messages by now and be curious. How he was going to explain this mess to them and also explain why he was taking the woman who had tried to damage their business home to Greece was beyond him.

With a grimace, he picked up the phone and dialed Theron's number.

He spoke rapidly in Greek when his brother answered. "How did the groundbreaking go?"

"Chrysander, finally," Theron said dryly. "I wondered if I was going to have to fly over to beat answers from you."

Chrysander sighed and grunted in response.

"Do hold while I get Piers on the phone. It'll save you another call. I know he's as interested in your explanation as I am."

"Since when do I answer to my *younger* brothers?" Chrysander growled.

Theron chuckled and a moment later Piers's voice bled through the line. He didn't bandy words.

"Chrysander, what the hell is going on? I got your message, and judging by the fact you never showed up in London, I can only assume that you're otherwise occupied in New York."

Chrysander pinched the bridge of his nose between his fingers and closed his eyes. "It would appear that the two of you are going to be uncles."

Silence greeted his statement.

"You're sure it's yours?" Theron finally asked.

Chrysander grimaced. "She's five months pregnant, and five months ago, I was the only man in her bed. This I know."

"Like you knew she was stealing from us?" Piers retorted.

"Shut up, Piers," Theron said mildly. "The important question is, what are you going to do? She obviously can't be trusted. What does she have to say for herself?"

Chrysander's head pounded a bit harder. "There is a complication," he muttered. "She doesn't remember anything."

Both brothers made a sound of disbelief. "Quite convenient, wouldn't you say?" Piers interjected.

"She's leading you around by the balls," Theron said in disgust.

"I found it hard to believe myself," Chrysander admitted. "But I've seen her. She's here…in our—my apartment. Her memory loss is real." There was no way she could fake the abject vulnerability, the confusion and pain that clouded her once-vibrant blue eyes. The knowledge of her pain bothered him when it shouldn't. She deserved to suffer as she'd made him suffer.

Piers made a rude noise.

"What do you plan to do?" Theron asked.

Chrysander braced himself for their objections. "We're flying out to the island as soon as I feel she's well enough. It's a more suitable place for her recovery, and it's out of the public eye."

"Can't you install her somewhere until the baby comes and then get rid of her?" Piers demanded. "We lost two multimillion dollar deals because of her, and now our designs are going up under our competitor's name."

What he didn't say but Chrysander heard as loudly as if his

brother had spoken the words was that they had lost those deals because Chrysander had been blinded by a woman he was sleeping with. It was as much his fault as it was Marley's. He'd let his brothers down in the worst way. Risked what they'd spent years working to achieve.

"I cannot leave her right now," Chrysander said carefully. "She has no family. No one who could care for her. She carries my child, and to that end, I will do whatever it takes to ensure the baby's health and safety. The doctor feels her memory loss is only temporary, merely a coping mechanism for the trauma she has endured."

"What do the authorities have to say about her abduction?" Piers asked. "Do you know why yet, and who was responsible?"

"I spoke briefly with them at the hospital, and I have a meeting with the detective in charge of the investigation tomorrow," Chrysander said grimly. "I hope to find out more then. I'll also tell them of my plans to take her out of the country. I have to think of her safety, and that of the baby."

"I can see you're already decided in this," Theron said quietly.

"Yes."

Piers made a sound as though he'd protest but was cut off when Theron spoke once more. "Do what you have to do, Chrysander. Piers and I can handle things. And for what it's worth, congratulations on becoming a father."

"Thanks," Chrysander murmured as he pressed the button to end the call.

He set the phone aside. Instead of making him feel any better about the situation, his discussion with his brothers had only reinforced how impossible things were. He didn't doubt that Marley didn't remember him or the fact that she'd stolen from him. Her confusion couldn't possibly be that feigned.

Which left him with the only choice he had, one he'd made the instant he'd known she was pregnant with his child. He would keep her close to him, take care of her, ensure she had the best care possible. He'd hire someone to stay with her when he couldn't be there and to provide the more intimate details of her care. It would enable him to keep her at arm's length while still keeping a close watch on her progress. And he would set aside, for now, the anger over her betrayal.

Four

The next morning, Marley sat across from Chrysander as he watched her eat breakfast. He nodded approvingly when she managed to finish the omelet he'd prepared, and he urged her to drink the glass of juice in front of her.

Despite her anxiety and uncertainty, it felt good to be taken care of by this man. Even if she wasn't entirely sure of her place in his world. He was solicitous of her, but at the same time he seemed distant. She wasn't sure if it was out of deference to her memory loss, and he had no wish to frighten her, or if this was simply the normal course of their relationship.

She caught her bottom lip between her teeth and nibbled absently. The idea that this could be ordinary bothered her. Surely she hadn't desired marriage with someone who treated her so politely, as though she were a stranger.

And yet, for all intents and purposes, they were strangers. At least he was to her. A flood of sympathy rolled through her. How awful it had to be for him to have his fiancée, a woman he loved and planned to marry, just forget him, as though he never existed. She couldn't imagine being in his shoes.

He'd watched her closely through breakfast, and she knew she must be broadcasting her unease, but he said nothing until he'd cleared their dishes away and taken her into the living room. He settled her on the couch and then sat next to her, his stare probing.

"What is concerning you this morning, Marley?" Chrysander asked.

His gaze passed over her face, and his expression left her faintly breathless.

"I was just thinking how perfectly rotten this whole thing must be for you."

One eyebrow rose, and he tilted his head questioningly. He looked surprised, as though it were the last thing he'd expected her to say.

"What do you mean?"

She looked down, suddenly shy and even more uncertain. He reached over and touched his fingers to her chin. He slid them further underneath and tugged until she met his gaze.

"Tell me why things are so horrible for me."

When put like that, it sounded ridiculous. Here was a man who could have, and probably did have, anything he wanted. Power, wealth, respect. And yet she presumed to think it was so terrible that his mousy fiancée couldn't remember him. It would have been enough to make her laugh if she hadn't felt so forlorn.

"I was trying to imagine myself in your place," she said sadly. "What it feels like when someone you love forgets you." His thumb rubbed over her lips, and a peculiar tingling raced down her spine. "I think I would feel…rejected."

"You're worried that I feel rejected?" Faint amusement flickered in his eyes, and a smile hovered near the corners of his mouth.

"You don't?" she asked. And did it matter? She hated this lack of confidence. Not only was her memory of this man stolen, but any faith she had in who she was to him had been erased, as well. She hated the idea that she couldn't speak of their relationship frankly because she worried that she might make errant assumptions and look a fool.

Embarrassment crept over her cheeks, leaving them tight and heated as he continued to stare at her.

"You cannot help what happened to you, Marley. I don't blame you, and neither do I harbor resentment. It would be petty of me."

No, she couldn't see him as petty. Dangerous. A little frightening. But not petty. Was she afraid of him? She shivered lightly. No, it wasn't him she was afraid of. It was the idea that she could have been so intimate with a man such as him and not remember it. She couldn't imagine ever forgetting such an experience.

"What happened to me, Chrysander?" A note of pleading crept into her voice. Her hands shook, and she clenched them together to disguise her unease.

He sighed. "You had…an accident, *pedhaki mou*. The doctor assures me your memory loss is only temporary and that it's imperative for you not to overtax yourself."

"Was I in a car accident?" Even as she asked, she glanced down, searching for signs of injury, bruising. But she had no muscle soreness, no stiffness. Just an overwhelming fatigue and a wariness she couldn't explain.

His eyes flickered away for the briefest of moments. "Yes."

"Oh. Was it very serious?" She raised a hand to her head, feeling for a wound.

He gently took her hand and lowered it to her lap, but he didn't relinquish his hold. "No. Not serious."

"Then why…how did I lose my memory? Did I suffer a concussion? My head doesn't hurt that way."

"I'm very glad your head doesn't pain you, but a head injury isn't what causes memory loss."

She cocked her head to the side and stared at him in puzzlement. "Then how?"

"The physician explained that this is your way of coping with the trauma of your accident. It's a protective instinct. One meant to shield you from harmful memories."

Her forehead wrinkled as her eyebrows came together. She

pressed, trying to struggle through the thick cloak of black in her mind. Surely there had to be something, some spark of a memory.

"Yet I wasn't harmed," she said in disbelief.

"A fact I'm very grateful for," Chrysander said. "Still, it must have been very frightening."

A sudden thought came to her, and her hand flew from his in alarm. "Was anyone else hurt?"

Again his gaze flickered away from her for just a second. He reached up and recaptured her hand then brought it to his lips. A soft gasp escaped her when he pressed a kiss to her palm. "No."

She sagged in relief. "I wish I could remember. I keep thinking if I just try a little harder, it will come, but when I try to focus on the past, my head starts to pound."

Chrysander frowned. "This is precisely why I do not like to discuss the accident with you. The doctor warned against causing you any upset or stress. You must put the incident from your mind and focus on regaining your strength." He placed his other hand over her abdomen and cupped the bulge there protectively. "Such upset cannot be good for our baby. You've already gone through too much for my liking."

She tugged her hand free and placed both of hers lightly over his hand that was still cupping her belly. Beneath his fingers, the baby rolled. He snatched his hand back, a stunned expression lighting his face.

Her brows furrowed as she gazed curiously at him. His hand shook slightly as he returned it to her stomach. His fingers splayed out, and once again her belly rippled underneath his palm.

"That's amazing," he whispered.

He looked so completely befuddled that she had to smile. But on the heels of that smile came confusion. He acted as though he'd never experienced their baby kicking.

She licked her lips and cursed the fact that she couldn't remember. "Surely you've felt it before, Chrysander."

He continued his gentle exploration of her stomach. It was a long moment before he spoke. "I was often away on business," he said with a note of discomfort. "I had only just returned when I learned of your accident. It had been…a while since we'd been together."

She let her breath out, relief sliding over her and lightening her worry. If they had been separated for a time, it would explain a lot.

"I don't suppose it was the homecoming you expected," she said ruefully. "You left a woman who knew you, who was pregnant with your child and planned to marry you. When you came back, you faced a woman who treats you like a stranger."

She glanced down at her finger automatically as she spoke. No ring adorned it. She frowned at it before she quickly looked back up, trying to make the uneasiness disappear once more.

"I was only happy that you and our baby were unharmed," he said simply. He eased away from her, shifting his body until more space separated them. His gaze still drifted back to her belly as though he was fascinated with the tiny life making itself known there.

A buzz sounded, and Chrysander stood and strode to the call box on the wall. Marley strained to hear who he was speaking to, but she only heard his command to come up.

He returned to her and sat down, collecting her hands in his. "That was the nurse I hired to look after you. I have a meeting that I can't miss in an hour's time."

Her eyes widened. "But Chrysander, I don't need a nurse. I'm perfectly capable of remaining here while you attend to your business."

His grip on her hands tightened. "Humor me, *pedhaki mou*. It makes me feel better knowing I'm leaving you in capable hands. I don't like to think of you having need of anything in my absence."

A smile curved her lips at his insistence. "How long will you be gone?" She hated the hopeful, almost mournful quality to her voice. She sounded pathetic.

He stood as the sound of the elevator opening filtered into the living room. "Stay here. I'll return with the nurse."

Marley relaxed against the back of the couch and waited for Chrysander to return. His attentiveness was endearing, even if unnecessary.

A moment later, he walked back in with a smiling woman dressed in slacks and a sweater. She beamed at Marley as she stopped a few feet away from the sofa.

"You must be Marley. I'm so pleased to meet you. I'm Mrs. Cahill, but please do call me Patrice."

Marley couldn't help but return the older woman's smile.

"Mr. Anetakis has discussed his wishes with me, and I'll do my utmost to make sure you're taken care of."

Marley pinned Chrysander with a stare. "Oh, he did, did he? May I ask what his instructions were?"

Chrysander made a show of checking his watch. "Her instructions are to make sure you rest. Now, I'm sorry, but I must go out for a while. I'll return in time for us to have lunch together."

"I'd like that," she softly returned.

He leaned down and stiffly brushed a kiss across her forehead before turning to walk away. Her gaze followed him across the room, and she realized how clingy she must look.

With effort, she dragged her stare from his retreating back and looked up at Patrice. "I'm really quite fit," she explained. "Chrysander makes it sound like I'm a complete invalid."

Patrice smiled and winked. "He's a man. They're famous for that sort of thing. Still, there's no harm in a little rest, now is there? I'll see you to bed, and then I'll see about making us a nice cup of tea for when you wake."

Before Marley even realized what was happening, the other woman was effectively shuttling her toward the bedroom. She blinked when Patrice tucked her solidly into bed and arranged the covers around her.

"You're quite good at this," Marley said faintly.

Patrice chuckled. "Getting my patients to do what they don't want to is part of my job. Now get some rest so that man of yours is happy with me and with you when he returns."

Marley heard the light sounds of Patrice's shoes as she walked from the bedroom. When the sound faded away, Marley glanced to the fireplace on the wall opposing the foot of her bed. Chrysander had started the flame the evening before, more for cozi-

ness than actual warmth, because the apartment suffered no chill.
Even the floors were heated, which she loved, because she hated
to wear shoes indoors.

The thought hit her even as a burst of excitement swept over
her. What else could she remember about herself? She concentrated hard, but the effort caused her head to ache again.

The baby moved, and she slid her hand down to rest over her
swollen abdomen. The movement eased the discomfort in her
head, and she smiled. Despite the temporary loss of her past, she
had a future to look forward to. Marriage and a child. She just
wished she could remember how she'd gotten to this point.

With a sigh, she resigned herself to living in the moment.
Hopefully her memories would return and fill in the gaps.

She dozed, and when she awoke, she looked at the clock by
her bed and saw that an hour had elapsed. She felt refreshed and
drew away the covers, wanting to get up and move around. The
constant rest was starting to make her restless.

Though she was dressed in soft pajamas, she nevertheless
reached for the silk dressing robe lying at the foot of her bed.
Tying it around her body, she walked out of the bedroom and into
the living room, where she found Patrice.

She smiled at the other woman and assured her she was feeling
well when Patrice prompted her. Patrice nodded approvingly, and
as if sensing Marley's need to be alone, excused herself.

Marley took the opportunity to explore the spacious penthouse. She walked from room to room, acquainting herself with
her home. Only it didn't *feel* like home. She could see Chrysander
in the style and makeup of the decorations and furnishings, but
she couldn't see anything that made her feel as though she'd
made any mark on the apartment. For some reason, that discomfited her. She felt like a guest intruding where she didn't belong.

When she entered the master suite, her frown grew. Chrysander had placed her in what apparently was one of the guest
rooms. She hadn't given any thought when he'd put her to bed
and seen to her comfort in the extra bedroom. She'd been too
overwhelmed, too focused on trying to process everything.

She retreated, unable to shake the thought that she was somehow trespassing. Next to the master suite was a large office. It was obviously Chrysander's work space. The furnishings were dark and masculine. Bookcases adorned the back wall, and a large mahogany desk sat a few feet in front of them. Her feet brushed across a plush rug as she walked farther into the middle of the room.

A laptop rested on the desk, and she sat down in the leather executive chair in anticipation of browsing the Internet. She only hoped he had a wireless connection since she could see no evidence of a cable line connected to the computer.

She touched the keypad, and the monitor lit up. At least she wasn't a useless vegetable and had retained knowledge of the basics. As frustrating as her memory loss was, she was relieved to know it was confined to her personal history and not to the world around her.

She shook her head, plagued by the sheer absurdity of it all.

For the first half hour, she did countless searches on memory loss, but wading through the mass of conflicting opinions only gave her a vile headache. So she turned her attention to looking up information on Chrysander.

It was a bit frightening to see just how powerful and wealthy Chrysander was. He and his two brothers were a formidable presence in the hotel industry. There wasn't much personal information, though, and that was what she craved.

She sat back, irritated with her cowardice. What she needed was to ask Chrysander for the information she wanted. For goodness' sake, he was her fiancé, her *lover.* They'd created a child together, and he'd asked her to marry him. If only she could remember those events, she would feel more sure of herself.

"What are you doing?"

Chrysander's whiplike voice lashed over her, and she jerked in surprise and fright. She stared up to see him standing in the doorway, anger and suspicion glittering in his eyes. His mouth was drawn into a tight line. He strode toward her before she could even formulate a response.

"Chrysander, you scared me." Her hand went to her chest to try and calm the erratic jumping of her pulse.

"I asked you what you were doing," he said coldly as he walked around the desk to stand beside her.

Hurt and confusion settled over her. "I was just surfing the Internet. I didn't think you'd object to me using your laptop."

"I prefer if you leave the things in my office alone," he said curtly, even as he reached out and closed the computer.

She slid out of the chair and stood staring at him in shock. Tears burned the corners of her eyes. He looked at her with such…loathing. A shiver took over her body, and she desired nothing more than to be as far away from him as possible.

"I'm sorry," she managed to choke out. "I was just trying to discover something about me…you…this horrid memory loss. I won't bother you or your things again."

She turned and fled the room before she embarrassed herself and broke into sobs.

Chrysander watched her go and cursed under his breath. He dragged a hand through his hair before he sat down and reopened the laptop. A quick check of the browsing history showed she'd done nothing more than research memory loss and a few articles about his company. Another check of his files indicated none of his business documents had been accessed.

He cursed again. He'd reacted badly, but seeing her using his computer had immediately put him on guard. In that moment, he'd wondered if her memory loss was all a ruse and she was plotting again to betray him.

He propped his elbows on the desk and held his head in his hands. His meeting with the detective in charge of the investigation into Marley's abduction had been an exercise in frustration. They had little to no information to go on, and the one person who could supply it couldn't remember.

Marley hadn't been rescued as the news had led viewers to believe; rather, she'd been abandoned by her kidnappers, and an anonymous caller had alerted police to her presence in the rundown apartment building. When they'd arrived, they'd found a frightened pregnant woman obviously in shock. When she'd awoken in the hospital, she'd remembered nothing. Her life, in essence, began on that day.

So many questions, so much unknown.

What had been made clear to him, though, was that he couldn't take chances with her safety. Whatever threat there was to her was still out there, and he'd be damned if he let anyone get close enough to hurt Marley or his child again. He'd expected the authorities to balk when he said he was taking Marley out of the country, not that he cared, because her well-being was his top priority and he would do whatever it took to ensure it.

Instead, they'd agreed that it was the best choice and advised him to step up his security. They wanted to be notified the moment her memory returned, so they could question her. Chrysander supplied them with his contact information and told them he would be leaving with her the next day.

There was much to do to prepare for their departure. He'd already alerted his security team both here and on the island. Preparations were under way, but he still had many phone calls to make. Yet the sight of Marley's tears and the hurt in her voice gave him pause. He should shove it aside and continue with his plans. Her safety was important. Whether she was upset was not.

Even as he thought it, he was on his feet and going after her.

Marley stood in the closet of the bedroom Chrysander had given her, staring blindly at the row of clothing hanging in front of her. She wiped the tears with the back of her hand and concentrated on what to wear.

She rummaged through the many outfits, but none of them felt like her. With an unhappy frown she turned to the row of shelves that lined the right side of her closet and saw a stack of faded jeans next to several neatly folded T-shirts.

She reached for the jeans, knowing that this was what she felt comfortable in. But when she unfolded the first pair, she saw that they weren't maternity pants. A quick search of the rest yielded the same results.

She turned back around and flipped through outfit after outfit on the hangers and saw that they, too, were not suitable clothing for a woman in the more advanced stages of pregnancy. Why did she have nothing to wear? She glanced down at the bulge of her stomach. While she wasn't huge, the waistlines of the clothing in her closet were too confining for a woman five months along.

She felt his presence before he ever made a sound. Slowly, she turned to see Chrysander standing in the doorway of her closet. His expression softened when she swiped at her face and turned quickly away.

He stepped forward and captured her wrist in his hand. "Marley, I'm sorry."

She stiffened and raised her chin until she met his gaze. "I shouldn't have meddled in *your* belongings." She raised her hand to gesture at the closet full of clothes. "We obviously keep a very separate lifestyle. You'll pardon me while I relearn the ropes."

He frowned darkly and stared at her in confusion. "What are you talking about? There will be no separation of our lifestyles."

She shrugged indifferently. "The evidence is here. It doesn't take an idiot to figure it out. You've put me in my own room. My clothes are separate. Our things are separate. Our beds are separate. It's a wonder I ever got pregnant," she added wryly. She swallowed and then pressed on with the question burning uppermost in her mind. "Why are you marrying me, Chrysander? Was my pregnancy an accident? Was I some lascivious bitch who trapped you into a relationship?"

She knew she sounded hysterical even as the words tumbled out, but the hurt was eating away at her insides. She needed reassurance, some sign that the life he claimed was hers was a happy place and not one filled with dark gaps like the holes in her memory.

"*Theos!* Come with me."

Before she could protest, he was dragging her from the closet. He ushered her over to the bed and sat her down before settling beside her.

She glanced uncomfortably around. "Where is Patrice?" She had no wish to have a disagreement in front of anyone else.

"I dismissed her when I arrived," he said impatiently. "She is only here when I cannot be until we leave for Greece. She'll remain on the island with us for as long as you have need of her."

Marley couldn't keep the disappointment from her expression. "But Chrysander, I don't need her at all, and I thought we would be alone once we reached the island."

His look told her that he wanted anything but, and hurt crashed in again at his seeming rejection.

"You may think she isn't needed, but I won't take chances with your recovery. Your health is too important to me." His voice became softer, and his eyes lost some of their hardness. "You're pregnant, and you've undergone a great deal of stress. It's only natural that I would want the best care possible for you."

She swallowed and slowly nodded.

He stared intently at her. "Now, as for my earlier rudeness…I apologize. I had no right to speak to you that way."

She snorted, which caused his eyebrows to rise. "I don't think rude adequately covers it. You were a first-class jerk."

Color rose in his cheeks, and he swallowed. "Yes, I was, and for that I apologize. I have no excuse. I've been busy making arrangements for our travel, and I took my frustrations out on you. It's unforgivable, but I ask for your forgiveness nonetheless."

"I accept your apology," she said coolly.

"And as for your other assertions." He took one of his hands away from hers and dragged it carelessly through his dark hair. "We do not lead separate lives. Nor will we. You did not trap me into a proposal, and I won't have you say it again." He paused and sighed. "I put you in this room out of deference to your condition. I didn't think it fair of me to expect you to share a room and a bed with a man who is a stranger to you. I had no wish to put such pressure on you."

In that light, her worry seemed silly. What she'd perceived as a slight had in fact been an act of caring on his part. Her shoulders sagged as her breath escaped in a sigh.

"I thought…"

"What did you think, *pedhaki mou?*"

"I thought you didn't want me," she said lamely.

He let out a curse and cupped her face in his palm. For a long moment, he stared at her. Light blazed in his golden eyes, and then he lowered his head to hers. Her breath caught in her throat and hung there as his lips hovered over hers.

A fierce longing ignited within her, and suddenly she wanted nothing more than his mouth on hers. When their lips met, a bolt of electricity shot down her spine and rebounded, spreading through her body like wildfire.

Instinctively, she arched into him, working her body into the shelter of his as his fingers fanned across her cheek and he deepened the kiss. Her breasts tightened as desire hummed through her belly. His chest brushed across her taut nipples, and she flinched in reaction.

Her arms snaked around him, and her fingers dug into the hair at his nape. Peace enveloped her. A sense of rightness she hadn't experienced since waking in the hospital bed lodged in her mind.

A low groan worked its way from his throat as he pulled away. His breath came in ragged spurts, and his eyes shimmered with liquid heat.

"Your body remembers me, *pedhaki mou,* even if your mind does not." Pure male satisfaction accentuated his statement. It sounded arrogant, self-assured, but it gave her flagging confidence a much-needed boost. He sounded very pleased at the idea that she recognized him, if only on a physical level.

"I don't have any suitable clothing," she blurted, then blushed at the absurdity of her statement. Her brain had gone to mush as soon as he'd kissed her, and now she scrambled to cover the awkwardness.

One brow went up again.

"Why don't I have any maternity clothes?" she asked. "Did I not buy any?" She reached for any plausible explanation as to why she wouldn't have appropriate clothing among the closet-ful of outfits she owned.

Chrysander frowned. "I am sorry, *pedhaki mou.* I did not think of this. Of course you cannot go around in your jeans." He smiled a slow, sensual smile. "Even if I do love to see you in them."

She cocked her head to one side.

He chuckled, and the sound, sexy and low, vibrated over her hypersensitive body. "You do not like to wear them around me. Something about looking nice when we are together, but I assure you, you would look beautiful in a sackcloth if you chose to wear one."

Heat bloomed in her cheeks, and she smiled at the compliment.

He shook his head ruefully. "I am not doing a good job of taking care of you since your release from the hospital. I've upset you and not seen to your needs. This is something I must remedy at once. I admit, though, that your safety and well-being, not your clothing, was uppermost on my mind."

"Don't say that," she protested. "You've been wonderful. Well, except the brief stint as a big jerk." She smiled teasingly at him as she spoke. "This can't have been easy for you, and yet you've been incredibly patient. I'm sorry for being such a shrew."

He touched her face again, and for a moment, she thought he'd kiss her once more. "I won't let you apologize, Marley. You keep worrying about how hard this is for me, when you are the one who has suffered." He took his hand away and stood. "Now I must make some phone calls so I can have more appropriate clothing arranged for you."

She blinked in surprise. "Couldn't we just go shopping?"

He frowned. "You are not up for a shopping trip. I want you to rest. We're leaving for the island tomorrow morning, as soon as you have seen the doctor and he gives his approval for you to travel."

"Tomorrow?" she parroted. "So soon?"

He nodded. "Now you know why I must hurry if I am to have your clothing delivered on time."

She put her hands up helplessly. He said it as though he had much experience in making things happen in accordance with his wishes. If he could have clothes delivered to her on such short notice, then who was she to argue?

"Now—"

She held up a hand to silence him. She knew enough about

the look on his face and the tone of his voice to know that an order to rest was about to follow.

"If you tell me to rest again, I may well scream."

His gaze narrowed, and he was about to protest.

"Please, Chrysander. I feel well. I napped while you were gone. Now, you promised me lunch when you returned from your meeting, and I find myself starving. Can we go eat?"

He cursed again and clenched his fingers into fists. "Of course. Apparently, I strive to be thoughtless in all things. Come and sit down at our table. I'll get us something to eat."

Five

The next morning, Marley dressed in one of the chic outfits that had been delivered straight to their penthouse by a local boutique specializing in maternity wear. Chrysander had insisted she see an obstetrician before they departed for his island, and so, accompanied by Chrysander and flanked by several members of his security team, they entered the medical building where the doctor's offices were housed.

She felt conspicuous and faintly embarrassed, but she also glowed under Chrysander's constant attention and his apparent concern for her well-being.

To her surprise, there was no waiting once Chrysander announced their arrival to the receptionist. His security detail remained in the lobby, and Marley smiled at the image of the big, burly men standing amidst a dozen pregnant women.

She and Chrysander were ushered to an exam room by a young nurse who assured them that the doctor would attend them shortly.

When the nurse retreated, Chrysander lifted Marley and

settled her on the exam table. Instead of sitting in the chair to the side, he stood in front of her and rubbed his hands up and down her arms in a comforting manner.

She leaned into his arms, unable to resist the pull between them. She rested her cheek on his broad chest and closed her eyes as his hands slipped around to caress her back.

The door opened, and Marley quickly pulled away. But Chrysander seemed in no hurry to relinquish her. He slipped an arm around her shoulders and pulled her against him as the doctor introduced himself.

After a few preliminaries and a discussion of her condition, the doctor looked over his clipboard and said, "I'd like to perform an ultrasound just to make sure everything is as it should be."

Chrysander frowned. "Do you have cause for concern?"

The doctor shook his head. "It's purely precautionary. Given the fact that you're traveling out of the country, and that Miss Jameson has recently suffered a trauma, I'd just like to take a look at the baby and make sure everything is well."

Chrysander nodded and took Marley's hand. As the doctor left the room, he turned to her. "I will be with you, *pedhaki mou.* There is nothing to fear."

She smiled and squeezed his hand. "I'm not worried. I wasn't even injured in the accident, so there's no reason anything should be wrong with the baby."

His expression became unreadable, but his hand remained tight around hers.

A few moments later, the doctor returned and instructed Marley to recline on the table. When he asked her to tug her pants below her waistline and to raise her shirt, Chrysander frowned fiercely.

"Her belly must be exposed in order to perform the scan," the doctor said, amusement twinkling in his eyes.

Chrysander himself arranged her clothing, only baring the minimal amount of flesh, and he hovered close, his hand resting above the swell of her stomach.

When the probe slid over her belly and the screen lit up with a blurry image that resembled a blob, Marley reached a shaking hand for Chrysander's. Chrysander bent over her, his face close to her ear as he strained to see the monitor.

"Would you like to know what you're having?" the doctor asked with a broad smile.

Chrysander looked at Marley, and she held her breath for a moment, excitement making her pulse race. "I do," she whispered to Chrysander. "Do you?"

He smiled and brought her hand to his lips. "If that is what you wish, *pedhaki mou*. I, too, would like to know whether we're having a son or a daughter."

Marley turned her head to look at the doctor. "Yes, please. Tell us."

She watched as the screen changed, blurring in and out as the probe moved over her belly. A few seconds later, the image slowed and then became clearer.

"Congratulations, you're having a boy."

Marley's breath caught in her throat. "Is that him?" she whispered as she viewed what appeared to be two legs and round buttocks.

"Indeed it is. Handsome devil, isn't he?"

"He's beautiful," Chrysander said huskily. He bent and brushed his lips across Marley's cheek. "Thank you, *pedhaki mou*."

She twisted to look up at him. "Why are you thanking me?"

"For my son." His gaze was riveted to the screen, and delight shone deeply in his eyes. He was clearly enthralled with the tiny baby, and her heart squeezed with emotion.

"We're finished here," the doctor said.

Chrysander gently arranged Marley's clothing and then put an arm behind her back to help her sit forward again.

"Was everything all right?" Chrysander asked the doctor.

"Quite so. Make sure she checks in with an obstetrician when you arrive in Greece. I don't anticipate any problems. She and the baby appear perfectly healthy, but it's a good idea if she has regular care during her pregnancy."

"I've arranged for a private physician as well as a nurse to remain on the island as long as we do," Chrysander said. "She will be well looked after."

The doctor nodded his approval and then smiled at Marley. "Take care, young lady, and best wishes on your pregnancy."

Marley returned his smile then took Chrysander's hand as he helped her from the table. He ushered her out moments later and helped her into the waiting limousine.

"Are you feeling all right?" Chrysander asked as they pulled away. "The plane is waiting at the airport, but if you're tired from your appointment we can take the flight after you've rested."

"Are our bags already there?" she asked in surprise.

He nodded. "I had them brought over while you were at your appointment."

"We can leave now. I can rest on the plane."

He leaned forward to tell the driver to take them to the airport, and then he closed the privacy glass between them.

She gazed at him, suddenly a little shy. "Are you happy about our son, Chrysander?"

He looked startled by her question. Then he pulled her closer to him, until she was nearly in his lap. He cupped his hand to her belly and rubbed tenderly over the swell.

"Have I given you reason to think I am not happy about our child?"

She shook her head. "No, I just wondered. I mean, now that I know what I'm having, it suddenly seems so *real*."

"I couldn't be happier about our son. I would have loved a daughter just as well. As long as our child is healthy and safe, I am very content."

"Yes, me, too." She sighed. "Now if only I could remember, things would be so perfect. It's been such a good day."

He put a finger over her lips. "Don't spoil it by lamenting over things that are out of your control. It will come. Don't rush it."

She grimaced. "You're right. I just wish…"

"What do you wish, *pedhaki mou?*"

"I wish I could remember loving you," she said quietly.

His eyes darkened, and for a moment, what she saw sent a

shiver down her spine. There was such conflicted emotion in the golden orbs.

"Maybe you can learn to love me again," he finally said.

She smiled. "You're making it easy." She settled against him, content. But then an uneasy thought assailed her. She'd spoken of loving him, something she couldn't remember, but felt that she had, but there had been nothing said of his love for her. Not once had he voiced words of love, and shouldn't they have come? When she was in the hospital. Weren't reaffirmations of love common after a scare? Wouldn't he seek to reassure her that he loved her when she couldn't remember their life together?

She raised her head to ask him, to seek confirmation of that fact, but the question died on her lips when she saw his attention was already focused on the small television screen in the corner of the large compartment of the limousine.

She let the question die and contented herself with remaining snuggled into his body. The next thing she knew, they were arriving at the airport.

"We are here," Chrysander said.

She nodded, and Chrysander stepped from the limousine. He reached in and helped her out, and she blinked as the bright sunshine hit her eyes. The wind blew, and she shivered against the slight chill.

Chrysander wrapped an arm around her and hurried her toward the waiting plane. The inside was warm and looked extremely comfortable.

As he guided her toward a seat, he said, "There is a bed in the back. Once we've taken off, you can go lie down."

"That sounds lovely," she said with a smile as he settled into the seat next to her. She turned and looked out the window and then glanced toward the front of the plane as she saw several of Chrysander's security detail file into the cabin.

"Chrysander, why do you have so many security people?"

He stiffened beside her. "I am a very wealthy man. There are those who might seek to harm me...or those important to me."

"Oh. Is the danger very high?" she asked as she turned her gaze on him.

"It is the job of my men to ensure there is no danger. Do not worry, Marley. I will see to the safety of you and our child."

She frowned. "I didn't mean to imply that you wouldn't. I'm merely trying to understand your world."

"Our world." He stared pointedly at her. "It's our world, Marley. One that you are very much a part of."

A blush colored her cheeks. "I'm trying, Chrysander. I'm trying very hard. It's difficult when I'm in a place but can't remember any part of it. Please be patient with me."

"If I spoke too harshly, then I apologize," he said soothingly. He reached across her lap to pull her seat belt over her waist. With a click, he secured it then pulled it snug. "We'll be taking off soon."

A few minutes later, the plane began to move, and she settled back in her seat, trying not to think too hard about the uncertainty that lay ahead.

They landed at a small airstrip in Corinth several long hours later, and Chrysander helped her down the few steps onto the concrete runway. He urged her toward a waiting helicopter several feet away. When she looked questioningly at him, he leaned in close and said, "The island is a fifteen-minute ride by helicopter."

She glanced appreciatively out the window of the helicopter as it rose over Corinth and headed out to sea. In the distance, she saw ancient ruins and turned to question Chrysander about them. When she had no luck making him hear over the noise of the rotors, he slid a pair of earphones with an attached microphone over her head and suddenly she could hear him clearly.

"The Temple of Apollo," he explained. "If you like, we can fly back and tour the ruins when you've recovered from your journey."

"I'd like that."

She turned her attention to the brilliant blue expanse of sparkling water, but already in the distance she could make out a small dot of land. "Is that it?" she asked, pointing.

He nodded.

"Does it have a name?"

"Anetakis," he responded.

She laughed. "I should have known." She shook her head. It

seemed unreal that he'd own an entire island. But his naming the island Anetakis didn't surprise her in the least. He wore arrogance like most people wore clothing.

As the island loomed larger on the horizon, she curled her fingers into tight balls. Her anxiety must have been evident to Chrysander, because he reached over and took one of her hands in his. "There's nothing to worry over, *pedhaki mou*. You'll like it on the island, and it will be good for you to have time to relax and concentrate on regaining your strength."

She didn't argue with him over her condition, knowing full well it was a useless expenditure of energy. But she had no intention of spending her time on the island "resting."

They landed on a small concrete helipad situated at the rear of a palatial house. Chrysander curled a protective arm around her as they ducked and walked away from the helicopter.

He touched her shoulder and indicated that she wait while he spoke to the pilot. She stood, staring up at the sprawling house, waiting for some flicker of recognition. A cool breeze blew off the water, and a chill raced up her arms. Still, she remained, staring, hoping, but she was convinced she'd never been here.

"Come," Chrysander said as he took her hand. "You're getting cold."

As the helicopter droned away, she took a step to follow Chrysander and then paused again. He turned and looked inquisitively at her. "What is wrong?"

She swallowed as she continued to gaze over the grounds. There was a sense of wonder, as though she'd stepped into some wild paradise, but no feeling of home, that this was a place she had any knowledge of. It terrified her.

Chrysander closed the distance between them and touched her face in concern. He cursed when she trembled.

"I've never been here," she said in a low voice. She looked to him for confirmation.

He nodded. "This is so. This is your first visit to the island."

"I don't understand," she said faintly. "We're engaged, and I've never been to the place you call home?"

His lips pressed together. "We made our home in New York, Marley. I told you this."

The cloud of confusion grew around her. Would they not have visited? Even once? She allowed him to take her hand, and they walked up the long, winding path toward the house. As they neared the gate, Marley could see the sparkling waters of a swimming pool.

A large patio extended from the back of the house, and the pool was carved in the middle. To her surprise, the pool entered the house under an elaborate archway.

"It's heated," Chrysander explained as he drew her inside the house. "It's too cool this time of year for outdoor swimming, but you can enjoy a light swim indoors if the doctor gives his permission."

She rolled her eyes and allowed him to tug her along with him. They entered a huge room that looked to be in actuality three separate areas. They stood in the living room but the floor plan into the kitchen and dining area was open, and they flowed seamlessly into one another.

Marley's gaze wandered to the glass doors leading onto a patio where yet another pool was situated with a view of the ocean in the distance. To her shock, a woman in a skimpy bikini appeared at the entrance and stepped inside the house.

She recognized her as Chrysander's personal assistant, but why would she be here? And it was certainly too cold to be out sunbathing in such a suit.

Roslyn looked up, and it was apparent to Marley that she feigned surprise at seeing them. Though she had a wrap draped over one arm, she made no move to put it on as she hurriedly crossed the floor toward Chrysander.

"Mr. Anetakis, I didn't expect you until tomorrow!"

Her long blond hair trailed seductively down her back, and Marley gaped as she saw the bottom of Roslyn's bikini was actually a thong.

"I hope you don't mind that I took advantage of the facilities," Roslyn rushed to say as she put well-manicured fingers to Chrysander's arm.

"Of course not," Chrysander said smoothly. "I did tell you to avail yourself of whatever you liked. Did you set up my office as I requested?"

"Of course. I do hope it won't be a problem for me to remain one more night? I didn't arrange for the helicopter to fetch me until tomorrow morning."

Roslyn's wide, innocent eyes didn't fool Marley, and she felt the beginnings of a headache drumming in her temples. She pulled her hand from Chrysander's and merely walked away, having no desire to listen to the mewings of his assistant any longer.

"You are welcome to stay, Roslyn. I do hope you'll have dinner with us tonight," Chrysander said politely as Marley mounted the stairs.

She really had no idea where she was going, but upstairs seemed as good a place as any, and it would put her solidly away from the source of her irritation. She was nearly to the top when Chrysander overtook her.

"You should have waited for me," he reproached. "I don't like you navigating the stairs by yourself. What if you were to fall? In the future, someone will escort you up or down."

Her mouth fell open. "You're not serious!"

He frowned, clearly not liking her tone of disbelief. "I'm very serious when it comes to your well-being and that of our child."

She blew out her breath in frustration as Chrysander escorted her from the landing of the stairs down the hall to a spacious bedroom. Clearly this was the master suite. She set aside the protests forming on her tongue and stared at Chrysander in question.

"Is this to be my room?"

"It is *our* room."

Heat rose in her cheeks. Her throat suddenly went dry as she imagined sharing the big bed with Chrysander. Satisfaction gleamed in his eyes as he observed her reaction.

"Do you have any objections?" he asked softly.

She shook her head. "N-no. None."

A slow smiled curved his sensual mouth. A predatory gleam entered his eyes. "That is good. We are in agreement then."

"I—w-well, not exactly," she stammered.

He cocked one imperious brow. "We are not?"

She shook herself from the intimate spell he was weaving over her. The one that had her reduced to a mass of writhing stupidity. She lifted her chin and stared challengingly at him. "I don't need an escort to get up and down the stairs, Chrysander. I'm not an invalid, and I don't wish to be treated like one."

"And I would prefer you had someone with you." His voice became steely and determination creased his brow.

"I will not spend our time here as a prisoner, only allowed out whenever someone can make the time to fetch me back and forth." She crossed her arms over her chest and glared mutinously at him.

To her surprise, his shoulders relaxed and laughter escaped him.

"What's so funny?" she demanded.

"You are, *pedhaki mou*. You sound just like you always have. Always arguing with me. You've always accused me of being too set on having things my way." He gave a shrug that said he accepted as much.

"Well, since we're arguing, what is that woman doing here parading around in next to nothing?"

She hadn't meant it to come out quite like that. She'd wanted to sound more casual and less like a jealous shrew, but she'd failed miserably.

Chrysander's expression hardened. "You never liked her, but I would appreciate it if you weren't rude."

Marley raised a brow. "Never? And you don't wonder why?" She turned her back to Chrysander and walked to the window that overlooked the pool and the garden to the left that separated the two swimming areas. "Why is it she is here and seems so comfortable, and yet this is my first visit?"

She tensed when Chrysander's hands cupped her shoulders. "Roslyn often travels with me. This time I arranged for her to stay in Corinth so she is available if I need her, but her presence won't be an issue for you." His lips brushed across her temple. "As to why you've never been here, I can only say that it has never come up. When I would return to New York after being away for weeks at a time, I was more interested in spending that time with you, not wasting it traveling."

Marley turned around and without thinking wrapped her arms around Chrysander and buried her face in his chest. "I'm just so frustrated. I won't apologize, however, for not liking the fact that my fiancé's personal assistant is cavorting around with barely a string covering her assets, or that she seems perfectly at home in a place that I should, but don't."

"If it makes you feel better, I did not notice her assets." There was a tone of amusement in his voice, and it only served to irritate her further.

When she tried to wrench away from Chrysander's arms, he gripped her shoulders and held her fast. His eyes glistened with a need that made her stomach do odd flips. Nervously, she wet her lips, and he groaned just before he slanted his mouth over hers.

She felt as though someone had lit a match as she went up in flames. Oh, yes, her body recognized, craved his touch. His tongue swept over her lips, demanding she open to him. Her mouth parted on a sigh, and his tongue laved hers, hot, electrifying.

She went weak and sagged against him, but he caught her, holding her tightly against him. A low moan worked from her throat, and he swallowed it as it escaped. Her hands scraped across his shoulders, clutching and seeking his strength.

Her nipples beaded and tingled when his fingers skimmed underneath the waist of her shirt, feathering across her belly and up to where the lacy bra cupped her breasts. Before she could fully process what his intentions were, her bra fell loose, and his thumb rolled across one taut point.

Uncontrollable shudders wracked her small frame as his mouth slid down her throat and lower. He blazed a molten trail to the curve of one breast, and when he took the sensitive nipple in his mouth, she nearly shattered in his arms.

"Please," she begged.

His head came up at her plea, and shock was reflected in his golden eyes. "*Theos mou!* I would have ravaged you on the floor," he said in disgust. He quickly rearranged her bra and settled her shirt back over her body.

Her hand shook as she raised it to her swollen lips. Every nerve-ending in her body screamed in want. Her reaction to Chrysander frightened her. It was intense. Volatile. How easily she'd gotten carried away as soon as he'd touched her.

"Do not look at me that way," he said in a near growl.

"How?" she asked, her voice shaking.

"Like you want nothing more than for me to carry you to our bed and make love to you all night. I only have so much control."

She laughed, a hoarse and needy sound. She attempted to calm her response to his words by smoothing her hands down her sides. "And if that was what I wanted?"

He reached out to cup her chin. "The doctor will arrive in a few moments. I want him to examine you and make sure you haven't overexerted yourself with our travel. Your health is my first priority."

"I do believe I've been shot down," she murmured ruefully.

He moved so quickly she barely had time to blink. One minute they were a foot apart, and the next she was hauled against his chest, his eyes burning into her.

"Don't mistake my hesitation for disinterest," he said in a soft, dangerous tone. "I assure you, as soon as the doctor has given his approval on the state of your health, you *will* be in my bed."

He slowly let go of her, and she stepped back on faltering feet. "I believe I hear the helicopter now. That will be the physician and Mrs. Cahill. Why don't you freshen up and make yourself comfortable. I'll send the doctor up to see you."

Marley nodded like a dolt then watched as he strode away. As soon as he disappeared, she sagged onto the bed and clenched her trembling fingers together in her lap. How could she react so strongly to a man who was, for all practical purposes, a stranger? It was as he said, though. Her body recognized him even when her mind did not. She should find comfort in that, but the intensity of her attraction to him frightened her. In just a few moments, she'd so easily lost herself to his touch.

Remembering that the doctor would be up in a few moments, and not wanting to give him any excuse to send her straight to bed, she hastened to the bathroom, where she splashed cool water on her face in an effort to rid herself of the flush that still suffused her cheeks.

She dragged a hand through her curls and frowned at her reflection in the mirror. Her hair didn't look right. A brief image flashed across her mind. It was her, laughing, but with shorter hair. Hair that curled riotously around her head in an unruly cap. Even with such a brief glance into her memories, she knew she preferred her hair short. So why had she let it grow long? She shook her head and vowed to get it trimmed as soon as she was able.

A knock sounded at her door, and she rushed out of the bathroom. Chrysander walked in, an older man following closely behind him. Patrice entered after them and smiled at Marley across the room.

"Marley, this is Dr. Karounis. He is a leading obstetrician in Athens, and he has graciously agreed to see to your care while we are here on the island," Chrysander said as he curled one arm around her waist.

"Miss Jameson, it is my pleasure to provide what assistance I may," the doctor said formally.

She smiled a little nervously. "Thank you. Chrysander fusses a bit much. I'm sure it wasn't necessary for you to come all this way."

"He wants the best for you and his child," Dr. Karounis said with an easy smile. "I can hardly fault him for that."

She smiled ruefully. "No, I suppose you can't. Do whatever it is you need to do to persuade him I'm quite all right." She aimed a glare at Chrysander. "And that I'm perfectly capable of navigating the stairs by myself."

Chrysander's expression never wavered. "You will do this for me, *pedhaki mou*. It is a small thing I ask. Having someone assist you up and down the stairs will take no longer than if you were to go by yourself, and I would feel more at ease."

Oh, he knew just how to make her feel about an inch tall. She sighed. "Very well." She looked pointedly at the doctor and then made shooing gestures at Chrysander and Patrice.

Chrysander pulled her hand to his lips and kissed her palm. "After the doctor has finished, why don't you take a long bath and rest before dinner. I'll come up for you when it's time to go down."

She nodded, and Chrysander's eyes gleamed in triumph. He turned and walked out of the room, shutting the door behind him.

Six

Somehow, between the visit with the physician and a very long, relaxing bath, Marley had managed to forget all about Roslyn's presence at the house. When Chrysander walked into their bedroom to escort her down the stairs, she smiled welcomingly.

He stopped in front of her and studied her for a moment. Then he brushed his lips across hers and folded her hand in his. "You look beautiful. Your color is much better, and you look rested."

"The good doctor has proclaimed me fit as a fiddle. So there's no cause for concern."

"That is good, *pedhaki mou*. Your health is important to me."

He tucked her arm underneath his, and they headed out of the bedroom and down the stairs. As they neared the bottom, Marley looked up and saw Roslyn standing in the entrance to the formal dining room.

Marley stiffened. The woman was immaculately turned out in a designer dress that molded to every single one of her curves. She looked down self-consciously at her own very casual slacks and maternity blouse. She felt a sudden desire to race back up the stairs and change.

Not willing to allow the woman to know how much she had rattled her, Marley tightened her grip on Chrysander's arm and plastered a smile on her face.

"If I had known we wouldn't be dressing for dinner, I would have chosen different apparel," Roslyn said. She made a gesture at her outfit that drew attention to the plunging bodice. "You usually like a formal dinner." She made her last remark directly to Chrysander and cut her eyes toward Marley as if gauging her reaction to the fact that she knew more about Chrysander's likes than Marley did.

Chrysander ushered Marley forward, curling his arm around her waist in a casual manner. "Marley's comfort is what is most important, and since we intend to enjoy a great deal of privacy while we're here, it makes no sense to be so formal."

Marley relaxed and wanted to throw her arms around Chrysander. Roslyn didn't seem to be too affected by his statement, however.

"Come, *pedhaki mou*. Mrs. Cahill and Dr. Karounis are waiting on us to begin dining."

They walked past Roslyn, leaving her to follow. Marley could feel the other woman's malevolent stare boring into her back.

The food, she imagined, was delicious, but she didn't register the taste for all the attention she paid it. She smiled until her jaw ached and nodded appropriately when Patrice or Dr. Karounis spoke, but her focus was on the quiet conversation between Chrysander and Roslyn.

Chrysander's head was bent and his expression intent as the two spoke in low tones. When dessert was served and Chrysander showed no signs of turning his attention from the woman who sat a little too close, Marley scooted back in her chair, tossed her napkin down and rose.

Chrysander jerked his gaze to her. "Is everything all right?"

"Just fine," she said tightly. "Don't let me disturb you. I'm going upstairs." Before he could respond, she turned and walked away as calmly as she could.

When she reached the foot of the stairs, Patrice caught up to her. "Mr. Anetakis doesn't want you to go up the stairs alone," she said as she took Marley's elbow in her gentle grip.

Marley turned but saw no sign of Chrysander. He wasn't so worried that he'd see to the task himself. Obviously Roslyn's company was a little more important than his posturing over Marley's safety.

Fatigue beat at her as she entered the master suite and Patrice returned downstairs. The long, hot bath she'd taken before dinner had relaxed her, and she could have gone to bed then. Dinner had just brought back the tension she'd managed to rid herself of, and she knew she wouldn't sleep now.

She gazed down at the pool and gardens from the large window. The entire area shimmered under bright moonlight. It glowed with a magical quality, one that called to her. Maybe a walk in the garden would soothe her irritation.

She pulled a sweater from the closet and tugged it over her shoulders as she left the bedroom and headed for the stairs.

Not sparing one iota of guilt over the fact that her *doting* fiancé wouldn't be pleased that she was ignoring his dictate, Marley eased down the stairs. She held tightly to the banister, cursing the fact he'd made her paranoid with his concern.

She could still hear the murmur of voices filtering in from the dining room as she stepped down into the living room. She turned left and hurriedly crossed the floor to reach the French doors leading to the patio.

When she opened the door and slipped out, a chill blew over her face and raised goose bumps on her neck. Still, it was a lovely evening, and the moon shone high overhead.

She followed the stone pathway that led beside the pool and then veered right into the winding walkway of the garden. In the distance, the faint sound of the ocean soothed her ears. As she walked farther into the garden, the sound of running water overrode the distant waves. To her delight, as she rounded the corner of a thick row of hedges, she found a fountain, illuminated by spotlights angled from the ground.

Marley moved closer and inhaled the brisk night air. The salty breeze tasted tangy on her lips, and her fingers crept higher to pull the sweater more firmly around her body. She shivered with the cold but was reluctant to depart the scenic spot so soon.

"You should not be out here."

Chrysander's voice startled her even as his hands closed around her shoulders, spinning her around to face him. Anger glinted in his eyes, and displeasure tightened his jaw.

"How did you find me so quickly?" she asked, refusing to apologize for her flight.

"I've known where you were as soon as you left the house," he said calmly. At her confused expression, he said, "I have security posted all over the island. I was notified the moment you stepped onto the patio. You've been closely watched ever since."

Her mouth turned down into a frown even as she looked around, trying to ferret out the security he mentioned.

"You were not to navigate the stairs alone, and you should not come outside in the darkness unless I am with you."

"You could hardly accompany me anywhere, glued as you were to your personal assistant," she said dryly. She wanted to be flip and sound like she couldn't care less, but hurt registered in her voice, and she clenched her fingers together.

"I neglected you at dinner. For this, I am sorry. I had several things I needed to go over with Roslyn before she leaves in the morning. I will be away from my offices during our stay, and while I can work from here, I'd rather devote the time to you."

He drew her closer as he spoke, and she felt herself go weak. She hated jealousy and would like to believe she wasn't a jealous person, but how was she to know? Did she always feel such burning insecurity when it came to Chrysander? She hoped not. It had to be a miserable existence.

She leaned her forehead on his chest and closed her eyes. His spicy scent surrounded her, blocking out the salt in the air and the fragrance of the garden. Warmth enveloped her and bled into her body. "I'm sorry," she whispered.

He pulled her away and tilted her chin up with one finger. "Promise me you won't go off like this again. I cannot protect you and our child if you won't heed my precautions."

She stared up at him, watched slow desire burn its way through his eyes. Her breath caught in her throat, and all she could do was nod. She wanted him to kiss her again, touch her.

"I have spoken with Dr. Karounis," he said huskily. His finger trailed up her jaw and then over her cheek and back to her lips.

"What did he say?" she asked breathlessly.

He reached down and swept her into his arms. She let out a startled gasp as she landed against his hard chest.

"He saw no reason I could not make love to you."

"You asked him that?" she squeaked. Mortification tightened her cheeks, and she buried her face in his neck.

His low chuckle vibrated against her mouth. "I would not endanger you or our child, so I had to be sure I would not hurt you by taking you to my bed."

He strode back up the path toward the patio, bearing her weight without the slightest difficulty.

"Chrysander," she protested. "If there are all these security men around who see everything we do, then you shouldn't be carrying me off like this. They'll know what you're doing!"

He laughed but continued on. "You are cute when you're embarrassed, *pedhaki mou*. They are all men. They understand very well what it is I do."

She groaned and kept her face firmly planted, unable to bear the thought of looking up and seeing one of the security men milling about.

He nudged the French doors open with his foot then shouldered them aside as he ducked inside with her. As he climbed the stairs, Marley's nervousness grew. She wanted what was about to happen, but she also feared it. How could she retain any amount of control when he shattered it with one touch?

Her physical reaction to him made her feel vulnerable, as though she couldn't shelter any part of herself from him. She wasn't even entirely sure she wanted to, but until she could fully remember the scope of their relationship, she needed to be able to protect her emotions.

Chrysander laid her on the bed and stared down at her with glittering eyes. He touched her cheek and then let his hand trail down her body and over the swell of her stomach.

He bent and tugged her shirt up then touched his lips to her belly. There was a tenderness to the gesture that made her heart ache. He placed his hands on either side of her head and held his body over hers.

"Is this what you want?"

"Yes, oh yes," she breathed. She twisted restlessly, wanting him to fulfill the promise in his eyes.

"In many ways this is our first time together," he said huskily. "I don't want to frighten you."

She reached for him, pulling him down to meet her kiss. Her uncertainties evaporated under the heat of his lips. He took command of her mouth, leaving her to clutch desperately at his shoulders.

"I want you," she whispered when he pulled away from her, his chest heaving.

He stood to his full height, and she stared up at him from her position on the bed. Her lips were full and trembling. Her pulse ratcheted up, and excitement raced through her veins as he reached for the buttons at his neck.

Slowly, with exacting precision, he divested himself of his shirt. It fell to the floor, and he began to undo his pants. Her breath caught in her throat at the familiarity of his actions. He'd done this for her before. Teased her. Taunted her until she was crazy for him.

"You've done this before," she murmured.

A predatory smile curved his lips as the pants fell down his legs. "It is something you enjoy, or so you've told me. I like to please my woman."

Finally the silk boxers inched down his thighs, and she swallowed as his erection bobbed into view. He was simply beautiful. All powerful male. Strength rippled through the muscles in his body as he leaned forward once again.

"And now to rid you of your clothes, *pedhaki mou.*"

She curved her arms over her chest in a moment of panic. Would he find her beautiful? Would he react to her as she'd reacted to him? She strained to remember more of their lovemaking, seeking more familiarity than the fact that he'd undressed for her before.

He gently took her wrists in his hands and pulled them away until they were over her head, pressed against the mattress.

"Don't hide from me. You're beautiful. I want to see all of you."

She licked her lips as little goose bumps raced across her skin. Her nipples tightened against the confines of her bra, and suddenly she ached to be skin to skin with him, without the impediment of her clothing or her doubts.

Chrysander lowered one hand and began to pull at her shirt. His mouth found the soft skin of her neck, and he began nibbling a path to her ear. The room went a little fuzzy around her, and she struggled to keep up with the need for oxygen. She simply couldn't breathe.

Amazingly, he'd removed every stitch of her clothing. Her mouth rounded in shock, and he smiled arrogantly at her as he tossed the last of her undergarments over his shoulder.

He lifted her and positioned her on the pillows in the middle of the bed then followed her down, pressing his hard body to hers. He cupped her belly protectively then slid his hand lower, finding her most sensitive flesh.

"Chrysander!" she gasped as she arched into him.

Hot, breathless and aching, her body tightened as his mouth closed around one hard nipple. A sob escaped her as his fingers brushed across the tiny bundle of nerves at her center.

"I want you so much," he whispered. "I've missed this. We're so good together. Give yourself to me. Give me your pleasure."

He covered her, his skin pressed to hers. He inserted one thigh between her legs and positioned himself. She wrapped her arms around him as he slowly entered her body.

Even as he possessed her, he cradled her tenderly against him, taking care not to put too much of his weight on the swell that rested below her heart.

He took her to paradise, and in that moment, for the first time, she felt like she was truly home. That she belonged and wasn't living someone else's life. Tears streamed down her cheeks, and only when she found completion in his arms did he shudder above her and slowly come to rest on her body.

When he tried to move, she uttered a weak protest.

"I'm too heavy," he murmured as he settled beside her. He drew her into his arms and tucked her head underneath his chin. He ran a hand down her side and came to a rest over the curve of her hip. His fingers tightened possessively as she snuggled further into his chest.

For a long moment, they breathed in silence. Warm lethargy stole over Marley, and sleepy contentment weighed on her eyelids.

"Chrysander?"

"Yes?"

"Was it always like this?" she asked softly.

He went still against her. "No, *pedhaki mou*. This…this was much better."

A smile curved her lips as she drifted off, the smell and feel of Chrysander surrounding her.

Seven

Morning sun streamed into the bedroom and cast a warm glow on the bed where Marley lay. She opened her eyes and promptly burrowed more deeply underneath the covers. Her hand sought Chrysander, but she found only an empty spot.

She frowned and sat up, looking around the bedroom, but he was nowhere to be found. The unmistakable whir of the helicopter caught her attention, and she got out of bed and walked to the window.

Chrysander stood with Roslyn a short distance from the helicopter, his hand on her arm. She nodded and ducked down to hurry into the helicopter. A few seconds later, it lifted and headed toward the mainland. Marley couldn't help but breathe a sigh of relief.

She stood watching a moment longer before she turned and hurried toward the bathroom. After a quick shower, she pulled on her robe and walked back into the bedroom to dress. Chrysander was waiting for her.

She eyed him nervously and pulled her robe tighter around her.

"I'll leave you to dress," he said shortly. "I'll send Mrs. Cahill up to escort you down in half an hour."

Without another word, he turned and walked out of the bedroom, leaving Marley to gape after him. Hurt trickled up her spine. He'd acted as though he couldn't wait to be away from her, and after last night, his behavior certainly wasn't what she'd expected.

And sending Patrice to collect her? If he was so bent on her not navigating the stairs alone, then he could at least see to the task himself rather than foist her off on the hired help like she was some undesirable chore.

She drew her shoulders up and went to the closet to choose an outfit. There were enough concerns she had to deal with without adding a surly, moody man to the equation. Whatever the reason for his fit of temper, he could damn well get over it.

All warm and floaty feelings from the night's lovemaking evaporated as she walked out of the bedroom. She wasn't going to stand around like a lapdog and wait to be summoned. It was ridiculous that he insisted on having her helped up and down the stairs like a child.

She was halfway down when she saw Chrysander standing at the bottom, his jaw set and anger flashing in his eyes. She faltered for a moment but gripped the railing and continued downward. It made her feel childish and a little petty to defy him over such an insignificant matter, but at the moment she didn't mind irritating him in the least.

She met his gaze challengingly as she navigated the final step. His lips thinned, but he said nothing. He put a hand to her elbow to guide her to the breakfast table, but she firmly moved her arm forward and walked ahead of him.

They ate in silence, although she couldn't really say she ate anything. She pushed the fruit around on her plate and sipped mechanically at her tea, but the stony silence emanating from Chrysander had her wanting to flee.

Several times she opened her mouth to ask him what was the matter, but each time, something in his expression kept her silent. Finally, she gave up any pretense of eating and shoved her plate away.

Chrysander looked up and gave a disapproving frown when he noted the food still on her plate. "You need to eat."

"It's rather difficult to eat when a black cloud resides at your breakfast table," she said tightly.

His lips thinned, and his eyes flickered. He looked as though he would respond, but then she heard the sound of a helicopter approaching.

"It's a regular airport this morning," she murmured.

Chrysander stood and tossed down his napkin. "That will be the jeweler. I'll return in a moment."

Jeweler? She watched him go, confusion running circles through her head. What the devil did he need a jeweler for? She sat back with a sigh and wondered where Patrice or Dr. Karounis was. At least with them present, she wouldn't have to face Chrysander's stormy silence.

She stood and looked around for a moment before finally deciding to venture outdoors. The sun looked warm and inviting, and she had yet to see any of the island in daylight.

She stepped out onto the terrace and immediately closed her eyes in appreciation as the sea breeze blew over her face. It was cool but not uncomfortably so, and sunshine left a warm trail over her skin as she sought out the stone path leading to the beach.

The farther she walked from the house, the sandier the pathway became. She stopped on the walkway and shed her sandals, wondering how the warm sand would feel sliding over her feet.

At the end of the pathway, there was a short drop off to the beach. When she stepped down, her toes sank into the loose grains, and she smiled.

The waves beckoned, and so she ventured toward the frothy foam spreading across the damp sand at the water's edge. The sea was so blue it took her breath away. Paradise. It was simply paradise. And Chrysander owned it.

The wind picked up the curls at her neck and blew them

around her face. After several attempts to tuck the wayward strands behind her ears, she laughingly gave up and let them fly.

She glanced back toward the house, but seeing no one coming, she continued to walk down the beach, paralleling the water. The sounds of the incoming waves soothed her, and soon the tension in her shoulders began to unravel. She felt at peace here, but more than that, she felt safe.

The word startled her, and she stopped where she was, her forehead wrinkling in consternation. Why wouldn't she feel safe? Chrysander had a veritable mountain of security that he insisted on taking everywhere with them. If anyone was safe, she was. And yet, until they'd landed on the island, she'd felt uneasy, panic just a heartbeat away.

"You're losing your mind," she muttered. "Well, you've already lost that. Maybe the sanity isn't far behind."

Marley spied a large piece of driftwood wedged against a mound of sand, and she walked toward it. There was a place on the end that was relatively smooth, so she dusted off the sand and settled down to sit.

She sighed contentedly. She could sit here for hours watching the waves roll in and listening to the soothing sounds of the ocean. If it was warm enough to swim, she'd be tempted to shed her clothing and wade in. But then she had no idea where all the lurking security men were, and she had no desire to give them a free show.

Movement out of the corner of her eye caught her attention, and she turned her head to see Chrysander striding down the beach.

She grumbled under her breath even as he approached. Stopping in front of her, he fixed her with a frown. He pursed his lips then shook his head before moving to sit down beside her on the log.

"I can see you're going to keep my security team very busy, *pedhaki mou.*"

She shrugged but didn't say anything.

"What are you doing out here?" he asked mildly.

"Enjoying the beach. It's very beautiful."

"If I promise to bring you out again, will you come back to

the house with me? The jeweler is waiting for us, and he must return to the mainland soon."

She glanced sideways at him. "Why is a jeweler here, and why must we meet with him? Doesn't one usually visit a jeweler in his shop?"

Chrysander stood and gave her an arrogant look that suggested everyone came to him, not the other way around. He held out his hand to her, and she extended hers in resignation.

"You're really no fun," she muttered as he pulled her up to stand beside him.

"I can see I will have to change your opinion of me."

She tried to pull her hand away as they started back toward the house, but he held it fast. Hot then cold. At this rate, she'd never figure out the man. Memory loss or not, she couldn't imagine not wanting to tear her hair out around him.

They walked into the library, where an older man was arranging velvet-covered trays on Chrysander's desk. When they entered, he looked up and beamed.

"Sit, sit," he encouraged as he walked around the desk to grasp Marley's hand. He raised it to his lips and brushed a polite kiss over her skin.

When Chrysander had settled her into a chair, he took the one beside her, and the jeweler hastened around the desk.

Marley took in the stunning rings, the dazzling array of diamonds, in front of her, and gasped. She turned a questioning gaze to Chrysander.

"He is here so we can choose your ring," Chrysander said matter-of-factly. As if having a jeweler personally come out was an everyday occurrence.

"I don't understand," she began lamely.

Chrysander picked up her left hand and raised her fingers to his lips. "It is important to me that you wear my ring, *pedhaki mou*. We had not gotten around to choosing one when you had your…accident. I want to rectify that matter now."

"Oh." As responses went, hers wasn't terribly brilliant, but it was all she could manage.

Chrysander urged her to turn her attention to the rings, and she did so a little nervously. They were so huge. And expensive! She didn't even want to know how much they cost. After trying several on, she spotted one that she loved, but then wondered if he'd be offended by her choice.

Her gaze kept wandering to it even as she continued to try on the rings the jeweler pressed on her.

"That one," Chrysander said, pointing to a ring to the far right.

To her surprise, the jeweler plucked the one she'd been staring at and handed it to Chrysander. Chrysander slid it onto her finger, and it fit perfectly. It was smaller than the others, and simple, but it suited her. A single sapphire-cut solitaire sparkled on her finger, and suddenly she had no wish to take it off.

"You like it," Chrysander said.

"I love it," she whispered, then looked quickly up at Chrysander. "But if you'd prefer another, I don't mind."

"We'll take this one," Chrysander told the jeweler.

If the jeweler was disappointed, he didn't show it as he smiled broadly at the couple. He efficiently boxed the jewelry back up and stored it in a briefcase that he locked. A few minutes later, Chrysander walked the jeweler out to the waiting helicopter but not before issuing Marley a stern order not to move from her spot.

She giggled as he left. He looked so exasperated, but then he was probably used to people obeying his every command and staying where they were put. A sudden thought horrified her. Had she been one of those people? Surely not. She may have lost her memory, but she hadn't had a personality transplant.

With that in mind, she left the library and went in search of something to eat. Her nonbreakfast was now a regret as her stomach protested.

Before she could open the refrigerator, she heard Chrysander enter the kitchen.

"How did I know you would not be where I left you?" he said.

She turned around and smiled sweetly. "Because you didn't ask nicely?"

He let out a low laugh, a sexy sound that vibrated right up

her spine. "I've asked the helicopter to return in an hour's time. If you are feeling well enough, I thought we could go visit the ruins you were interested in and maybe take in some of the other sights."

"Oh, I'd love to!" Forgotten was food or anything else as she hurried across and threw herself into Chrysander's arms. She hugged him tightly in her excitement.

Chrysander chuckled again. "Am I forgiven then for being no fun?"

She pulled back and made a face. "Trust you to throw my words back at me. But yes, you are forgiven. Let me just go change."

"Bring a sweater," he cautioned. "It will grow cooler toward evening."

She started to hurry off, but he caught her hand and pulled her back to him. She landed against his chest and looked up to see his mouth just inches from her own.

"Surely I deserve a reward?" he murmured.

She licked her lips, and he groaned. "I suppose a little one wouldn't be remiss," she said huskily.

His mouth closed over hers, and she melted into his arms. She trembled as he deepened his kiss, and a small moan escaped her lips.

He pulled away, his eyes blazing. "I better take you upstairs to change, or we will not be going anywhere but to bed."

She grinned impishly then pulled away and headed for the stairs. Not that she thought she'd get far, and she didn't. He caught up with her before her foot hit the first step.

She gave him an exasperated look as they climbed the stairs. "I am perfectly capable of navigating the stairs on my own, Chrysander. I'm not completely helpless."

"I can be a reasonable man. Just not in this matter," he said arrogantly. "I'm sorry, but you'll have to live with the fact that I intend to take care of you."

She rolled her eyes, but a smile twitched at the corners of her mouth. She could tell she strained his patience, and for some reason that amused her.

He waited while she changed and handed her a sweater when she was finished. She laid it over her arm, and once again he took her down the stairs and out to the helipad, where the helicopter waited.

Soon they were flying over the water and a while later landed in Corinth. A car was waiting, and to her surprise, Chrysander put her into the passenger seat of the Mercedes then slid into the driver's seat himself.

"I do know how to drive," he said dryly when she looked at him questioningly.

She laughed. "It's just that I've never seen you do so." She frowned as she realized what she'd said. "What I mean is, I haven't seen you drive since…"

He laid a hand over hers. "I know what you meant, Marley. True, I don't drive very often. I'm usually occupied with business matters, but I have a car both here and in New York."

She settled into the soft leather seat as he drove away from the airport.

They spent much of the morning walking among the ruins. He explained the history, but she was more focused on the fact that it was a beautiful autumn day and they were together. No annoying personal assistants, no doctors or nurses, no business calls or faxes. It was, in a word, perfect.

"You're not paying a bit of attention, *pedhaki mou*." Chrysander's amused voice filtered through her haze of contentment.

She blushed and turned to look at him. "I'm sorry. I'm enjoying it, truly."

"Are you ready to return to the island?" he asked. "I'm not overtiring you, am I?" The amusement had turned to concern, and if she didn't dissuade him of the notion that she was not well, she'd find herself bundled back on the helicopter and her perfect day would be at its end.

"Tell me about your family. You've said nothing about them. I realize the information may be redundant, but since I can't remember any of it, perhaps you could humor me."

"What would you like to know?" he asked.

"Anything. Everything. Are your parents still living? You don't talk about them."

A flash of pain showed in his eyes, and she immediately regretted the question.

"They died some years back in a yachting accident," he said.

She slipped her hand into his and squeezed comfortingly. "I'm sorry. I didn't mean to bring up such a painful subject."

"It's been a long time," he said with a shrug. But she could tell speaking of them bothered him.

She opened her mouth to change the topic when he suddenly frowned and lowered his other hand to his pocket. He pulled out his cell phone and studied it for a moment before opening it and putting it to his ear.

"Roslyn," he said shortly, after a quick glance at Marley.

Marley stiffened and pulled her hand away from Chrysander's. Trust his assistant to know just when to call. She must have radar.

She could see the tension rise in Chrysander, and when he looked in her direction, it was as though he stared right through her.

"Everything is fine here," Chrysander said. "Find out from Piers how things are going for the Rio de Janeiro hotel and report back." There was a long pause. "No, I don't know when we'll return to New York." He glanced again at Marley, and she got the distinct impression Roslyn was talking about her. "No, of course not," he said in a soothing voice. "I appreciate your diligence, Roslyn. You'll be the first to know when I plan to leave the island."

Marley looked away in disgust, no longer able to listen to his part of the conversation. A few moments later, he snapped the phone shut and put it into his pocket. As expected, when she turned back to him, his entire demeanor had changed for the worse. He looked at her almost suspiciously, though she couldn't imagine why. But she wasn't imagining it. There was a distinct change in his mood.

"I'm sorry for the interruption," he said almost formally. "What were we talking about?"

"Tell me about your hotels," she said impulsively, wanting to steer him away from his concerns.

His expression froze and wariness stole over his face. "What would you like to know?"

She found a place to sit that overlooked the tall pillars and tugged him down beside her.

"I don't know. Anything. Where do you have hotels? Imperial Park in New York is one of yours, isn't it?"

He nodded.

"Where else do you have hotels? Are you very international? I heard you say something about Rio de Janeiro. Do you have a hotel there?"

He'd gone completely stiff, and she puzzled over why. Did he not like to discuss his business? In truth, she craved whatever details about him she could get. He hadn't been very forthcoming about his work life, a fact she found odd.

"We have hotels in most major international cities. Our largest are in New York, Tokyo, London and Madrid. We have several others, slightly smaller, across Europe. We're currently working on plans for one in Rio de Janeiro."

"But not in Paris? I think I'd like for you to have one in Paris so we could visit." She grinned teasingly at him.

Her smile faded when his eyes went cold and hard. A shiver worked its way up her spine, and a knot formed in her stomach. He looked angry. No, he looked *furious*.

"No, we do not have one in Paris."

His clipped tone had her backing away. She slid several inches down the bench. "I'm sorry…." She didn't even know what she was apologizing for. His mood had gone black in an instant, and she had no idea why. She seemed to have a penchant for dredging up the wrong subjects. First his parents and now his business. Was there any safe topic for them to discuss?

She stood and clenched her fingers into tight balls. "Perhaps you're right. Maybe we should go back now." She turned swiftly, her intention to walk back toward the car, but she moved too fast and the world spun dizzyingly around her.

She thought briefly of her missed breakfast before her knees buckled and she blacked out.

When Marley regained consciousness, the first thing she heard was a furious voice rapidly firing in Greek. As her eyes opened and her gaze flickered around her surroundings, she realized she was on an exam table in what appeared to be a clinic.

Chrysander's back was to her, and he was interrogating the doctor standing in front of him.

"Chrysander," she murmured weakly.

He spun around immediately and hurried over to where she lay. "Are you all right?" His hands swept over her body even as his eyes bored intensely into hers. "Are you in pain?"

She tried to smile, but she felt shaky. The doctor moved in front of Chrysander and held a cup toward her.

"Drink this, Miss Jameson. Your blood sugar is too low, but I think some juice will set you to rights."

Chrysander took the juice then curled an arm underneath her neck to help her sit up. He held the cup to her lips as she cautiously sipped at the sweet liquid.

"When was the last time you ate, Miss Jameson?"

The doctor pinned her with an inquiring stare, and she felt her cheeks warm with embarrassment. She ducked her head. "I didn't eat breakfast," she admitted.

Chrysander bit out a curse. "Nor did you eat much dinner last night. *Theos,* but I should not have brought you here today. I knew you hadn't eaten properly, and yet I didn't think to remedy the situation."

She gave him a wan smile. "It isn't your fault, Chrysander. It was foolish of me. I didn't give it much thought in my excitement over our trip to the ruins."

"It is my job to take care of you and our child," he said stubbornly.

The doctor cleared his throat and smiled at them. "Yes, well, no harm was done. A proper meal, and she'll feel like a new woman. I'd suggest being off your feet for the rest of the day. No sense in chancing things."

"I'll personally see to it," Chrysander said stiffly.

Marley sighed. He was taking her fainting spell personally. He fairly bristled with guilt, and she knew there'd be no swaying him from his course. She might as well resign herself to the rest of the day in bed.

"Can I take her home now?" Chrysander asked the doctor.

The doctor nodded. "Just make sure she eats promptly and that she rests."

"You can be certain I will," Chrysander said grimly.

Marley made to slide off the exam table, but Chrysander put out a hand to prevent her movement. Then he simply plucked her up into his arms and strode out the door.

When they got outside, a dark car pulled immediately in front of them, and a man jumped out to open the door for Chrysander. He ducked in, still holding Marley close to him.

"So much for you driving," she muttered as they were whisked away toward the airport.

"I cannot drive and hold you at the same time," Chrysander said patiently.

"I wasn't aware of the need to be held."

"I *will* take care of you."

It was said with ironclad resoluteness, his voice solemn, and she knew he took his vow very seriously. Realizing she wouldn't win any arguments with him today, she relaxed against his chest and curled her arms around his body.

He stroked her head and murmured softly in Greek. She was nearly asleep when the car came to a halt. Soon after the door opened, and a shaft of sunlight speared her eyes as she looked up.

Chrysander threw his arm up to shield her then gently turned her head back into his chest. He got out of the car still holding her and walked rapidly toward the helicopter.

"Go back to sleep if you can, *pedhaki mou*," he murmured as he climbed in.

But when the whir of the blades started, the fog of sleep disappeared. She contented herself instead with snuggling into the curve of his neck as they lifted off toward the island.

He'd obviously called ahead and issued a montage of orders, because when he walked into the house with her, Patrice had a meal waiting, and Dr. Karounis stood by to monitor Marley's condition. After an initial fuss, Patrice and the doctor, once they'd assured Chrysander that Marley was well, excused themselves, leaving the two alone.

Marley dug into the bowl of soup first and sighed as it coated her empty stomach.

"You will not skip any more meals," Chrysander said reproachfully as he watched her from across the table.

"I didn't intend to skip any," she said. "I just got sidetracked."

"I'll make sure that doesn't happen again."

She raised an eyebrow then grinned mischievously. "So it's back to being no fun then?"

He glowered at her.

That glower reminded her of what had transpired right before she'd fainted. She sobered and looked pensively at him.

"What is the matter?" Chrysander asked.

She fiddled with her spoon then set it down. "Before, when we were at the ruins. Why did you become so angry?"

His expression remained neutral, but she could tell he had no liking for the question. "It was nothing. I was just thinking about work," he said dismissively.

She stared doubtfully at him but didn't pursue the matter. When she had finished eating, Chrysander once again swept her into his arms and carried her up the stairs to the bedroom.

He settled her onto the mattress and methodically removed her clothing. By the time he'd pulled away her pants, she lay in only her bra and filmy panties. She heard the catch in his breath just as he turned away.

"Chrysander," she whispered.

He turned back, the muscles rippling through his body as if he were under a great strain.

"Stay with me. Could we take a nap together? I find I'm very tired after all."

If he didn't look so tortured, she'd laugh. She worked to keep her expression neutral as he grappled with her request. Finally he began working the buttons to his shirt. In silence he undressed to his boxers then crawled onto the bed with her.

Then he cursed. She looked inquiringly at him as he stared down at her.

"Would you like something to sleep in? You cannot stay in your bra. It doesn't look comfortable."

She blushed but nodded. "A nightshirt will do."

He got up and returned with one of his shirts. He helped her sit up and unclasped her bra. His hands shook slightly as he pulled the shirt over her head and let it fall to her swollen belly.

With gentle hands, he urged her back down and knelt above her. "Better?"

"Much," she said huskily.

He settled down beside her and tucked her into his arms. She twisted about, trying to find just the right spot. When she scooted her behind into his groin, she froze, feeling his arousal there against her skin. She started to move away, when Chrysander growled in her ear.

"Be still."

He clamped his arms around her, rendering her immobile. Her cheeks flaming, she tried to relax. The moment he'd touched her, her fatigue had fled. Now she faced trying to sleep with him wrapped around every inch of her body.

His warmth bled into her. He stroked her hair and murmured in her ear. Greek words she couldn't understand, though the comfort they intended was well recognized. She sighed in contentment as his hand glided down her arm, to her hip, coming to rest on her thigh.

She felt a wave of such utter rightness, and she was stunned to realize the nameless emotion she'd been grappling with was love. Her eyes fluttered open even as she heard Chrysander's even breathing signal his slumber.

She loved him. It shouldn't surprise her, but now that she'd acknowledged it, she realized that she hadn't immediately recognized it after her memory loss. Shouldn't she have known on some level that she loved this man?

He was complicated, there was no disputing that. Complex, hard and reserved. Well, if she'd broken down his barriers once, then surely she could do so again.

She settled down to sleep, purpose beating a steady rhythm in her mind.

Eight

Warm lips kissed a line from her shoulder down her arm. Marley stirred and opened her eyes to see Chrysander's dark head move sensuously down her body.

"That's a very nice way to wake up," she murmured.

His head came up, and she met the liquid gold of his eyes. "How are you feeling, *pedhaki mou?*"

She rolled onto her back and lifted her hand to thread it through his short hair. "Much better. I'm full and had a nap. What more could a pregnant woman want?"

"Our child did not sleep much," Chrysander said as he slid his hand over her rippling abdomen.

She smiled. "No, he's been very active lately. The obstetrician said they do the most moving in the second trimester."

He stared intently at her rounded belly, fascination lighting his eyes. "They don't move in the last trimester?"

"Yes, just not as much. There isn't as much room. In the last month, they do very little as their environment gets even more cramped."

"I would think it would be easier for you to rest then."

She yawned then covered her mouth with her hand as her jaw nearly cracked with the effort.

"You're still tired," he said reproachfully.

"I'm pregnant. I expect I'll be tired for the next eighteen years. I feel much better though. Truly, Chrysander. Let's get up."

He straddled her body, putting one knee on either side of her hips. He looked down at her, his eyes gleaming with a predatory light. "You're so eager to rise. Why is this?"

She blushed and smacked his chest with her fist. He leaned down and tugged her lips into a kiss. He nipped at the fullness of her bottom lip until it was swollen and aching.

"I have half a mind to keep you in bed until tomorrow morning," he murmured.

Putty. She was complete putty in his hands. If he so much as breathed on her, she went to mush. She twined her arms around his neck and returned his kiss hungrily. She could feel his erection straining against her, knew he wanted her as badly as she wanted him.

With obvious reluctance he pulled away and climbed off the bed. She looked at him in confusion. Why was he withdrawing?

He reached down and touched her hair, smoothing the tendrils away from her cheek. "You've been through an ordeal today, *agape mou*. I don't want to tire you any more."

He seemed as surprised as she was when the endearment slipped out of his mouth. Her eyes widened, and he tensed. Then he turned around and strode to the closet.

She watched him dress and then disappear from the bedroom. He'd called her my love, and while it had given her an indescribable thrill, it was obvious that it wasn't something he meant to say.

But he had said it. She held tight to that truth as she got out of bed to dress. Not knowing how he felt about her and why he took such pains to hold himself distant had puzzled her from the beginning. Was it because of her memory loss? Did he fear that her feelings for him couldn't possibly be considered valid while he was still a stranger to her?

She'd focused so much on her own problems that arose from the gaping hole in her past, but it was obvious that he, too, had difficulties with the situation.

If only she could remember. If only she could reassure him that she loved him whether or not she could remember loving him in the past.

All she could do was show him. And hope that her memory was restored before too much longer.

Chrysander sat in his office, staring out the window that overlooked the beach. Marley stood close to the water, her feet bare and the maternity dress she wore rippling in the breeze. He kept careful watch over her and had instructed his security team to do the same. He wouldn't take any chances after her fainting spell of the day before.

Just moments earlier, he'd hung up after speaking to the lead investigator on Marley's case. There had been no arrests made yet. No leads. The men who had abducted her were still out there. Still a danger to her and their child. It was unacceptable.

The detective had promised to stay in touch and to inform him the moment there was a break in the case, but Chrysander still wasn't satisfied. He wanted results. He wanted to make the men who'd dared to touch Marley pay.

He focused his attention back on Marley, who was still staring out to sea. Every once in a while she raised her hand to shove the curls from her face, only for them to blow back. She lifted her chin and laughed, and Chrysander could feel the impact from where he sat.

She was beautiful and carefree. Unguarded in the moment. He searched his memory for the times when they had been together. Happy. He hadn't appreciated it at the time, but their relationship—he now admitted to himself that they'd had a relationship—had been open and undemanding.

So what had driven her to betray his trust? He'd almost have preferred she'd betrayed him with another man; but no, she'd gone after his family, his brothers. And that he couldn't forgive…could he?

Indecision wracked his brain. A large part of him was still conflicted and angry. But another, smaller part was ready to move on. To forget what she had done and embrace a new beginning. Maybe she'd never remember, and if he was honest, it would make things easier if she never did.

He continued to watch her, and his gaze moved beyond her to where one of his security detail stood on guard at a distance. She continued to defy him, and he pretended annoyance, but all he did was make sure his men shadowed her at every turn. Her determination to go against his wishes amused him because he didn't sense any real irritation on her part. She liked goading him.

And he knew he was being overprotective, but the fact that her kidnappers were still out there, that they still posed a threat to her and their child, sent dark fear through his veins. She was his. He'd failed her once. No matter that she had betrayed him. He'd sent her and his child unprotected into the hands of her kidnappers because he'd allowed emotion to cloud his judgment.

He turned in annoyance when his phone rang. Tearing his gaze from Marley, he put the phone to his ear.

"Mr. Anetakis." Roslyn's voice broke clear over the line.

"Roslyn, have you spoken to Piers about the status of the Rio de Janeiro deal?"

"Yes, sir, and he said to tell you that if you'd answer your phone he'd let you know how things were going himself."

Chrysander chuckled. "I will deal with my younger brother."

"If at all possible, you need to attend a conference call tomorrow evening, seven our time. I'll send out an e-mail with the details. Theron and Piers will both be on hand, but Mr. Diego specifically wished to speak personally with you."

"I'll make it," he said.

"And how are things with you?" Roslyn asked hesitantly.

Chrysander frowned and glanced back to the beach, where Marley stood watching the waves roll in.

"Has she regained her memory yet?" she continued.

"No," he said shortly.

There was a moment of silence, and he could hear Roslyn's

soft breathing as though she battled over whether to say what was on her mind.

"If that's all," he said in an effort to end the call.

"Have you considered that she's faking her memory loss?" Roslyn said in a rush.

"What?"

"Think about it," she said impatiently. "What better way to circumvent your anger than to pretend to have forgotten it all? You can't even be sure the child is yours. She was in captivity for months. Who's to say what went on during that time?"

Ice trickled down Chrysander's spine. "That's enough," he said tersely.

"But—"

"I said enough."

"As you wish. I'll phone you if anything changes."

Chrysander hung up and yanked his gaze back to the beach, but Marley was gone. Could Roslyn be right? Could Marley be faking her amnesia? The thought had crossed his mind when they'd still been in New York and Marley was fresh from the hospital. His instincts said no, but then he'd already been so wrong about her in every way. If someone had told him six months ago that she was capable of betraying him as she had, he would have cut them down to size.

Anger and confusion took turns battering his head. He rubbed a weary hand across his face and closed his eyes. It didn't really matter what he thought at this point. She was pregnant with his child and that took precedence above all else. He could overlook a lot for his son.

A sound at the door made him look up. Marley stood just inside his office, a sparkling smile on her face. Her eyes glowed with…happiness.

He found himself relaxing, the turmoil of a few minutes ago dissipating.

"You grew tired of your walk on the beach?"

Her lips twisted ruefully as she walked forward. "I should have known you knew exactly where I was."

He gestured toward the window. "I had a prime view. You looked to have enjoyed yourself. Are you feeling well today? You haven't overdone it?"

She stopped at his desk, and he nearly gestured her around to settle on his lap, but he refrained, needing to maintain a distance while he felt so volatile, so uncertain. He didn't want to think of her as a deceiver, nothing more than a practiced actress bent on escaping retribution.

"I'm fine, Chrysander. You worry far too much. I don't need to be coddled. You would think I was the first woman to ever be pregnant."

"You are the first woman to bear my child," he pointed out.

She laughed. "And so I am. I'll make allowances for your overbearing ways because this is your first child. When we have our next, I expect you to act sanely."

Every muscle in his body stiffened, and he fought the darkness that spread across his face. Another child. It suggested permanence. A lasting relationship. Yes, he planned to ask—no, insist—she marry him, but he hadn't given thought to what it would mean. A permanent place in his life for her. More children.

Were his brothers right? Should he have installed her in an apartment, hired suitable staff to look after her until the baby was born and then removed her from his life?

"Chrysander? Is something wrong?"

He glanced up to see her staring at him with worried eyes. There, again, as it had so many times before when she looked at him, was a flash of uncertainty. Of fear almost. He cursed under his breath. He had not intended to frighten her, nor did he want to upset her.

He reached for her. "No, *pedhaki mou*. Nothing is wrong."

She hesitated the briefest of seconds before she finally walked around and into his arms. She settled on his knee, and he watched as she worked her lower lip between her teeth.

"Don't you want more children?" she asked.

He cocked his head to the side, trying to adopt a casual air. "I don't suppose I'd considered it yet. Our first son is still to be born."

She nodded. "I know. I suppose I just assumed since you have brothers that you'd want more than one child. Have we discussed it before? Did I want more than one? I look ahead now and feel like I'd love several more. Maybe four total. But I don't know if I've always wanted that many."

Unable to resist her worried brow, he pressed a kiss to her forehead. "Let's not worry about it now. We have plenty of time. First you have to marry me," he said teasingly. "Let's wait until our son is born to think about adding more to our family."

A beautiful, captivating smile lit up her face and knocked the breath from him all in one moment.

"That sounds so lovely when you say it," she breathed.

"What's that?"

"Family. I don't have family, or so I was told. To know that you and I will have a family of our own means so much. Sometimes I feel so lonely, like I've been lonely forever."

She shivered lightly against his chest as the haunting words left her lips.

"You aren't alone," he said softly. "You have me, and we have our son."

It was a vow. One that he felt only passing discomfort over making. Part of him wondered at the ease with which he committed himself to a woman who'd done so much damage, but the other part could no sooner turn away than he could cut off his arm.

"You should go rest," he said firmly, more because of his need to distance himself from her before he totally succumbed to the pull between them than a real concern over her health. The doctor had assured him she was fit and well, that her fainting spell had been nothing more than a product of missed meals. "I'll summon Mrs. Cahill to help you up the stairs."

Her lips turned down into a frown. She struggled up from his lap even as he put a hand to her arm. "I'm perfectly rested, Chrysander. The walk on the beach was very refreshing."

"Still, a short repose wouldn't be unreasonable," he said. "I have some work to finish. I'll come for you when I'm done, and we can have dinner together."

Disappointment dulled her eyes before she looked away. She nodded but said nothing as she left the room.

Marley closed Chrysander's door quietly and glanced up as Patrice approached. She tried to look welcoming, because after all she did like Patrice. She was just doing her job.

"Are you ready to go up?" Patrice asked with a smile.

Marley sighed. "Honestly? I'd like to smother Chrysander with the pillow he insists I rest on."

Patrice tried to stifle her laughter, but a chuckle escaped. "Could I interest you in a cup of tea on the terrace instead?"

Marley immediately brightened. "That sounds wonderful."

She fell into step beside Patrice as the two headed toward the glass doors. A cool breeze, scented by the ocean, blew over Marley's face when she stepped outside.

"I hope you don't mind if Dr. Karounis joins us." Marley noticed the way Patrice's cheeks turned pink as she spoke. "He and I take tea here every afternoon."

"Of course not," Marley replied as she settled into one of the chairs surrounding the small table overlooking the gardens.

When Patrice ducked back inside to prepare the tea, Marley was left alone. She leaned back and stared out over the grounds. Even with the constant company that Patrice and Dr. Karounis afforded, loneliness surrounded her like a cloak. That and frustration.

Every time Chrysander relaxed around her and they shared any sort of intimacy, he immediately backed away, as if he became aware of what was happening and rushed to correct it.

She was convinced that Patrice and Dr. Karounis were here more as a barrier between her and Chrysander than they were here over any worry he had of her health. Not that he didn't care. She wasn't petty enough to think he wasn't genuinely concerned for her and their child. But at the same time, she couldn't discount the convenience of him pawning her off on Patrice whenever things got too personal.

It seemed that when she actually started to relax, he only grew more uptight. Nothing about her supposed relationship with this man made any sense to her. If only she could remember.

If only she knew someone she could ask. Had she truly been so closed off from the rest of the world during her relationship with Chrysander?

"Surely things aren't that bad," Patrice said as she set a tray down on the table in front of Marley. "You look as though you have the weight of the world on your shoulders."

Marley managed a faltering smile. "Oh, nothing so serious. Just thinking."

Dr. Karounis walked up behind Patrice and nodded a greeting to Marley. Patrice smiled broadly and urged the doctor to sit down while she poured tea.

Despite her own inner turmoil, Marley couldn't help but smile at the older couple. They were obviously enjoying a mild flirtation. It was good to see someone happy and content. She'd give anything to enjoy a moment's peace.

With another sigh, she collected her cup and brought it to her lips as she looked out again over the beautiful garden. Maybe she was expecting too much in too short a time. Maybe she was pushing too hard, which precipitated Chrysander pushing her away. So much would be solved if she could only remember.

At any rate, she couldn't expect an overnight miracle. There had to be a way to break through Chrysander's defenses. She just had to find it.

Nine

Their days slowly began to settle into a routine much as their nights did. Once he was assured of her health, Chrysander made love to Marley every night, possessing her with passion that left her breathless. But in the mornings, he was always gone before she woke up.

She'd made it a habit to seek him out, bothered by the fact that he left their bed so early. More often than not, she'd find him in the library, either on the phone, on his computer or poring over contracts and faxes. He'd look up when she entered, and for a brief moment, she'd see fire flare in his eyes before his expression became more controlled, and after murmuring a polite good-morning, he'd return to his work. And she was summarily dismissed.

So she spent most mornings alone or in the company of Patrice and Dr. Karounis who seemed quite content to spend their time together. At lunch, Chrysander would make his appearance as if he hadn't just spent hours sequestered in work. To his credit, he devoted the afternoons to Marley.

She'd cajoled him into taking walks with her on the beach,

though he grumbled about the chill and her tiring herself. She looked forward to these times because she had Chrysander all to herself, and at least in those few short hours, he seemed to lose his cautious reserve with her.

It was during one of those walks that Chrysander pulled her down to sit on the log she often sat on to watch the ocean. He stared out over the water for a moment then turned to her, his expression serious.

"We should get married soon."

She twisted the engagement ring around her finger with her thumb and wondered why this wasn't a happier conversation.

"I wanted to give you time to recover and regain your strength. The doctor feels you are strong and healthy now."

She relaxed a little under his intent gaze. "When were you thinking of?"

"As soon as I can arrange it. I don't want to wait any longer. I don't want our child born a bastard."

She frowned and twisted her neck to gaze up at him. It was hardly a romantic declaration of love and devotion. But then she didn't want her child to be born out of wedlock, either. She suddenly felt selfish for wanting a more flowery reason for the hastiness of their marriage.

"Will you marry me, *pedhaki mou?* I'll take care of you and our child. You'll want for nothing, I swear it."

She worked to keep another frown from her face. The more he talked, the less desirous she was for marriage. He made it sound like a bargain. She didn't want their marriage to be cold and clinical.

He tipped her chin up with his finger and stared down into her eyes. "What are you thinking about so hard?"

She didn't want to tell him the truth. So instead, she slowly nodded.

One of his eyebrows lifted in question. "Is that a yes?"

"Yes," she whispered. "I'll marry you as soon as you can arrange it."

Satisfaction glinted in his eyes. He leaned down to brush his lips across hers. "You won't regret this, *pedhaki mou.*"

Such an odd choice of words. Why would she have reason to believe she'd regret marrying the man she loved, the father of her child? She wondered if he'd always been so cryptic and that she'd learned to love him in spite of it. Obviously she had.

As they walked back to the house, she slid her hand into his. There was a need for comfort in her action. After only a slight hesitation, he curled his fingers around hers and squeezed. Bolstered by the small gesture, she shrugged away the doubts tugging at her.

That night, Marley was dressing for bed when Chrysander came up behind her and curled his arms around her waist. His hands rested over the swell of her stomach as he nuzzled a line from the top of her shoulder to the sensitive region just below her ear. Goose bumps danced and scattered along her skin, and she trembled against his chest.

"I much prefer you naked, *pedhaki mou,*" he said as he slid one hand up to pluck at the string of the gown she'd just slipped on.

His words speared through her mind, sparking a distant remembrance. For a moment, she had an image of him standing before her, staring at her with glowing eyes, saying those exact words. She struggled to remember more, but it slipped away as fast as it had slipped in.

She closed her eyes in frustration even as she gave way to the pleasure of his touch.

He slid the strap over her shoulder, following it with his lips until it tumbled down her arm. Then he turned his attention to the other side, giving it the same thorough attention. He thumbed the thin string down her arm until the satin material spilled from her body and landed in a pool on the floor.

Uncertainty and vulnerability washed over her as she stood naked save for the lacy panties she wore. She jumped when he placed his hands over her belly again and then did a slow walk up and over her curves. His palms smoothed up her sides and then curved around to her breasts, where he cupped both soft mounds. His lips found her neck again, and she shivered uncontrollably as his thumbs caressed her taut nipples while he landed light nips with his teeth.

"I want you," he said in a guttural voice. "You're so beautiful, *agape mou*. Come to bed with me."

It was so easy to forget her doubts and insecurities in the shelter of his arms. When they made love, they truly connected. There were no barriers, no stiffness and no reluctance. She lived for these moments, when he made her his, when he showed her far better than words what she meant to him.

She turned, allowing his hands to slide over her skin. When she was facing him, she leaned up on tip toe and linked her arms around his neck. "Kiss me," she whispered.

With a low growl, he swooped in and captured her lips with barely controlled restraint. His movements were impatient tonight, as though he couldn't get enough of her, as if he couldn't wait to possess her.

She allowed him to urge her toward the bed, his body pressed tightly to hers. He eased her onto the mattress, his lips never leaving hers. He lifted himself off her, his eyes blazing in the dim light. With jerky motions, he stripped out of his clothing before lowering himself once more.

"Make love to me, Chrysander," she said as she reached up to touch his face.

He bent, and his lips moved heatedly down her jaw to her neck and then lower to her breasts. He tugged one taut nipple with his mouth before going to the other. Lightly, his tongue rolled over the crest, sending shock waves to her throbbing center.

His dark head bobbed as he continued a path downward to the rise of her belly. Scooting his body down, he framed the mound between his hands with a reverence that brought tears to her eyes. Then he pressed his mouth to her stomach in a gentle kiss.

Emotion knotted in her throat until it became hard to breathe around it. If only they could stay this way. Here, where there were no words, no defenses, she felt loved and cherished. No walls, no barriers, no secrets.

His mouth moved lower, and she gasped when he nudged her thighs apart and touched his mouth to her pulsing core.

"Chrysander!" she cried out as he licked over her sensitive bundle of nerves.

"You taste so sweet, *agape mou,*" he said as he moved up her body again.

He fit himself against her damp heat and then slowly slid inside her body. She closed her eyes and reached for him with a sigh of pleasure. Her hand threaded through the short hair at the back of his head and down to his nape where she caressed as he moved back and forth with exquisite gentleness.

Then his lips found hers again, and he swallowed her abrupt cry as he sank deeper than before.

"Give me your pleasure," he said against her mouth. "Only to me."

She arched against him, her body tightening as the first stirrings of her release began deep and rushed in a thousand different directions. Her soft cry split the night, and he gathered her tightly to him. His hand smoothed down her side to her hip and then to the curve of her belly.

"I can never get enough of you," he admitted in a voice that sounded strangely vulnerable.

She opened her eyes to see him staring down at her, his expression fierce and haunted. And then he began to move harder, more demanding. Wordlessly he took her to indescribable heights. She floated freely, her body cocooned in bliss.

So began the night. She'd barely come down from the peaks he'd driven her to when he began making love to her all over again. He possessed her tirelessly, commanding her body with a practiced ease that left her gasping. Throughout the night he was insatiable, and just before dawn, they both fell into an exhausted sleep.

Even as Marley hovered in the euphoric aftermath, her sleep was troubled. There was a familiarity to Chrysander's demanding lovemaking, as if for the first time he'd shown her part of her past life with him.

In her dreams, she struggled to open a firmly shut door,

knowing that on the other side lay her life, her memories, everything that had happened to her in her lifetime. She pulled at it then beat on it, sobbing for it to open and show her.

She clawed at it, and finally, she managed to pry it open the barest amount. Light poured from the crack, and then, as suddenly as it had shone, brilliant and white, it was doused by an overwhelming feeling of fear and despair. She knew without a doubt that she didn't want to see what was on the other side.

In her shock, she loosened her grip and the door slammed shut, leaving her kneeling and shaking against the cold wood. No! She needed to know. She had to know. Who was she and what had happened to her?

"Marley. Marley!" Chrysander's urgent tones intruded on her dream. "You must wake up, *pedhaki mou*. It's just a dream. You're safe. You're here with me."

She opened her eyes to see Chrysander over her, his eyes bright with concern. He'd turned the lamp on beside the bed, and for that she was grateful. She felt suffocated by the darkness of her dream.

She felt wetness on her cheeks and realized she'd been crying in her sleep. Her heart still raced with panic, and she couldn't dispel the awful feeling of foreboding that had gripped her.

She tried to speak, to tell Chrysander she was all right, but a cry wrenched from her throat. He gathered her tightly in his arms and held her close as her body shook with sobs.

"You're going to make yourself ill, Marley. You must stop."

For a long time she gripped his arms, not wanting him to pull away from her. When she finally managed to regain control of herself, he gently eased her back onto the pillows.

"What has frightened you so badly, *agape mou?*"

The images from her dream came roaring back, but she was hard-pressed to make sense of them. Thankfully, the awful panic had receded so that she could breathe normally again.

"I was at a door," she said, her speech faltering. "And I knew that on the other side of the door were my memories. But I couldn't open it no matter how hard I tried. Finally, I managed to crack it but then…"

"Then what?" he asked gently.

"Fear," she whispered. "So much fear. I was afraid. I let go of the door, and it slammed shut."

He lay back down beside her and curled his arms around her. "It was just a dream, *pedhaki mou*. Just a dream. It can't hurt you. You fear the unknown. This is natural."

She slowly began to relax against him. He stroked her back, his palm gliding up and down her spine.

"Are you all right now? Do you want me to call for Dr. Karounis?"

She shook her head against his chest. "No. I'm fine. Really. I feel so silly now."

"You're not silly. Try and go back to sleep. I fear I kept you awake far too long tonight."

His voice had deepened to a husky timbre, and her body tightened all over as she remembered the ways he'd kept her up.

With a yawn, she burrowed as tightly as she could against his hard body and let herself fall into what was this time a dreamless sleep.

Chrysander rose at dawn the next morning. He hadn't slept since Marley had awakened with her nightmare. After he'd soothed her, and she had fallen into a more peaceful rest, he'd lain awake, staring at the ceiling as he realized the impossibility of their situation.

Careful not to wake Marley, he showered and dressed. After checking to make sure she hadn't been disturbed, he went quietly down the stairs. He bypassed his office, though it was his custom to begin the day with business matters.

This morning something drove him to the beach where Marley so often visited. The air was chilly blowing off the water, but he took no notice as he stood watching the waves break and slide into shore.

Marley's past, *their* past, threatened her in sleep. Her memories waged war at her most unguarded moments, and what would he do when it all came back?

The terrible conflict that ate at him was wearing him down. He should be angry, and at times he was. But it was also easy to forget. Here on the island, safeguarded from the rest of the world, it was easy to pretend that it was just him and Marley and their unborn child. No past betrayals, no lies, no deceit.

He shoved his hands into his pockets and bowed his head in resignation. Never before in his business or personal life had he felt so out of control, so indecisive. Could he forgive her for trying to destroy him and his brothers? That was the million-dollar question, because if he couldn't, they had no future. When she remembered, things would irrevocably change, and he could either hold on to the acid taste of betrayal, or he could forge ahead and offer his forgiveness.

Theos mou, but he didn't have the answer. He didn't know if he had it in him to be so generous. He wanted her, no question. He was drawn to her, even knowing her sins. She was pregnant with his son, but could he honestly say that if she weren't pregnant, he could so easily cast her aside?

Small arms circled his waist, and a warm body burrowed against his back. He looked down to see Marley's hands clasped around his middle, and he brought his up to cover hers automatically.

She hugged him tightly, and he could feel her cheek pressed against his spine. She felt…right.

Slowly he eased her hands away so that he could turn in her arms. She looked up at him with warm and welcoming eyes before she dove into his arms and nuzzled against his chest.

"Good morning," he said, unable to prevent the surge of desire from racing through his body.

"I stopped by your office but didn't find you. I was worried," she said as she pulled away.

He cocked his head. "Worried?"

"You're never not in your office," she said lightly. "And then I couldn't find you anywhere in the house. I thought…I thought you might have left."

He ran his hands up to her shoulders and squeezed reassuringly. "I wouldn't leave without telling you, *pedhaki mou.*" Was he so distant, so caught up in his efforts to avoid her that this was what she thought of him? If she did think so, he could hardly blame her. Between Mrs. Cahill and Dr. Karounis, he'd erected a veritable arsenal of people to put between them.

"Would you like to take a walk with me?" she asked. "I always walk on the beach in the mornings when you're working. That is, if you aren't too busy?"

He caught her hand and brought it to his lips. "I'm not too busy for you and our child. But should you be resting?"

An exasperated shriek left her lips, startling him with her ferocity. She yanked her hand from him and parked both of her fists on her hips.

"Do I look like I need to be resting?" Anger and disappointment burned in her eyes. "Look, Chrysander, if you don't want to spend time with me, just say so, but stop throwing out your pat 'You need to be resting' line."

She turned and stalked farther down the beach, leaving him there feeling like she'd punched him in the stomach. He ran a hand through his hair as he watched her hurry away, and then he strode after her, his feet kicking up sand as he closed the distance between them.

"Marley! Marley, wait," he called as he caught her elbow.

When he turned her around, he was gutted by the tears streaking down her cheeks. She turned her face away and swiped blindly at her eyes with her other hand.

"Please, just go away," she choked out. "Go do whatever it is you do with your time. I'll wait for my *appointment* with you in the afternoon."

It came out bitter and full of hurt, and he realized that he hadn't fooled her at all with the distance he put between them.

He reached for her chin and gently tugged until she faced him. With his thumb, he wiped at a tear that slipped over her cheekbone.

"You aren't an appointment, Marley."

"No?" She yanked away from his touch and retreated a few feet until there was a respectable distance between them. "I've tried to be patient and understanding even though I don't understand any of it. Us. You or even me. I can't figure you out, Chrysander, and I'm tired of trying. I've tried to be strong and undemanding, but I can't do it anymore. I'm scared to death. I don't know who I am. I wake up one day to find myself pregnant, and there's a stranger by my bed who says he's my fiancé and the father of my child. One would think this would tell me that at least I was loved and cherished, but nothing you've done has made me feel anything but confusion. You run hot and cold, and I never know which one to expect. I can't do this."

Coldness wrapped around Chrysander's chest, squeezing until he couldn't draw a breath. "What are you saying?" he demanded.

She looked at him tiredly. "Why are you marrying me? Is it just because of the baby?"

He frowned, not liking the corner she was backing him into. "You're tired and overwrought. We should go back in and continue this conversation where it's warm—"

She cut him off with a furious hand. "I am *not* tired. I am not overwrought, and I want you to stop with the overprotective hovering. I don't even buy that you're that concerned, only that it's a convenient barrier you can hide behind when I start asking questions."

He opened his mouth to refute her words but then paused. He couldn't very well deny it when it was true. Still, he had no desire for her to become distraught. Surely *that* couldn't be good for the baby.

"What in my past am I so afraid of?" she whispered. "Last night terrified me. I woke this morning with a feeling of such fear, and not because I can't remember, but because I'm afraid to remember."

She stared earnestly at him, her eyes pleading.

"Tell me, Chrysander. I need to know. What were we like before? How did we meet? Were we very in love?"

He turned toward the water and shoved his hands back into his pockets. "You worked for me," he said gruffly.

She moved beside him, not touching him. But she was close enough that he could feel the soft hiccups of her breaths.

"I did? At your hotel?"

He shook his head. "In the corporate offices. You were my assistant."

She looked at him in shock. "But Roslyn is your assistant, and she seems awfully comfortable in that role. Like she's been there for years."

He offered a small smile. "You weren't my assistant for long. I was too intent on having you in my bed. I convinced you to quit and move in with me. You were too much of a distraction for me at work."

She didn't look pleased by his statement. A worried frown worked over her face, and her lips turned down into a dissatisfied moue.

"So you've made it a practice to put me where it's most convenient for you," she murmured.

He cursed softly under his breath, but again, he couldn't very well deny that he'd been intent on having his way when it came to her.

"And I allowed this?" she asked. "I just quit my job and moved in with you?"

He shrugged. "You seemed as happy to be with me as I was with you."

She frowned harder and curled her hands protectively over her waist. "Was our baby planned?"

He drew in his breath. Here was an area he had to tread lightly. "I wouldn't say planned, but your pregnancy certainly wasn't unwelcome."

If possible, she looked more miserable. She hunched her shoulders forward and turned away, but not before he saw the reemergence of tears.

He sighed and reached for her, pulling her into his arms. "Why are you so sad this morning, *pedhaki mou?* What can I do or say to make you feel better?"

She glanced up at him, her eyes shining with moisture. "You can stop avoiding me. You can stop using concerns over my health and that of the baby as an excuse to treat me as an invalid. You can stop treating my past like it's something I have no right to know."

He pressed his lips tightly together. "I will try to be less conscientious of your…health, though I reserve the right to be concerned."

She smiled then, and the relief that hit him almost caused him to stumble. He hadn't realized just how much her happiness was important to him. Was he crazy to be so concerned when she'd had no regard for his happiness in the past?

She leaned up to kiss him, and he caught her against him, holding her possessively as he devoured her lips.

"Thank you," she said as she pulled back. "I just want…" She stopped, and longing flooded her eyes before she look away.

"What do you want, *pedhaki mou?*"

Her gaze flickered back to his. "I want us to be happy," she said huskily. "I want to be sure of my place in your life. I want to remember, but more than that, I want to feel like I have more than just a small piece of you and your time."

He regarded her thoughtfully. She'd never been so direct before her memory loss. She'd been shy and hesitant about voicing her wants and desires. But had she felt like this before? Had she resented his prolonged absences? The way he fit her into his life at his convenience? Was that why she'd lashed out? Had it been a bid to gain his attention?

"I want you to be happy, too, Marley. I want this very much. And while I can't convince you of your place in my life with mere words, hopefully I can prove it to you over time."

Her smile warmed him to his toes. It was like watching the sun break over the horizon. She reached for his hands and slid her palms into his grip.

"Come walk with me," she invited.

Unable to deny her anything in that moment, he gathered her close and began walking down the beach.

Ten

Marley knelt in the cool soil of the garden and plucked the few weeds from around the flowers and greenery. With Chrysander's morning ritual of working, she'd found other ways to occupy her time, much to the dismay of the gardener who flew out twice a week to tend the grounds.

Ever since her outburst on the beach, Chrysander had ceased to push Patrice and Dr. Karounis at her for every little health concern. Instead, they stayed firmly in the background on an as-needed basis, and Chrysander had relented on her traveling the stairs alone.

Despite the fact that he continued to work in the mornings, he came out to have breakfast with her before returning to his office. Then the fun began for Marley. Each day she found a new method of driving him insane. He'd come looking for her when work was finished, and invariably she tried the restraint he'd promised to exercise when it came to demanding that she rest.

When Chrysander had found her in the garden on her hands and knees, she thought he was going to burst a blood vessel. He'd promptly carried her inside and up the stairs, stripped her down and put her into the bathtub.

She'd giggled at his ferocious scowl, listened with pretended solemnity to his decree that she not endanger herself in that manner anymore and promptly plotted to return as soon as he was caught up in work again.

It began a fun game between them, although the amusement was entirely hers because Chrysander failed to see the hilarity in her continued disobedience.

So here she sat, waiting with amused delight for his arrival.

She heard his sigh behind her and grinned even as she found herself lifted into the air. She tumbled against Chrysander's hard chest and smiled serenely up at his dark expression.

He strode for the house, grumbling the entire way.

"I promised to ease up on my *overprotective tendencies*. I stopped insisting you rest and even allowed you to walk unaided up and down the stairs."

Marley rolled her eyes.

"But you would try the patience of a saint," he growled.

As he had done before, and as she was counting on, he stripped her down and deposited her into an already drawn bath. He glared balefully at her, and she giggled as she sank lower into the water. He watched intently as she slowly washed herself, hunger glittering in his eyes.

Relishing the fact that she had his full attention, she took advantage as she worked the cloth over every inch of her body. When she was finished, she glanced innocently up at him as he towered over her. She flashed him her best smile, but he continued to glower at her.

"Your cuteness is not going to get you out of trouble, *pedhaki mou*," he said.

"Well, at least I'm cute," she said pertly.

"Why do you insist on provoking me? My hair is turning gray, and it is solely your fault."

She glanced up at his dark hair, not marred by a single gray strand, and raised an eyebrow. "You poor baby. Are you too old to keep up with one little pregnant woman?"

"I'll show you old," he growled as he plucked her from the bathtub.

He barely took the time to dry her before he strode into the bedroom and deposited her on the bed. Her eyes widened appreciatively as he began stripping his clothing from his muscled body.

"Clearly I need to be bad more often," she murmured. "I could learn to live with the punishment."

"Little minx," he said as he lowered himself into her waiting arms.

He was always in control in their lovemaking, and she knew this was the way it had always been, but now she had a sudden desire to turn the tables. To make him as crazy as he made her.

She pushed at him, and he withdrew with a frown. She followed him up and placed her hands on his shoulders, forcing him to lie on his back. She straddled his legs and stared at his shocked expression, a mischievous grin working at her lips.

"I want to touch you, Chrysander," she said softly. She placed her palms on the tops of his thick legs and smoothed them slowly upward.

His eyes smoldered and sparked. "Then by all means, touch me, *agape mou.*"

With a little nervousness, she touched his male flesh, and he jerked in reaction. Feeling a little bolder, she wrapped her fingers around the turgid length and stroked lightly.

A groan worked from his throat, and she could see sweat beading on his brow. He was beautiful. Hard, male, his strength rippled through his every muscle.

She leaned down and pressed a kiss to his taut abdomen and then worked her way up to his flat nipples. A thin line of hair dusted his midline, and she ran her fingers over it, liking the feel of it on her skin.

She knew what she wanted to do but was unsure of exactly how she would accomplish it. He must have sensed her uncertainty and her hesitation, because he reached down with his strong hands and grasped her hips.

He lifted her then eased her down over the length of his erection. She closed her eyes as he slid inside her.

"You're killing me, *pedhaki mou,*" he rasped. "God, it's so good. You're so sweet."

Encouraged by the satisfaction and approval in his voice, she made love to him, raining kisses over his chest as his hands helped guide the movements of her hips.

Her body trembled, and she knew she was nearing her release, but she wouldn't succumb until he went with her. He tensed beneath her, and suddenly his hands tightened around her hips. He arched into her, and with a cry, the world exploded around her.

She fell forward, but he caught her with gentle hands. He lowered her to his heaving chest and stroked her hair as they struggled to catch their breaths.

He turned so that he could position her beside him, and he eased out of her body, eliciting another soft moan from her. She cuddled against him, warm and replete.

"Was I any good?" she asked, her words muffled by his chest.

He shook with laughter then turned her face up so she could see him. "If you were any better, you really would make me an old man before my time."

"But did you like it?" she asked softly. "Or do you think I'm a brazen hussy now?"

He tweaked her on the nose then kissed the same spot. "I liked it very much. I liked it so much that I might consider letting you go play in your garden again tomorrow."

She rolled her eyes and yawned sleepily. He drew his finger down her cheek. "Sleep now. I'll wake you for dinner."

"I don't need a nap," she grumbled, but she was already drifting off.

Not wanting to be entirely predictable, Marley forewent the garden the next day and opted instead for the heated pool. She'd been eyeing it with longing since they'd arrived, and thanks to boutiques only too willing to deliver to the island, she had a simply decadent swimsuit she was dying to try out.

As she pulled the skimpy suit on, she realized that in essence she was trying to seduce Chrysander. Not that she hadn't already, but she was attempting to make him fall in love with her.

She frowned back at herself in the mirror. Wasn't this backward? He was the one with the memory. Shouldn't he be trying to make her fall in love with him? She knew she loved him but hadn't said the words. Something had held her back, and now she pondered what it was that made her unwilling to take that jump.

There was a hesitation about him that niggled at her, as though he wanted to keep a certain amount of distance between them. She didn't want that. She wanted him to love her as she loved him.

She sighed. If only she could remember.

She wiggled a bit and readjusted the bikini until she was satisfied with the result. The top cupped her small breasts and did a remarkable job of making them seem more impressive than they actually were. The bottom… She smiled as she turned at an angle to view the back of the bikini. It wasn't a thong…exactly, but it did draw attention to her gently rounded bottom.

Straightening again, she smoothed a hand over the swell of her belly. Chrysander seemed to enjoy her pregnancy. He touched and kissed her belly frequently and seemed entranced by the mound. She hoped he'd find the suit, and her, sexy.

Recognizing that she was stalling, she reached for the silk robe and tugged it on. She wanted no chance that someone else would see her in such a scandalous suit. This was for Chrysander's eyes only.

She slipped down the stairs and made it through the living room unseen. She walked into the smaller room that housed the indoor portion of the pool and eyed the rippling water with anticipation. Chrysander or no Chrysander, she was looking forward to a swim.

Shedding the wrap, she tossed it over one of the loungers and walked to the edge of the pool to dip her toe in. It was wonderfully warm. She moved to the steps and carefully descended into the water.

Oh, it was marvelous. She swam toward the back glass enclosure that overlooked the outdoor portion of the pool. She was tempted to duck under the divider and swim outside, but the breeze would be cold on her damp skin.

She floated lazily on her back for a while then did a few laps, gliding underneath the water for as long as she could hold her breath. She came up with a gasp and grabbed on to the side of the pool. And then she saw a pair of leather loafers.

She glanced up to see Chrysander watching her, arms folded across his chest, a mock scowl on his face. Even she could see that his lips were twitching suspiciously.

With an innocent blink, she smiled and offered a hello. He squatted down and put a finger underneath her chin, nudging it upward.

"Enjoying yourself, *pedhaki mou?*"

"Very much," she returned.

"And to think I was looking forward to hauling you out of your garden today," he murmured.

Her face heated as she recalled all that had happened yesterday when he'd done just that. She extended her hand. "Help me out?"

He grasped her hand, and she reached to grip his wrist with her other hand at the same time she planted her feet against the side of the pool and pulled with all her might. He gave a shout of surprise as he toppled over and hit the water with a gigantic splash.

He came up sputtering, and for a moment, she worried that he was truly angry. He scowled ferociously at her before glancing down at his soaked clothing. Then he started laughing.

Before he could think retaliation, and since she still wanted him to see her suit, she swam over to the steps and exited the pool in slow, deliberate movements. She glanced over her shoulder to see his mouth drop open as he viewed the back of her suit.

When Marley reached the top, she turned so he could see her profile, and she heard him suck in his breath. She turned away again and began walking toward where her wrap was laying.

"Oh no you don't, you little tease," he growled.

She blinked at how quickly he got out of the pool. She gave a shriek of surprise when he closed in on her then laughed when he gathered her into his arms and headed back toward the pool.

"Chrysander, your clothes!"

"As if they matter now. You've quite ruined them."

"I'm sorry."

He laughed. "No, you're not." He bent down at the side of the pool and gently eased her back into the water. Then he stood and fixed her with a glare. "You stay right there."

She giggled. Her laughter died in her throat, though, when he began peeling his clothing off his body. First his shirt came off, revealing his muscular chest. Then he kicked off his shoes and yanked off the soaked socks. When he reached for the fly of his trousers, she blushed but couldn't look away to save her life.

The discernible bulge in his boxers as he stepped out of his pants told her that she'd certainly been successful in her quest to make him a little crazy. But now she wondered what exactly he'd do about it.

He hopped over the side, landing next to her with a minimal splash. Then he hauled her against him, kissing her hungrily.

"That suit should be illegal," he said as he worked his mouth down her neck.

"You don't like it?" she asked innocently. "I could always get rid of it."

"Oh, I like it," he murmured. "I'm going to like taking it off of you even better."

She broke loose and dove beneath the water, swimming away from him as fast as she could. She surfaced after a short distance but didn't immediately see him. She looked down, too late, to see his glimmering body. He grabbed her legs and yanked her underneath.

His lips closed over hers, and he propelled them both above

the water. She wrapped her arms around his neck and smiled up at him. "I suppose I'm going to have to take back what I said about you being no fun."

"It would seem so."

"I wouldn't object to you hauling me out of the pool and taking me upstairs," she said with pretended innocence.

He kissed her again, hot, breathless. His hands slid around her waist to cup her bottom. He lifted her upward, and she latched her legs around his waist.

"Hold on to me, *pedhaki mou*," he murmured. "I'm hauling you out of the pool right now."

He mounted the steps and carefully climbed out of the pool. As he neared one of the loungers, she noticed that he'd brought two towels with him. Apparently he had planned to come in all the while. She grinned impishly at him. He wasn't so serious all the time.

He put her down in one of the loungers then reached for a towel. He dried her hair and her body, allowing his hands to linger in some of her most sensitive areas. He touched and caressed until she was squirming in the chair.

"Now who's teasing?" she said breathlessly.

He straddled the lounger and lowered his body to hers.

"Mmmm, you're warm."

"Are you cold?" he asked huskily. "I wonder what I can do to warm you."

She pulled him closer, wrapping her arms around him. She threaded her fingers into his wet hair and kissed him. A sound of contentment purred from her throat as he returned her kiss with equal ardor.

His erection strained against her belly, hot, like steel. Warmth shot through her body, leaving her flushed and aching. She wanted him. Wanted him so badly.

"Take me upstairs," she whispered as his lips scorched down her neck and to the swell of her breasts.

The sound of a door closing startled them both. Chrysander let out an oath as he rolled away from Marley and yanked up a towel to cover her. Marley stiffened when she saw Roslyn over Chrysander's shoulder.

Her surprise turned to anger. The woman had barged in, intruded on their privacy without so much as a call to let them know she was coming out to the island. They hadn't even heard the helicopter land, but then they'd been occupied with other matters.

"What are you doing here?" Chrysander said icily.

"I'm sorry to interrupt, Mr. Anetakis," Roslyn said, though her expression said she was anything but. Her gaze skimmed Marley in triumph, but the look was gone when she turned her attention back to Chrysander. "There were several things that needed your attention, and I thought it best to see to them personally rather than rely on the phone or e-mail."

"They certainly haven't failed in the past," Chrysander said stiffly. "If you'll excuse us, I think perhaps it would be better for you to wait in my office."

"Yes, of course, Mr. Anetakis. Again, my apologies for the disturbance."

Marley shivered, this time the chill setting in deep. The woman had impeccable timing.

"I'm sorry," Chrysander said as he helped her from the lounger. He wrapped the towel around her shivering body and tucked her against his side. "I'll take you upstairs so you can change into something warmer. This shouldn't take but a moment, and then I'll return."

Marley nodded, but for her, the moment was ruined. Gone was Chrysander's fun-loving mood. The passion that had sizzled between them just minutes ago was now a cold blanket thrown by his trusty assistant.

He took her upstairs and ushered her into the shower. When she stepped out, he'd already dressed and gone back downstairs. With an unhappy sigh, she gathered the towel around her and sat down on the edge of the bed.

Chrysander entered his office, irritation replacing his earlier good mood. He stared hard at Roslyn, who stood to the side. "I do not appreciate this intrusion," he said crisply. "There was no call, no warning, no *permission* asked to come out to the island."

Roslyn paled and her eyes widened.

"This is my private living area, and as such, you do not have free rein as you do in my business settings. Are we understood?"

"Yes, sir," she said stiffly.

"Now, what was so important that it didn't warrant a phone call?" he demanded.

"I've discovered that another design was stolen," she said softly.

"What?" Curses spilled from his lips, and it took a moment for him to realize he was speaking in Greek, and Roslyn didn't understand a word of it. He shook his head and put both hands down on his desk. "What design? Tell me everything."

Roslyn's expression hardened. "It's an older one, a design you discarded. It was the original plan for the Rio de Janeiro hotel. But still, she must have sold it to Marcelli with the others, because his hotel going up in Rome bears a remarkable likeness. I saw the proofs myself just two days ago."

Rage burned like acid in Chrysander's veins. "Do my brothers know of this yet?"

Roslyn shook her head. "I thought you would want to tell them."

He nodded and closed his eyes as he turned to look out the window to the beach. Every time he thought he had come to terms with Marley's betrayal, the past came back to haunt him. As much as he wanted to forget, to move on, to put the past behind them, it always came back, insidious and unrelenting.

He struggled to remember how Marley could have gotten access to the hotel plans. He certainly hadn't guarded himself at home. As careful as he was in the office and in all other aspects of his life, he'd been relaxed and free with her, never thinking to protect his interests from her.

How could he build a life with her when he could never trust her? Was he a fool for building a temporary relationship when it would all come tumbling down the minute she remembered? When she'd have to face the sins she'd committed and reap the consequences of her betrayal?

Through it all, he could only remember one thing. The way she'd looked the night he'd confronted her in their apartment. The absolute shock and horror on her face. Could anyone fake such a reaction that well?

For the first time, he took a long, hard look at the woman she'd been during their time together before her abduction and the woman she'd been since. There was no marked difference. The only inconsistency was her betrayal.

"Chrysander." Roslyn spoke up in a soft voice.

His eyes narrowed at her use of his name. It was not something he ever tolerated from his employees, though he wasn't sure why it bothered him coming from someone he had worked closely with for some time.

"You won't allow her to do it again, will you?"

He turned around to face her. "No, it won't happen again," he said tightly, anger creeping up his spine. His anger wasn't totally at Marley. For some reason, it rankled that Roslyn would think to warn him away from Marley.

Roslyn looked uncomfortable. "I just hope she doesn't ruin things for you with this hotel deal. Not again. It's too important."

"I don't think that's any of your concern. I will handle Marley."

She flinched at his tone. "I apologize. This company, this job, is very important to me. I've worked hard for you, sir. I worked hard on the Paris deal."

Chrysander let go of some of his anger and blew out a sigh. She had worked hard, and he could see why she would harbor some anger toward Marley even if he wouldn't tolerate it. Even if he didn't feel she was justified in that anger. That thought struck him hard, because it meant on some level he didn't believe Marley capable of her crime.

"I appreciate your concern, Roslyn. However, it is not your business. If that is all you wanted, then I'll call for the helicopter to return you to the mainland."

She looked as though she would protest, but then she nodded.

Thirty minutes later, Chrysander escorted her out to the

helipad, and as soon as the helicopter lifted off, he turned and strode back into the house.

His anger and uncertainty evaporated when he entered the bedroom and found Marley sitting on the bed, wrapped only in a towel, her expression sad and distant.

He knelt in front of her and touched her cheek. "What is it, *agape mou?* Are you all right?"

She smiled, though it didn't reach her eyes. Her beautiful blue eyes that had sparkled just a short time ago with laughter. He wanted them to sparkle again. He wanted that stolen moment at the pool back. Before Roslyn had arrived and given him news that could very well change everything between him and Marley. Again.

"I'm in an impossible situation," she confessed.

His brow wrinkled in confusion. He didn't like the sadness in her tone. The resignation.

"What do you mean?" he asked softly as he trailed a finger down the silken curve of her cheek.

She looked into his eyes. "I don't like the way she has free rein in our lives. This is our home. We should be able to make love, have fun together, without fear of being caught in a compromising situation by a stranger. But if I voice this, if I say I don't like her and I don't want her here, it makes me a catty bitch. There is no way for me to come out the winner and every way for me to be the loser in this."

She looked down for a moment then stared back up at him, emotion shimmering in her eyes. "I don't like the way you back away from me every time she appears. She sweeps in on some pretext of business, then she leaves and you become distant. The last weeks have been so utterly wonderful, and now she barges in and I can already feel you pulling away from me. I don't know that I can bear it."

Tears pooled in her eyes, and he was struck speechless, for what she said, all of it, was completely true. He hadn't realized how it would look to her, had thought he'd hidden the conflicting emotions he experienced when reminded of the fact she'd stolen from him, lied to him, betrayed him.

He raised one of her hands to his mouth and pressed it firmly to his lips. "I'm sorry, *agape mou*. I'm sorry her presence has bothered you and that I've ignored it. It won't happen again. I've already informed her that under no condition is she to just arrive here without at least phoning."

"I could stand her presence. I won't lie and say I like the woman, but I could tolerate her. What I cannot bear is the way you pull away from me every time she appears. Without any memories to bolster my confidence, I have nothing to point to and say, Marley, you're being ridiculous. Of course there's nothing going on between him and his assistant."

His mouth fell open in surprise. "You think I'm having an affair with her?" He couldn't control the shudder of distaste that rolled down his spine.

She shook her head emphatically. "Oh, I've made a mess of this. I'm only trying to say that for me, this is all new. Our relationship is new. I can't remember our time together before, so in essence, we're building new, starting all over. I can't help the insecurity I feel when I look at her and know she's trying to undermine our relationship."

He gathered her in his arms, having no idea what to say to her. He couldn't very well deny that Roslyn probably did want to keep him from Marley. She knew Marley had stolen from the company, a company that Roslyn was devoted to and had put in a lot of long hours for in preparing the deal that had disappeared along with the plans for the Paris hotel. And now he'd learned that yet another of the Anetakis designs would be going up under the Marcelli name. No matter it was one he'd discarded. Marley couldn't have known that at the time.

What an impossible situation. Surprising to him was the anger that Roslyn's words had caused. His first reaction had been to defend Marley and to chastise Roslyn for speaking out against Marley. But how could he when Roslyn was right?

All he knew was that he didn't want Marley to hurt. As stupid as that sounded given the hurt she'd caused him, he wanted to wipe away the sadness in her eyes. While he couldn't do anything to erase the past, what he could do was make sure that Roslyn wasn't a source of contention between them. He would honor Marley's wishes in this, for they mirrored his own. He didn't want anything to come between them here on the island. Roslyn wouldn't return.

Eleven

Chrysander hung up the phone with a grimace and leaned back in his leather chair. He put his hands behind his head and stared up at the ceiling.

He had to return to New York. Piers had called him with the news just moments ago, and Chrysander greeted the fact with a discomfort that was alien to him. Worse, he'd had to inform Piers and Theron that another of their designs had been stolen. They were understandably furious. With Marley. How would they react when they learned he had every intention of marrying her as soon as possible?

He was torn between wanting Marley to go with him and wanting to keep her sheltered here on the island. Away from any chance she might remember. Away from the judgment and animosity of his brothers.

The beginnings of a headache plagued him as he considered the selfishness of that particular thought. He knew, though, that when she remembered, and the doctors had assured him she would, things would irrevocably change between them.

He should still be furious with her, and he should be working to maintain distance between them, but she'd chipped away his resistance during their time on the island. As much as it shamed him, it no longer mattered to him that she'd lied, that she'd stolen from him and his brothers. He wanted things to remain as they were, and if she remembered, then they would be forced to face the events of the past.

And he'd likely lose her.

It bothered him more than it should. She was pregnant with his child, he told himself, and that should be reason enough not to want things to sour between them.

His time here with Marley had brought him back to the times they'd spent together before the night he'd discovered her betrayal. He hadn't really appreciated her before. He'd taken her and her presence in his life for granted, but now he knew how much he'd liked having her there when he returned from business.

She was fun and carefree. Gentle and loving. All the things he'd wish for in the mother of his child.

But she'd betrayed him. It always came back to that even as he wanted to forget it.

"Chrysander?"

He looked up on hearing his softly spoken name to see Marley standing in the doorway, her hand resting on the frame as she peered in. He shook himself from his grim thoughts and hoped his expression wasn't as brooding as he felt. Things had been strained and tense between them since Roslyn had come to the island. A fact he regretted but was unable to fully remedy when he still carried his own doubts and uncertainties where Marley was concerned.

"What is it, *pedhaki mou?*"

"Are you all right?" She let her hand fall and started forward, her steps hesitant.

He guessed he did look brooding.

"Come here," he said, holding out his hand to her as she neared. He pulled her down onto his lap, suddenly wanting her close. "I have to return to New York."

A shadow crossed over her face. "When?"

"In the morning. My brother called, and a dignitary we are courting for a hotel project is going to be at a reception at our New York hotel. Piers and Theron thought to handle it, but the man wished to meet with all three of us. It's something I cannot miss, I'm afraid."

She looked disappointed, and even as the uneasiness over her going back to New York lingered in his mind, he found himself saying, "You could go with me."

Her eyes lightened. "I wouldn't be in the way?"

He frowned. "You are never in the way, *agape mou*. This would be good, I think. We could announce our wedding plans. My brothers will want to meet you," he said, warming to the subject. "We could even be married in New York with my family around us and then return here."

In his mind, the sooner they married, the better.

"I'll arrange for Dr. Karounis to return to Athens. I don't think we need him any longer."

Her smile broadened. "And Patrice? Not that I don't love her, but she and Dr. Karounis seem to have gotten along extremely well. Maybe she'd like to take a trip to Athens."

"I'll extend the offer," he said with a smile.

"Then yes, I'd love to go." She threw her arms around him and kissed him exuberantly on the lips. Before he could deepen the kiss, she scrambled off his lap. "I have to go pack!"

He chuckled and caught her hand. "You have plenty of time."

But still she hurried away, and he stared after her, long after she'd disappeared through the doorway. He should feel relieved that soon they'd be married, and she'd be bound to him, but he couldn't dispel the uneasy feeling that gripped him.

Chrysander's jet touched down in New York in the late afternoon, and a limousine was waiting for them when they stepped off the plane. A tall, formidable-looking man stood by the car, and as they drew closer, Marley could see a strong resemblance between him and Chrysander.

"Theron," Chrysander called out. "I did not expect you to meet us. This is a surprise."

Theron gave a half smile. "Can I not greet my brother?"

Chrysander put an arm around Marley's waist and drew her forward. "Theron, this is Marley. Marley, this is my younger brother Theron."

She smiled. "I'm very glad to meet you."

His gaze flickered impassively over her, and he didn't return her smile. Slowly hers faded as she read the unwelcoming look on his face. Instinctively, she shrank into Chrysander.

Then Theron's gaze dropped to the hand on which she wore the engagement ring, and he outright frowned. He stared back up at Chrysander, his jaw tight.

"You will be courteous," Chrysander said in a very low tone. Even so, she could hear the bite in his voice.

"I'm pleased to meet you," Theron said stiffly, though his body language said just the opposite. He turned on his heel and walked toward another car parked a short distance away.

Marley looked up at Chrysander in bewilderment. "What was that all about?"

"It is nothing, *pedhaki mou*. I am sorry he was rude. It won't happen again."

"But *why* was he rude?" His behavior baffled Marley. And then another thought occurred to her. "Have we met before? Of course we would have. He's your brother. Did I do something to offend him in the past? Has he always disliked me?"

Chrysander ushered her into the car and slid in beside her. "No, you haven't met before. You needn't worry that you've done anything. It's just Theron's way." He sounded a bit strangled, and her gaze narrowed at what she thought must be a lie.

When his cell phone rang, he lunged for it in his haste to answer. She put her lips together and seethed in silence. Something didn't add up. Why would his brother dislike her so intensely on sight? And for that matter, why had she never met him before? It couldn't be normal for her not to have met the family of the man she was going to marry, the father of her child.

She leaned back against the seat and blew out her breath in frustration. While in New York, she fully intended to seek answers and maybe try to dislodge the block that seemed permanently embedded in her mind. There had to be some way to break her memories free. And if there was, she was going to find it. Preferably before she got married.

Yet more was in store when they reached the penthouse. She very nearly growled her frustration when the lift opened and she caught sight of Roslyn. Was she doomed to find this woman in her home at every turn?

Roslyn smiled warmly in greeting, and Marley did not miss that it extended only to Chrysander. She stood beside him while his assistant outlined the schedule of meetings, phone calls he needed to return and contracts that needed his attention. She wouldn't retreat this time and allow Roslyn any victory, implied or otherwise.

Roslyn spoke in low, sultry tones and touched Chrysander's arm frequently. She laughed huskily at something he said, all the while overtly ignoring Marley's presence. The woman had brass. Marley had to admit that. If she weren't pregnant, she'd give serious consideration to throwing the woman out of the penthouse on her ear.

It was good as fantasies went, but Chrysander would be horrified. She sighed even as the image of the beautifully coiffed woman banned from the apartment cheered her considerably.

Finally, Roslyn made to leave, and Marley's shoulders sagged in relief. But as the elevator opened to admit her, another man, also bearing a strong resemblance to Chrysander strode off.

She wanted to ask Chrysander just how many people had access to their private quarters but bit her lip.

"It would seem our apartment is a revolving door today," Chrysander said dryly, and Marley wondered if he'd read her mind.

While Theron's disapproval of her might have been more subtle, there was nothing left to imagine about this man's opinion of her. He scowled openly even as Chrysander introduced him to her as his brother Piers.

"A word if you don't mind, Chrysander," Piers said, his jaw clenched tight.

"Don't let me interrupt," Marley said. She turned and walked toward the bedroom, having had enough of the chilly reception she'd received.

Even as she closed the door, she could hear raised voices and Chrysander's angry tone. She hesitated a moment, wondering if she should listen to their conversation. Would she want to hear what they were saying? With a sigh, she turned to survey the room that Chrysander had given her upon her release from the hospital.

Not knowing what else to do, she slipped out of her shoes and sat down on the bed. The trip hadn't been tiring, but sliding under the covers and hiding appealed to her. Her head was beginning to ache from tension, and if she could just get away for a few minutes, she might feel better. And maybe when she woke, there wouldn't be anyone in their apartment anymore.

When she did wake, she was in a different bed. She blinked the sleep-induced fog away and realized that she was in Chrysander's bedroom. She stretched and was glad not to feel the pressure in her head any longer.

She sat up and saw Chrysander standing across the room looking at her. For some reason, she felt unsure of herself in that moment.

"I must have been more tired than I realized," she said lightly. "I didn't even wake when you moved me."

"You will sleep in our room, in our bed."

She blinked. "Well, okay. I just didn't think. That was the room I had before."

He closed the distance between them and sat down on the bed next to her. "Your place is here. With me."

She cocked her head. She had the distinct impression he wasn't just speaking to the fact that she'd gone to bed in another room. It was almost as though he was convincing himself, and others, that she belonged with him.

"Your brothers don't approve of me," she said quietly.

His face became a stone. "My brothers have no say in our relationship. I will announce our forthcoming marriage at the reception two nights from now, and we'll marry in a week."

And that was that, she thought. The law laid down by Chrysander Anetakis.

He leaned down to kiss her. "Why don't you dress? We'll go out for a nice dinner."

"Lobster?" she asked hopefully then realized what she'd said. Her eyes widened in excitement. "Lobster! Chrysander, I remember that lobster is my favorite."

He smiled tightly and kissed her again. "So it is, *pedhaki mou*. I used to have it delivered here, and we'd sit naked on the bed to eat it."

She flushed to the roots of her hair but had to admit the image was appealing. Chrysander helped her up, and she went into the bathroom to shower and change. Thirty minutes later, Chrysander escorted her down the elevator and out to the waiting car.

He took her to an elegant restaurant, and they sat in an intimate corner set away from the main dining area. The lighting was low, and it reminded her of Christmas. A warm feeling of nostalgia took hold as she recalled how very much she loved the holiday season.

In another month, decorations would be going up, and many of the shops and restaurants would twinkle with lights and holly. She smiled dreamily as she imagined spending Christmas with Chrysander.

"You look lost in thought, *agape mou*. With such a sweet smile on your face, I can only hope that I am what is occupying your thoughts."

She looked across the table to see Chrysander studying her, his bronze skin illuminated by soft candlelight. "I was imagining spending Christmas with you. I was remembering how much I love the holidays."

"Your memories seem to be coming back," he said, though there was no joy in his tone.

Her lips twisted into a rueful smile. "Not very quickly, I'm afraid. Just a snippet here and there, and it's more of an awareness, not a true memory."

"It will come. You must be patient."

She nodded, but she could feel the frustration creeping over her. Determined not to let the evening go the way the rest of the day had, she forced herself to relax and enjoy the wonderful meal and being with Chrysander. With no interruptions from family members or personal assistants.

"Would you like to go shopping tomorrow?" Chrysander asked.

She blinked in surprise at the sudden change in topic.

"I have a meeting first thing, but then we could eat lunch together and shop for the things you will need for the reception we will be attending. You could also look for a wedding dress."

She couldn't wrap her brain around the image of Chrysander shopping, and she was sure no amount of searching her memory would find one. He simply wasn't a man to do such a thing.

"Are you sure you want me there?"

He cocked one eyebrow. "As I plan to announce our upcoming wedding, it would be strange if you weren't. Unless you have no wish to go."

"No, that isn't it at all. I'd love to go. I just wasn't sure…." She trailed off, determined not to dig her hole any deeper.

"Then it is settled. We'll go out shopping tomorrow after I've fed you properly."

She grinned. "You make me sound like a pet."

A slow, sexy smile curved his mouth. "I like the sound of you being my pet. My own personal, pampered pet," he purred.

Heat sizzled through her body like an electric current. She swallowed and took a sip of her water in an attempt to assuage the tingling warmth.

Then he laughed, and the sound sent a flutter of awareness over her nerves. "You like the idea, too, I see."

She blushed and ducked her head. "I like the idea of being your anything," she said honestly.

He reached across the table and tugged her fingers into his hand. "You are mine, *agape mou*. That is what you are."

"Then take me home and make love to me," she whispered.

Twelve

The next morning, Chrysander left their bed early. He kissed her softly on the brow and told her he would come for her at noon. Marley yawned sleepily, murmured her goodbye and turned over to go back to sleep. His soft chuckle echoed in her ears as she drifted off.

When she woke again, she squinted against the sunlight and glanced over at the clock. She still had hours until her lunch date with Chrysander, and she had no desire to spend them sitting around the apartment.

With so many of Chrysander's security men milling about, surely one of them would have access to transportation. She could commandeer one of them and go out on her own a bit, though she had no idea where she'd go exactly.

And then another thought occurred to her. With Chrysander being such a stickler for tight security, she doubted she'd gone anywhere without it in the time they were together. If that was the case, then surely one of them would have an idea of the places she'd visited and the things she liked to do.

Considerably cheered by that realization, she hurried into the shower. Thirty minutes later, she rode the elevator down to the lobby and got off. She could see a burly-looking man standing by the door and recognized him as the man Chrysander called Stavros.

He snapped to attention when he saw her walking toward him.

"Miss Jameson," he said in a heavy Greek accent. "Is there something I can do for you?"

She noticed the way he subtly moved to bar the door so she could not exit and nearly laughed.

"I'm sure Chrysander has told you that I…that I've lost my memory."

He nodded, and his expression softened.

"What I was wondering is if you could tell me whether or not I had security assigned to me before my accident."

"I personally saw to your protection," Stavros said.

"Oh, good! Then maybe you can help me. I'd like to go out, but I don't really know where. I mean, I don't know what places I liked to go, and since you no doubt followed me everywhere I went, maybe you could take me to some of those places today."

He paused for a moment as if considering her request. Then he dug out a cell phone from his pocket, punched a button and stuck the phone to his ear. He spoke rapidly in Greek, nodded a few times then extended the receiver to her.

"Mr. Anetakis would like to speak to you."

"Oh, for heaven's sake," she huffed as she took it. "You didn't waste any time ratting me out, did you?" She stared accusingly at Stavros, who didn't look the least bit apologetic.

Chrysander laughed in her ear. "What sort of trouble are you causing, *agape mou?*"

She sighed a little ridiculously. After that first awkward time he'd murmured the endearment, he'd used it with increasing frequency. It turned her to mush every time it slid over her ears, warm and vibrant.

"I wanted to go out for a while. I'll be back in time for our lunch, I promise."

"Enjoy your morning, but be careful and don't overexert

yourself. If you find you're running late, have Stavros call me, and I can meet you for lunch so you don't have to return to the apartment."

She smiled and murmured her agreement. They rang off, and she handed the phone back to Stavros. "You and I need to have a conversation about tattling."

He didn't bat an eyelash. "I assure you, Miss Jameson, we've had such conversations in the past."

She grinned and then watched as Stavros put a hand to the small earpiece he wore and barked out several orders in Greek.

Within moments a car rolled around the front, and yet another security man got out to open the door for her. Stavros ushered her out of the building and settled her comfortably in the vehicle before he and the other man took seats in the front.

The privacy glass between the front and backseats lowered, and Stavros turned to look at her over his shoulder.

"Where would you like to go, Miss Jameson?"

"I don't know," she said with a laugh. "Can you give me a tour of some of the places I used to go?"

He nodded, and they drove onto the busy New York streets.

Their first stop was a small coffee shop a few blocks away from the apartment. It was clear that Stavros hadn't expected her to want to get out, because when she made the intention known, his lips drew into a disapproving line. Still, he and the other man with him escorted her inside the small café.

It was cozy and brimming with conversation and laughter. It felt inviting, and she could well see herself in a place like this. But it didn't spark any memories. With a sigh, she turned and told Stavros she was ready to leave.

Next they pulled up to a small market, and she looked at Stavros in surprise.

"You liked to cook for Mr. Anetakis, particularly when he'd been out of the country for an extended period of time. We would come here to shop for the necessary ingredients. Then you'd make me carry back all the sacks," he added with a small smile.

"Was I so very trying?" she teased.

"It was my pleasure to accompany you on your outings," Stavros said.

"Why, it sounds like you like me." She grinned up at the burly man, trying to gain any sort of recognition, some flicker that maybe they'd bantered like this in the past. "Where to next?"

They visited a library and a small art shop, and while she could see herself in those places, she recalled nothing. When the car rolled to a stop in front of a park, for a moment panic quivered in her stomach.

"Are you all right?" Stavros demanded.

She looked up to see him standing at the open door, waiting for her to climb out.

"Maybe we should return now. It's nearly time for your lunch with Mr. Anetakis."

"No," she said as she hastened out of the car. No, she wanted to be here. Needed to be here. Something about this place had caused a tremor in her mind even if it was uncomfortable.

She walked down the pathway and gathered her coat tighter around her. In truth, it wasn't that cold. The afternoon sun shone warmly, but she felt a chill, one that reached far inside her.

Behind her, Stavros and his second flanked her, and she had the brief thought that she appeared far more important than she was. Her gaze locked on to a stone bench that overlooked a statue, and she moved toward it, not sure why she was so drawn by it.

Marley sat down and spread her hands over the cool stone. She stared ahead and felt a glimmer of sadness. It made no sense, but she knew she had sat here before, and she knew that she had felt fear. Uncertainty.

She raised her hands to cup her face and leaned over, huddled on the bench. It was there, just out of reach, so close she could feel the heavy weight of sadness, of indecision.

A hand touched her shoulder, and Stavros's concerned voice reached her. "Are you all right? Do I need to call Mr. Anetakis? Perhaps I should take you to the hospital."

She shook her head and looked up. "No. I'm fine. It's just that I've been here before. I can feel it."

Stavros nodded, though the concern didn't leave his eyes. "You often said this was your thinking spot."

"It would appear I had a lot to think about," she murmured.

He checked his watch. "Let me call Mr. Anetakis and tell him to meet us at the restaurant. By the time we return to the apartment, you could already be eating."

She didn't object when he gently helped her up, and instead of walking just behind her, he held her elbow as they walked back to the car.

"Stavros, please don't concern Chrysander," she said as he put her into the car. "He'll have me back at the apartment in bed."

"Which is perhaps where you should be," Stavros said.

She made a face. "You're seriously no fun. I'm supposed to go shopping. For a wedding dress no less. I can't very well do that if I'm in bed."

Stavros looked to be fighting a smile as he closed the door. A moment later, the privacy glass slid down and Stavros turned to look at her. "If Mr. Anetakis asks, I'll simply say we had a quiet day on the town."

"I knew there was a reason I liked you," she said cheekily, her good spirits restored.

When they arrived at the restaurant, Chrysander met them at the car and promptly dismissed Stavros, saying he would have his driver take him and Marley home when they were through shopping.

Over lunch, Chrysander asked how her morning had gone, and she explained about all the places Stavros had taken her. But when she asked him about his morning, he grew silent and vague.

Not wanting to cast a pall over the day, she swiftly changed the topic to their shopping.

"Exactly how fancy is this reception we're attending?" she asked as she savored another bite of the rich pasta.

He quirked one eyebrow. "That depends on your definition of fancy."

"Oh, then I can wear my blue jeans and maternity top," she said sweetly.

He laughed. "While I certainly would not object to you

wearing your blue jeans, I do not want others seeing you in something that cups your bottom so lovingly."

"Am I supposed to dress up then?" she asked with a sigh.

"Don't concern yourself with it, *pedhaki mou*. I will choose the perfect dress for you."

"I won't wear high heels," she said resolutely. "There is no way I'm waddling around on toothpicks."

"Of course not," he said in a tone that suggested she was crazy for even mentioning it. "I'm certain it's not advisable for a pregnant woman to put herself through such torture. What if you fell?"

"Maybe I could go barefooted," she said mischievously.

He laughed. "And maybe I should stick to a plan of keeping you at home solidly under lock and key."

She swallowed the last bite of her pasta and reluctantly pushed the plate away. "That was so wonderful, and I ate far too much."

"You need to gain some weight. You are too slight as it is. It is good that you ate well."

"And if I eat any more, I won't fit into whatever dress you plan on buying me." She glanced down at her rounded belly. "Do they make ultra-chic wear for pregnant women?"

Chrysander gave her a patient look. "Trust me, Marley. We will find you something suitable."

"Just how do you know so darn much about buying dresses anyway?" she grumbled as he took her out to his waiting car.

"Surely you don't expect me to answer that?" he said with barely suppressed amusement.

She shot him a withering look and settled into the car.

As it turned out, he did indeed have a skill for choosing the perfect dress. He nailed it with the second one she tried on. White silk in a very simple design. It had spaghetti straps with a conservative bodice, and the material hugged her belly, drawing attention to the soft mound.

"It makes me look…well, very pregnant," she said as she turned to allow Chrysander to look.

"You look absolutely exquisite," he murmured. "I think every pregnant woman should like to look as you do right now."

The appreciation in his eyes sold her on the dress. She had no desire to look any further. It was carefully wrapped and set aside along with the low-heeled shoes that she had chosen.

"Tell me, *agape mou*, do you want a traditional wedding dress?"

She pursed her lips then shook her head. "No, I'd prefer something simpler, I think."

The saleslady set several really gorgeous selections in front of them, and Marley watched Chrysander closely for his reaction.

She fell in love with a peach-colored gown that scraped the floor and fell in soft waves from her waist. It accentuated her pregnancy in such a way that she truly felt beautiful and feminine. It was clear by the look on his face that Chrysander agreed.

To her surprise, instead of returning to the car, he walked her next door to a jeweler and proceeded to choose a stunning set of diamond earrings and a matching necklace to go with her wedding dress. Already speechless, she was reduced to a mere croak when he next selected a sapphire necklace and earrings that he suggested she wear with the white silk dress to the reception.

"They will look beautiful with your eyes, *agape mou*," he murmured next to her ear. "And later, I'd love nothing more than to see you in these jewels and nothing else."

Her face exploded in heat, and she looked around to make sure no one could see her furious blushing.

"You spoil me, Chrysander," she said as they left the jewelry store.

"It is my right to spoil my woman," he said with a shrug.

"I find I quite like it," she said with a smile.

"That is good, because it would be a shame for you not to enjoy something I intend to be doing a lot of."

Impulsively, she scooted against him in the seat and kissed him full on the lips. A staggered breath escaped him as his hands went out to grip her arms. Her cheek slid down his until she nuzzled against his neck and she hugged him tightly.

"Thank you for today. I had so much fun."

His hand went to her hair and stroked softly as he hugged her back with his other arm. "You are quite welcome."

She raised her head and started to move away, but Chrysander held her fast against him.

"Am I a good cook?" she asked, cocking her head at him.

His face registered surprise. "I'm sorry?"

"Cook. Stavros informed me that I liked to cook for you and frequently went to the market for ingredients. I wondered if I was any good at it."

A peculiar expression lit his face. "That's right. You did. I hadn't thought about it in a while, but yes, you did often cook a meal for me on my first night home."

"Were you gone very often?" she asked.

He paused for a moment then slowly nodded. "I'm afraid I was. I was often out of the country on business. Sometimes we went weeks without seeing each other."

"I can't imagine it," she said softly. "I missed you in just the few hours we were apart this morning."

He kissed her again. "And I missed you, *pedhaki mou*."

She settled against his side as they continued the ride home. She was a bit tired, but there was no way she'd tell him that. The day had been nearly perfect, and they still had the evening together.

Thirteen

Marley fidgeted and tugged at her dress as she surveyed her appearance in the mirror. Sapphires glinted from both ears, and the matching necklace lay against the skin of her neck.

"You look beautiful, *agape mou*."

She turned to see Chrysander behind her. She sucked in her breath as she took in his appearance. The excellently tailored black suit fit him to perfection, drawing attention to his muscular build. The white shirt contrasted with his bronze skin, dark hair and golden eyes, and quite frankly, she felt like drooling.

"So do you," she finally managed.

He chuckled and walked toward her. "Beautiful? Surely you can do better than that."

"Gorgeous? Devastatingly handsome? So good-looking that I'm tempted to fall on you and tear your clothes off?"

"I like the way you think."

"I wasn't joking," she muttered.

"Are you ready? The car is waiting for us below."

She took a deep breath and twisted her engagement ring around her finger with the pad of her thumb. "As ready as I'll ever be."

He reached for her hand and tugged her into his arms. "It won't be so bad. I will be with you the whole night."

She reached up on tiptoe to kiss him. "I'm a coward. I fully admit it."

He took his time exploring her lips, moving with a sensual thoroughness that left her weak and breathless. When they drew apart, she could see he was as affected as she was.

"I think we should leave now," he said hoarsely. "Otherwise we won't be going anywhere for a very long time."

They rode to the hotel, and Marley could see several limousines lining the circular drive outside the main entrance as they pulled up. She swallowed nervously as she saw the glitz and glamour of the people stepping from the cars and entering the hotel. She suddenly felt underdressed and unprepared.

When they reached the front entrance, the doors were opened and Chrysander stepped out, extending his hand to help her from the car. He tucked her arm securely underneath his, and they walked inside the hotel.

Butterflies performed a rendition of the River Dance in her stomach as they entered the large ballroom. A jazz band played softly from a small stage at the back of the room. Waiters circled with trays of wine and champagne while others offered a selection of hors d'oeuvres.

Chrysander murmured to one of the waiters as he took a glass of wine from the tray, and a few moments later, he returned with a glass of mineral water for Marley.

As she scanned the room, glass in hand, she mentally groaned as she saw Theron and Piers and then Roslyn. While she knew they'd be in attendance, she'd truly hoped to avoid them as much as possible. That wasn't going to happen, she mused as she saw Theron start across the room toward Chrysander.

Her first reaction was to excuse herself to the ladies' room, but Chrysander's grip tightened on her fingers as though he knew of her impending flight.

"Chrysander," Theron said by way of greeting. His gaze skimmed quickly over Marley, and he offered the briefest of nods. At least it wasn't a full-blown snub, nor did he scowl at her.

She listened as the two exchanged pleasantries, and then Theron gestured toward Piers and a distinguished older gentleman who was standing beside him. She hung back as Chrysander started toward his brother, but he tugged her along with him, and her dread increased.

Piers frowned when she and Chrysander approached. The older gentleman smiled broadly and uttered a polite greeting to Chrysander. A woman Marley assumed was his wife also offered an enthusiastic hello from his side.

Chrysander urged her forward. "Senhor and Senhora Vasquez, I'd like you both to meet Marley Jameson. Marley, this is Senhor Vasquez and his wife. They're here from Brazil on business."

Marley smiled and exchanged pleasantries with the older couple then relaxed against Chrysander. Piers was being polite, and Theron had joined the group minus the complete indifference he'd shown in her presence a moment earlier. Maybe she could endure the evening after all.

Chrysander reached down and squeezed her hand, and then he faced the others, odd tension on his face. "Marley has agreed to be my wife. We plan to marry while we're here in New York. We'd be honored if you all could attend."

A gasp sounded behind Chrysander, and Marley whirled around to see Roslyn standing a few feet away, shock reflected on her face. She recovered quickly, but not quick enough for Marley to wonder what she could possibly have found so shocking about the announcement. As she turned and looked at the others, only the Vasquezes looked congratulatory over the news.

Piers's and Theron's expressions both mirrored Roslyn's shock. Then their surprise turned to outright distaste. Chrysander shot them warning looks, but Marley was at a complete loss. She trembled against Chrysander, and his grip tightened on her hand as if he understood her desire to flee.

How could their engagement possibly be news? They were

engaged before her accident, and yet everyone acted as though it was a recent development. An unpleasant one at that.

After the obligatory well wishes from the Vasquezes and more from a few people nearby who'd overheard, the conversation switched to more mundane topics. Marley remained silent, numb to the talk around her. Chrysander loosened his hold on her hand, but he slid his arm around her waist and anchored her firmly against him. There was no escaping, no matter how much she might wish it.

The conversation turned to the possible building of a hotel in Rio de Janeiro, and while Marley remained silent, only observing the others, Chrysander's arm never strayed from around her waist.

As the evening wore on, more people offered their congratulations on the upcoming wedding, and soon the room buzzed with the news. The constant smile Marley wore was starting to wear on her. As if sensing her strain, Chrysander whirled her onto the dance floor as a slow jazz song floated melodiously in the air.

She sighed as she melted into his arms. "Thanks. I needed that."

He smiled and leaned down to nibble at the corner of her mouth. "You are the most beautiful woman in the room. The men all look at you with lust in their eyes, and it's enough to make me want to pound them into the ground."

"Mmm, as much as I like the macho act, I'd much prefer if you took me home and worked off some of that male arrogance in another way."

"You tempt me."

She smiled up at him. "I was very serious."

He sighed. "As much as I would like to do just that, I'm afraid I am stuck here for the evening. If it becomes too much for you, I can have Stavros take you back to the apartment."

As if she'd leave him here with Roslyn, Miss Super Assistant.

Despite the fact that Chrysander's brothers and Roslyn seemed determined to treat her as a pariah, there were many others who went out of their way to be gracious to Marley and include her in conversation. She actually found herself enjoying the festive atmosphere despite the evening's inauspicious start.

It was growing late when Chrysander leaned in close to her ear and murmured, "I need to speak with my brothers. Will you be all right for a few moments?"

"Of course, silly," she said with a smile. "I'm going to visit the ladies' room. You go on."

He kissed her then strode toward his brothers. Marley took her time in the bathroom. It was a nice reprieve from the endless chatter and the dark glances thrown her way by the Anetakis contingent.

"You can't hide in here forever," she said to herself. Squaring her shoulders, she exited the bathroom and walked back toward the ballroom. As she passed one of the smaller meeting rooms, she heard Chrysander's voice through the open door. She faltered and came to a stop, debating whether to continue or stay and wait for him.

The next words she heard made her decision for her.

"Damn it, Chrysander, there is no need to marry her. Put her up in an apartment somewhere until the child comes. Don't tie yourself to her and give her access to everything you own."

Her mouth rounded in shock at Piers's angry words.

"She is pregnant with my child," Chrysander said icily. "That I choose to marry her is none of your concern."

She moved closer to the door, not caring whether they saw her. What right did Piers have to talk to Chrysander so?

"You can't mean to marry her!" Roslyn's shrill voice rose. "Do you forget how she stole from you? That she tried to ruin your company? If you need any reminders, just look at the new hotels going up in Paris and Rome. Your hotels, Chrysander. Only they're going up under your competitor's name."

A haze blew through Marley's mind. Red hot. Like a swarm of angry bees, tidbits of information began buzzing in her head. And suddenly it was as if a dam broke. The locked door in her mind that she'd tried so hard to budge simply opened, and the past came roaring through with vicious velocity.

She swayed and gripped the door frame tighter. Nausea boiled in her stomach as each and every moment flashed like a movie in fast-forward.

Chrysander's angry accusation of thievery. His ordering her from their apartment, his life. Her abduction and the months she'd spent in hopeless fear, waiting for Chrysander to answer the ransom demands. Demands he'd ignored.

Oh God, she was going to be sick.

He'd left her. Discarded her like a piece of rubbish. The half million dollars, a paltry sum to a man of Chrysander's means, was an amount he'd been unwilling to part with to ensure her return.

Everything had been a lie. He'd lied to her nonstop since she'd awoken in the hospital. He didn't love her or want her. He *despised* her.

She hadn't been worth half a million dollars to him.

Pain splintered through her chest as she shattered. As everything she'd known as true suddenly turned black. Her heart withered and cracked, falling in pieces around her.

He hadn't tried to save her.

The tortured cry that ripped from her mouth echoed through the room. She clamped a hand over her lips, but it was too late. Everyone looked her way. Theron flinched, and an odd discomfort settled over Piers's face. She met Chrysander's gaze, and she could see the truth in his eyes as he realized that she remembered.

As he started across the room toward her, she backed away, stumbling as she did. Oh God, she couldn't face this. Tears blurred her vision. The image of his pale face only spurred her on.

Marley fled down the hallway toward the lobby. Chrysander called her name, but she didn't stop. Sobs bubbled from her chest and exploded outward. She stumbled but regained her footing and pushed herself forward. Behind her, Chrysander cursed and called out to her again.

She was running for the exit, no clear destination in mind. She was nearly there when she met with a mountain. Stavros stepped in front of her and held her, and she exploded in fury, kicking and shoving. Her only thought was to get away, as far away from this place as she could.

She broke free but stumbled backward and fell to the floor. Stavros was down beside her, asking her if she was all right, and she knew she was trapped.

Pain cycled through her body, an unending stream of agony. She closed her eyes as Chrysander's strong hands slid over her body. In an urgent voice, he demanded to know if she was hurt, but she was incapable of answering him. She curled into a ball, uncaring that she was in the middle of the hotel lobby.

Chrysander picked her up, and she could hear him saying her name. Curses fell from his lips, and then he barked orders for someone to summon a doctor. He strode away from the noise of the lobby, and a few moments later, he entered an empty hotel room.

As soon as he lowered her to the bed, she curled herself into a tight ball again and turned away from him. She flinched when he put his hand on her, his touch light and concerned.

"You must stop crying, *agape mou*. You're going to make yourself ill."

She was already sick, she thought dully. Utterly sick at heart. She closed her eyes, but still hot tears streamed down her cheeks, even as Chrysander wiped them away with his fingers.

She wanted to escape. Go some place where it didn't hurt so much. Through the fog, she heard Chrysander conversing with the doctor. A moment later, she felt a prick in her arm, but she didn't react. She didn't care. And then she floated away, so grateful that the pain had receded. Her mind grew fuzzy as the veil of sleep descended over her. Oblivion. She reached for it. Embraced it and wrapped it around her as she slipped away to a place where there was no hurt and no betrayal.

Chrysander paced back and forth at the foot of Marley's bed while the hotel physician administered the sedative. She was beyond distraught, and the doctor had moved immediately to prevent further upset.

As the doctor stood and backed away from the bed, he looked at Chrysander, a grim expression on his face.

Fear tightened Chrysander's chest. "Is she all right? Is the baby all right?"

The doctor motioned him across the room and away from where Marley now quietly lay. "Her injuries are not physical. If they were, perhaps I would be of use. Her distress is mental. If it is as you said, and she has regained her memory, it is that which has caused her immeasurable pain."

Chrysander stirred impatiently. "What can be done? She cannot be left as she is. There must be something we can do." The sight of her pale face and her eyes, so huge with devastation, twisted his gut painfully.

"You should return her to your home, to a place that is more familiar. She needs a doctor, not for her physical well-being, but one who can help her mentally."

"A therapist you mean?" Chrysander asked grimly.

"This is a very delicate time," the doctor warned. "She is extremely fragile, and remembering such traumatic events could cause an emotional breakdown."

His face twisted in sympathy, and he reached out to grasp Chrysander's shoulder. "This will be hard, but perhaps it is for the best. It is good that her memory returned, even if it causes her such distress."

Chrysander wasn't so sure of that. With her memory regained, she also knew that he'd tossed her out of their apartment, basically put her into the hands of her kidnappers. She would also recall the cruel words he'd thrown at her. And she would remember her own part in the whole mess.

He ran a hand wearily through his hair. Part of him wished she would have never regained those memories. They had started fresh, without past deceptions and betrayals. Something niggled at him even as those thoughts passed through his mind.

Wouldn't she have greeted her memory's return with guilt? All he'd seen in her eyes was hurt. Deep and horrific hurt. There was no guilt, no embarrassment over the fact she'd stolen from him. Just distress so keen that he still felt the knife deep in his chest from the tortured sound of her cry and the memory of her stumbling away from him.

An uneasy sensation took hold of him. He couldn't help but think that there were things buried in Marley's memories that he wasn't going to like.

Fourteen

Marley was only vaguely aware of the things going on around her. After that first pass into oblivion, she registered being carried into a car. She heard Chrysander's worried voice as he murmured to her, but she closed herself off from him, folding inward.

When she next awoke, she knew she was in a bed. As she looked around the room, recognition sparked, and with it, a surge of fresh agony, hot and raw, seared through her body and robbed her of breath.

He wouldn't do this. Surely even he could not be so cruel as to bring her back to the place they'd shared and the place he'd brutally shoved her from.

She reached for the tears, expecting them to come, but curiously all she felt was an odd detachment, a void of nothingness coupled with the need to get out of this place.

When she sat up, her gaze flickered to a chair by the window occupied by Chrysander's sleeping form. He was slouched against the arm, his clothing rumpled and the stubble of over a day's beard shadowing his jaw.

She waited for the rush of anger, of fury, but again, she felt nothing but overwhelming numbness and a need to escape.

She got out of bed, not paying attention to her own rumpled clothing. It occurred to her that maybe she should change, but she couldn't risk waking Chrysander. No, she needed to be away. She couldn't look him in the eye knowing that he'd made such horrible accusations and then left her to the mercy of her kidnappers.

Her thumb brushed across the thin band of her engagement ring, and she wrenched it off. It felt cold in her hand. She gently laid it on the nightstand beside the bed then turned and walked away.

On bare feet, she walked out of the bedroom and to the elevator. Her stomach churned as she relived the night she'd gotten on this elevator as her world crumbled around her, Chrysander's accusation ringing in her ears. How could he? It was the only thought that played over and over in her mind until she wanted to scream at it to stop.

When she reached the lobby, she paused, realizing that not only would Chrysander's security people likely be manning the front entrance but that also the doorman would never let her walk out as she was.

She turned and hurried for the back entrance. To her dismay, one of the men she recognized from Chrysander's detail was standing at the door. She quickly ducked into a service entrance and made her way down the hallway that housed rooms for laundry and building maintenance. A few minutes later, she opened the door and walked out into the pale, predawn light.

Chrysander woke with a monster catch in his neck and shifted in the too small chair to alleviate his discomfort. He'd wanted to spend the night with Marley tucked into his arms, but she'd resisted his touch at every turn, becoming so distraught that he'd had no choice but to retreat.

He'd taken the doctor's advice and phoned a therapist as soon as he'd returned to the apartment with Marley. The therapist was due to arrive this morning to speak with her. Chrysander just hoped she would be able to.

His gaze moved to the bed, and when he saw it empty, he shot to his feet. He started to bolt from the room, but a glimmer of something on the nightstand caught his eye. When he saw her engagement ring lying there, dread tightened his chest. He ran from the room in search of her. As he went from room to room, his panic grew. She wasn't anywhere to be found.

Even as he hurled himself into the elevator, he dug out his cellular phone. As soon as the doors opened in the lobby, he ran out and nearly collided with Stavros.

He grasped the man's shirt in his hands and pulled him up close. "Where is she?"

Stavros blinked in surprise. "We haven't seen her, sir. No one has. She was with you."

Chrysander pushed him away with a violent curse. "She's gone. Call your men in. I want her found immediately."

He strode to the entrance to question the doorman, but he seemed as baffled as the security man. He turned around to see several of his detail gather in the lobby as they were questioned by an angry Stavros.

Theos! Where could she have gone? She was in no state to be wandering around New York, and the people who had abducted her were still at large.

Worry settled hard into his chest. He turned to go out the door in search of her himself when he saw Theron walk in.

"Chrysander," he said in greeting. "I was on my way up to see you. How is Marley?"

"She's gone," he said grimly.

Theron raised one brow. "Gone? But how?"

"I don't know," he said in frustration. "She's disappeared. I have to find her."

Theron put a firm hand on Chrysander's shoulder. "We'll find her, Chrysander."

"There is something about this situation," Chrysander said in a hollow voice. "Something that doesn't add up. I saw no guilt in her face when she remembered everything. All I saw was complete devastation, as if she were the one who was betrayed. She was so distraught that she had to be sedated, and she becomes extremely upset when I get close to her. She isn't herself right now. I fear where she may have gone. Her frame of mind is not good."

"I will help you, Chrysander," Theron said quietly. "Do not worry. We will find her."

Marley shivered as she eased down onto the cold stone bench and clutched her arms around her trembling body. She glanced down at her feet but couldn't summon any rebuke for having gone out in the chill without shoes or a coat. The only thought she'd had was to get away as quickly as possible. She couldn't face Chrysander now.

Now she knew why she'd been drawn to this place. Her thinking spot, indeed. Just hours before that last night, she'd sat here, afraid of how Chrysander would react to her pregnancy. She'd been right to be afraid. He didn't trust her. He didn't love her. And he'd left her to her fate with the kidnappers.

She refused to allow the memories to roll back in her mind. They simply hurt too much. At least now she realized why she'd chosen to forget. All those weeks of living in fear as her kidnappers waited for their demands to be met had paled next to the betrayal Chrysander had handed her when he'd refused.

How could anyone be so cold? Wouldn't he have been willing to pay such a meager amount of money to free anyone? Even a complete stranger? She'd never imagined him to be so heartless. But he'd cast her aside with little regard for her. She'd been his mistress, someone to slake his lust and nothing more. The fool was her for falling in love with him, not once, but twice.

A small moan escaped her lips, and she closed her eyes as the ache built within her once more. Never had she felt so hurt, so utterly lost.

Her hands closed around the bulge of her stomach, and the tears that she'd thought locked under the ice began to well to the surface.

How could he be capable of such a despicable deception? He had to know she'd remember eventually, and yet he'd spent weeks wooing her, making her love him all over again. Pretending affection for her. And passion. The question was, why?

Was it all an elaborate ruse to punish her? To make her suffer more than she already had? She'd never imagine Chrysander to be so cruel, but it just proved how little she'd known about the man she'd given herself to.

She sat there, rocking back and forth, her arms wrapped protectively around her abdomen. The wind picked up, chasing a chill down her spine, but she ignored the discomfort.

"Marley?"

Her name came out cautiously and sounded distant, yet when she looked up, the man was standing just a few feet away, concern lighting his eyes. She recognized him. Theron. No wonder he'd been so resistant to Chrysander marrying her. He thought her the thief that Chrysander did. It was more than she could bear.

She hugged herself tighter and looked down, determined that he not see her tears.

He squatted down in front of her and put a hand on her wrist. "I need to take you back, *pedhaki mou*. It's not safe for you to be out here," he said gently.

She flinched at the endearment. It was Chrysander's pet name for her, and she wanted no part of it. She shook her head and pulled her hand up in a protective manner.

He glanced down at her feet and swore under his breath. "It's cold, and you shouldn't be out here in your bare feet. Let me take you back home."

She recoiled violently. "No." She shook her head vehemently. "I won't go back there." She slid to the end of the bench, the rough stone scratching against her clothing.

Theron put a hand out to prevent her flight. "Marley, think of your baby. Let me take you back. You're cold."

"I won't go back to that apartment," she said desperately. She stood, prepared to bolt.

Theron look at her with regret. "I cannot allow you to run. You're clearly upset and are not dressed for the weather."

Tears filled her eyes. "Why do you care? I stole from you,

remember? I'm just the harlot who snared your brother and tried to ruin his company," she said bitterly.

Theron's eyes softened. "If I promise not to return you to the apartment, will you come with me? I won't leave you like this, Marley."

She swayed, and he caught her as her knees gave out. He picked her up and began striding away.

She stiffened in his arms. "Please, just leave me alone," she begged.

"I cannot do that, little sister."

"I'm just your brother's whore," she said, allowing more of the anguish in.

His grip tightened around her. "*Theos!* Never say that again."

She turned her face into his shoulder, and hot tears flooded her eyes. "It's true," she whispered.

She closed her eyes and allowed herself to drift away once again. It was easy to flee from reality when it represented so much she wanted to escape. She cursed that she'd ever regained her memory. Doing so had destroyed her.

Fifteen

Chrysander strode into the Imperial Park Hotel, waving off members of the staff as they hastened to greet him. The elevator was being held open for him, and he got in and rode it to the top floor.

A few moments later, he walked into the luxury suite usually reserved for VIP guests. His brother met him in the sitting area, and Chrysander scowled furiously at him.

"Why didn't you bring her back to the apartment?" he demanded.

"She became hysterical at the mere mention of it," Theron said. "She was set to run as far and as fast as she could. I had to promise I wouldn't take her back to the penthouse."

Chrysander swore and closed his eyes. He brought his hand to his face and pinched the bridge of his nose between his fingers in a weary gesture.

"She's about to break," Theron said quietly. "Bring your therapist here to talk to her. Maybe she can help."

Chrysander looked sharply at his younger brother. "You seem concerned about her."

"She carries my nephew." His lips pressed together in a grim line. "It is as you said. There is no guilt in her expression, her actions. She acts as though she has suffered the deepest of hurts. It was uncomfortable for me to see. I suddenly wanted to do all I could to shield her from such pain."

"Where is she now?" Chrysander demanded.

"Asleep," Theron replied. "She fell asleep on the way here and never stirred when I carried her up the elevator and put her into bed."

Chrysander headed for the bedroom, determined to see for himself that she was safe. He made his way through the dimly lit room and stopped at the head of the bed. Even in sleep, her brow was creased in an expression of despair.

He reached down and touched her cheek, tucking a curl behind her ear. She didn't stir. Her pale face lay against the pillow, framed by her dark curls. Deep shadows smudged her eyes, and he could tell from the redness that she had been crying. His chest twisted painfully at the signs of her distress.

As he walked back into the sitting room, he pulled out his cellular phone to call the therapist and have her come to the hotel. When he was done, he closed his phone and turned to Theron.

"Where did you find her?"

Theron handed him a drink. "She was in a garden a few blocks from your apartment." He winced as he looked at Chrysander. "She was barefoot, with no coat or sweater. She looked lost and unaware of her surroundings."

Chrysander swore. "It has been so since she regained her memory. *Theos mou,* but I don't know what to do." He'd never felt so helpless.

"Do you still believe she is guilty?" Theron asked quietly.

"I don't know," Chrysander admitted. "I think sometimes that it doesn't matter." He looked bleakly up at his brother, expecting to see condemnation. Instead, Theron looked at him with understanding.

"When I saw her on the bench, it did not matter to me, either," Theron said softly.

The therapist arrived a few minutes later, and Chrysander filled her in on everything that had happened since arriving in New York.

Despite the discomfort he felt over providing such personal details to the woman, he wanted her to know whatever she needed in order to help Marley. So he told her everything. From the confrontation he'd had with Marley so many months before, to the present.

To her credit, the woman did not react. She took the information in stride and asked to see Marley.

"She is resting, but you can go in and wait for her to awaken. I don't want her to grow upset and try to leave."

The therapist nodded and followed Chrysander to the bedroom. As they entered, Marley stirred. Chrysander automatically stepped forward, but the therapist held up her hand to halt him.

"Leave me to speak to her," she said softly.

Chrysander weighed his desire to be near her with the therapist's request. Finally, he nodded curtly and turned to leave. He didn't go far, though. He stepped from the bedroom and closed the door, but left it slightly ajar so he could hear what was being said within.

There was a long period of silence, and then the slight murmur of voices filtered from the room. The therapist did most of the talking at first as she soothed Marley. After a long while, he could hear Marley's trembling voice, and he strained closer to hear what she said.

"I went to the doctor the day Chrysander was due back from overseas. When I discovered I was pregnant, I was shocked. I worried how Chrysander would react. I wanted to ask him about our relationship…how he felt about me."

"Go on," the therapist encouraged.

Marley's questions that night now made sense to Chrysander. And then he flinched at her next words.

"He told me we had no relationship. That I was his mistress. A woman he paid to have sex with," she said hollowly.

He wanted to protest. He wanted to march into the bedroom and tell her that he'd never considered her someone he paid to have sex with.

"Then he accused me of…" Her voice trailed off, and he could hear a quiet sob rise from the room.

"It's all right, Marley," the therapist soothed.

"He said I had stolen from him. He said I took plans for one of his hotels and gave them to his competitor. He told me to get out."

"And did you steal them?"

"You're the first person to actually ask," Marley said wanly.

Chrysander flinched. She was right. He hadn't asked. He'd judged and condemned her.

"I was stunned. I still don't understand. I'd never even seen the papers he threw at me. I don't know why he thought I took them or how he could even think such a horrible thing."

The tears he heard in her voice felt like little daggers to his chest. The tension grew until he felt he would explode. Dread skated up his spine. What had he done?

"And then…" She broke off as sobs took over.

There was another long period of silence as the therapist murmured words of comfort to Marley.

"Tell me what happened next, Marley."

"I left the apartment, but I knew I had to come back the next day after he'd calmed down so I could make him see reason and tell him I was pregnant. I felt if I could just have the chance to talk to him that he would see what a mistake it was."

"And what happened?" the therapist asked gently.

Chrysander pushed against the door, his body tense with anticipation.

"A man pulled a bag over my head and forced me into a car. I was taken to another place in the city and told that I was being held for ransom. I was terrified. I was pregnant and was so scared that they would hurt me or my baby."

Chrysander's hands curled into fists as he fought the rising rage within him.

"They sent two ransom demands," Marley whispered. "He refused both. He left me there. Oh God, he left me to those men. I wasn't even worth half a million dollars to him!"

Sobs ripped from her throat as she dissolved into tears. Chrysander stood in stunned disbelief. Mother of God. He'd never received a ransom demand. He hadn't! His stomach boiled as acid rose in his throat. He turned and laid his forehead against the wall and brought his clenched fist to rest a few inches away. He felt wetness on his cheeks but made no move to wipe it away.

A few moments later, the therapist eased out of the bedroom and looked at Chrysander. He expected condemnation in her eyes but saw only a faint sympathy.

"I've sedated her. She was nearly hysterical. She needs rest above all else. Her reality is very painful, so she retreats. That same self-preservation is what prompted her amnesia. Now that she no longer has that protective buffer, she struggles to cope in the best way she knows how. Be gentle and understanding with her. Don't push her too hard."

She patted him on the arm as she walked past.

"Call me if you need me. I'll come at once."

"Thank you," Chrysander said hoarsely.

When she left, Chrysander turned and shuffled farther into the sitting room and sagged onto the couch.

"Dear God," he said bleakly.

"I heard," Theron said with a grimace.

"She never stole anything." Chrysander closed his eyes and dragged a hand through his hair. "*Theos*. I never got a ransom demand. She thinks…she thinks I left her to those animals, that I didn't care enough to pay half a million dollars for her return."

Theron put a comforting hand on Chrysander's shoulder. "There is much we need to investigate."

Chrysander nodded. His thoughts hardened as he turned from the anguish over Marley's revelation and forced himself to play back the events of that night.

The realization, when it came, was so startlingly clear that he cursed himself for not having pieced it together before. He'd been too angry, too wounded by what he perceived as a betrayal by Marley.

"Roslyn," he said tersely.

Theron raised a brow. "Your assistant?"

"She was there. Just before I found the papers in Marley's bag. She must have planted them."

Another thought occurred to him, one that sickened him and made him want to empty his stomach. Any ransom demand would have gone to his office. His residences were highly guarded secrets. Marley had said that he'd ignored ransom demands, but now he realized they could have been delivered and intercepted. By Roslyn.

He stood and whirled around to face his brother. "You will stay here with Marley. Make sure she goes nowhere and that she is well cared for. I'll send a physician over to monitor her condition."

Theron also stood. "Where are you going, brother?"

"I'm going to find out if what I suspect is true," he said in a dangerously low voice.

"Chrysander, wait."

Chrysander paused and stared back at his brother.

"You should call the authorities. If you confront her and gain a confession, it won't do any good. Only you will know."

Chrysander clenched his fists in frustration, but he knew his brother was right. He didn't want Roslyn to get away with what she'd done. He could make her life miserable, but she would still be free. He wanted justice.

Chrysander paced the confines of his New York office as he waited for Roslyn to arrive. He didn't want to be here. He wanted to be with Marley. Theron had stayed with her, and Chrysander simmered with impatience. Her condition hadn't changed. Even when she'd awakened, she'd been distant, unfocused, there but not there. It was as if she'd gone to a place where he couldn't hurt her anymore.

He closed his eyes and tried to focus on the task at hand. When he heard Roslyn enter, he stiffened. It was all he could do not to rage at her, not to break her skinny neck. It took everything he had to smile and act as though nothing was wrong, as though he didn't loathe the very ground she walked on.

"You wanted to see me?" Roslyn said breathlessly.

"I did," Chrysander murmured. He let his gaze run suggestively over her body even as his flesh crawled.

Her eyes brightened, and her stance immediately became suggestive.

"I've only just become aware of the lengths to which you went to try and get my attention," he said with a chuckle. "Men can be thick, so you women say, but I think maybe I was thicker than most."

Confusion rippled across her face, and she struggled to retain a look of innocence. She couldn't be sure what he was talking about yet, but it would soon be clear. He watched her body language, her eyes, the windows into the soulless bitch that she was.

"Why did you not just say you wanted me?" he purred. "It would have saved us a lot of trouble. Instead, I was trapped in a relationship I didn't want, though I appreciate the efforts you made to rid me of that problem."

Roslyn relaxed, and a cold smile flashed across her face. It was strange, but Chrysander had never realized just how ugly she was.

"How did you arrange it?" he asked silkily.

He listened in horror as she outlined what she'd done to make it appear as though Marley had stolen the plans. The kidnapping had been an added bonus, but when she'd received the ransom demand at his office, she'd seen her opportunity to be rid of Marley once and for all.

So anxious was she to prove her devotion to Chrysander, that she didn't realize she'd admitted to selling his plans to his competitor.

"So you stole the plans and gave them to Marcelli." His voice was like ice, and she flinched at his tone. Her face whitened as she realized just what she'd confessed to.

"You then framed Marley, thinking not only would you have the proceeds from selling me out to my competitor, but then you would have Marley out of the way so you could move into her place."

Her mouth opened and closed, and he could see the realization settle in that he'd duped her and was furious.

"And then when the ransom demands were delivered to my office, you destroyed them, hoping what, Roslyn, that they would kill her? Permanently remove her from the picture?"

He was shaking he was so angry. She simmered before him in a red haze. All he could see was Marley alone and frightened. Pregnant with his child and vulnerable. Thinking that not only did he hate her but that he'd simply left her to her fate. He wanted to weep.

Roslyn seemed to recover her composure, and she looked scornfully at him. "You'll never prove it."

"I don't have to," he said softly. He pressed the small intercom button on his desk. "You may come in now, Detective."

Roslyn swayed as three policemen entered the room, their expressions grim.

"You can't do this!" she shrieked. "I love you, Chrysander. I would have done anything for you."

He shook his head and turned away from her rantings as she was escorted away in handcuffs. He had no desire to listen to her. He wanted to return to Marley.

"Forgive me, *agape mou*," he whispered.

Marley was dimly aware that she was being carried yet again. It wasn't Chrysander. She was intimately familiar with his touch. For a moment she panicked, and then she heard comforting words being spoken in Greek and then in English.

"Rest easy, little sister. You are safe."

"Where are we going?" she asked weakly.

"Someplace safe," he soothed. "Chrysander won't allow anything to happen to you."

She wanted to protest that Chrysander wouldn't do anything for her, but she couldn't muster the energy. At some point, she heard Chrysander, and she cursed the fact that she immediately felt safer and that some of the panic abated.

She felt the brush of lips against her forehead and then firm hands tucking her into bed. Fingers stroked through her hair, and warmth enveloped her.

"You are safe, *agape mou*. I'll never allow anyone to hurt you again."

"Don't call me that," she cried. "Never again." But she held to Chrysander's promise even as her heart screamed in protest. He'd lied to her. She couldn't believe anything he said. And yet she relaxed and settled into a dreamless sleep.

When Marley next awoke, there was a crispness to her mind that had been absent since the day she'd regained her memory. No longer did fog shroud her memories. She both welcomed and cursed the new awareness. Gone was any confusion, but with that new clarity came inevitable heartbreak.

She felt alert, as though she'd slept a week. And maybe she had. She had no idea how much time had passed, and while her past was no longer a mystery, the events of the last few days were hazy and fractured.

With a reluctant sigh, she pushed back the covers and eased her legs over the side of the bed. As she glanced around, she realized she had no idea where she was. The room was spacious and cheerful, with several windows to allow natural lighting.

She pushed herself up and walked into the adjoining bathroom, her eyes widening at the size and luxury. She eyed the Jacuzzi tub with longing. While she might not know how many days had passed—they'd all been a blur—she did know that she hadn't had a bath in a while, and she couldn't wait to feel clean and refreshed again.

Bracing her foot on the step to the tub, she leaned over and turned the handle to start the water. When she looked up, she saw Chrysander standing in the doorway. A startled gasp escaped her.

He started forward immediately and grasped her arm to steady her. "I'm sorry for frightening you, *pedhaki mou*. It was not my intention. I worried when I came in to check on you and you were not in bed."

"I just wanted a bath," she said in a low voice.

"I do not want you to be in here alone," he said. "I'll

summon Mrs. Cahill so that if you have need of anything, you can just call out."

She closed her eyes for a moment and drew in a steadying breath. Then she met his gaze. "Please, Chrysander, let's not have any further lies between us. There's no need for you to pretend that I'm important to you…that I matter."

Bleakness entered his eyes, and his face grayed underneath the olive tone of his skin. "You matter very much to me, *agape mou.*"

Before she could respond, he retreated from the bathroom, and a moment later, Patrice bustled in. In a matter of minutes, Marley found herself stripped and settled into a warm bath. Not too hot, Patrice assured, since overly hot baths were not good for a pregnant woman.

As Marley settled into the fragrant bubbles, she leaned her head back against the rim of the tub and glanced over at Patrice. "Where are we? And how did you get here? I thought you were in Athens with Dr. Karounis."

"Mr. Anetakis asked me to fly back so I could be with you," she said soothingly. "He was quite desperate. The idea of return- ing to the apartment upset you so badly that he brought you here."

"And where is here?" Marley asked.

"His house," she explained patiently. "We're about an hour from the city. It's quieter here, more peaceful. He thought you'd prefer it."

Tears blurred Marley's vision. And she thought she hadn't any more tears to shed. She hadn't known he owned a house outside of the city, and like the island, it was one more place she'd never visited in all the time she'd been with Chrysander. Further proof that she'd never occupied an important place in his life.

"He's been very worried about you," Patrice said, her face softening in sympathy. "We all have been."

Marley shook her head in denial. Chrysander hated her. He'd never loved her, and she'd been too stupid to realize it.

"What am I going to do?" she whispered to no one in particu- lar. She'd been an idiot to give up her apartment, her job, every means she had of taking care of herself when she moved in with

Chrysander. She'd been too blinded by her love and convinced that she had a future with him.

"Come out of the tub," Patrice said gently. "You need to get dried off so you can go down to eat."

Marley allowed Patrice to mother her. She was dried off and pampered then clothed in comfortable slacks and a maternity shirt. She rubbed a hand over her belly and whispered an apology to her unborn son.

She couldn't afford to fall apart. Her child was depending on her.

Chrysander was waiting for her when she exited the bedroom. He said nothing, but he cupped her elbow and helped her down the stairs, and she let him, too numb to protest. Marley also remained silent, her emotions too much in turmoil to try and have a reasonable conversation.

They sat at a small table that overlooked a beautifully manicured garden. Bright morning sun shone through the glass doors, and she felt warmed by the sun's rays.

Chrysander set a plate piled high with food in front of her then settled into a seat across from her. She piddled with her fork and toyed with the food, pushing it around the plate as she avoided his gaze.

He sighed, and she looked up to see him staring at her. His expression was somber, as though he was enduring the worst sort of hell. She nearly laughed at the absurdity. To her horror, she felt the prick of tears, and his face swam in her vision.

"We must talk, Marley. There is much I need to say to you." His voice sounded oddly strangled. "But first you must eat so you can regain your strength. Your health and that of our child must come first."

She bowed her head again, refusing to meet his stare any longer. She concentrated on eating, and once she started realized she was actually quite hungry.

As she was finishing the last of her juice, she heard a door slam in the distance, and then she heard the determined stride of someone walking across the floor. She turned to see Theron enter the room, a grim look on his face.

Before he could speak, Chrysander locked his gaze onto his brother and said in a steely voice, "Whatever it is, I'm sure it can wait until Marley has finished eating."

Theron cast a concerned glance her way and nodded his understanding to Chrysander. Anger tightened her throat and made swallowing difficult. Whatever it was they wished to speak about, it was obvious they didn't want to do so in front of her. But then why would they? She was someone they believed had stolen from them.

She stood abruptly and tossed down her napkin. Without a word to either man, she stalked away.

"Marley, don't go," Chrysander protested.

She turned and pinned him with the force of her glare. "By all means, have your conversation. I'd hate to intrude. After all, someone who has stolen from you and betrayed your trust isn't someone you want around when you're talking."

"*Theos,* that is not the issue here. Marley? Wait, damn it!"

But she ignored him and continued walking.

Chrysander watched her leave and cursed. He felt strangled by helplessness. How could he ever hope to make things right between them? She hated him, and she had every right to.

He turned to Theron, who had also watched Marley go, a frown etched on his face. "What brought you here in such a hurry?" Chrysander demanded.

Theron reached into the jacket of his suit and pulled out a folded newspaper. He tossed it onto the table in front of Chrysander. "This did."

Chrysander opened it and immediately cursed in four languages. On the front page was a picture of Marley being carried by Theron on the day she'd run from the apartment. Underneath were pictures of himself and of Roslyn with a story outlining the soap-opera saga that highlighted every single facet of his relationship with Marley.

He threw the paper across the room with vicious force. "It had to be Roslyn. None of my men would have spoken to the press."

Theron nodded his agreement. "Since you had her arrested for her theft and her duplicity in keeping the ransom demands from you, she likely thought she had nothing to lose and everything to gain by giving the public her spin on your supposed relationship with her."

Chrysander sank into the chair and rested his elbows on the table. "I curse the day I ever hired that woman. Marley could have died because of my stupidity."

"You love her."

It wasn't a question, and Chrysander didn't treat is as such. It was simply a statement of fact. He did love her. But he'd managed to kill her love for him not once, but twice.

He nodded and buried his face in his hands. "I wouldn't blame her if she never forgave me. How can she when I cannot forgive myself?"

"Go to her, Chrysander. Make this right between you."

Chrysander stood. Yes, it was time to try and make things right with Marley. If he could.

Sixteen

Marley stood in the bedroom, staring out the window with unseeing eyes. Nothing Chrysander did at this point should hurt her, but he still had that power over her, much to her dismay.

"Marley."

She swung around to see Chrysander standing in the doorway. He looked tired, his features drawn and his eyes worried. There was something else in his expression. Sadness and…fear?

He started forward, a little hesitantly. "We need to talk."

She tensed then braced herself for what she knew would come. His repudiation of her. She turned her face away but nodded. Yes, they needed to talk and get it done with.

His fingers curled around her chin, and he gently turned her to face him. "Don't look like that, *agape mou.* I do not like to see you so sad."

"Please," she begged. "Just say what it is you want to say. Don't draw it out."

He lowered his hand to capture her wrist. His thumb brushed across her pulse, which jumped and sped up at his touch.

"Come, sit down."

She let him lead her over to the bed. He eased down beside her and sat stiffly, his posture screaming discomfort. Suddenly she couldn't wait for what he would say. Her anger bubbled like an inferno within her.

"You lied to me," she seethed. "Every single thing you've said to me since that day in the hospital has been one lie after another. You don't care about me. All those things you said, everything was a *lie*. When you took me to bed, you despised me, and yet you made love to me and made me believe you cared. Who does that sort of thing?"

She shuddered in revulsion and put her hands to her face.

"You are wrong," he said softly. He pulled her hands away from her face and lifted one to his lips to kiss her upturned palm. "I care a great deal about you. I didn't despise you when I made love to you. Yes, I lied to you about details. I was told not to do or say anything to upset you and to let your memory come back on its own. I lied, Marley, but about the little things. Not the important things. Like how much I care about you. *S'agapo, pedhaki mou.*"

She bowed her head. Her nose stung, and tears burned her eyelids. How she wanted to believe him. But he'd done nothing to earn her trust.

"I have wronged you greatly, Marley."

She raised her head to stare at him in shock. Chrysander admitting that he was wrong?

Shame dragged at his eyes, and deep sorrow had pasted shadows under them.

"There are things you must know. I never received any ransom demands. I would have moved heaven and earth to free you. No price would have been too high. I did not know that you had been abducted."

Her mouth fell open. "How could you not know?"

His eyes grew stormy. "Roslyn destroyed the ransom notes. You were right to dislike her, and because I ignored your feelings about her, I placed you in terrible danger."

Marley's mind reeled with all he had told her. She raised a shaking hand to her mouth. He hadn't gotten the ransom demands? "I thought—" She broke off and shook her head, emotion overwhelming her.

"What did you think, *agape mou?*" he asked softly.

"That you hated me," she whispered. "That you wouldn't pay to free me because you thought I had stolen from you. That I wasn't even worth half a million dollars to you."

He groaned and pulled her into his arms. His hands trembled against her back as he stroked up and down. "I am a fool. I was wrong to accuse you as I did. I have no defense."

She pulled away and gazed up at him. "You don't believe I stole from you?"

He shook his head sharply. "No. It was Roslyn. She planted the papers in your bag to make me think it was you." He paused and swiped a hand through his hair. "Even though I thought you had stolen from me, it no longer seemed to matter after your abduction. All that mattered to me was that you were back where you belonged. With me." His mouth twisted. "That night when you asked me about our relationship…I was frightened."

She raised one eyebrow. The idea of anything frightening Chrysander was laughable.

"I thought you were unhappy, that you wanted more than I was giving you," he admitted. "And then I was angry because it scared me. I was determined that you not be the one to decide our relationship, so I pushed you away by telling you that we had no relationship, that you were my mistress."

Her heart sped up as she viewed the vulnerability on his face. Her chest tightened, and it became harder to breathe as her pulse raced. "What are you saying?" she whispered.

"That I love you, *pedhaki mou. S'agapo.*"

Her eyes widened as she realized what the words he'd said a few minutes ago meant. She couldn't even formulate a response, so she stared at him in shock.

Self-derision crawled across his face. "I have a terrible way of showing it. I was proud, too proud to just tell you how I felt. I didn't even know it then. I just knew I didn't want you to leave and was angry that I thought you were unhappy in our current relationship. And then when I saw those papers in your bag, I was shocked and furious. I couldn't believe that you would steal from me."

"But you did," she said painfully.

He looked away, sorrow creasing his features. "I was angry. I've never been so angry. I thought you had used me so you could help our competitor. So I sent you away."

He ran a hand around to clasp the back of his neck. "And God help me, I sent you straight into the kidnappers' hands."

She closed her eyes, not wanting to remember the fear and despair she'd experienced during her captivity. Even though her memory had returned, that part was still very much a blur. Maybe she'd forever block it out.

"You *love* me?" She was still back on those words. The rest of the conversation seemed a muddle, and she was fixated on those three words.

He gathered her in his arms again and held her as delicately as a piece of hand-blown glass. "I've not done a good job of showing you, but I do love you. I want the chance to prove it to you. I want you to marry me. Please."

She shook her head in confusion at his humble plea. "You still want me to marry you?"

He tugged her closer to him until his lips pressed against the top of her head. "I don't expect you to answer now. I know I have said much to shock you. But give me a chance, Marley. You won't regret it, I swear. I'll make you love me again. I'll never abuse your precious gift as I have done."

She'd gone mad. She'd finally lost her mind. Chrysander was holding her in his arms, declaring his love for her and wanting her to marry him. For real this time. No pretense. No lies or half-truths between them.

Gently, he pulled her away and pressed a light kiss to her lips. "Think about it, *agape mou*. I'll wait as long as it takes for your answer."

He stood as if sensing her desire to be alone. He walked to

the door but turned to look at her one last time before disappearing from view.

Marley sat there for a long time simply staring at the now-empty doorway. Her hands shook and her stomach rolled. He loved her? Roslyn had planted the papers in her bag and then destroyed the ransom demands?

She shivered. Had Roslyn hated her so much? Or had she just wanted Chrysander that badly? Maybe both. Or maybe Roslyn had just been working for Chrysander's competition all along.

The events of the last few days still weighed heavily on her. She couldn't just forget everything because he apologized and offered her love and marriage, could she? She couldn't even return that declaration because he'd never believe it if it came now.

She sighed and lay on her side, curling her knees to her swollen belly. She was so tired. So very worn out, both physically and emotionally. She rubbed her stomach, smiling when her son rolled and kicked beneath her fingers.

"What should I do?" she whispered. She was so afraid to trust Chrysander with her love again. She was also afraid to be without him. As much damage as he'd done to her heart, she ached at the thought of leaving him.

She closed her eyes for just a moment. Exhaustion permeated every pore. She couldn't make such a monumental decision in a few minutes' time. Too much was at stake. She had a child to consider. She had herself to consider.

Over the next few days, Chrysander saw to her every need. He coddled her, pampered her and fussed endlessly over her. He told her often that he loved her, though he was careful to keep a respectable distance between them.

It would seem he went to great pains not to pressure her in any way. He wouldn't use the passion that sparked between them as a means to sway her, and for that she was grateful.

Two days after Chrysander had asked her to marry him again, his brothers came to visit. Marley tried to excuse herself, thinking that they'd want to discuss business with

Chrysander, and to be honest, she still felt awkward and shamed in their presence even though she'd done nothing to deserve their censure.

But it was her they asked to speak to, and she stared at them in bewilderment as they looked gravely at her.

"We have acted unforgivably toward you, little sister," Theron said.

Piers nodded in agreement. "It is understandable if you never forgive us. We were harsh. There is no defense for our treating you, especially since you are pregnant with our nephew, as we have."

Guilt was etched heavily into their faces, and they looked so uncomfortable, but she had no idea what to do or say to ease the situation.

Theron moved forward and put his hands gently on her shoulders. He kissed her on both cheeks then stepped back as Piers did the same.

She glanced toward Chrysander, who watched her with solemn eyes. His face was drawn and seemed thinner as though he'd lost weight. He looked…unhappy. It wasn't guilt, though there was a lot of that floating around the room. He genuinely looked as though he'd lost the one thing that mattered most to him.

Her?

The thought nearly paralyzed her. She smiled shakily at Theron and Piers and then excused herself, nearly running from the room in her haste to get away.

She threw open the door to the patio and welcomed the chilly air. She stepped outside taking deep breaths and trying to settle her rioting emotions.

Her mind skated back over everything she'd felt for the last several days. Betrayal. She'd been lied to. She stopped there, because now she wondered if Chrysander really had lied to her about his feelings.

He looked like she felt. Lost. They were both obviously hurting. If he hated her, truly hated her, then why would he enact such an elaborate charade when she lost her memory? Why would he feel obligated to someone who had stolen from him?

"You're pregnant with his child," she murmured. And yes, she could see how a fair amount of care would be due the mother of his child, but why wouldn't he have done as Theron suggested and merely set her up in an apartment somewhere? Why would he woo her, make love to her, act as though she mattered to him?

Did he love her? The declaration couldn't have been easy for him to make. Chrysander wasn't a man prone to sharing his emotions. In all the time they were together before her kidnapping, he'd never spoken to her of his feelings. But he'd shown her in a dozen ways that she had mattered to him.

Could she trust him again? The thought frightened her, and at the same time it offered her a measure of peace. The choice was hers. Her future would be of her own making.

Even as her options rolled over and over in her mind, she knew what she would do. She knew what she wanted, even knowing it might not be the best choice for her. The heart didn't always choose wisely, she thought with a grimace.

Still, she found herself returning inside and going in search of Chrysander. Worry knotted her belly, but she knew she was making the right decision, even if it didn't feel quite right at this very moment.

She found him in the room she'd left him in, staring out the window, a drink in his hand. His brothers were gone and heavy silence lay over the room. She paused for a moment, gathering her courage. He looked as though he hadn't slept in days. His slacks were wrinkled and his shirt sleeves were unbuttoned and rolled partway up his arms. A shadow of a beard covered his jaw, and his hair was rumpled.

And still, he looked so desirable to her. She wanted to cross the room and melt into his arms. She wanted him to hold her and coax away her fears and doubts. The knot in her throat grew bigger, and she knew she had to speak now or risk being unable to.

"Chrysander," she called softly.

He whirled around. He set his drink down and hurried toward her. "Are you all right, *agape mou?* Is there anything I can get you? I'm sorry if my brothers upset you."

She tried to laugh, but it ended in a small sob. She drew in a deep breath and worked to compose herself.

"I'll marry you," she said.

A dark fire sparked in his eyes, making the amber glow more golden. He grasped her shoulders in his hands and stared down at her. "Yes?" he asked in a hoarse voice.

She nodded.

He closed his eyes and then crushed her to him. For a long moment, he just held her, and then he stepped back to stare intently at her.

"You mean it? You'll marry me?"

She licked her lips nervously. "I want a small ceremony. No fuss. As quiet as we can make it."

He nodded and cupped her chin in his hand. "Whatever you'd like."

"And I want…" She looked away and drew her bottom lip between her teeth.

"What do you want, *agape mou?* Tell me. There's nothing I won't do for you. You have only to ask."

"I don't want to stay here," she said quietly. "I'd like to go back to the island." She gripped her fingers together until the tips shone white.

His expression softened, and he dropped his hands to hers and gently uncurled her fingers until they were twined with his.

"We'll fly there as soon as we're married."

Relief surged through her veins. "You mean it? You don't mind?"

"Your happiness is everything to me. You ask such a small thing. How could I not grant it? We'll make the island our home if that is your wish."

She nodded. "I'd like that."

"Then I'll make the arrangements at once."

Chrysander wasted no time in finalizing plans for their wedding and preparing for them to travel to the island. He single-handedly rearranged his business schedule, made sure everything Marley could possibly need was purchased, though they'd already shopped for her wedding gown. She stood in awe of all he could accomplish in such a short time.

The authorities questioned her now that she'd regained her memory, and she spent several exhausting hours providing them with the few details she could remember. The kidnappers hadn't harmed her and had actually shown her consideration when her pregnancy became obvious. They had watched her, knowing she was close to Chrysander, and had struck when the opportunity arose. They'd asked for a small ransom, certain they would get it with no fuss. When no ransom had been forthcoming, they abandoned the kidnapping and arranged for Marley to be found.

It was the realization that Chrysander had ignored the ransom that had pushed Marley beyond her limits. It was that moment in the kidnapping that she blocked out her past, so devastated was she over his betrayal. Overwhelming emotion had crippled her— fear of being abandoned by the kidnappers, the terror of being left alone and having nowhere to go, no one to turn to.

Marley became distraught during the retelling, and Chrysander suffered the agony of being confronted by all she'd gone through. Because of him. He hovered protectively throughout, and finally called a halt when it was clear she was past all endurance.

The police were given their contact information so that Marley could be reached if arrests were made or there was a need for her to testify.

Two days later, they were married. Theron and Piers both attended, and Patrice was the only other witness to the ceremony. Afterward, Piers gave her a somewhat reserved welcome to the family while Theron's was more warm and enthusiastic.

"You've made him very happy, little sister," Theron murmured as he gathered her in his arms for a hug.

She offered a small smile, but she knew Theron wasn't fooled by it.

Soon after, Piers and Theron left, Theron to return to London and Piers to fly to Rio de Janeiro to oversee plans for the new hotel. Patrice returned to Athens, where she'd be met by Dr. Karounis. While Chrysander wanted to wait a day for their own departure, Marley was adamant that they leave as soon as the ceremony was done. She wanted to return to the island, a place she'd been happy even if only for a short time. New York held too many unhappy memories, and she just wanted to be away.

Chrysander bundled her on the plane and insisted she sleep for the duration of the flight. It was late when they landed and later still by the time the helicopter touched down on the island. But Marley felt relieved that she was home.

Chrysander carried her into the house and didn't relinquish her until they were upstairs in the bedroom. He set her down on the bed and then busied himself undressing her and tucking her underneath the covers.

When he crawled in beside her and merely held her lightly against him, as though he was afraid of touching her, she frowned in the darkness. She rose up and reached across him to turn on the light he'd extinguished a moment earlier.

"Marley, what is wrong?" he asked as she stared down at him.

She studied him, the lines around his mouth, the worry in his eyes. In that moment, she understood. He was afraid.

"Make love to me," she whispered.

His eyes darkened and turned to liquid. A ragged breath tore from his mouth.

"I need you to make love to me."

"You have to be sure about this, *agape mou*. I don't want to pressure you into doing anything you aren't ready for."

"I'm sure."

With a tortured groan, he rolled her beneath him. Every kiss, every touch was so exquisitely tender. He touched and stroked her with infinite care.

Her gown was removed, and he slid out of his boxers. His body, hot and straining, covered hers. Pleasure streaked through her body in waves when he closed his mouth over her nipple. He sucked lightly, tonguing the small bud, then he turned his attention to her other breast.

His hand cupped her belly protectively, cradling her against him as he kissed his way up her neck and finally to her lips.

"*S'agapo, pedhaki mou. S'agapo*," he murmured in a voice so husky, so emotional, that it brought tears to her eyes.

She cried out as he moved over her. "Please," she begged. "I need you."

He entered her slowly, his movements careful and measured. But she didn't want him to treat her so carefully. She wanted all of him. She arched into him and wrapped her legs around his hips.

Sobs of need, of pleasure, ripped from her throat, and for once, pain had diminished to a distant memory. There was only here and now and the man who loved her.

She raced up a mountain slope and hurtled into a free fall of ecstasy. Chrysander was there to catch her, gathering her close against him as he murmured words of love against her lips.

She snuggled into his embrace, melding herself as close to him as she could. She needed this. Needed him.

"Don't let me go," she whispered.

"Never, *agape mou*," he vowed. He stroked her hair, her back, the swollen mound of her belly as she drifted off to sleep. The last thing she was aware of was him telling her he loved her.

Marley slipped out of bed and pulled on her robe to cover her nakedness. Chrysander was still firmly asleep, his arm stretched out as though reaching for her.

He'd made love to her throughout the night, the two of them falling into an exhausted sleep just before dawn. Her body still tingled from his touch, his lips, his gentle caresses. As she stared at him, she knew that she couldn't hold off any longer. She couldn't torture them both. Her uncertainty was gone. Her fears would follow in time.

She padded down the stairs, smiling ruefully at the thought of how Chrysander would fuss that she hadn't waited for him. After a stop in the kitchen, where she nibbled at a bagel and drank a glass of juice, she ventured into the living room to enjoy the view of the ocean.

It was there that Chrysander found her. He slid his arms

around her, cupping her belly with his hands as he kissed the curve of her neck.

"You're up early, *agape mou*."

"I was thinking," she murmured. She swiveled in his arms and met his worried gaze.

They both stared for a long moment, and then finally Chrysander said in a hoarse voice, "Do I ever have a chance of you loving me, Marley? Have I ruined that chance forever?"

Her gaze softened, and her heart turned over again with the love that swelled within her. Love and forgiveness.

"I already do," she said softly.

Surprise flickered across his face, and then doubt crept in.

"I've always loved you, Chrysander. From the moment I met you there has never been another man for me. There never will be."

"You love me?" he said in wonder, hope flaring in his eyes.

"I couldn't tell you before," she explained. "Not in New York when things were so messed up. You wouldn't have believed it if I had said it on the heels of your declaration. I wanted to return here, where we were happy. I wanted our life to begin here."

He gathered her in his arms and held her against his trembling body. His voice shook with emotion as he murmured to her in Greek. He switched back and forth between Greek and English as he told her how much he loved her and how sorry he was for the pain he'd caused her.

Then he swept her in his arms and carried her up the stairs and back to their bed, where he made sweet, passionate love to her again. Later he tucked her against his body and stroked a hand through her hair.

"I love you so much, *yineka mou*. I don't deserve your love, but I am so very grateful for it. I'll spend the rest of my life cherishing it, I swear."

She hugged him to her. "I love you, too, Chrysander. So much. We'll be so happy together. I'll make you happy."

And she did.

Epilogue

Ironically enough, Marley discovered she was in labor halfway down the stairs. Alone. She gripped the banister and doubled over as a contraction rippled across her abdomen. Wasn't labor supposed to start out slow?

She wanted to laugh at the fact that fate was obviously cursing her for trying to sneak down the stairs without Chrysander knowing. While he'd relented about her taking the stairs in the earlier stages of her pregnancy, now that she was so close to her due date he'd once again insisted she not walk the stairs alone. He'd go insane now that she was nine months pregnant and, if the pain ripping out her insides was any clue, about to deliver.

She stood on the step, holding on to the railing and taking deep breaths. She'd have called out if she weren't so busy sucking air through her nose. Besides, Chrysander was busy with endless calls as he and Theron worked out Theron's relocation to the New York offices. Theron was taking over operations there so Chrysander could remain in Europe. They had been tied up for hours discussing security measures since her kidnappers were still at large.

When she heard footsteps above her, she straightened and tried her best to look as though nothing was wrong. She glanced guiltily up to see Chrysander standing at the top of the stairs, a disapproving expression marring his face.

He started down, grumbling in Greek all the way. "What am I to do with you, *agape mou?*" he asked when he got close.

"Take me to the hospital?" she asked weakly. She doubled over again as another contraction hit.

"Marley! *Pedhaki mou,* are you in labor?" He didn't even wait for a response, not that he needed one. He scooped her into his arms and hurtled down the stairs, shouting for the helicopter pilot, who had remained on the island for the last two weeks for just such an event.

"Do not worry, my darling," he said in uncharacteristic English. "We'll have you to the hospital in no time."

"Darling?" She laughed and then ended it in a moan. "It hurts, Chrysander."

He paled as he climbed into the helicopter with her.

"You aren't allowed to use English endearments," she panted. "Greek sounds so much sexier."

"*Pedhaki mou, yineka mou, agape mou,*" he whispered in her ear. My little one, my woman, my love.

"Much better," she sighed. She smiled then winced again as they lifted into the air. Chrysander was a basket case the entire way to the hospital. The pilot set down on the roof, and a medical team was waiting to usher her inside.

A mere hour later, with Chrysander hovering and holding her hand, Dimitri Anetakis squirmed his way into the world to the delight of his father and mother.

"He is beautiful, *agape mou,*" Chrysander murmured as he leaned in close to mother and child. Dimitri was nursing contentedly at Marley's breast, and Chrysander watched in fascination.

"He's perfect," she said in wonder. "Oh, Chrysander, everything's so perfect."

He kissed her tenderly, his love for her overflowing his heart. *"S'agapo, yineka mou."*

She cupped his face and smiled up at him. *"S'agapo,* Chrysander. Always."

* * * * *

THE TYCOON'S
REBEL BRIDE

BY
MAYA BANKS

To Fatin and Ali, two terrific ladies
I am very privileged to know and call friends

One

Theron Anetakis sifted through the mountain of paperwork his secretary had left on his desk for him to read, muttering expletives as he tossed letters left and right. Occasionally one would garner more than a brief glance and then he'd shove it to a separate pile of things requiring his attention. Others, he consigned to the trash can by his feet.

His takeover of the New York offices of Anetakis International hadn't been without its pitfalls. After the discovery that one of the staff members had been selling Anetakis hotel plans to a competitor, Theron and his brothers had cleaned house, hiring new staff. The culprit, Chrysander's former personal assistant, was behind bars after a plea bargain. They had been leery of replacing her and allowing another employee unfettered access to sensitive company information, but in the end, Theron had opted to bring in his secretary from the London office. She was older, stable and most importantly, loyal. Though after the debacle with Roslyn, none of the Anetakis brothers were keen to trust another employee implicitly.

Theron's arrival from London had been met by a pile of documents, contracts, messages and e-mails. Two days later, he was still trying to make sense of the mess. And to think his secretary had already weeded out the majority of the clutter.

He paused over one letter addressed to Chrysander and almost tossed it as junk mail, but yanked it back into his line of vision when he saw what it said. His brow furrowed deeper as he scanned the page, and stretched out his other hand for the phone.

Uncaring of the time difference, or that he would probably wake Chrysander, he punched in the number and waited impatiently for the call to go through. He spared a brief moment of guilt that he would also be disturbing Marley, Chrysander's wife, but hopefully he would pick up the phone before it wakened her.

"This better be damn good," Chrysander growled in a sleepy voice.

Theron didn't waste time with pleasantries. "Who the hell is Isabella?" he demanded.

"Isabella?" There was no doubt as to the confusion in Chrysander's voice. "You're calling me at this hour to ask me about a woman?"

"Tell me…" Theron shook his head. No, Chrysander wouldn't be unfaithful to Marley. Whatever this woman was to Chrysander, it must have been before he met Marley. "Just tell me what I need to know in order to get rid of her," Theron said impatiently. "I've a letter here informing you of her progress, whatever the hell that means, and that she's graduated successfully." Theron's lips thinned in disgust. "*Theos,* Chrysander. Isn't she a bit young for you to have been involved with?"

Chrysander exploded in a torrent of Greek, and Theron held the phone from his ear until the storm calmed.

"I do not like your implication, little brother," Chrysander said in an icy voice. "I am married. Of course I am not involved with this Isabella." And then Theron heard Chrysander's sharp intake of breath. "*Bella.* Of course," he murmured. "I'm not thinking clearly at this hour of the night."

"And I repeat, who is this Bella?" Theron asked, his patience running out.

"Caplan. Isabella Caplan. Surely you remember, Theron."

"Little Isabella?" Theron asked in surprise. He hadn't remembered her at all until Chrysander mentioned her last name. An image of a gangly, preteen girl with ponytails and braces shot to mind. He'd seen her a few times since, but he honestly couldn't conjure an image. He remembered her being shy and unassuming, always trying to fade into the background. She'd been at his parents' funeral, but he'd been too consumed with grief to pay attention to the young woman. How old would she have been then?

Chrysander chuckled. "She's not so little anymore. She will have just graduated. Was doing quite well. Intelligent girl."

"But why are you getting a report on her?" Theron asked. "For God's sake, I thought she might be a former mistress, and the last thing I wanted was her causing trouble for Marley."

"While your devotion to my wife is commendable, it's hardly necessary," Chrysander said dryly. Then he sighed. "Our obligation to Bella had temporarily slipped my mind. My focus of late has been on Marley and our child."

"What obligation?" Theron asked sharply. "And why haven't I heard of this before?"

"Our fathers were longtime friends and business partners. Her father extracted a promise from our father that if anything should ever happen to him that Isabella would be looked after. Our father preceded her father in death, so I assumed responsibility for her welfare when her father also passed away."

"Then you should know that, according to this letter, she's arriving in New York two days from now," Theron said.

Chrysander cursed. "I can't leave Marley right now."

"Of course you can't," Theron said impatiently. "I'll take care of it. But I need details. The last thing you need right now is to be saddled with another concern. New York is my responsibility. I'll count this as yet another problem I've inherited when we traded offices."

"Bella won't be any problem. She's a sweet girl. All you need to do is help her settle her affairs and make sure her needs are provided for. She doesn't gain full control of her inheritance until she's twenty-five or she marries, whichever happens first, so in the meantime Anetakis International acts as the trustee. As you are now the New York representative of Anetakis, that makes you her guardian of sorts."

Theron groaned. "I knew I should have bloody well made Piers take over the New York office."

Chrysander laughed. "This will be a piece of cake, little brother. It shouldn't take you long at all to make sure she's settled and has everything she needs."

Isabella Caplan had no sooner made it past the airport security checkpoint when she saw a man in a chauffeur's uniform holding a sign with her name on it.

She held up a hand in a wave and made her way over. To her surprise, two other men stepped forward to flank her. Her confusion must have showed because the chauffeur smiled and said, "Welcome to New York, Ms. Caplan. I'm Henry, your driver for today, and these gentlemen are from Mr. Anetakis's security detail."

"Uh, hi," she said.

"I've arranged for someone to collect your luggage from baggage claim," Henry said as he herded her toward the exit. "It will be delivered to the hotel shortly."

Outside, one of the security men held the limousine door open for her then got in after her, while the second climbed into the front seat with Henry. Privacy wasn't in the cards, and what she really wanted to do was wilt all over her seat.

Isabella leaned back as the limousine pulled away from the passenger pickup area en route to Imperial Park, the hotel owned by the Anetakis brothers. Chrysander had arranged a suite anytime she visited New York, not that it had occurred often.

This trip had been planned as nothing more than a brief stopover on her way to Europe, a fact she'd apprised Chrysander of in her correspondence. All of that had changed the minute she'd received a terse missive from Theron Anetakis informing her that he was now overseeing her affairs, and he would meet briefly with her in New York to make sure she had everything she needed for her trip abroad.

He didn't know it yet, but her trip was a thing of the past. She was going to stay in New York...indefinitely.

The limousine pulled up in front of the hotel and ground smoothly to a halt. Her door opened, and the security guard who'd ridden in front extended his hand to assist her out. Once inside the lobby, she was ushered immediately to her suite, bypassing the front desk altogether.

Within ten minutes, her luggage was delivered to her room along with a bouquet of flowers and a basket filled with an assortment of snacks and fruits.

If that wasn't enough, just as she settled onto the couch to kick off her shoes and catch her breath, another knock sounded. Grumbling under her breath, she went to open the door and found another hotel employee standing there. He extended a smooth, cream-colored envelope.

"A message from Mr. Anetakis."

She raised an eyebrow. "Which Mr. Anetakis?"

The young man looked discomfited. "Theron."

She smiled, thanked him and then closed the door. She turned the envelope over and lightly ran her finger over the inscription on the front. Isabella Caplan. Had he written it himself?

Experiencing a moment of silliness, she brought the paper to her nose, hoping to catch his smell. There. Light but undeniably his scent. She remembered it as though it were yesterday. He obviously still wore the same cologne.

She broke open the seal and pulled the card from the envelope. In a distinctly masculine scrawl, he'd written his instructions for her to come to his office the next morning.

An amused smile curved her lips. As arrogant as she remembered. Summoning her like a wayward child. At least Chrysander had dropped by her suite to check in on her. But then she'd been a mere eighteen, and he'd also provided a veritable nanny to chaperone her for her visit to the city.

She'd be more than happy to meet Theron on his terms. It would make it that more satisfying to rock him back on his heels. The basis for her big trip to Europe had been solely because that was where Theron lived. Or had lived. When Chrysander married, he and his wife moved to his Greek island on a permanent basis. Which meant that Theron had moved a lot closer to Isabella. Finally.

The trip to Europe was off. Her seduction of Theron was on.

She sank onto the couch and put her feet up on the coffee table. Vibrant red toenail polish flashed in front of her as she wiggled her toes. The delicate ankle bracelet flashed and shimmered with the movement of her foot.

Theron had only gotten more gorgeous over the last few years. He'd lost the youthful handsomeness and replaced it with raw masculinity. While she'd been waiting to grow up so she could stake her claim, he'd only become more desirable. More irresistible. And she'd only fallen more in love with him.

It wouldn't be easy. She didn't imagine he'd fall readily into her arms. The Anetakis brothers were hard. They could have any woman they wanted. They were ruthless in business, but they were also loyal, and honor was everything.

The phone rang, and she sighed in aggravation. The phone was across the room, and she was quite comfortable on the couch. Shoving herself up, she stumbled over to answer it.

"Hello?"

There was a brief silence.

"Ms. Caplan—Isabella."

She recognized the accented English, and a thrill skirted down her spine. It wasn't Chrysander, and given that Piers was out of the country and had never so much as had a conversation with Isabella, it could only be Theron.

"Yes," she said huskily, hoping her nervousness wasn't betrayed.

"This is Theron Anetakis. I was calling to make sure you made it in okay and are settling in with no difficulty."

"Thank you. Everything is fine."

"Is the suite to your liking?"

"Yes, of course. It was kind of you to reserve it for me."

"I didn't reserve it," he said impatiently. "It's my private suite."

She looked around with renewed interest. Knowing that she was staying where Theron spent a lot of his time gave her a decadent thrill.

"Then where are you staying?" she asked curiously. "Why would you give up your suite?"

"The hotel is undergoing renovations. The only available suite was…mine. I'm temporarily taking a different room."

She laughed. "I could have taken other accommodations. There was no need for you to move out for me."

"A few days won't make a difference," he said. "You should be comfortable before your trip to Europe."

She swallowed back the denial that she would be going to Europe. No sense in putting him on guard as soon as she arrived.

There'd be plenty of time to apprise him of her change in plans. Mainly when he had no chance of talking her out of it.

A mischievous smile curved her lips. "I received your summons."

He made a sound of startled exclamation that sounded suspiciously like an oath. "Surely I didn't sound so autocratic, Ms. Caplan."

"Please, call me Isabella. Or Bella. Surely you remember when we weren't so formal? Granted it's been a few years, but I haven't forgotten a single thing about you."

There was an uncomfortable silence. And then, "All right, Isabella."

"Bella, please."

"All right...Bella," he conceded.

He made an exasperated sound in her ear and then said, "Now what was it we were discussing again?"

He sounded distracted, and though he was unfailingly polite, she knew he wanted rid of her as soon as possible. She grinned. If he only knew...

"We were discussing your autocratic demand for me to appear at your office tomorrow."

"It was a request, Bella," he said patiently.

"And of course I will honor it. Shall we say ten in the morning then? I'm a bit tired, and I'd like to sleep in."

"Of course. Don't overtax yourself. Order in room service tonight for dinner. Your expenses are being taken care of."

Of course. She hadn't expected anything less and knew better than to argue. The Anetakis brothers were thorough if nothing else. And very serious about their perceived obligations.

"I'll see you tomorrow then," she said.

He uttered an appropriate goodbye, and she hung up the phone. A smile popped her lips upward as she hugged her midsection in delight. Oh, she'd planned to pay him a visit the next day, all right.

Two

Theron sat back in his chair and surveyed the skyline of the city from his window. After a busy morning of meetings and phone calls, he actually had a few minutes to breathe. He glanced at his watch and grimaced as he remembered that Isabella Caplan was due in a few minutes.

He felt like a revolving door. Isabella was in, and then she'd depart for Europe, while Alannis would be arriving in a week's time from Greece. Thankfully he'd be rid of his obligation to Isabella in short order. He'd make sure she was adequately provided for, arrange for someone from Anetakis International to meet her in London and have a security team see to her safety for the duration of her stay.

Alannis, on the other hand... He smiled ruefully. She was his own doing. He and Alannis had what could only be considered a close friendship. Perhaps an understanding was a better term, though he was open to the relationship growing into more. He knew he needed to settle down now that he was taking over the New York office. It was something he'd discussed candidly with Alannis a few weeks before.

They'd make a good couple. They understood each other. She was from a solid Greek family, old friends of his father's. Her own father owned a shipping company. They were well matched, and so it stood to reason that they'd gravitate toward each other.

She'd give him friendship and children. He'd give her security, protection.

Yes, it was time to settle down. His move to New York was in all likelihood permanent, as Marley had no desire to move from the island where she and Chrysander had made their home. And if he was going to be living here on a permanent basis, it seemed the best course to find a wife and start his family.

His thoughts were interrupted by a knock on his door. He frowned and looked up as he uttered the command to enter.

"Sir, Ms. Caplan is here to see you," Madeline, his secretary, said as she poked her head in the door.

"Send her in," he said brusquely.

As he waited, he straightened in his seat and drummed his fingers idly on the desk. He tried to draw on his vague memories of the girl but all he could picture was a very young Isabella with big eyes, gangly legs and braces. He wasn't even sure how old she was now, only that she'd graduated. Wouldn't that make her somewhere around twenty-two?

He summoned a gentle smile as the door swung open. No need to scare her to death. He was on his feet and walking forward to greet her when he pulled up short, all the breath knocked squarely from his chest.

Before him stood not a girl, but a stunningly beautiful woman. An invisible hand seized his throat, squeezing until he twisted his neck to alleviate the discomfort.

She smiled tentatively at him, and he felt the gesture to his toes. For a long moment, all he could do was gawk like a pimply-faced teenager experiencing his first surge of hormones.

Isabella was dressed in formfitting jeans that slung low on her hips. Her top, if you could call it an actual top, hugged her generous curves as snugly as a man's hands. The hem fell to just above her navel, and that, coupled with the low-slung jeans, bared her navel to his view.

His gaze was drawn to it and the glimmer of silver in the shallow indention. He frowned. She had a belly ring?

He looked up, embarrassed to be caught staring, but then he locked eyes with hers. Long, dark hair fell in layers beyond her shoulders. Long lashes fringed sparkling green eyes. A hint of a smile curved plump, generous lips and white teeth flashed in his vision. Two dimples appeared in her cheeks as her smile broadened.

This was not a woman who could ever escape notice. The past several years had wrought big changes. To think he'd remembered her as someone who faded into the background wherever she was. A man would have to be blind, deaf and dumb to overlook her in a room.

"What the hell are you wearing?" he demanded before he could think better of it.

She raised one dark brow, amusement twinkling in her eyes. Then she glanced down as she smoothed her hands over her hips.

"I believe they're called clothes," she said huskily.

He frowned harder at the playfulness he heard in her voice. "Is this the sort of thing Chrysander allowed you to run around in?"

She chuckled, and the sound skittered across his nape, raising hairs in its wake. It was warm and vibrant, and he derived so much pleasure from it that he wanted her to laugh again.

"Chrysander has no say in what I wear."

"He is—was your guardian," Theron said. "As I am now."

"Not legally," she countered. "You're doing a favor for my father, and you're the executor of his estate as it pertains to me until I marry, but you're hardly my guardian. I've managed quite well on my own with minimal interference from Chrysander."

Theron leaned back against his desk as he studied the young woman standing so confidently in front of him. "Marry? The terms of your father's will is that you gain control of your inheritance when you turn twenty-five."

"Or I marry," she gently corrected. "I plan to be married before then."

Alarm took hold of Theron as he contemplated all sorts of nasty scenarios.

"Who is he?" he demanded. "I'll want to have him fully investigated. You can't be too careful in your position. Your inheritance will draw a host of unwanted suitors who only want you for your money."

Another smile quirked at the corner of her mouth. "It's nice to see you again, too, Theron. My trip was fine. The suite is lovely. It's been awhile since I last saw you, but I'd recognize you anywhere."

Her reproach irritated him because she was exactly right. He was being rude. He hadn't even properly greeted her.

"My apologies, Isabella," he said as he moved forward. He grasped her shoulders and leaned in to kiss her on either cheek. "I'm glad to hear your trip was satisfactory and that the suite is to your liking. May I get you something to drink while we discuss your travel arrangements?"

She smiled and shook her head, and then moved past him toward the window. Her hips swayed, and her bottom, cupped by the too-tight denim bobbed enticingly. He sent his gaze upward so that he wasn't ogling her inappropriately.

It was then that a flash of color at her waist stopped him. He blinked and looked again, certain he had to be mistaken. As she stopped at the window, the hem of her shirt moved so that a tiny portion of what looked to be a tattoo peeked from between her jeans and her shirt.

His gaze was riveted as he strained to see what the design was. Then he scowled. A tattoo? Obviously Chrysander had failed miserably in his role as her guardian. What the hell kind of trouble had she gotten herself into? Tattoos? Talk of marriage?

He closed his eyes and pinched the bridge of his nose as he felt the beginnings of a headache.

"You have a wonderful view," she said as she turned from the window to look at him.

He cleared his throat and sent his gaze to her face. Anywhere but at the breasts hugged tight by the thin T-shirt. *Theos,* but the woman was a walking time bomb.

"Have you already made all the arrangements for your trip to Europe or would you prefer for me to see to them?" he asked politely.

She shoved her fingers into her jeans pockets, a feat he wasn't certain how she managed, and leaned against the window.

"I'm not going to Europe."

He blinked. "Pardon?"

She smiled again, the dimples deepening. "I've decided not to travel to Europe for the summer."

He put a hand to his forehead and massaged the tension. Damn Chrysander for getting a life and saddling him with Isabella Caplan.

"Does this have anything to do with your sudden desire for marriage?" he asked tiredly. "You still haven't answered my question about the intended groom."

"That's because there isn't one yet," she said mischievously. "I never said that I had a man lined out yet, just that I intended to be married before I turned twenty-five. As that gives me three more years, there certainly isn't a need to start ordering background checks."

"Then why aren't you going to Europe? It was your plan at least a week ago according to the letter you sent to Chrysander."

"I sent Chrysander no such thing," she protested lightly. "The man Chrysander hired to oversee my education and my living arrangements informed Chrysander of my trip to Europe. I simply changed my mind."

His hand slipped to the back of his neck as a full-blown migraine threatened to bloom.

"So what do you intend to do then?" He was almost afraid to hear the answer.

She smiled broadly, her entire face lighting up. "I'm getting an apartment here in the city."

Theron choked. Then he closed his eyes as he felt the cinch draw tighter around his neck. If she stayed here, then he would be stuck overseeing her affairs, checking up on her constantly.

Suddenly her impending marriage didn't strike such a chord of irritation. She was twenty-two. True, it was young to marry these days, but certainly not outside the realm of possibility. Perhaps the best thing he could do for her was to introduce her to a man well equipped to provide security and stability for her.

The thought was already turning in his head, gaining momentum, when she spoke again.

"I'm sorry?" he said when he realized he had no idea what she'd said to him.

"Oh, I only said now that we've gotten my arrangements out of the way, I need to be going. I have an apartment to find."

Alarm bells rang at the idea of Isabella traipsing around a city she wasn't intimately familiar with, alone and vulnerable. Hell, she could wind up in an entirely unsuitable neighborhood. And then there was the matter of her security. Now that she was going to be here and not in Europe, he'd have to scramble to get a team in place. The last thing he needed was for her to be abducted as Marley had been.

"I don't think this is something you should do alone," he said firmly.

Her expression brightened. "That's so sweet of you to offer to go apartment hunting with me. I admit, I wasn't looking forward to it on my own, and your knowledge of the city is so much better than mine."

He opened his mouth to refute the idea that he'd volunteered anything, but the genuine appreciation on her face made him snap his lips shut. He let out a sigh, knowing he was well and truly screwed.

"Of course I'll accompany you. I won't have you staying just anywhere. I'll have my secretary come up with a few suitable places for you to view and then we'll go. Perhaps tomorrow morning? You're welcome to stay in the suite for as long as you need it."

She frowned. "But I hate to put you out."

He shook his head. "It's no bother. Chrysander still has a penthouse here that I can use. I need to be looking for a place as well now that I've permanently relocated here."

Her eyes sparked briefly, but then her expression faded to one of neutrality.

"In that case, I appreciate the offer, and I'd love to go apartment hunting with you tomorrow. Shall we do lunch as well?" she asked innocently.

"Of course I'll feed you," he said with a grunt. Why did he feel as though he'd been run over by a steamroller? The idea that this mere slip of a girl had run so roughshod over him left him irritated and feeling like he'd been manipulated, but there was nothing but genuine appreciation and relief in her expression.

She hurried over and threw her arms around him. She landed against his chest, and he had to brace himself to keep from stumbling back.

"Thank you," she said against his ear as she squeezed him for all she was worth.

He allowed his arms to fold around her as he returned her hug. Her body melted against his, and he felt every one of those generous curves he'd noticed earlier. His hand skimmed over the small portion of flesh on her back that was bared by her shirt, and he wondered again over the tattoo he'd seen there. It was driving him crazy not to know what it was.

He shook his head and gently extricated himself from her grasp. "Let me call for the driver so he can return you to the hotel."

She kissed him on the cheek and then turned toward the door. "Thank you, Theron, and I'll see you first thing tomorrow."

He was left rubbing his cheek where her lips had brushed just seconds before. Then he cursed and strode around to the back of his desk again. He'd been so ready to condemn Chrysander for being involved with someone so young, and here he stood lusting over the same girl. Pathetic. It had obviously been way too long since he'd been with a woman.

He buzzed his secretary and quickly gave her instructions to find three or four possible apartments. If all else failed, he could give her Chrysander's penthouse to use.

After talking with Madeline, he then picked up the phone to arrange for a security detail for Isabella.

As he hung up, he remembered that Alannis would be arriving in a week, and he groaned. He'd counted on not having Isabella to contend with when his future fiancée arrived. One woman was always more than enough, and splitting attentions between more than one was a recipe for disaster.

But maybe Alannis would have ideas where Isabella was concerned. Together they could introduce Isabella to a few eligible men—men who'd passed muster with Theron, of course.

Deciding that this was another task suited for Madeline, he buzzed her and asked her to compile a list of eligible bachelors complete with background checks and a checklist of pros and cons. She sounded amused by his request but didn't question him.

Theron sat back in his chair and folded his hands behind his head. This wouldn't take long at all. He'd find her an apartment, find her a husband, and then he would turn his attentions to his own impending nuptials.

"Isabella!" Sadie cried as she threw open the door to her apartment.

Isabella found herself enveloped in her friend's arms, and she returned the hug just as fiercely.

"Come in, come in. It's so good to see you again," Sadie exclaimed as she ushered Isabella inside.

The girls sat down in the small living room, and then Sadie pounced. "So? Did you see him?"

Isabella smiled. "Just came from his office."

"And?"

Isabella shrugged. "I told him I wasn't going to Europe and that I was going to look for an apartment here. He's going to help me," she added with a small smile.

"So he took it well?"

Sadie flipped her long red hair over her shoulder, drawing attention to her pretty features. A year older than Isabella, she had graduated the term before and moved to New York to pursue a career on Broadway.

"I wouldn't say well," Isabella said in amusement. "I think it was more a matter of him wondering what on earth he was going to do with me. The Anetakis brothers take their responsibilities very seriously. They're Greek, after all. And I am one huge responsibility Theron needs to be rid of. I'm sure he was looking forward to herding me onto a plane for Europe as soon as possible."

"Okay, so spill," Sadie said eagerly. "What's your plan?"

Isabella grimaced. "I'm not altogether sure. I had planned

to go to Europe and be an all-around nuisance to him there. Now all of a sudden he's here in New York so I'm having to scramble with the change of plans. The good news is we're having lunch tomorrow when we go apartment hunting. I guess I'll see where things go from there."

"How did he react when he saw you?" Sadie asked. "It's been what, four years since he got a good look at you?"

"Ugh. Yes. Thank goodness I've finally blossomed."

"So? Did he appreciate your womanly charms?" Sadie asked with a wide grin.

"I'm sure he noticed, but I think it was a cross between interest and being appalled. You have to understand that Theron is very, uhm, traditional." She sighed and leaned back against the couch. "But if I had shown up dressed like a good, modest Greek girl, he wouldn't have given me a second glance. I would have been relegated to little sister status, just as Chrysander has done, and there would be no changing it."

"Ah, so better to throw out the challenge from the outset," Sadie acknowledged.

"Exactly," Isabella murmured. "If he never sees me as a nonthreatening entity, then it will be damn hard for him to turn a blind eye to me."

Sadie laughed and clasped Isabella's hands in hers. "I'm so glad to see you again, Bella. It has been too long and I've missed you."

"Yes, it has. Now enough about me. I want to hear all about you and your Broadway career. Tell me, have you landed any roles?"

Sadie twisted her lips into a rueful expression. "I'm afraid the parts have been few and far between, but I haven't given up. I have an audition next week as a matter of fact."

Isabella frowned. "Are you making it okay, Sadie?"

"I have a job. Not many hours. Just a couple of nights a week.

The money is fantastic and I get to look drop-dead gorgeous," Sadie said cheekily. "It'll do until I get my big break."

Isabella viewed her friend with suspicion. "What is this job?"

Sadie grinned slyly, her eyes bright with mischief. "It's a gentleman's club. Very posh and exclusive."

Isabella's mouth dropped open. "You're working as a stripper?"

"I don't always strip," Sadie said dryly. "It's not required per se. But I get better tips when I do," she added with a bigger grin.

Isabella stared for a long moment and then burst out laughing. "Maybe I should take lessons from you. Theron would have to notice me if I did a striptease in front of him."

Sadie joined in her laughter until the two of them were wiping tears. "If he didn't notice you, hon, then the man is dead."

Impulsively, Isabella leaned up and hugged Sadie. "I'm so glad I'm here. I've missed you. I have such a good feeling about being here in New York. Like maybe this will actually work and I can make Theron fall in love with me."

Sadie returned Isabella's hug and then pulled away, a gentle smile on her face. "I have every faith that Theron will fall hopelessly in love with you. But if he doesn't? You're young and beautiful, Bella. You could have your choice of men."

"I only want Theron," she said softly. "I've loved him for so long."

"Well then, we need to think of a way to catch him, don't we?" Sadie said with a grin.

Three

"Alannis," Theron greeted her smoothly. "I trust things are well with you?"

He listened as she uttered a polite greeting, somewhat distant and reserved, but then he expected nothing less. Alannis was steeped in propriety and would never offer a more effusive greeting. It simply wasn't her style.

"I've made arrangements for the Anetakis jet to fly you from Greece to New York a week from now. Will your mother be traveling with you?"

It was a senseless question, meant to be more polite than inquisitive since he knew well that Alannis's family would never allow her to travel to see an unmarried man unchaperoned.

"I'll look forward to your arrival then," he continued. "I've arranged for a night at the opera shortly after you arrive." If all went well, he'd request a moment alone to propose and then the two families could go ahead with the wedding plans.

Of course now he needed to apprise his brothers of his intentions.

He hung up the phone and stared at it for a long moment. He had no doubt Chrysander would, in his newfound loving bliss, be reluctant to encourage Theron to enter into a loveless marriage. Piers on the other hand would shrug and say it was Theron's life and if he wanted to mess it up, that was his prerogative.

In time he could grow to like Alannis very well. He liked her already and respected her, which was more than he could say for a lot of the women of his acquaintance. He knew better than to expect a woman to love him as deeply as Marley loved his brother. But he'd like to think he could be friends with his future wife and enjoy her companionship in and out of bed.

He frowned when he thought of Alannis naked and in his bed, beneath his body. He glanced down at his groin as if expecting a response. If he was, he was disappointed.

Alannis…she came across as cold and extremely stiff. He supposed he couldn't blame her for that. She was most assuredly a virgin, and it would be up to him to coax the passion from her. It was his duty as her husband.

With a sigh, he checked his watch, and to his irritation noticed that Isabella was late. He drummed his fingers impatiently on his desk. Madeline had provided three possible apartments, all in good areas and in close proximity to the Imperial Park Hotel. She hadn't as of yet provided a list of eligible men.

No matter. The first order of business was to see her settled. The sooner, the better. Then he'd worry about marrying her off.

When he heard his door open, he looked up, startled. Then he frowned when he saw Isabella stride inside. On cue, his intercom buzzed, and Madeline's voice announced somewhat dryly that Isabella was on her way in.

"Good morning," Isabella sang out as she stopped in front of his desk.

He swallowed and then his gaze narrowed as he took in her attire. It wasn't exactly immodest, and as such he couldn't offer a complaint. It covered her. Sort of.

His mouth went dry when she put her hands on his desk and leaned forward. Her breasts spilled precariously close to the neckline of her T-shirt, and he could see the lacy cups of her bra as they pushed the soft mounds upward.

He cursed under his breath and directed his gaze upward. "Good morning, Isabella."

"Bella, please, unless you have an aversion to the name?"

He didn't, though it somehow seemed more intimate, particularly when he took the meaning of the Italian form of her name. *Beautiful.* That she was. Stunningly so. Different from the usual sophisticated type of women he gravitated toward, but beautiful nonetheless. There was something wild and unrestrained about her.

He ground his teeth together and shifted his position. Where his groin had remained stoic when thinking of Alannis, it had flared to life, painfully so, as soon as Isabella had walked into his office.

He was her guardian, someone to look after her welfare, and here he sat fantasizing about her. Disgust filled him. Not only was it disrespectful to Isabella but it was disrespectful to Alannis. No woman should have to put up with her soon-to-be fiancé lusting after another woman.

"Bella," he echoed, taking her invitation to use her nickname. It suited her. Light and beautiful.

He rose from his seat and walked around the front of his desk. She eyed him curiously, and he found himself asking her why.

She laughed. "You're dressed so casually today. I'm so used to seeing you in nothing but suits and ties."

"When have you seen me?" he asked in surprise. He

thought back to the times when she would have seen him, and while he probably was wearing a suit, it was hardly a basis for her supposition.

She flushed, and he watched in fascination as color stained her cheeks. She ducked away, her hair sliding over her shoulder.

"Pictures," she mumbled. "There are always pictures of you in the papers."

"And you get these papers all the way out in California?" he asked.

"Yes. I like to keep up with the people looking after my financial well-being," she said evenly.

"As you should," he said approvingly. "Are you ready to go? I have a list of potential apartments. I took the liberty of scaling down the possibilities to a few more suitable to a young woman living alone."

And then he realized he'd made a huge assumption. There was certainly no reason to believe that a woman as beautiful and vibrant as Isabella would be living alone. He refused to retract the statement or ask her if she was currently involved with anyone. But he'd need to know because if she was involved, seriously, then he could forego the whole process of introducing her to prospective husbands.

"I'm ready if you are," she said as she smiled warmly at him.

As they walked from the building that housed the Anetakis headquarters, Theron put his hand to the small of Isabella's back. She felt the touch through her shirt. It seared her skin, and she was sure that if she could look, there would be a visible print from his fingers, burned into her flesh.

After loving him from afar for so many years, she'd been prepared for disappointment, that maybe the man he'd become wouldn't live up to the dream. She'd been so far removed from the truth that reality overwhelmed her. He was more, so much more than she could have imagined. Her feelings hadn't gone away when she'd seen him again. They'd cemented.

She sat next to him in the back of the limousine. In addition to the driver, Henry, there was one additional member of his security detail that rode up front. When they pulled up in front of the first apartment building, she noticed that another smaller car pulled in behind them, and two men got out and cautiously scanned the area.

"I don't remember the security being this tight the last time I visited," she murmured as they walked toward the entrance.

Theron stiffened. "It's a necessary evil."

She waited for him to say more but he didn't volunteer further information.

Three hours later, they'd toured the apartments on his list with him vetoing the first two before she could even offer an opinion. He was tight-lipped about the third but offered her the choice between it and the last on their list.

She stifled her laughter and solemnly informed him that she liked the fourth. He nodded his approval and set about securing it for her.

"Will you have your things shipped to the apartment?" he asked as they walked back to the limousine.

She shook her head. "I plan to shop for everything I need here and have it delivered. It will be quite fun!"

He growled something under his breath but when she turned to him in question, he pressed his lips together.

"I'll arrange for someone to take you shopping," he said grudgingly.

She raised an eyebrow. "I assure you, I have no need of a babysitter, Theron. Chrysander saddled me with one four years ago, and I had no more need of it then than I do now."

"You will not roam all over the city by yourself," he said resolutely.

She shrugged and offered a faint smile. "You could always go with me."

He gave her a startled look.

"No? You seem the logical choice given I don't know anyone else here." She purposely kept silent about Sadie. There was no reason for Theron to know about her, and he wouldn't approve if he knew she worked in a strip club. And find out he would, because the instant she let him know of someone she was spending time with, he'd perform an extensive background check and then forbid her to associate with Sadie any longer.

Not that she'd listen, but she intended for their relationship to get off to the best possible start. Lust was fine for now, but she wanted to make him fall in love with her. She wanted him to need her.

"You're right, of course," he said with a grimace. "I forget you've lived in California and have only been here to visit."

She slid into the limousine and smiled over at him as he got in on the other side. "Does that mean you'll go shopping with me?"

He grunted, and she couldn't hold the laughter in any longer. His eyes widened, and he stared openly at her as though he found the sound of her laughter enchanting.

All the breath left her as she saw for just one moment a look of wanting in his eyes. Just as soon as it flashed, he blinked and recovered.

"I'll see if my schedule permits such a trip," he said tightly.

"Where are you taking me for lunch?" she asked, more to remind him of their date than any real curiosity over their destination. She didn't care where or what they ate. She just wanted the time with him.

"We have an excellent restaurant at the hotel," he said. "My table is always available to me. I thought we could eat there and then you could retire to your suite to rest."

She resisted the urge to roll her eyes. He was smooth. Plotting the easiest way to get rid of her. She couldn't blame him. She was an unexpected burden, and he was a busy man.

She chewed her bottom lip and looked out the window at the passing traffic as she contemplated how to get him to see beyond the inconvenience to the woman who loved him and wanted him so badly.

"Is something the matter, Bella?"

She turned to see him staring at her in concern. She smiled and shook her head. "Just a little tired. And excited."

He frowned. "Maybe you should allow me to see to the furnishing of your apartment. If you would mark down your preferences, I could have a designer work with you so that you didn't have to go out shopping for all the things you need."

"Oh, no, that wouldn't be near as much fun. I can't wait to pick out everything for the apartment. It's such a gorgeous place."

"What are your plans, Bella?" he asked.

She blinked in surprise. "Plans?"

"Yes. Plans. Now that you've graduated, what are your career plans?"

"Oh. Well, I planned to take the summer off," she hedged. "I'll focus on the future this fall."

He didn't say anything, but she could tell such an approach bothered him. She smiled to herself. It probably gave him hives. He and his brothers all were intensely driven with a *take no prisoners* approach when it came to business. They weren't the world's wealthiest hotel family for nothing.

When they arrived at the hotel, Theron ushered her inside as his security team flanked them on all sides. It was odd and a bit surreal, almost like they were royalty.

A few minutes later, they were escorted to Theron's table at the restaurant. It was situated in a quiet corner, almost completely cutoff from the rest of the diners.

He settled her into her chair and then circled around to sit across from her. He dropped his long, lean body into his seat and stared lazily at her.

"What would you like to eat, *pethi mou?*"

Isabella cringed at the endearment. He'd called her the same thing when she was thirteen. *Little one.* It set her teeth on edge. Hardly something that evoked images of the two of them in bed, limbs entwined.

"What do you suggest?" she asked.

She studied his lips, the hard, sensual curve to his mouth and the dark shadow already forming on his jaw. She was tempted, so very tempted to reach across and run the tip of her finger along the roughness and then to the softness of his lips.

What would it be like to kiss him? She'd kissed several boys in college. She said *boys* because next to Theron, that's all they were. Some were very good, others awkward and "pleasant."

But Theron. Kissing him would be like chasing a storm. Hot, exciting and breathless. Her pulse jumped wildly as she imagined the warm brush of his tongue.

"Bella?"

She blinked and shook her head as she realized Theron had been calling her name for a few seconds.

"Sorry," she murmured. "Lost in my thoughts."

"I was suggesting you try the salmon," he said dryly.

She nodded jerkily and tilted her head toward the waiter who was standing beside the table waiting for their order.

"I'll have what he suggests," she said huskily.

Theron placed their order in succinct tones, and the waiter hurried away shortly afterward.

"Now, Bella," Theron said, as he sat back in his chair. He looked comfortable, at ease as he raked his gaze over her features, setting fire to every nerve receptor. "Perhaps we should talk about your future."

A nervous scuttle began in her stomach. "My future?" She laughed lightly to allay the pounding of her heart. If she had any say, her future would be inexorably linked to his.

"Indeed. Your future. Surely you've given it *some* thought?"

He sounded slightly scornful, impatient with someone who didn't have an airtight plan. If he only knew. She'd done nothing else for the past years but plan for her future. With him.

"I've given it a lot of thought," she said evenly.

"You mentioned marriage. Are you truly considering being married before you turn twenty-five."

"I count on it."

He nodded as if he approved. She almost laughed. Would he be so approving if he knew he was her intended groom? A sigh escaped her. She felt so evil, like she was plotting an assassination rather than a seduction.

"This is good," he said almost to himself. "I've taken the liberty of forming a list of possible candidates."

Her brow crinkled as she stared at him in puzzlement. "Candidates? For what?"

"Marriage, Bella. I intend to help you find a husband."

Four

Isabella eyed Theron suspiciously, wondering if he'd suddenly developed a sense of humor.

"You intend to do *what?*" she asked.

"You want a husband. After my initial misgivings, I've decided it's a sound idea. A woman in your position can't be too careful," he continued, obviously warming to his subject. "So I've taken the liberty of drawing up a list of suitable candidates."

She burst out laughing. She couldn't help herself. As absurdities went, this might well take the cake.

He blinked in surprise then frowned as she continued to chuckle. "What do you find so amusing?"

She shook her head, the smile not dropping from her lips. "I'm in the city all of two days, and already you're planning to marry me off. And tell me, what do you mean by *a woman in my position can't be too careful?*"

"You're wealthy, young and beautiful," he said bluntly.

"You'll have every man between the ages of twenty and eighty plotting to wed and bed you, not necessarily in that order."

She sat back in mock surprise. "Wow. And not a word about my intelligence, wit or charm. I'm glad to know I don't plan to wed for superficial reasons."

Theron sobered then reached over and took her hand. Warmth spread up her arm as his fingers stroked her palm. "This is precisely why I felt I should be involved in your search for a husband. Men will try to take advantage of you by pretending they're something they're not. Fortune hunters will pretend they know nothing of your wealth. They'll be swept away by your *kindness* and *generosity*. It's important that any man we allow close to you be carefully vetted by myself."

Her lips twitched, but she dare not laugh. He was utterly serious, and she had to admit that his concern was endearing. It would be quite sweet if he weren't so intent on marrying her off to another man.

"Don't be disheartened, *pethi mou*," he soothed. "There are many men who would give you the world. It's a matter of finding the right one."

It was all she could do not to cringe. If that wasn't a painful lecture, she'd never heard one.

"You're right, of course," she murmured.

Because what else was she going to say? What she really wanted to do was lean over and ask him if he could be that man. But she already knew the answer to that. He couldn't be that man. At least not yet. Not until he had time to get used to the idea.

Theron smiled his approval and slipped his fingers from hers as he leaned back in his chair. She glanced down at her open hand, regretting the loss of his touch.

"So tell me, what are your requirements in a husband?" he asked indulgently.

She gazed thoughtfully at him, her mind assembling all the

things she loved most about him. Then she started ticking items off on her fingers.

"Let's see. I'd like him to be tall, dark and handsome."

Theron rolled his eyes. "You've described the wishes of half the female population."

"I also want him to be kind and have a sense of responsibility. As I'd prefer not to have children right away, his agreement on that matter would also be important."

"You don't want children?" he asked. He seemed surprised, but then he likely thought all women aspired to pop out a veritable brood as soon as they got a ring on their finger.

"I didn't say I didn't want them," she replied calmly. "Let me guess, you'd want them immediately?"

He arched one brow. "We aren't discussing me, but yes, I see no reason to wait."

"That's because you aren't the one having them," she said dryly.

For a moment it looked as though he would laugh, but then he waved his hand and urged her to continue with her wish list.

She pretended to consider for a moment. "I want him to be wealthier than I am so that my money is a nonissue."

Theron nodded his agreement.

Then she let her voice drop, and she leaned forward. "I want him to burn for me, to not be able to go a day without touching me, holding me, caressing me. He'll be an excellent lover. I want a man who knows how to please me," she finished in a husky, longing-filled voice.

He stared at her, his eyes sharp. For a moment she imagined that there was answering passion in his eyes as they flickered over her exposed skin.

"Do you not agree that these are things I should expect?" she asked softly as she studied him.

He cleared his throat and looked briefly away. Was she affecting him at all or was he completely immune? No, there was something in his eyes. His entire body emanated sexual awareness. She might be young, but she wasn't naive, and she certainly wasn't stupid when it came to men. She'd had her share of interested parties. She could read harmless, flirty interest, and then there was the dark, brooding intensity of a man whose passions ran deep and powerful.

Never before had she felt the intense magnetism that existed between her and Theron. She'd spent years searching for something that even came close to the budding awareness that had begun in her teenage years.

She'd experimented with dates. Kisses, the clumsy groping that had inevitably led to her showing the guy the door. There was only one who ever came close to coaxing her to give him everything. In the end, it had been him who'd called a stop to their lovemaking. At the time, she'd been embarrassed and certain that she'd made some mistake. He'd kissed her gently, told her that he was greatly honored by the fact that he would be her first, but that perhaps she should save her gift for a man who held a special place in her heart.

Then, she'd seen it as a cop-out, a man running hard and fast from a woman who obviously equated sex with commitment or at least a deeper relationship. Now, she was just grateful that she hadn't blithely given away her innocence. Travis was right. Her virginity was special, and she'd only give it to a special man.

She blinked again when she realized Theron was talking to her.

"I think you are wise to place emphasis on…these qualities," he said uncomfortably. "You wouldn't want a man who'd mistreat you in any way, and of course you'll want someone who shares your vision of marriage and a family."

"But you don't think I should want a good lover?" she asked with one raised eyebrow.

His eyes gleamed in the flickering lamp situated in the

middle of the table. Her breath caught and hung in her chest, painful as her throat tightened. She swallowed at the raw power radiating from him in a low, sensual hum.

"It would indeed be a shame if a man had no idea what to do with a woman such as yourself, Bella."

He looked up in relief when the waiter came bearing the tray with their food. Isabella, on the other hand, cursed the timing.

Theron surprised her, however, when after the waiter retreated, he caught her eye and murmured in his sexy, accented voice, "Your mother died early in your childhood, did she not? Has there been no one else to speak to you about…men?"

She gaped at him in astonishment. Did he honestly think she'd reached the ripe old age of twenty-two without ever hearing the birds and the bees talk? She wasn't sure who was more horrified, her or Theron. He looked uncomfortable, and hell, so was she.

Picking up her fork, she cut into her fish and speared a perfectly cooked piece. It hit her tongue, and she nearly sighed in appreciation. It was good, and she was starving.

Theron was clearly waiting on her to answer his question. His really ridiculous question aimed more at a fourteen-year-old, pimply faced girl than a twenty-two-year-old woman.

"If I say no, are you volunteering to head my education?" she asked with a flash of a grin.

He shot an exasperated grimace in her direction. "I'll take that as a yes that someone has spoken to you of such matters."

"Next you'll be offering to buy my feminine products," she muttered.

He choked on the sip of wine he'd just taken and hurriedly set the glass back down on the table. "You imp. It's not polite to make someone laugh as they're taking a drink."

"I'll remind you that you started this conversation," she said dryly.

She watched him take a bite and then wipe his mouth with his napkin. He had really gorgeous lips. Perfect for kissing.

"So I did," he said with a shrug. "I merely wondered if you'd spoken to another woman about men and husbands and of course which men make the best husbands."

"And lovers," she added.

"Yes, of course," he said in resignation.

She sat back in her seat and stared at him in challenge. "You don't want the woman you marry to be a good lover?"

He gave her what she could only classify as a look of horror. "No, I damn well do not expect my wife to be a good lover. It's my duty to…" He broke off in a strangled voice. "We're not discussing my future wife," he said gruffly.

But her curiosity had been well and truly piqued. She sat forward, and placed her chin in one palm, her food forgotten. "It's your duty to what?"

"This is not a conversation that is appropriate for us to have," he said stiffly.

She sighed and nearly rolled her eyes. He sure didn't mind playing the guardian card when it suited him, and the last thing she wanted was to plant any sort of parent role into his brain. But she desperately wanted to hear just what he considered his duty to be to the woman who'd share his bed.

"You're my guardian, Theron. Who else can I talk to about such matters?"

He let out a long-suffering sigh and took another sip of his wine. "I don't expect my wife to be sexually experienced when she comes to my bed. It's my duty to awaken her passion and teach her everything she needs to know about…lovemaking."

Isabella wrinkled her nose. "That sounds so medieval. Have you ever considered that she might teach you a thing or two?"

He set the glass down again, a look of astonished outrage on his face. Clearly the thought had never occurred to him that any woman could teach him anything when it came to sex. So he fancied himself a good lover then. She had to fight off a full-body shiver. She wanted his hands on her body so badly. She'd be more than willing to be an eager pupil under his tutelage.

"I assure you, there is little a woman could teach me that I am not already well acquainted with," he said with a thread of arrogance.

"That experienced, huh?"

He grimaced. "I don't know how our conversation deteriorated to this, but it's hardly an appropriate conversation between a guardian and his ward."

And up went the cement wall again. At least he was struggling to put her back on a non threatening level which meant he considered her just that. A threat.

She dug cheerfully into the remainder of her meal, content to let silence settle over the table. Theron watched her, and she let him, making sure not to look up and catch his stare. There was curiosity in his gaze but there was also interest, and not the platonic kind. He might fight it tooth and nail, but his eyes didn't lie.

When they were finished eating, Theron queried her on her next course of action.

"I'll need furniture, of course. Not to mention food and staple items."

"Make a list of food items and any other household things you need. I'll have it delivered so that you don't have to go out shopping," Theron said. "If you can stand a few more days in the hotel suite, I'll see if I can fit in a furniture shopping trip later in the week."

"Oh, I need everything," she said cheerfully. "Towels, curtains, dishes, bed linens—"

He held up his hand and smiled. "Make a detailed list. I'll see that it is taken care of."

He tossed his table napkin down and motioned for the

waiter. Then he glanced at Isabella. "Are you ready to return to your suite?"

Isabella wasn't, but she also knew that she'd monopolized Theron's entire morning, and he was a busy man. She nodded and rose from her seat. They met around the table, and he put his hand to the small of her back as they headed for the exit.

"I'll see you up," Theron said when they walked into the lobby.

The elevator slid open and the two stepped inside. Even before it fully closed, Isabella turned to Theron. He was so close. His warmth radiated from him, enveloping her. She could smell the crispness of his cologne.

"Thank you for today," she murmured.

She reached automatically for his hands and knew that he was going to lean in to kiss her on either cheek. The elevator neared the top floor.

"You're quite welcome, *pethi mou.* I'll have my secretary call you about your apartment and also about our shopping trip."

As she thought, when the elevator stopped, he leaned down, his intention to kiss her quickly. She stepped into his arms, her body molding to his chest. Before he could react, she circled her arms around his neck and as his lips brushed against her cheek, she turned her face so that their lips met.

The air exploded around them. Their mouths fused and electricity whipped between them like bolts of lightning. At first he went completely still as she boldly kissed him. And then a low growl worked from his throat and he took control.

He yanked her to him until there was no space between them. His arms wrapped around her body, and his hand slid down her spine, to the small of her back and then to cup her behind through her tight jeans.

She was intensely aware of his every touch. His fingers felt like branding irons against her skin, burning through the denim of her pants. His other hand tangled roughly in her hair, glancing over her scalp before twisting and catching in the thick strands.

It wasn't a simple kiss, no loving caress between two people acquainting themselves. It was the kiss of two lovers who were starved for each other.

No hesitancy or permission seeking. It was like they'd been separated for a long period and were coming back together, two people who knew each other intimately.

The warm brush of his tongue coaxed her mouth further open and then he was inside, licking at the edge of her teeth and then laving over her tongue, inviting her to respond equally.

She went willingly, tasting him and testing the contours of his lips.

His hand moved from the curve of her bottom up underneath her shirt and to the small of her back where his large hand splayed out possessively as he crushed her to his hard body.

Her breath caught, and she gasped when his hand made that first contact with her bare skin. Her breasts swelled and throbbed against his chest.

She dare not say a word or make a sound, because if she did, the moment would be lost. He would remember who he was kissing. Instead she focused her energy on making it last as long as she could.

When his lips left hers and stuttered across her jaw and to her neck, she moaned, unable to remain silent. She shivered and quaked, her senses awakening after a long winter.

Never had she felt anything like his lips, whisper soft, across the delicate skin beneath her ear.

Her knees buckled, and she clutched frantically at him. Suddenly his mouth left her, and he cursed. She closed her eyes, knowing the moment was over.

He yanked her away, his hands tight around her arms. His eyes blazed, equal parts anger, self-condemnation and…hunger. She stared helplessly back at him, unable to say anything.

He cursed again in Greek and then shook his head before shoving her out of the elevator. He ushered her to the door where he jammed the card into the lock.

He held the door open with one hand, and she slowly entered. When she turned around to say something, he was already letting the door close. Before it clicked shut, she heard his footsteps hurrying away.

Turning until her back rested against the door, she closed her eyes and hugged her body as she relived those precious moments in Theron's arms.

Their passion had been immediate. The chemistry between them was positively combustible. The last unknown was unveiled. In every other aspect, Theron had proved himself to be her perfect match. All she hadn't known is if they were sexually compatible, not that she'd harbored any doubts, and now in the space of a few heated moments in the elevator, the last piece had fallen neatly into place.

Now all she had to do was make him see it.

Five

Theron pinched the bridge of his nose between his fingers and cursed long and hard. His head felt like someone had taken a hammer to it, he was tired, and he hadn't slept more than an hour the entire night.

Madeline kept staring at him throughout the morning as though he'd lost his mind, and maybe he had. He'd forgotten two meetings and had waved off three phone calls, one of which was from his brother Piers.

All that occupied his thoughts was a dark-haired minx with sultry green eyes. *Theos mou,* but he couldn't forget her kiss, the feel of her mouth on his, her body molded to his as though she were made for him.

He was her guardian. He was responsible for her well-being, and yet he'd damn near hauled her into the bedroom of her suite and made love to her. His body still ached to do just that.

He shook his head for what seemed like the hundredth time since he'd gotten to his office this morning. No matter what he did, though, he couldn't rid himself of her image. Her scent. She was destined to drive him crazy.

Impatient and more than a little agitated, he slapped the intercom. Madeline's calm voice filtered through as she asked what he needed.

"Do you have that list drawn up for me yet?"

"Which list would that be?"

"The list of eligible men I asked for. The men I intend to introduce Bella to."

"Ah, that one. Yes, I have it."

"Bring it in then," he demanded.

A few moments later, Madeline walked through his door holding a piece of paper.

He motioned for her to sit down in front of his desk. "Read them off to me," he said as he leaned back in his chair.

"Did you sleep at all last night?" Madeline asked, her eyes narrowing perceptively.

He grunted and closed his eyes as he waited for her to give up and do as he asked.

"Reginald Hollister."

Theron shook his head immediately. "He's an immature little twerp. Spoiled endlessly by his parents. Bella needs someone…more independent."

Madeline made a show of scratching him off. "Okay then, what about Charles McFadden?"

Theron scowled. "There's rumor that he abused his first wife."

"Bradley Covington?"

"He's an ass," Theron said.

Madeline sighed and quickly crossed him off.

"Tad Whitley."

"Not wealthy enough."

"Garth Moser?"

"I don't like him."

"Paul Hedgeworth."

Theron frowned as he tried to think of a reason why he shouldn't consider Paul.

"Aha," Madeline said when nothing was forthcoming. She drew a large circle around his name. "Shall I invite him to your cocktail party Thursday night?"

"He's too handsome and charming," Theron muttered.

Madeline smiled. "Good, then Isabella should be well pleased."

She glanced down her list then looked back up at Theron. "I think we should include Marcus Atwater and Colby Danforth, as well. They're both single, very good-looking and aren't currently in a relationship."

Theron waved his hand in a gesture of surrender. This was probably best left to Madeline anyway. She'd know better what Isabella would like than he would.

They were interrupted when the door burst open and Isabella hurried in, a bright smile on her face.

"Sorry to just barge in," she said in an out-of-breath voice. "I didn't see Madeline…oh, there you are," she said when she caught sight of his secretary.

Madeline rose and smiled in Isabella's direction. "Quite all right, my dear. I was just on my way out. I'm sure Mr. Anetakis has time for you. He appears to have canceled all his morning meetings."

He scowled at Madeline, not that she seemed particularly intimidated. She patted Isabella on the arm as she passed and then she turned as she reached the door. "I'll hold your calls and take messages."

"That won't be—"

But Madeline was gone, and he was left with Isabella. His gaze drifted over her to see that she was wearing shorts. Really short shorts that bared her long, tan legs.

A dainty ankle bracelet hung loosely at her foot. She wore sandals that showed off bright pink toenails. As his gaze drifted upward again, he saw that the T-shirt she wore was cut off so as to bare her midriff, and the belly ring she wore, and it molded to her breasts like she was planning to enter a wet T-shirt contest.

He wasn't going to survive this.

He cleared his throat and gestured toward the seat that Madeline had vacated. "I'm glad you're here, Bella. We need to talk."

She turned for a moment, and he caught a glimpse of the tattoo on her back. It sparkled almost. It was either a fairy or a butterfly. He couldn't tell and it was making him nuts. He wanted to go over and shove her shorts down so that he could see it.

A tattoo. He caught himself just short of shaking his head again. What had she been thinking? If she was his, she would have never done something so foolish. There was no reason to take such a risk with her body.

Theos, now he was sitting here considering what he would and wouldn't allow her to do if she was his. She wasn't his. Would never be his. He mustn't even entertain such a thought.

She settled into the seat in front of him which put her breasts right in his line of vision. He certainly couldn't accuse her of baring too much cleavage. The shirt covered her very well, but the shirt clung to the globes, outlining every curve and swell. It was far more enticing than the lowest cut neckline.

"What did you want to talk about?" she asked.

By now he was hanging onto his temper and control by a thread. And yet she stared calmly at him as though they were about to discuss the weather. He wanted to beat his head on the desk.

He rubbed his hand tiredly over his face and then focused his attention on the matter at hand.

"About last night…" he began.

She held up her hand, startling him into silence.

"Don't ruin it, Theron," she said huskily.

He blinked in surprise. "Ruin what?"

"The kiss. Don't ruin it by apologizing."

"It shouldn't have happened," he said tightly.

She sighed. "You're ruining it. I asked you not to."

He stared at her open-mouthed. How the hell was he supposed to hand her the lecture he'd carefully planned when she looked positively disgruntled over the fact that he'd brought it up?

"If you positively must regret it, I'd appreciate it if you did so quietly," she said before he could offer anything further. "You're allowed to forget it ever happened, you're allowed to regret it, you're allowed to swear on all that's holy that it'll never happen again. Just don't expect me to do the same, and I'd appreciate it if you didn't patronize me by making light of it. As kisses go, I thought it was damn near perfect. You saying differently doesn't make it any less in my mind."

He was speechless. A first for him. He who always had something to say. He was the diplomat in the family, always the level-headed one, and yet he'd been reduced to a mindless, gaping idiot by this infuriating woman.

She crossed one leg over the other and pressed her hands together in her lap. "Now, if that's all you had on your mind, I thought we could finalize the arrangements for the apartment and plan our shopping trip? I arranged for the papers I need to sign for the apartment to be faxed here since I was sure you'd want to look over everything first."

That was it? She could so easily shove what happened the night before out of her mind when he'd been consumed the entire morning? The memory didn't just consume him, it tortured him endlessly.

Even now he looked at her lips and remembered the lush fullness against his mouth. He could remember her taste and scent. The throb in his groin intensified as he imagined how she'd look, spread naked on the bed as he moved over her.

He cursed again and ripped his mind to present matters.

"Check with Madeline and see if she has the agreement. I'll have my lawyer look it over if you like. As for shopping, Madeline will know my appointments for the week. Stop on your way out and have her schedule a few hours for us to pick out your furniture."

She flashed him a smile that warmed parts of his body that didn't bear mentioning. With a toss of her long hair, she rose gracefully from the chair. She gave him a small wave bye then turned and walked to the door.

A fairy. Her tattoo was a fairy with a sprinkling of glittery dust and sparkles radiating from the design.

It suited her.

But it brought up another very intriguing thought. Did she have any other tattoos? Maybe one or two that could only be seen when she wore no clothing? It made him twitchy as he imagined going on a hunt with her body as the map.

Isabella left Theron's office, biting her lip to keep from smiling. He'd certainly been prepared to give her an endless lecture on how they could never again do what they'd done the night before. It wasn't anything she hadn't expected which was why she'd been prepared to head it off before he ever got started.

She mentally patted herself on the back at the expert way she'd diffused the situation. He was probably still off balance and trying to figure out just what had happened.

She approached Madeline's desk and politely asked if Madeline had received a fax for her.

Madeline tapped a stack of papers at the edge of her desk and then smiled up at Isabella.

"Did he tell you about the party?" Madeline asked.

Isabella picked up the rental agreement and frowned. "No, he didn't mention it."

Just then Theron stuck his head out the door. "Bella, I forgot to tell you that I have a cocktail party planned this Thursday that I'd like you to attend. Seven p.m. at my penthouse. Madeline will arrange for a car to pick you up at the hotel."

Before she could respond, he withdrew into his office again and closed the door.

"Well, there you have it," Madeline said in amusement. "I don't suppose he's also told you the occasion?"

Isabella turned back to the older woman, her frown deepening. "Why do I get the idea that I'm being royally set up?"

"Because you are?" Madeline said cheerfully.

Isabella flopped down in the chair beside Madeline's desk. "Tell me."

Madeline pulled out a sheet of paper and thrust it toward Isabella. "I wasn't told to keep this secret so I'm not violating anyone's confidence, and I figure if I was invited to a party where my future husband was in attendance, I'd at least want the opportunity to buy a gorgeous dress for the occasion."

Isabella snatched the paper and stared back at Madeline in astonishment. "Husband?"

Madeline's eyebrows went up. "He didn't tell you that he was searching for a husband for you? I'd have to think that came up in conversation at least once."

"Well it did, briefly I mean. Just yesterday. He's already found someone?"

Isabella tried to keep the horror from her voice, but she wasn't entirely certain she'd been successful judging by the sympathy she saw in Madeline's eyes. She'd gone along with it because she hadn't really thought that Theron was serious, and even if he was, she figured she had plenty of time.

"Maybe he's in a hurry so that he can concentrate on his own upcoming wedding," Madeline said in a soothing voice.

"What?" Isabella croaked.

"He didn't tell you that, either?" Madeline asked cautiously. "Well then, you didn't hear that from me."

Isabella leaned forward. "Tell me," she said fiercely. "Is he really getting married? Is he engaged?"

Madeline looked stunned for a moment and then understanding softened her expression. "Oh dear," she breathed.

She got up and walked around to where Isabella sat stiffly, her hands gripped tightly in her lap. "Why don't we go into the conference room," Madeline said quietly.

Isabella let Madeline lead her into the other room where Madeline shut and locked the door. "Have a seat," she directed Isabella.

Numbly Isabella complied and Madeline took the seat next to her.

"Now, how long have you had this crush on Theron?"

"Crush?" Isabella asked in a mixture of amusement and devastation. "A crush is a passing fancy. I've been in love with Theron ever since I was a young girl. Back then it might have been considered a crush, but now?"

Madeline shook her head and patted Isabella's hand. "He has the right idea to introduce you to potential husbands then. He has an arrangement with the Gianopolous family to marry their daughter Alannis. She and her mother arrive in New York in less than a week's time. I'd hate to see you...hurt. Perhaps the best thing to do would be to focus on the men Theron has in mind for you. This fascination with Theron can only end in disappointment."

Isabella knew that Madeline was nothing but well-intentioned, but she also had no idea of the depth of Isabella's feelings and her determination.

Still, the thought of Theron already being engaged, of having a commitment to another woman... She closed her eyes against the sudden stab of pain. No wonder he was so put off by the kiss they'd shared the night before.

"When do they marry?" she asked in a soft voice.

"Well, he has to propose first, but from what I understand

that's a mere formality. He didn't want a long engagement, so I imagine it will be this fall sometime."

"So he hasn't even proposed yet?"

Relief filled Isabella. If he hadn't asked, then there was time to make sure he didn't.

Madeline frowned. "I don't like the look you're giving me."

Isabella leaned forward and grabbed Madeline's hands. "You have to help me, Madeline. He's making a huge mistake. I need to make him see that."

Madeline shook her head vehemently. "Oh, no. I'm not getting involved in this. Theron has made his choice, and I make it a point never to get involved in my employer's personal life. You're on your own."

Isabella dropped Madeline's hands with a sigh. "You'll thank me for this when he's a much happier man."

Madeline stood and regarded Isabella with reservation. "Don't make a fool of yourself, Isabella. No man is worth losing your self-respect over. If your mother was alive, she'd probably tell you the same thing."

"My mother loved my father very much," Isabella said softly. "He loved her, too. They'd both want me to be happy. They'd want me to marry the man I loved."

"Then I'll wish you luck."

Isabella smiled, though it was completely forced. "Thank you, Madeline."

They left the conference room, and Isabella quickly signed the rental agreement before handing it over to Madeline. "Let him read over it and if he has no objections, fax it back for me, please."

"And your shopping trip? When would you like to schedule that?"

Isabella shook her head. "I'll go by myself. When is the cocktail party again?"

"Thursday night. Seven."

Isabella slowly nodded. "Okay, I'll be there."

She turned to walk out of the office, her mind reeling from the unexpected shock of Theron's upcoming proposal. She flipped open her cell phone and dialed Sadie's number.

"Sadie? It's me, Isabella," she said when Sadie answered the phone. "Are you busy? I need to come over. It's urgent."

Six

"This is a disaster," Isabella groaned as she flopped onto Sadie's couch.

Sadie sat next to her, concern creasing her pretty features. "Surely you aren't giving up. He hasn't even proposed to her yet."

"*Yet.* That's the problem," Isabella said glumly. "*Yet* means he fully intends to, so for all practical purposes, he's engaged."

"She might not say yes," Sadie pointed out.

Isabella gazed balefully at her. "Would you say no to Theron Anetakis?"

"Well, no...."

"Neither will she," Isabella said with a sigh. She stared up at the ceiling as she raced to come up with a plan. "She's no doubt a good Greek girl from a good Greek family. She'll have impeccable breeding, of course. Her father probably has loads of money, and she would probably drink battery acid before ever going against her parents' wishes."

"That exciting of a girl, huh?"

Isabella laughed as she looked back at Sadie. "I'm not being very charitable. I'm sure she's lovely."

"Now you make her sound like a poodle," Sadie said in amusement.

Isabella covered her face with her hands and tried not to let panic overtake her. Or despair.

"Oh, honey," Sadie said as she wrapped her arms around Isabella. "This doesn't change anything. Truly. You still have to do the same thing as always. Get him to see you. The real you. He won't be able to resist you once he spends time with you."

Isabella let herself be embraced by her friend. At the moment she'd take what comfort she could get. Being alone had never really bothered her, but now she was faced with the possibility of not being with the one person she wanted.

"We kissed last night," she said when Sadie finally drew away.

"See? I told you," Sadie exclaimed.

"Don't celebrate yet," Isabella said glumly. "He gave me the lecture this morning, or at least he tried."

Sadie's eyebrow went up. "The lecture?"

"Oh, you know, the whole *this can never happen again, it was a mistake* lecture."

"Ah, that one."

"At least now I know why."

"Okay, so it won't be as easy as you thought it might be," Sadie said. "That doesn't mean you won't be successful. From what you've said, it hardly sounds like a love match."

Isabella sighed again. "So what do I do, Sadie?"

Sadie squeezed her hand and smiled. "You make him fall in love with *you.*"

"Which requires me to make him see past this whole guardian-ward thing. The kiss was…" She took a deep breath

and smiled dreamily. "It was hot. I need him to see me like
he did in that moment."

"If I can make this all about me for a moment, I might
have a somewhat devious method for getting him to see you
sorta naked."

Isabella reared her head back in surprise. "You certainly
have my attention now."

Sadie grimaced. "I'd planned to ask you this anyway, and
it sounds awfully self-serving, but it *could* work. Maybe."

"So, tell me," Isabella said impatiently.

"I have an audition Saturday night. Well, it's not exactly
an audition but it could turn into one if I play my cards right."

"Will you just get on with it?" Isabella said. "The suspense
is killing me."

Sadie grinned. "I have to work this Saturday. It's a pretty big
deal. A group of rich out-of-towners who only come through
once a year. Well this weekend is it and they've rented out the
entire club for the night. All of the dancers are expected to be
there, no excuses. Only I have this party I was invited to. Howard
Griffin is going to be there and Leslie is going to introduce me."

"Who is Howard? And who is Leslie?" Isabella asked.

"Howard is producing a new Broadway musical. And, he's
opening auditions next week. They're by invitation only.
People would kill to get an invite from him. Including me.
Leslie has an invite but then she's all over Broadway right now.
Everyone wants her. I met her a couple of weeks ago, and we
became friendly. She's doing me such a huge favor by basically recommending me to Howard. I can't miss that party."

"Okay, so what does that have to do with me?"

Sadie gave her an imploring look. "If I don't show up for
work, I'll lose my job, and until I land enough steady roles—
big roles—I can't afford to lose the kind of money I make at
the club. So I thought you could fill in for me just for a few
hours Saturday night."

Isabella burst into laughter. "You want me to pose as you in a strip club? Sadie, we look nothing alike. I'm a terrible dancer. I'd get you fired in two seconds."

Sadie shook her head vigorously. "First of all, I wear a blond wig. We're of similar height and with the right makeup, no one would be able to tell the difference if you wear the same clothes. No one looks at your face in that place anyway," she added dryly.

"And how does this have anything to do with Theron? He'd have heart failure if he knew I even went into a strip club, much less worked there for a night."

Sadie's eyes twinkled in amusement. "Just think about it. If he knew where you were, he'd blow a gasket, and he'd no doubt go haul you out by your hair which would of course force him to see you half naked."

"How does this not get you fired?" Isabella asked pointedly.

A frown creased Sadie's forehead. "Damn," she muttered. "I hadn't thought of that."

Isabella instantly took pity on her friend. "How about I cover for you without Theron knowing, and I'll figure out another way to get his attention."

"Are you sure?" Sadie asked anxiously.

"I'll give his security team the slip. Apparently he's hired a team to follow me around New York. If you ask me, he's taking this guardian thing a bit far."

Sadie's mouth gaped open. "You have a security team?"

"Yeah, I know, ridiculous isn't it? I'm to report to his office bright and early in the morning to meet them, and then, according to Theron, I'm to go nowhere without them."

A mischievous smile curved Isabella's lips.

"Why do I get the impression you'll see this security as a challenge?" Sadie asked.

Isabella's grin broadened. "It'll make Theron crazy. See, I can give them the slip to cover for you at the club. Word will get back to Theron. He'll never know where I went, but it'll give him another chance to lecture me. I'll think of some way to get his attention. If the lecture gets too bad, I'll just kiss him again."

"You know, I hope he's worth all this trouble you're going to," Sadie said. "My first thought is that no man is worth all this effort."

"He's worth it," Isabella said softly.

Isabella climbed out of the taxi in front of Theron's office building and walked briskly toward the entrance. She took the elevator up to his floor, and when she entered his suite of offices, she saw a pile of luggage in the hallway.

She walked into Madeline's office to ask what was going on, but saw that the area was full of people. She approached Madeline's desk and leaned over to whisper.

"What's going on?"

Madeline cleared her throat. "Alannis and her mother arrived early. That is your security team," she said, pointing in the direction of three intimidating-looking men. "And the others are this morning's appointments which are waiting because Alannis and company are in his office."

Frowning, Isabella straightened and glanced toward Theron's closed door. Without another word, she headed for his office, ignoring Madeline's calls.

Part of her wanted to run as fast and as far away as she could, but another part of her wanted to see for herself the woman that Theron wanted to marry.

She threw open the door and walked in. Theron who was standing in front of his desk looked up and frowned when he saw her. Not good. An older woman also turned, and her frown was much larger. The last, who had to be Alannis, picked up her head and stared curiously at Isabella.

Of course she wouldn't be homely, because that would be

asking far too much. Alannis and her mother both were extremely beautiful in a classy, elegant way. While her mother wore her hair upswept in a neat chignon, Alannis's hair fell to her shoulders in a dark wave. Her brown eyes were warm and friendly, and she smiled tentatively in Isabella's direction.

"Bella," Theron said gruffly. "Did Madeline not tell you I was occupied?"

The reproach was clear in his voice, but Isabella ignored it. She was too busy trying to find fault with Alannis. Unfortunately for her, unless Alannis's voice was grating, the woman was darn near perfect. She and Theron even looked fabulous together.

"She might have mentioned that you were busy," Isabella murmured.

"Who is this?" Alannis's mother asked imperiously.

Theron turned and smiled reassuringly. "This is the girl I told you about, Sophia." Then he looked back at Isabella. "Isabella, I'd like you to meet Alannis Gianopolous and her mother, Sophia. Ladies, this is Isabella Caplan, my ward."

Sophia immediately lost her guarded look and smiled warmly at Isabella. To Isabella's further surprise, the older woman approached her, holding her hands out.

"It's a pleasure to meet you, Isabella. Theron has told us so much about you. I think it's wonderful that he's taking the time to introduce you to potential husbands."

Sophia kissed her on either cheek while Isabella murmured her stunned thanks.

"I'm very happy to meet you, Isabella," Alannis offered with a shy smile.

"Likewise," Isabella said weakly. Her gaze found Theron's again. She looked for any sign that he was miserable, but his expression was unreadable.

"Was there something you needed?" Theron prompted.

She made a show of checking her watch. "You told me to be here this morning. Well, here I am."

He frowned for a moment and then remembrance sparked in his eyes. "Ah, yes, of course. You'll have to forgive me." He flashed a smile in Alannis's direction. "In the excitement of Alannis's arrival, I completely forgot about your security team. They're waiting out front. I've briefed them on my expectations. Madeline can go over the rest with you."

He walked over to his intercom and proceeded to tell Madeline that he was sending Isabella out to meet her security force.

And just like that, she was dismissed.

Sophia hugged her warmly while Alannis gave her a friendly smile. A moment later, Isabella found herself all but shoved from the office.

Numbly she made her way back to Madeline's desk. Madeline gave her a quick look of sympathy before getting up and circling her desk.

"Come with me," she directed as she all but dragged Isabella after her.

Isabella allowed herself to be led into the same conference room as the day before. Madeline shut the doors behind them and then turned on Isabella.

"I've changed my mind. I've decided to help you."

Isabella looked at her in surprise. "What do you mean?"

Madeline sighed. "Alannis is a lovely girl."

"Now you're making her sound like a poodle," Isabella pointed out, remembering that Sadie had told her the same.

"She's truly lovely, but she's all wrong for Theron. I knew it the moment I met her and her forceful mama. Alannis is a mouse while Theron is more of a lion."

"Maybe he wants a mouse," Isabella murmured.

"Have you given up then?" Madeline asked as she tapped her foot impatiently.

Isabella gave her an unhappy frown.

Madeline shook her head in exasperation. "This marriage

would be a disaster. You know it and I know it. Theron has to know it somewhere behind that thick skull of his."

"I thought you had a strict policy against interfering in your employer's personal life?" Isabella said.

Madeline snorted. "I'm not going to interfere. You are."

Isabella raised her eyebrows.

"He plans to propose this Friday night after the opera. He has the tickets, the ring, the entire evening planned. I've given you the information. What you do with it is up to you," she said with a shrug.

"So soon?" Isabella whispered.

"Yep, which means you have to move fast," Madeline said cheerfully.

Isabella slowly nodded. Her mind was already racing a mile a minute.

"While you're pondering, let me introduce you to your security team," Madeline said as she herded Isabella back toward the office where the men waited. "They have strict instructions to accompany you wherever you go." She turned to Isabella and grinned. "Should make things interesting for you."

Isabella only half heard the introductions. She had to crane her neck to look up to the three really large men. They certainly fit the part of security, though she couldn't imagine that subtlety was their strong point. But then subtlety wasn't one of Theron's strong points, either.

As Madeline introduced the last man, Theron's door opened and he and Alannis and her mother came out. Alannis's arm was linked with Theron's, and his head was bent low as he listened to something she said.

Isabella stared unhappily at them until Madeline elbowed her in the ribs.

"You're being far too obvious, my girl," Madeline whispered. "Smile. You don't want mama bear to be suspicious. I get the impression she can be a barracuda when it comes to her daughter."

Isabella forced a smile to her lips just as the three approached.

"I trust you found your security team to your liking?" Theron asked politely.

Isabella nodded and smiled more broadly. Then in an even bigger effort to kill them all with kindness, she turned her attention to Alannis. "How was your trip? Everything went well, I hope."

Alannis's smile lit up her entire face. "It did," she said in only slightly accented English. "I'm very happy to be here." She glanced up at Theron, and Isabella flinched at the open adoration in her expression.

"We look forward to seeing you again Thursday evening," Sophia said.

"Thursday?" Isabella parroted. She glanced at Theron in confusion.

"The cocktail party," Theron said smoothly. "I, of course, extended an invitation to them, as well."

"Of course," Isabella said faintly.

Though his almost fiancée stood at his side, clinging to his arm like seaweed, Theron's gaze was on Isabella, his dark eyes probing. His eyes traveled a path of awareness over her skin.

Did he love Alannis? Did he feel a certain affection for her? She was older than Isabella, but not by much. Maybe a few years? There was youthful innocence in Alannis's eyes that made Isabella feel older and more jaded.

Isabella swallowed the rising knot in her throat and she turned brightly to Sophia. "I too look forward to seeing you again. Perhaps you can tell me all about Greece. I've heard it's such a lovely place to visit. Maybe I can honeymoon there after I marry."

Sophia beamed at her while Theron's face darkened.

"We should go now," Theron said to Sophia. "You and

Alannis have had a long trip. I'll have your luggage delivered to the hotel at once."

He nodded in Isabella's direction as he and the other women walked past. "Let me know if you have any problems, Bella."

She nodded, unable to speak past the lump in her throat that she couldn't quite make go away.

Seven

He couldn't stop thinking about her. Theron rubbed his face in annoyance as he focused on what Alannis and Sophia were talking about. He'd taken them to lunch after they'd settled into their suite, but he was only reminded of having eaten with Isabella at this same table just before kissing her senseless in the elevator.

Sophia was overjoyed with his plan to propose to Alannis after the opera. He'd planned the evening meticulously, buying tickets for Alannis's favorite performance with a plan to end the evening with an after-party at his hotel.

So why wasn't *he* more enthused?

Alannis was obviously excited. Theron was sure Sophia had hinted broadly of his plan to ask Alannis to marry him, although he'd asked Sophia to keep the details secret.

It seemed everyone was thrilled except him.

"Have you found suitable candidates for Isabella?" Sophia asked.

"Pardon?" Theron asked as he shook himself from his thoughts.

"You mentioned that you were trying to find her a husband," Sophia said patiently. "I wondered if you'd found a suitable match yet."

"Oh. Yes, of course. I plan to introduce her to a few carefully screened men at the cocktail party Thursday night."

Sophia nodded approvingly. "She's a beautiful young girl. She seems lonely, though. I doubt she'll have any problem in finding a husband."

Theron frowned. No, she wouldn't have any trouble in that area. Men would line up for a chance to be her husband.

Sophia leaned forward, excitement lighting her eyes. "You know, Theron, I'd love to sponsor Isabella myself. She could return to Greece with me. Myron would be more than happy to introduce her to any number of fine young men from good families."

"That's a wonderful idea, Mama," Alannis said.

"I'll bring it up to her when I speak to her next," Theron said. He wasn't sure why, but the idea of her leaving the country and marrying someone so far away left a very bad taste in his mouth.

Not that her marrying closer made him feel any better.

He listened as Alannis recounted the details of her trip and her excitement over visiting New York for the first time. But his mind simply wasn't on the present. His thoughts were occupied by a vibrant, dark-haired temptress with a smile that would melt a man at twenty feet.

As if he'd conjured her, he glanced up and saw her across the room. She was walking beside the host as he directed her to a table by the window.

Remembering Sophia's assertion that she seemed lonely, he took the opportunity to study her. Sophia was right. Isabella did look lonely. Even a little sad.

She was dressed in jeans and a plain T-shirt. Her hair was drawn into a ponytail, and the smile that he'd just pondered over was absent.

She was seated by herself, and then she smiled up at the waiter as he attended her. But her smile didn't quite reach her eyes.

For the first time he reflected on her circumstances. How difficult it must be for her to be alone in an unfamiliar city. No family, and if she had friends, he hadn't been made aware of them. Guilt crept over him as he remembered his eagerness to rid himself of her.

Now he was glad he'd planned the cocktail party for Thursday night. Maybe instead of making it a bland gathering at his penthouse with polite conversation, he could turn it into a party at the hotel welcoming Isabella to New York. He could still introduce her to the men on Madeline's list, but at least she would have some fun if he livened things up a bit. A girl her age would be bored silly at the kind of gathering he'd first envisioned.

Feeling marginally better, he refocused his attention on Alannis and reminded himself that in a few days' time, he'd be asking her to be his wife. She'd be his lover and the mother of his children. She was the woman he'd spend the rest of his life with.

Cold panic swept over him until sweat beaded his forehead. Instead of infusing comfort and contentment, the idea of making such a commitment filled him with dread.

Why was he reacting so badly now when a week ago he looked forward to a life with Alannis? It didn't make any sense.

Again his gaze wandered to where Isabella sat. She stared out the window, a pensive expression on her face. Her fingers twined in a strand of her hair as she twirled it absently. She sipped at a glass of water, her gaze never breaking.

Theron reached into his pocket and pulled out his Black-

Berry. He thumbed a quick message to Madeline asking her when his shopping trip was scheduled with Isabella. After all, he didn't want to commit to an appointment with Alannis at the same time.

After a moment, Madeline returned his message. He frowned when he read it and then glanced up at Isabella again. She was going alone? She didn't want him to go with her?

Still frowning, he keyed in his response to Madeline.

Find out when she's going. Clear my schedule.

As soon as Isabella left her suite, a man fell into step beside her. She still hadn't gotten used to this whole security team thing, and it made her nervous to have men dogging her heels everywhere she went.

He got onto the elevator with her and stood in the back as they rode down. When they got to the lobby, they were joined by the other members. Trying to pay them no mind, she headed out the front where the taxis waited.

Before she got two steps toward the first in line, one of the men stepped in front of her, barring her path. She drew up short and sighed in exasperation.

"Look…what is your name?" They had been introduced to her yesterday, but she'd been reeling from the news of Theron's upcoming engagement. "Or should I just call you Huey, Louie and Dewey?"

The man in front of her flashed white teeth as he grinned. So they did have another expression besides the stone statue look.

"You can call me Reynolds." He gestured to the two men on either side of her. How had they gotten there anyway? "The one on your left is Davison and the other guy is Maxwell."

"Okay, Reynolds," she said patiently. She addressed him because he seemed to be in charge, and he was the one blocking her way to the taxi. "I need to get into that taxi. I'm going shopping. There isn't any need for you guys to follow me on a girly trip. You could wait here at the restaurant."

He smiled again. "I'm afraid I can't do that, Ms. Caplan. Our orders are to go everywhere you go."

She muttered an expletive under her breath and watched as amusement crossed his face again. "Even to the bathroom?" she asked sweetly.

"If necessary," he said, wiping the smile right off her face.

"Well, hell," she grumbled. And then she pointed out the obvious. "There's no way we'll all fit in that cab." She smiled as she waited for him to agree.

He looked sternly at her. "We have strict instructions that when you go anywhere, you're to take the car that Mr. Anetakis provided for you. This morning, however, you're to wait here for Mr. Anetakis to arrive."

She frowned and then stared at Davison and Maxwell. If she expected confirmation or denial from them, she was sorely disappointed. They simply stood, their gazes constantly moving around and beyond her as though looking for potential danger.

"You must be mistaken," she said to Reynolds. "I'm not meeting Theron today. I'm going shopping for my apartment."

Reynolds checked his watch and then looked up as a sleek, silver Mercedes vehicle pulled up and stopped just a few feet from where they stood.

To her never-ending surprise, Theron stepped from the car and strode in her direction. As he drew abreast of her, he pulled his sunglasses off and slipped them into the pocket of his polo shirt.

He reached for her hand, his fingers curling firmly around hers. Then he turned to Reynolds. "Is there a problem?" he asked with a frown.

Reynolds gave a quick shake of his head. "Ms. Caplan was about to leave in a cab. I was in the process of explaining to her why she couldn't."

Theron nodded his approval and then turned back to look

at Isabella. "It's important that you heed my instructions, *pethi mou*. The arrangements I have made are for your well-being and safety."

"Of course," she murmured. "I won't keep you. I'm sure you're here to see Alannis." She glanced over at Reynolds. "Will you call for the car since I'm not allowed in a taxi?"

Theron raised one eyebrow. "A few days ago, you wanted me to accompany you. Have you changed your mind?"

Confusion crowded her mind, and she scrunched up her brow as she stared up at him. "I assumed that since you have guests here, that you wouldn't have time to go with me."

"Ah, but you're my guest, too," he said as he pulled her hand. He guided her toward the still waiting Mercedes and gestured for her to get into the back. Then he spoke to Reynolds over the door. "You're excused until we return. My team will handle her security."

Isabella scooted over and settled into the comfortable leather seat. Theron ducked in and sat down next to her. As the driver pulled away, Isabella shook her head and smiled ruefully.

"When was the last time you didn't get your way about something?"

He gave her a puzzled look.

"And why all the security?" she asked in exasperation. "It seems a little pretentious."

His face immediately darkened. "Before they were married, Chrysander's wife was abducted and held for ransom. She was pregnant at the time. Her kidnappers have never been apprehended. I take no chances with the safety of those under my care."

"How are Chrysander and his wife?" she asked softly.

"They are well. Marley prefers the island so they stay there. Chrysander occasionally leaves for business purposes but he doesn't leave Marley or their son very often."

"I can't imagine Chrysander so in love," she said with a laugh. "He seems so intimidating."

"You obviously don't feel the same around me," Theron said dryly.

She let her gaze wander slowly up his body until she stared into his eyes. "The way I feel about you in no way compares to how I feel around Chrysander."

There was a surge in his expression, an awareness that he fought. Such conflicting emotions shooting across his face. Before he could respond to her enigmatic statement, she turned to look out the window.

"So what made you come along this morning?" she asked cheerfully.

Though she was no longer facing him, she could feel his every move. She could feel him breathe so tuned into his body was she.

"I would have thought you'd be far too busy with work and entertaining your…guests."

"I'm not too busy to renege on a promise I made," he said. "I told you I'd go shopping with you and here I am."

She turned then and smiled. "I'm glad. Thank you."

They spent the morning going down the list of items she wanted for her apartment. Theron seemed appreciative of the fact that she didn't take forever making her selections. But the fact was, she didn't really labor over furniture styles because if things went the way she wanted, then she wouldn't be staying in the apartment long term. And if they didn't go her way, she wasn't going to stick around New York City only to watch Theron with another woman.

By two in the afternoon, she was tired and hungry and told Theron so. He suggested they eat at the hotel again. She was thrilled that he didn't seem intent on rushing back to Alannis as soon as the shopping was done.

When they got back to the hotel, they were met by

Reynolds who told Theron he and the others would stand by in the restaurant while they ate. Already, she was growing used to the small entourage of people who followed Theron wherever he went.

If he was this protective over someone he deemed "under his care," then how much more so would he be when it came to someone he loved?

She smiled dreamily as they were escorted to Theron's table. She could handle his overprotective tendencies if it meant he loved her.

"You look well pleased with yourself, *pethi mou*."

Theron's voice broke through her thoughts.

"Are you happy with your purchases?"

She nodded and smiled. "Thank you for going with me."

"It was my pleasure. You shouldn't be alone in such an unfamiliar place."

After placing their orders, Theron sat back in his seat, glass of wine in hand and stared over the table at her.

"So tell me, Bella. Why New York? Did you not have friends in California you preferred to stay close to? And have you given more thought to what you will do now that you've graduated from university?"

She smiled patiently. "My indecision must drive someone such as yourself insane, but I really do have a well-thought-out plan for my future."

"Such as myself?" he asked. "Dare I ask what that's supposed to mean?"

"Just that I imagine your life is planned out to the nth degree and that you have no patience for people who aren't as organized as you. Am I right?" she asked mischievously.

He struggled with a scowl before finally relaxing into a smile. "There's nothing wrong with having one's path planned out in advance."

"No, there isn't," she agreed. "I have mine quite mapped

out, however, things don't always go according to plan. The real test is how you manage when your plans fall apart."

"Very wise words coming from someone so young."

She wrinkled her nose and rolled her eyes. "Do you keep reminding yourself of my age so that you aren't tempted to do something outrageous like kiss me again?"

He blinked at her, his mouth falling open. Then he snapped it closed and his jaw tightened. "I thought we agreed to forget that ever happened."

"I agreed to do no such thing," she said lightly. "You can do as you like, however."

He was saved from making his response when the waiter returned bearing their food. Isabella watched Theron all through the meal. His agitation was evident in his short, jerky motions as he dug into his food and ate. Several times he looked up and their gazes connected. There was such fire in his eyes. He wasn't immune to her. Not by a long shot. If she had to guess, he was very affected.

She'd already shoved her plate aside when she heard Theron's name called from a few tables away. She glanced over to see a handsome man approach their table. He was well dressed, he screamed wealth and refinement, and he looked at her with undisguised interest even though it was Theron's name he spoke.

Theron looked less than pleased by the interruption, but it didn't seem to bother the man who now stood at their table.

"Theron, it's good to see you. I was happy to receive your invitation for Thursday night."

He glanced over at Isabella as he spoke and she stared back, wondering if this was one of the men on Theron's infamous potential husband list. She cocked her eyebrow in question but Theron ignored her.

"Are you coming?" Isabella spoke up, offering the man a bright smile. "I have it on good authority that Theron is using Thursday's little soiree to find me a husband."

She grinned at the man's look of surprise. Then he laughed while Theron scowled even harder.

"You must be Isabella Caplan. I'm Marcus Atwater, and yes, I'll be attending. Now that I know my attendance puts me in the running, I wouldn't miss it for the world."

Isabella smiled and extended her hand. "Please, call me Bella."

Marcus took her hand but instead of shaking it, he raised it to his lips and kissed it.

"All right, Bella. A beautiful name for an equally beautiful woman."

"Is there something you wanted, Marcus?" Theron asked pointedly.

His glare could melt steel, but Marcus didn't seem to be too bothered—or intimidated.

Isabella sat back. Maybe Theron seeing another man openly flirt with her would bring out those protective instincts. Maybe, just maybe if he suddenly had a little competition…

"Nothing at all," Marcus said congenially. "I saw you with a beautiful woman, and I merely wanted to make her acquaintance and see for myself if this was the mysterious Isabella Caplan, the same woman you were throwing the party for. I'm glad now that I came over." He glanced back at Isabella again. "Save me a dance Thursday night?"

She smiled and nodded. "Of course."

She watched him walk away before turning back to Theron. "So tell me, how did he rate among the other men you considered for my husband?"

Theron gave her a disgruntled look. "He's toward the top," he mumbled.

"Oh good, then you won't mind if we spend time together at your cocktail party."

"No," he said through gritted teeth. "He would be a good

choice. He's successful, doesn't have any debt, he's never been married before, and he's healthy."

"Good God, tell me you didn't hack into his medical records," she said in disbelief.

"Of course I did. I wouldn't suggest you marry a man who was in ill health or had defects that could be passed on to your children."

He seemed affronted that she'd ask such a question.

She stifled her laughter and tried to look serious and appreciative. "So can I assume that any man at your party has been carefully screened and has your stamp of approval then?"

He nodded slowly but he didn't look happy about the fact.

"Well then, this should be fun," she said brightly. "A room full of wealthy, good-looking men to choose from." She leaned forward and pretended to whisper conspiratorially. "Did you also find out if they were good in bed?"

Theron choked on his drink. He set it down and growled in a low voice, "Of course I didn't question their sexual prowess."

"Pity. I suppose I'll have to find out myself before settling on one man in particular."

"You'll do no such thing," Theron snarled.

Her eyes widened innocently as she viewed his obvious irritation. He looked near to bursting a blood vessel.

His phone rang, and he looked relieved as he fumbled for it. After a few clipped sentences, he rang off and looked over at her.

"You'll have to excuse me, but I have to go. I have an important meeting I can't miss."

She shrugged nonchalantly. "Don't mind me. I was going up to my suite anyway."

Theron motioned for Reynolds and then rose from his chair.

"Your security detail will see you up to your suite. And Bella, don't try to go anywhere without them."

Eight

Theron's admonishment still rang in Isabella's ears the next morning as she plotted her path past her security team. It wasn't that she minded them going shopping with her. They might even be able to offer a male perspective on which dress looked best on her. She wanted to look good for the cocktail party, and not because of the men Theron had invited with her in mind.

As soon as she stepped out of her room, Reynolds fell into step behind her.

"Good morning," she offered sweetly.

"Good morning," he offered in return. "Where would you like to go this morning?" He pulled out his cell phone to call for the car.

"I want to do a little sightseeing," she said. "I don't know my way around the city very well, so I'll have to rely on you."

"What interests you?" he asked politely.

She pretended to think. "Museums, art galleries, oh, and I'd like to see the Statue of Liberty."

He nodded even as he relayed her wishes to the driver.

The elevator opened into the lobby where they were joined by Davison and Maxwell. She halted in front of them, took one look and shook her head.

"Is there a problem?" Reynolds asked.

"Look, if you guys are going to shadow me, I'd prefer you didn't look like something out of a mafia movie. Not to mention, I'd rather not broadcast the fact that I'm going around with three bodyguards. That will only make me more conspicuous."

"What do you suggest then?" Maxwell muttered. He didn't look entirely pleased with her assessment.

"Well, you could lose the shades. They make you look like secret service wannabes."

Maxwell and Davison both removed the sunglasses, and Davison glared at her. She grinned in return.

"Now get rid of the tie and the jacket."

All three men shook their heads. "The jackets stay." Davison spoke up for the first time. To get his point across, he pulled the lapel, opening the jacket enough that she could see the pistol secured by a shoulder holster.

Her mouth fell open. She wasn't a screaming ninny about guns. She well understood the need for them. She just hadn't realized that Theron was that concerned over her safety. For a moment she wavered. Maybe breaking away wasn't such a great idea. But then in her mind, having three hulking men made her much more noticeable than if she zipped to the department store and back for her dress.

"Okay, definitely leave the jackets," she muttered.

They walked outside where the car had pulled around. Davison got into the front while Maxwell walked around to the opposite passenger door and climbed in. Reynolds opened the passenger door closest to her and waited for her to get in.

She faked exasperation and slapped her forehead with her open palm. "Wait right here. I forgot my purse," she said.

"I'll get it for you. You get in," Reynolds said.

But she was already striding toward the hotel entrance. She turned back holding up a finger. "I won't be a minute."

Reynolds started after her, but she quickly rounded the corner and ducked into the men's bathroom. He'd most definitely search the women's room when he figured out she'd disappeared, but hopefully he wouldn't think to look in the men's.

She cracked the door just enough that she could look out. Reynolds hurried by and then he barked into a small receiver that hung from his shirt.

Seconds later, Maxwell and Davison ran by the bathroom, their faces grim. She slipped out with no hesitation and ran for the hotel entrance, hoping they didn't look back in the time it took her to get to a taxi.

She slid into the cab at the front of the line and offered the driver double his fee if he got the hell out fast. Only too happy to comply, he peeled out of the entryway and rocketed in front of two other cars. Horns sounded and angry shouts filled the air but the driver shook his fist and then grinned.

"Where you going, miss?"

She glanced up to see him staring at her in the rearview mirror.

"I'm not completely sure," she admitted. "I need a dress. A really gorgeous dress that'll make a man drool at a hundred yards."

"I know just the place," he said, nodding his head.

Not completely willing to forego any precautionary measures, she asked if he'd wait while she shopped, meter running of course.

He dropped her off in front of the upscale department store then gave her his cell number.

"Give me a ring when you're checking out, and I'll pull up and pick you up here," he said.

"Thank you," she said as she climbed out.

Making sure to keep in a clump of people, she entered the store. She wasn't a complete idiot when it came to safety. She avoided corners, anything off the beaten path and stayed in plain sight of the security cameras. When it was time for her to try on her dresses, she had the extremely helpful saleslady accompany her to the dressing room. After all she needed an opinion.

After trying on six dresses, she found the one. It slipped over her body, hugging every curve like a second skin. The genius of the dress was in its simplicity. There weren't any ruffles or frills, nothing to take away from the shape of her body. It was sheer with spaghetti straps, and it fell two inches above her knee. With a pair of killer heels, she'd have the men eating out of her hand.

She frowned as she realized it didn't really matter what the other men did. Theron was the only one who mattered, and it was anyone's guess how he would react.

She stepped out of the dressing room to show the saleslady. Her entire face lit up.

"It's perfect, Ms. Caplan. Just perfect. With the right shoes, you'll be a knockout."

Isabella smiled. "Would you happen to have a pair of black shoes in a three-inch heel that would go well with this dress?"

The saleslady smiled. "I'll be right back."

A few minutes later, Isabella twirled and glanced down her legs at the shoes. The heels were basically toothpicks, but they did look gorgeous on her.

Not content to sell her an outrageously expensive dress—the shoes were nearly as expensive—the saleslady also insisted she accessorize with just the right jewelry—and handbag of course.

Two hours after she'd ditched her security team, Isabella settled into her cab and headed back to the hotel. When they pulled up, she collected her bags and leaned up to pay the driver.

"Thank you so much. I truly appreciate you waiting for me."

"It was no problem, miss. Good luck at your party tonight. I'm sure you'll knock their socks off."

She smiled and got out then waved as he drove away. With a smile, she entered the hotel and headed for the elevator. The absence of her security team gave her pause, and then guilt crept in. She'd been so caught up in her shopping that she hadn't even considered phoning Reynolds to assure him that she was okay, and she hadn't ever provided him or Theron *her* cell number, so it wasn't as if they could have called her.

With a sigh, she pulled out her cell as she inserted the key to her hotel room. She entered, punching Reynold's number. Then she looked up and saw four very angry men staring at her from inside her room.

Theron rose from where he was sitting on the couch, his eyes sparking. He motioned to the other three men. "Leave us," he said shortly.

Isabella let the bags slide from her fingertips as the three men filed by. Reynolds shot her a disapproving look, and she smiled tentatively.

When they were gone, she glanced over at Theron who had closed the distance between them. He glowered menacingly, his face a veritable storm cloud.

"You didn't fire them, did you?" she asked uneasily.

"Rest assured I know exactly where the blame lies," he gritted out.

She bent down to collect her bags and walked around him toward the couch.

"Taking off from your security team was a foolish thing to do, Bella. Did I not impress upon you the need for them? What were you thinking?"

She turned and regarded him thoughtfully. "I had my reasons," she said simply.

He threw up his hands in exasperation. "What reasons?" he demanded.

She smiled. "Nothing you would approve of. I didn't stay long, and I took precautions. The very nice cabdriver looked out for me quite well, and the saleslady never left my side. Well, except when she went to get me shoes."

Theron's face went gray. "Cabdriver? You entrusted your well-being to a cabdriver?"

"Relax," she said with a grin. "He was a perfect gentleman. He drove me to the department store and waited for me until I was through."

Theron swallowed and looked as though he was fighting to keep his temper in check. Hmm. Theron losing his cool. That might be worth the price of admission.

"Why did you leave without your security team? What was so important that you would risk yourself in this manner?"

She held up her shopping bag. "I needed a dress for the party tonight."

He drew in a deep breath, closed his eyes and then reopened them. He strode over to where she stood and gripped her shoulders. "A dress? You gave me the fright of my life for a dress?"

He shook her as he spoke and she gripped his waist to keep her balance.

"It wasn't just any dress," she murmured as she tried to keep the smile from her face. She probably shouldn't bait him as she was, but making him lose his composure had suddenly become her mission. "I could hardly meet my future husband in anything but a truly spectacular dress."

"You are the most infuriating, frustrating woman I've ever had the misfortune to meet," he growled.

And then he crushed her to him, slanting his lips over hers in a forceful kiss that took her breath away. She moaned as his hands gripped her arms then slid over her back like bands of steel.

He tasted her hungrily, like a man starving, as though he couldn't get enough. Tingling awareness snaked up her spine.

Her breasts throbbed, and her nipples became taut points, pushing at his chest.

The sounds of their kiss, hot and breathless filled the room. One of his hands slipped to the waist of her jeans, and he yanked at her shirt until it came free. Then he slid his fingers over the bare skin of her lower back, right where her tattoo rested. He traced patterns over the small of her back as though he was aware of what was there.

Eager to taste him, she traced his lip with her tongue until he reached out to duel delicately with his own. Warm. So masculine, he tasted of strength, of heady power.

She lost herself in his arms, melted against his mouth. Her pulse sped up and bounced erratically. How she craved him.

His hand crept higher until it collided with her bra strap. He fumbled over the clasp and then he froze.

With a muffled curse, he broke away, his breaths coming hard and ragged. His eyes blazed like an out-of-control fire, and then he dropped his hands from her body like she'd burned him.

He swore again, a mixture of Greek and English and then ran a hand through his hair.

"*Theos mou!* We can't…not again. This mustn't happen again. I'm sorry, Bella."

He held up his hands and then backed away. He paused at the door, his motions haphazard, like he was drunk. Then he turned to stare at her, his eyes still burning with unresolved desire.

"Your security team goes *everywhere* with you. Are we understood? From now on, they even go to the bathroom with you."

She nodded, unable to do anything more. She was shaking too badly. As he left her hotel room, she gripped her arms and rubbed up and down to make the chill bumps go away.

"You can deny it all you want," she whispered to the empty room. "You want me every bit as much as I want you."

Nine

Theron rubbed the back of his neck in an effort to relieve the enormous tension that gripped him. Isabella still hadn't arrived, and he felt equal parts relief and disappointment.

He glanced around the ballroom of the Imperial Park Hotel, taking in the guests milling around, talking and laughing as a jazz band played softly from an elevated platform.

Alannis stood at his side, her hand resting on his arm. Sophia stood on Alannis's other side, her pride in her daughter evident.

He ducked his head to hear what Alannis was trying to tell him and nodded appropriately though his concentration was shot. When he stood to his full height again, his gaze went to the doorway, and his breath caught in his throat.

She was here.

Isabella stood as she gazed nervously over the room. Theron swallowed when he took in her attire. The term *little black dress* could have been coined for this occasion.

The material molded to her every curve and settled a few

inches above her knees. She wore her hair up, drawing attention to the shape of her neck. Stray tendrils escaped the elegant knot and whispered against her skin.

His fingers itched to let her hair down and watch it fall to her shoulders. He wanted to run his hands through the silken mass, feel it twine around his knuckles.

"Oh, look, there's Isabella," Sophia exclaimed.

As if he wouldn't be aware the moment she stepped into the room.

"Excuse me," he murmured to Alannis.

She let him go with a smile, and he made his way to where Isabella stood.

There wasn't an easy way to address the awareness between them, so he chose to ignore it—and the fact that he'd kissed her just hours before.

"Bella," he greeted as he stopped in front of her.

She gazed up at him with wide green eyes, her mouth curving into a smile of welcome.

"Sorry I'm late," she said in a breathy voice. "I don't suppose you saved me a dance?"

He nearly groaned. The thought of having her pressed that close to his body was torture.

"The dancing hasn't begun yet," he said as he turned to look at the band. "Perhaps we can kick it off together, and then I'll introduce you around."

He motioned to the pianist who nodded in return. A slow, sultry melody started, and Theron offered his hand to Isabella. Her fingers trembled slightly in his grip, and he squeezed to reassure her.

When they reached the middle of the area that was the designated dance floor, he turned, and she went willingly into his arms. The moment she melted against him, he went completely rigid.

Her scent surrounded him as the warmth from her touch

invaded his body. There wasn't a single inch that wasn't aware of her feminine form. He glanced down as they made a slow turn and swallowed hard. She wasn't wearing a bra and the lush mounds were pressed tightly against his chest, thrusting upward, straining against the neckline of her dress.

It was all he could do not to haul her out of the room so that no one else could see her.

He blew out his breath as inconspicuously as possible and reminded himself that she wasn't his, and he had no right to be possessive.

It still didn't help the rise of irritation when he saw how many men were staring avidly at Isabella. No, she wouldn't have any shortage of suitors after tonight. He should have been relieved, but he was anything but.

It was all he could do to keep the scowl from his face.

"The party is lovely," Isabella said with a smile as she gazed over his shoulder. "Thank you for putting it on."

"You're quite welcome, *pethi mou*. I want you to enjoy yourself."

"How are your guests settling in?" she asked innocently.

His eyes narrowed. Did she know of his plans for Alannis? It wasn't as if she wouldn't know in a short time, but for some reason he was reluctant to tell her of his impending engagement. Or maybe he was a first-class slimeball who'd kissed another woman within days of asking another woman to marry him.

"They're settling in quite well," he muttered as he swung her around so that she wasn't facing Alannis and her mother.

Guilt filled him. What kind of a man took advantage of a young woman when he had an agreement with another? Even Piers, who was never without a woman, would frown on seducing his ward when he had a soon-to-be fiancée waiting in the wings.

Chrysander wouldn't hesitate to kick his ass all the way back to Greece for pulling this kind of stunt with Isabella.

"So which ones are my potential husbands?" she asked as she craned to see around him.

She wore a mischievous smile that only made her sparkle all the brighter.

"I'll introduce you as soon as our dance is over," he said.

For this moment, she was his, in his arms, and he wasn't in any hurry to relinquish her to her waiting suitors. They'd gathered around the perimeter of the dance area like a bunch of vultures.

For the first time, he regretted his hasty decision to assist Isabella in her search for a husband. She was too young to think of marriage. She should be out having fun, not thinking of making a lifelong commitment.

And yet he was poised to do just that. Panic scuttled up his spine. Then he firmly tamped it down. Before Isabella came bursting into his life, he was more than content over the idea of marrying Alannis and settling down to have children. Isabella was a temporary distraction, nothing more. As soon as things were settled between him and Alannis, and he had Isabella on her path to security and stability, he was confident that he'd embrace his future without hesitation.

When the song died, Theron dropped his hands and then enfolded Isabella's in his. "Come, *pethi mou*. Your party awaits."

Isabella donned her best smile and allowed Theron to lead her through the assembled guests to where the band was set up. Theron held a hand out, and the music stopped. Then he turned to face the guests.

"I appreciate you coming for the occasion to welcome Isabella Caplan to our city," Theron said in a congenial tone.

A waiter approached and handed Isabella a glass of champagne then turned to offer Theron one. He held it at waist level as he continued to address the crowd.

"We're here to enjoy an evening of entertainment, dancing

and conversation. You're welcome to stay as long as you want, or until the booze runs out," he added with a smile.

Laughter rang out.

He turned to Isabella and held out his glass. "A toast to Isabella."

"To Isabella," the guests echoed.

Theron touched his glass to hers and their gazes locked. For a long moment they simply stared. And then Theron broke away and took a long swallow.

Though she had no desire to wade through the eligible men assembled at Theron's request—it reminded her of choosing steaks at a butcher shop—she knew she'd have to play the part, particularly if she had any hope of making Theron jealous. It was a long shot, because he'd have to feel more for her than simple lust, but at the moment, it was her only hope.

The toast seemed to have signaled a return to normal activities. The band struck up a song, and people swirled onto the dance floor.

"Come with me, Bella. It's time to introduce you around."

"You mean it's time for me to meet the men you've assembled for me," she said dryly.

He glanced questioningly at her. "Would you prefer not to meet them? There's nothing to say you have to."

He sounded almost hopeful, a little too eager, which was strange considering the time he had to have spent putting together his group of bachelors. The background checks alone would have been an enormous undertaking. And he wouldn't have left a single stone unturned.

She nearly grinned at the thought.

"No, let's do it. My future awaits and all that," she said lightly.

She curled her hand around his arm and allowed him to lead her into the crowd. Unsure of what she could expect, and maybe she'd thought there would be a stampede, she was pleasantly surprised by how civilized the whole process was.

Theron took her around from group to group, introducing her to business acquaintances and friends. It was easy to immerse herself in the fantasy that she and Theron were together, and he was acting as her escort and not a man bent on marrying her off. It was also easy to forget that just a few feet away, Alannis and her mother stood, observing the goings-on.

Still, Isabella wasn't ready to let reality intrude, and she clung to Theron's arm all the while offering a smile or a laugh as she engaged in conversation. After awhile she found herself relaxing and genuinely enjoying the festive gathering.

She glanced up as an attractive man made his way in her direction, a determined look on his face. She recognized him as Marcus Atwater, the man who'd introduced himself in the restaurant the day before.

"Isabella, my apologies for my late arrival," he said as he approached. He flashed her a charming smile that she couldn't help but respond to. "I was unexpectedly tied up with a client."

He took her hand, and as he'd done in the restaurant, he lifted it to his lips. Then he cast a questioning look in Theron's direction—Theron who stood there looking as though a black cloud had parked itself right over his head.

"I'd like to borrow Isabella. I promise to keep her safe, and you can return to your own date, who, if you don't mind me saying, looks very much like she'd like to dance."

Theron scowled, and Isabella glanced over to see Alannis eyeing the dancing couples with what could only be construed as a wistful glance. Isabella didn't want to feel pity. She wanted to dislike Alannis. If she was a complete ogre it would be so much simpler, but the fact was that both mother and daughter had been extremely nice to her.

"Are you borrowing me for a dance or for some other purpose?" she asked teasingly as she slipped her hand into Marcus's.

"How about we dance first and we can discuss other purposes later," he said with a teasing glint in his eye.

Theron's expression was glacial. She released his arm to go with Marcus, but he caught her free hand, pulling her between the two men.

She stared at him for a moment, waiting for him to speak, but he seemed to be at a loss for words, or maybe he hadn't intended to pull her back.

"Was there something you wanted?" she asked.

He released her hand and shook his head even as he glanced in Alannis's direction. "No. Have fun, *pethi mou*. This is your night."

With one last look in his direction, she turned and let Marcus lead her back to the dance floor. He spun her in an expert move, and she landed against his chest. Laughing blue eyes shone down at her, and she smiled in return.

"Are you still husband hunting or have I arrived too late for consideration?" he asked with mock seriousness.

"Aren't men supposed to run in the other direction when marriage is mentioned?"

"Not if he doesn't mind being caught by the woman in question."

"You're a total flirt," she said with a laugh. "I can't possibly take such a charming man seriously."

He grinned but didn't refute her claim. They danced among the crowd of couples, and every chance she got, she snuck a peek Theron's way.

He and Alannis were dancing on the far side. She stared laughing up into his eyes, and it didn't take a genius to see how starstruck she was by Theron. Isabella knew that feeling well.

"So," Marcus said casually as he spun her around. "Are you going to let him get away?"

She yanked her gaze guiltily away from Theron to meet

Marcus's amused smile. When she realized she hadn't a hope of playing ignorant, she sighed.

"Am I that obvious?" she asked in resignation.

"Only to another man who's scouting the territory for competition."

Her shoulders slumped downward. "I knew I shouldn't have agreed to this farce. This was Theron's idea in case you haven't guessed. He's decided that it's his duty to marry me off with all possible haste."

Marcus touched her chin and gently tugged upward until she looked him in the eye. "Have you told him how you feel?"

She glanced back over at Theron then shook her head. "It's complicated."

"Tell you what. Why don't we head to that corner over there. I'll get us a drink and you can tell me all about it."

Theron's gaze found Isabella again as he listened politely to Alannis and Sophia and the small group of people who stood in the loosely formed circle to the side of the dance floor. He ground his teeth together as Marcus leaned in close to Isabella, his lips hovering precariously close to her ear as he murmured to her.

She laughed and the seductive sound rose over the clink of glasses and the murmur of conversation. Marcus's fingers drifted over her bare shoulder, lingering there much longer than Theron thought appropriate.

He had to swallow the sound of anger that bubbled up in his throat when Marcus trailed one finger down her cheek and then seductively down the side of her neck and around to the hollow of her throat.

Isabella leaned toward Marcus as if seeking his touch, and then he angled in and pressed his lips very softly to the expanse of skin just below her ear.

"*Theos mou,*" Theron growled. "Enough is enough."

"Theron, is something wrong?" Alannis asked.

She touched his arm and he turned to see concern reflected in her eyes.

"It's nothing," he said shortly.

Alannis glanced at Isabella and then back to him. "She seems to be having a good time."

"Yes." His gaze drifted back, his annoyance growing as Marcus grew bolder in his advances. "Excuse me a moment, will you, Alannis?"

He nodded to Sophia and walked as calmly as he was able over to where Marcus was standing with Isabella. He all but had her trapped in the corner, his body moving in like a predator closing in on a kill.

Just as Theron started to speak up, Marcus lowered his head to nuzzle Isabella's neck. Rage exploded over Theron. He closed the remaining distance and grabbed the other man by the shoulder, tearing him away from Isabella.

"What the…" Marcus began but broke off mid sentence. "Theron, is there a problem?"

"Come here, Isabella," Theron bit out. He held his hand out as Isabella stared at him agape.

"What on earth is wrong?" she asked even as she slid her hand into his.

He pulled until she was against his side then he focused the full force of his glare at Marcus.

"Keep your hands off her," he snarled. "You aren't to touch her. You aren't to so much as think about her. Understand?"

Marcus surprised him by grinning and then backing away, hands up. "Whatever you say." Then he winked at Isabella. "I guess I'll go. Something tells me I've overstayed my welcome."

"Oh, no, Marcus, stay." She glanced back up at Theron with a puzzled expression. "I'm sure Theron has no objections."

"I have plenty of objections. He was mauling you in plain view of a roomful of people." Then he turned again to Marcus, as he pulled Isabella even closer. He dropped his voice low enough not to be overheard. "If I find you near her again, I'll take you apart. Are we clear?"

He ignored Isabella's stunned gasp. Marcus merely smiled and continued to back away, his expression smug.

"I'll see you another time, Bella."

"Goodbye," she said softly.

"Come on," Theron said, half dragging her along with him. "You're not to leave my side for the rest of the night."

To his surprise, she didn't offer any argument. Halfway back to where Alannis and her mother still stood, Isabella stumbled, and he turned back quickly to catch her.

"Slow down," she said. "I can't walk that fast in these shoes."

"Sorry," he said gruffly as he righted her. He held her arms until he was sure she had her footing. "Better?"

She nodded and they started back again.

"Isabella, are you all right?" Sophia asked in concern when they walked up.

Isabella offered a smile. "Yes, Mrs. Gianopolous. I'm fine. Thank you for asking."

"Please, do call me Sophia." Sophia reached out and took Isabella's hand from Theron's. "Can I get you something to drink? Have you had anything to eat since you arrived?" She turned to Alannis. "Will you excuse us for a minute, dear? You stay here with Theron while I take Isabella over to grab a bite to eat."

Theron held up his hand to stop the endless stream of chatter. His head was pounding, and what he really wanted was to go pound on Marcus for touching Isabella, for putting his lips on her.

"Just stay here. I'll have a waiter bring around a tray. I'd prefer that Isabella remain with me for the remainder of the evening," he said brusquely.

The older woman's eyes widened in surprise. Alannis

moved closer to Isabella and touched her arm. "Are you sure you're all right, Isabella?" she asked softly.

Isabella's smile seemed strained when she looked back at Alannis. "I'm absolutely fine. Theron overreacted." She shot him a challenging look. "I'm not sure how he expects me to find a husband when he flips his lid the moment a man pays attention to me."

Theron took a deep breath. "I don't think what he was doing could be classified as paying attention to you. *Theos!* He was making love to you for all to see."

She raised her eyebrows and a slow smile formed on her lips. "Is that what they call kissing these days?" she taunted.

His nostrils flared at the reminder of the kisses they'd shared. He was well and truly caught in a trap of his own making.

"His actions were inappropriate," he gritted out. "You are under my protection. You'll heed my instructions."

She turned cheekily to Sophia and Alannis. "I suppose he'll mark that one off the list of potential husbands now." Then she sighed dramatically and dropped her hands helplessly to her side. "I didn't even get to dance again."

"Theron will dance with you," Alannis urged. "He's a marvelous dancer as I'm sure you determined earlier."

"Yes, do go on," Sophia said. "I'll make sure there is food when you return."

Theron's mouth went dry. He wouldn't survive another dance with her lush body molded to his. One torture session was enough for the night.

But then the alternative was letting her dance with the circling pack of men. Men he'd hand-selected.

Over his dead body.

Without another word, he snared Isabella's hand and dragged her toward the dance floor.

"You're hell on these shoes," she murmured as he pulled her into his arms.

For the first time since Marcus had arrived, Theron relaxed as Isabella's soft body molded so sweetly to his. There was an innate sense of rightness. He loved touching her. It was difficult to keep his hands from roaming up and down her soft curves.

"You feel it, too," she said softly as she gazed up at him. "You don't want to. You fight it, but you feel it every bit as much as I do. It's why you've kissed me." She laughed softly. "You can't help but kiss me, just as I'm unable to resist. I don't want to resist."

He shook his head even as his body hummed agreement.

She smiled and put a finger over his lips as they swayed with the music. Then turning, so that his back was to Alannis, she let her hands run down his chest. Her eyes narrowed to half slits, and she parted her lips in a hungry gesture.

He groaned. "We mustn't, Bella. You make me so crazy. You have to stop with the teasing."

"Who says I'm teasing," she asked as she arched one eyebrow.

He took her hands and pulled them away from his body before turning her around again so that they were sideways to Alannis.

"You see her? Alannis. I'm going to ask her to marry me, Isabella."

She greeted his announcement with calm. No visible reaction. Had she already known?

"This must stop between us," he pressed on. "We're going to marry different people."

"And yet you keep kissing me," she said with a slight smile.

"I won't do so again," he vowed.

Instead of deterring her, a sparkle lit her eyes. "If I have anything to say about it you will."

Before he could respond, she pulled away. "I'm starving." Then suddenly she leaned close and murmured so only he could hear. "You say you don't want me, yet you don't want another man to have me. Pretty strange wouldn't you say?"

She turned and walked away, her hips swaying gently as she navigated her way back to where Sophia waited with a plate of food.

Ten

"He still plans to propose tonight?" Isabella asked in dismay. She held the phone tightly to her ear as she listened to Madeline.

Somehow she'd hoped that after last night Theron would have realized he felt *something* for her. Maybe not love. Not yet, but she'd thought he'd wake up to the attraction between them.

Okay, maybe he wasn't completely unaware, but he certainly seemed determined to ignore it.

She closed her eyes as she listened to Madeline confirm that according to Theron, the proposal was still on.

"Thanks, Madeline," she said slowly.

She hung up the phone and sunk lower into the bed. Theron with Alannis. She just couldn't imagine it. Theron needed… someone to shake him up, someone who wouldn't let him get too serious and organized.

He needed someone like her.

Alannis wouldn't challenge him. There was no spark of

chemistry between them. Alannis may as well be his daughter for all the attraction that existed.

Maybe Theron wanted a comfortable, dull marriage.

She shook her head. No, she wouldn't believe that, because if she did, then she'd have to give up, and she wasn't ready to do that yet.

Reaching for the phone again, she dialed the number that Marcus had given her the night before.

"Marcus, hi, it's Isabella," she said when he answered.

"Isabella, how are you?" he greeted.

She sighed. "Word is the proposal is still on."

"Sorry to hear that. I was certain he was ready to beat me into a pulp after our little act last night."

"He frustrates me," she said glumly. "I can't figure the man out. He's so controlled in all things except when he's alone with me."

Marcus laughed. "I can't say I blame the man. I have a feeling you'd try the patience of a saint and the vows of a priest."

"I don't suppose you could get tickets to the opera tonight? I hate to ask, but I'm desperate. He and Alannis are going to the opera and then to an after-party at the hotel where he plans to pop the question."

"I'm sure I could arrange it, but how do you plan to stop him from proposing?"

Isabella sucked in a deep breath. "I'm not sure," she said softly. "But I'll think of something."

"I don't suppose now would be a good time to admit that I hate the opera," Marcus said with a laugh.

She smiled faintly. "I'm not much of a fan myself, but apparently, it's Alannis's favorite performance."

"Then might I suggest an alternative?"

Her brow puckered, and she sat up in bed, the covers gathering at her waist. "What did you have in mind?"

"How about a date? You inform that security team of yours

of your plans for the evening, that you'll be out with me. I have no doubt that they report to Theron regularly." Amusement threaded through Marcus's voice. "It'll drive him crazy that he's stuck at the opera with Alannis, and he'll have no idea what we're up to, whereas if we're both at the opera, he'll be able to see us."

"But what about the party and his plans to propose?"

"I'll have you to the party before Theron arrives. Maybe by then you'll have come up with a plan."

"I don't know," she said slowly.

"Come on," he cajoled. "We'll have a nice dinner. It'll drive Theron crazy. Then you show up at the party. He'll be putty in your hands."

"All right," she conceded.

"Great. I'll pick you up at seven then. I'll call right before I arrive so you can come down."

They rang off, and Isabella swung her legs over the edge of the bed. Once again, she was in need of the perfect dress. Something gorgeous. She wasn't sure they sold dresses for the occasion of preventing a marriage proposal.

She had a sudden, alarming thought. Did this make her the other woman? Was she a femme fatale breaking up a relationship? The thought was an uncomfortable one, and it didn't give her a good feeling. But on the other hand, she knew that she and Theron were right for each other. Even if he didn't know it yet.

Besides, nothing was settled yet. Alannis wasn't wearing a ring, and no commitment had been made. Until that happened, all was fair in love and war.

She almost groaned at the cheesy cliché. Clearly she needed to come up with something more worthy.

Pushing herself up, she headed for the shower. She only had until tonight to figure out how she was going to prevent Theron from making a huge mistake. And to prevent her own heartbreak.

* * *

Theron picked up the phone as Madeline called back to say that Reynolds was on the phone to give his daily report. He listened as Isabella's head of security listed the morning's activities which consisted of shopping and lunch alone at the hotel.

His hand tightened around the receiver when Reynolds got to her plans for the evening. An outing with Marcus Atwater.

He swore in Greek and then quickly recovered. What was she thinking? Surely she couldn't be attracted to a man such as Marcus. He was smooth, too smooth, and he'd been all over her at the party.

Not to mention he had a different woman on his arm every week.

"You are to keep a close watch on her," Theron ordered. "I don't trust this man she's going out with. Under no circumstances are they to be left alone."

"Yes, sir," Reynolds replied.

Theron hung up the phone, his lips compressed into a tight line. Was she just trying to drive him insane? She had to know he wouldn't approve of her spending time with Marcus after what had happened the previous night.

And maybe she could care less what he approved of. She hadn't exactly paid him any heed in any other area.

He leaned back in his chair and opened his desk drawer, reaching for the small black box that nestled in the corner. His fingers touched it, and then he picked it up and opened it.

The diamond ring sparkled in the light as he studied it. Tonight he'd put it on Alannis's finger. So why wasn't he more enthused? Why wasn't he looking forward to his future?

This time next year he could even have a child, a family. He'd be settled. And yet he felt decidedly unsettled about her—about everything.

His intercom buzzed again, and Madeline announced that

he had another important call. She cut the connection before he could ask who. Shaking his head, he picked up the phone.

"Have you lost your damn mind?" Piers's demand made Theron frown.

"Give him a chance," Chrysander said dryly. "Then we'll ascertain whether he's lost his sanity."

"You told Madeline not to tell me it was you two calling, didn't you?" Theron accused.

"Damn right," Piers said. "You wouldn't have answered if you'd known. Coward."

"There's nothing to say I won't hang up," Theron said idly.

"Your sister-in-law wants to know why you didn't tell her you were thinking of getting married," Chrysander said.

Theron winced. "It's not fair of you to use Marley to make me feel guilty, and you know it."

"What are you doing?" Piers asked impatiently, cutting through the banter. "What could you possibly be thinking?"

"What our brother is trying to say is that we were caught by surprise, and we'd like to offer you our congratulations, just as soon as we understand why we're only just now finding out," Chrysander said diplomatically.

Piers made a rude noise. "Not me. If he tells me he's really doing this, I can only offer my condolences."

"What's wrong with me getting married?" Theron asked, surprised by Piers's reaction.

"Besides the fact that I think anyone willingly entering the institution of matrimony has a few screws loose, there is the fact that you're marrying Alannis Gianopolous. She's so wrong for you," Piers said bluntly.

Theron frowned. "Alannis is a perfectly acceptable choice."

There was a long silence, and then Chrysander cleared his throat. "*Acceptable choice?* That's an odd way of putting it."

"I'm more interested as to why you believe she's so wrong for me," Theron said, ignoring Chrysander's remark.

"Hell, Theron, apart from the fact that her father has been angling for her to marry one of us for years, she's…she's…"

"She's what?" Theron cut in.

"Just tell us why the sudden urge to get married," Chrysander said calmly. "And why you felt the need to include such momentous news in an e-mail."

"Probably because of the reaction I'm getting now," Theron said pointedly.

"Since when did you become so worried about what we thought?" Piers asked.

"Does anyone find it ironic that not so long ago, it was me and Piers having this talk with Chrysander about Marley? We were wrong about her, and you two are wrong about Alannis."

Chrysander sighed, and Theron knew he had him. What could he say when it was the truth? Theron and Piers had been quite vocal in their opposition of Marley. They'd also been dead wrong.

"Just be sure this is what you want," Chrysander said in resignation. "And keep us apprised of your plans. Marley will want to make it for the wedding."

Piers wasn't quite so ready to throw in the towel. "Think about what you're doing, Theron. This is the rest of your life you're talking about here."

"I appreciate your concern," Theron said dryly. "I am capable of making my own decisions."

"Tell me how things are going with Isabella," Chrysander broke in, an obvious attempt to change the subject. "Did you get her off to Europe?"

Again, there was a long silence. Theron wiped a hand through his hair wishing he'd pressed Madeline harder about who was on the phone.

"She didn't go to Europe," he said.

"Who is Isabella?" Piers demanded. "Are we talking about little Isabella Caplan?"

"I'll fill you in later," Chrysander said. "Why didn't she go to Europe? Where is she then?"

"She's here. She's decided to stay in New York," Theron said. "And she's not so little anymore," he added, though he was unsure why he felt the need to make that point.

Chrysander chuckled. "Poor Theron. Saddled with women on all sides. I imagine you're cursing me about now."

If he only knew.

"I've seen to Isabella's needs, and gotten her settled in. Everything is fine. *I'm* fine. You two can get off my back now."

"He sounds a little defensive, does he not?" Piers said smugly. "I smell something here. Something rotten. I only wish I was in New York to see for myself."

"You just stay the hell where you are," Theron muttered. "You have a hotel to build."

Piers's laughter flooded the line.

"I'm hanging up now," Theron said before lowering the receiver.

Now he knew how Chrysander had felt when he and Piers had given him such a hard time about Marley. Well-meaning relatives were always the worst.

Eleven

"Have any idea what you're going to say yet?" Marcus asked Isabella as he picked up his wineglass and brought it to his lips.

Reluctantly she shook her head and stared down at her barely eaten entrée. "I don't want to make an ass of myself, but at the same time I have to make him see that I'm not teasing. I'm not playing some silly game nor is he a passing infatuation."

When she looked up, she saw sympathy in Marcus's dark eyes.

"Put yourself in his shoes," she murmured. "You're about to ask a woman to marry you. You've kissed another woman twice, and you're fighting the attraction hard. What could this other woman say to you to convince you not to marry someone else?"

Marcus set his glass down, leaned back and blew out his breath. "Boy, you don't ask the hard ones, do you? I guess it would depend on whether I truly loved the woman I was about to marry, but then I wouldn't propose unless I was certain of that. And if I was certain, and I intended to propose, then nothing would sway me."

"I was afraid you'd say that," Isabella muttered.

"All you can do is try," he said gently. "Nothing ventured, nothing gained, and all that jazz."

A smile cracked through her lips. "Between you and me, we have all the trite clichés wrapped up."

He reached over and took her hand. "Are you sure this is what you truly want, Bella? I hate to see you hurt or disappointed."

"You're sweet," she began.

"Lord, but a man hates to hear those words from a woman's lips," he said with a groan. "It's as bad as hearing *you're just like a brother to me.*"

She laughed and relaxed her shoulders. Tension had crept into her muscles until her entire body had gone stiff with it. Marcus was right about one thing. All she could do was try. Whatever happened afterward was out of her control.

"You look fantastic tonight," he said as he relinquished her hands.

"Thank you. You really *are* too sweet."

She glanced down at the royal blue evening gown she'd chosen on her whirlwind shopping trip she'd dragged her bodyguards on earlier that day. She was dressed to kill, or to do battle at the very least. Without false modesty, she knew she looked her best.

High-class, posh, a far cry from her preferred jeans and flip-flops and brightly polished toes. Tonight, she fit into Theron's world. Her world too, for that matter, just one that she'd never fully embraced. She had the money and pedigree, just not the desire to fit in.

"What time should we leave?" she asked anxiously.

She couldn't help the surge in her pulse when she imagined

making it to the party too late. It made her want to break into a cold sweat that she'd arrive only to see the happy couple already engaged.

Marcus smiled reassuringly. "The opera has only just begun. We have quite awhile yet. Not to worry, I'll have you there in plenty of time. Try to relax and enjoy your dinner. It would be a terrible thing if you got to the party and promptly fainted at Theron's feet from hunger."

"Then again, it might be just the thing to stop the show," she said mischievously.

He chuckled and shook his head. "I'm almost sorry I agreed to help you, Bella. I would have rather pursued you myself."

"And if my heart weren't already lost to Theron, I would most gladly lead you on a very merry chase," she said with a grin.

"Then let me say this, and I won't broach the subject again," he said. "Should things not go the way you'd like...I ask only that you remember me."

She reached over to take his hand this time. "Thank you, Marcus. You've been a wonderful friend in the short time of our acquaintance. I hope you'll remain my friend no matter what. This is a lonely city when you know no one."

"I'd be honored. Now eat. I insist. They have the most wonderful desserts here."

Theron sat broodingly in his chair as the performance yawned on before him. Beside him, Alannis watched the stage with rapt attention, her face aglow with delight. Sophia was less enthused, but she still focused her attention forward.

Just before the performance had begun, Reynolds had reported that Isabella was meeting Marcus Atwater for dinner after a day of shopping. There wasn't a whole lot Theron could do at that point given that he was firmly entrenched in his evening. In the end, he gave Reynolds strict instructions to stick to Isabella like glue and make damn sure that Atwater didn't take advantage of her.

He was tempted to send a message to Reynolds from his BlackBerry, but he wasn't sure that Alannis was so ensconced in the performance that she wouldn't notice, and he'd promised that no business would interfere tonight.

Still, he'd requested periodic updates from Isabella's security team, and he'd find a way to check his messages even if it meant a trip to the bathroom.

For the entire next hour, he fidgeted, ready to be done. It irritated him that on a night he should be relaxed, that he was forced to think about Isabella's well-being. She was seeping into his life in a manner that didn't sit well with him. What did it say when he couldn't enjoy an evening with his future wife for thinking about Isabella Caplan?

Alannis touched his arm, and he was jerked from his thoughts.

"Theron, it's over," she whispered.

He glanced quickly to see the curtain drawn. Had he missed the encore entirely? Another nudge from Alannis had him rising to his feet. He offered her his arm and filed out of his box, Sophia and two of his security team following behind.

"And how did you enjoy the show?" he asked as they made their way to the waiting limousine.

"It was wonderful," Alannis gushed. "I do so love the opera. There was a time…"

She ducked her head, but not before he saw a bright blush form on her cheeks.

"There was a time, what?" he prompted.

"Oh, there was a time that I wanted to be an opera singer," she said self-consciously.

"And why didn't you pursue it?"

She smiled and shook her head. "I wasn't good enough. Besides, father wouldn't have had it. He thinks it's a vulgar career."

Theron raised an eyebrow. "I wouldn't have thought such talent could be considered vulgar."

"Oh, he thinks any career that lands you on stage is inappropriate for a young girl. He'd much prefer that I marry well and give him grandbabies."

Something flashed in her eyes before it quickly vanished into blandness.

"And what do you want?" Theron asked curiously.

"I like children," she said simply before turning to her mother.

Theron ushered them into the car and settled in himself as they started for the hotel. His hands were clammy, and he shook his head in disgust over his apparent nervousness. He prided himself on his control and his calm. Nothing about this situation should cause him any anxiety. He had his future mapped out, and everything was proceeding exactly as planned.

After that reminder, he relaxed in his seat. He felt in his pocket for the ring then let his hand fall when he reassured himself that it was there.

Traffic moved quickly, and a half hour later, they arrived at the hotel. Alannis yawned as Theron helped her out of the car.

He smiled and took her hand. "I hope you aren't too tired for the party."

"What party?" she asked in surprise.

Sophia smiled and tucked her arm in Alannis's. "He's planned a party in your honor, dear. It's a very special night." She winked at Theron behind Alannis's back, and Theron felt his unease increase.

"A party for me? It sounds so exciting," Alannis said, her eyes sparkling in delight.

She really was quite lovely, in a quiet, understated way. For some reason, however, he couldn't chase the image of another woman from his mind when he looked at her.

He glanced away, his jaw tight as they walked through the

lobby toward the ballroom. When they entered, the band struck up and confetti fell from the ceiling.

Alannis looked up, her eyes rapt. She held her fingers up to catch the flurries as they spiraled down like crazy, neon snow.

"Oh, it's wonderful, Theron," she breathed.

He nudged her forward again, his heart pounding with each step they took. His hand drifted into his pocket as they neared the center of the room. The edges of the box scraped against his fingers, and he fumbled with it, coaxing the velvet box inside free.

Would she be as excited when he asked her to be his wife? Would he? Or was he about to make the biggest mistake of his life?

"Alannis…" he began, cursing the fact that his voice was so shaky.

She turned and looked up at him, eyes shining and a smile curving her lips. Lips that he had no desire to kiss. "Yes, Theron?"

Isabella sat forward in her seat, straining to see out the front window. "What's the hold up?" she asked desperately. "Why aren't we moving?"

Marcus took hold of her shoulder. "It's a wreck, Bella. Calm down, sit back. We'll get there. He won't propose as soon as the party starts."

She stared out the window at the sea of cars all at a dead stop. They'd never get out of this in time.

In a burst of frustration, she reached for the door handle and yanked the door open.

"Bella, what are you doing? Get back in the car. You can't go running through the streets of New York City," Marcus exclaimed as she clambered out.

She turned and bent to stare back into the car where he sat. "I have to go, Marcus. We'll never make it in time and you know it. I have to get there before he proposes. I can't…" She swallowed and looked away for a moment. When she looked back, tears clouded her vision. "I have to go. Thank you for everything."

She closed the door, picked up the long skirt of her dress in her hands and ran through the traffic, ignoring the honks as she cut in front of cars trying to inch forward. She heard the shouts of Reynolds and glanced back to see that he was hotfooting it down the street after her. Turning, she kept on running. She didn't have time to stop and explain.

Unsure of where she was going, she kept to the sidewalk, paralleling the traffic. When she saw an unoccupied taxi, she ran to the window and tapped.

The cabbie gave her a disgruntled look and rolled down his window. "Look lady, no one's going anywhere in this mess."

She held up a hand. "Please, can you tell me how to get to Imperial Park Hotel? How far am I?"

His eyes narrowed as he stared back at her. "As the crow flies, not far. If you cut over from this street a block then up two, you'll be six or so blocks from the hotel. Just head straight for five blocks, turn left and you'll see it as soon as you round the corner."

With a murmured thanks, she gathered her dress, shed her shoes and took off running as fast as she could go.

"Hey, lady, you left your shoes!" the man shouted from behind her.

By the time she'd gone three blocks, it had started to rain lightly. Not that it mattered. She already looked a fright, and her hopes of looking like a million dollars when she burst into Theron's engagement party were doomed.

When she rounded the corner of the last block, the heavens opened and it began to pour. Blinking the water from her eyes, she dashed toward the hotel, avoiding the puddles that were already forming beneath her feet.

Please, oh please, let me be on time.

Her hair was plastered to her face by the time she made it under the awning. Water dripped from her body and from the sodden mass of her ruined dress. Her feet ached, and she was sure she'd cut her right foot on something.

Ignoring the inquisitive looks thrown her way, she rushed past several people who were trying to hurry inside. Skidding on the polished floor, she righted herself and ran as fast as she could with a wet dress wrapped around her legs.

As she neared the ballroom, she heard cheers from inside and then mad clapping. *No.* She couldn't be too late, she couldn't.

She thrust herself inside the door, her gaze wildly searching the crowd gathered. There, in the middle, stood Theron and Alannis. Alannis was beaming from head to toe as she gazed lovingly up at Theron who was smiling down at her. Around them people clapped and then they brought their glasses up in a toast.

The words were lost to Isabella. She heard nothing except the buzz in her ears. She saw nothing but how radiant Alannis looked. It was a stark contrast to how dead Isabella felt in that moment.

Slowly, every part of her aching, she turned, tears swimming in her eyes, and walked slowly back out of the ballroom. She nearly ran into Reynolds as he hurried up to her. Keeping her head down, she continued on, ignoring his demands to know if she was all right.

All right? Nothing would ever be all right again.

Gradually the sounds of laughter and happiness diminished, and she was left with only the murmur of the people milling about the lobby.

A tear slipped down her cheek, and she made no move to wipe it. Who would notice? It would look like she was caught in the rain as she had been.

As she neared the entrance, Marcus ran in and stopped abruptly in front of her.

"Isabella, are you all right?" he demanded. "That was a foolish thing you did."

He caught her shoulders and spun her so that she looked at him. And then he must have seen the misery in her eyes because his tirade ceased, and gentle understanding shone in his eyes.

"You were too late?" he asked needlessly.

She nodded and squeezed her eyes shut as more hot tears escaped.

He gathered her in his arms. "I'm so sorry, Bella. I promised I would have you here on time."

"It wasn't your fault," she whispered.

"Come on, let me get you up to your room," he urged as he turned her toward the elevator. "You're soaked through." He nodded tersely at Reynolds. "I'll take her up."

Numbly, she let him escort her into the elevator. As they rode up, images of Alannis and Theron filtered through her mind. They'd looked so happy.

Happy.

Almost like…they were in love.

She closed her eyes again. Why couldn't he love her?

Marcus took the key from her shaking fingers and unlocked her door. Cool air immediately washed over her, eliciting a chill.

"You're soaked, too," she said as she became aware of his wet shirt and slacks.

He gave her a wry smile. "I took off after you and got caught in the downpour."

She tried to smile and failed miserably. "Sorry."

He sighed. "Why don't you go take a hot bath? I'll order up room service and see if they can't also get me some dry clothing brought up from the boutique."

She nodded and shuffled toward the bathroom.

* * *

Theron slipped his hand in the inside pocket of his suit and pulled out his BlackBerry. He frowned when he saw his last message had gone unanswered.

Excusing himself from Alannis with a smile, he nodded to the other guests assembled around them and backed away. He walked out of the ballroom and headed to the men's room just two doors down. As he was about to enter, he looked down the hallway and saw Reynolds standing next to his men. He was soaking wet.

With a frown, Theron stalked toward the three men. Reynolds glanced up as he heard Theron approach.

"Where's Isabella?" Theron demanded.

"In her room with Atwater," Reynolds replied.

Sure he had heard wrong, Theron's eyes narrowed. "With who?"

"She went up a few minutes ago with Atwater," Reynolds said calmly. "They were both soaked."

Theron's pulse pounded against his temple. It was all he could do not to charge up to her room and drag Marcus out. Then he'd beat the hell out of him.

With a muttered curse, he spun around and headed for the elevator. Anger rushed like lava through his veins. What the hell was Marcus thinking? Theron knew damn well what he was thinking, and what he was thinking with.

When he finally reached Isabella's door, he rapped sharply. A few seconds later, the door opened to a smiling Marcus who wore just a bathrobe.

He looked startled to see Theron standing there, and then his eyes narrowed to slits. "Sorry, I thought you were room service," Marcus said. Then he turned his head toward the bathroom. "Stay in the tub a little longer, sweetheart. Food's not here yet."

Turning back to Theron, Marcus did a slow up and down

perusal, and then he asked in a bored voice, "Now, what can I do for you?"

"You arrogant…" Theron said in a menacing voice.

"You broke away from your engagement party to come up here and call me names?" Marcus asked in amusement.

A sound down the hallway had Theron looking to see the room service cart being wheeled toward Isabella's door. Marcus pressed forward and stared as well.

"Ah, there's the food now. If you'll excuse me. Or was there something you wanted?" Marcus asked pointedly.

Theron backed away, unsettled and feeling like he'd just gone a round in the boxing ring. Without a word, he turned and stalked away, his fists clenched into balls at his sides.

His gut churned as he got back onto the elevator. Why did it matter? He'd set Marcus up to be a choice in Isabella's hunt for a husband. Why then did he feel absolutely sickened by the prospect that Isabella had made her choice?

Twelve

Isabella was wakened by a loud knock at her door. She opened her eyes, wincing at how scratchy and dry they felt. Her hands went to wipe the swollen lids, and she remembered that she'd cried herself to sleep the night before.

Theron had proposed to Alannis. She'd been too late. And they'd looked so *happy*.

Fitting that she was completely miserable.

A knock sounded again, prompting her to slide her legs from the covers and push herself from the bed. Gathering her robe that lay over the chair a few feet away, she pulled it on and tied it as she walked to the door.

When she stared through the peephole, she saw Sadie standing outside, or at least someone who resembled Sadie. It was hard to tell with the platinum blond wig adorning her head. She opened the door, and Sadie brushed by talking a mile a minute.

"Thank goodness you're here," Sadie said. "For a minute I thought you'd forgotten about tonight."

Isabella closed the door and turned to look at Sadie.

"I've got everything in my bag, and we have plenty of time to prepare," Sadie chattered on. "It'll be a snap."

Then Sadie stopped as she got a good look at Isabella. Her brow creased in confusion, and her lips parted.

"Bella, what's wrong? Have you been crying?"

To Isabella's dismay, she felt the sting of more tears. Irritated, she blinked them away, determined not to shed a single one.

Sadie closed the distance between them and slung an arm around her friend, guiding her toward the couch. Isabella found herself seated, and then Sadie plopped down beside her.

"What happened?" she asked. "Is it Theron?"

Isabella closed her eyes and nodded.

"Oh, honey, I'm sorry." Sadie enfolded her in her arms. "Did he propose to Alannis? Is that it?"

Isabella nodded against Sadie's shoulder. Sadie pulled away and brushed the hair from Isabella's face.

"Let's forget all about tonight. We'll order in some really good takeout and binge on desserts that have a gazillion calories."

Isabella smiled. "You can't miss your party, Sadie. It's too important. Just because my life is in shambles isn't a reason for you to lose your job and your chance at Broadway."

Sadie looked doubtfully at her. "I'm not sure you're up for this, Bella."

Bella forced a broader smile to her lips. "How bad can it be? I'll dress like you, dance some and attract male attention. It won't last long, and you'll keep your job."

"Are you sure?"

Isabella nodded. "Let's order something to eat. I'm starved. Then you can teach me the moves I need to know." She glanced at the bright wig Sadie was wearing. "Is that what I'm wearing out of here tonight?"

Sadie grinned. "It's the perfect way past your security guys. I made sure they saw me come in, and honestly, who could miss this?" she said as she slid her hands suggestively down the curves of her body.

Isabella cracked up. "No false modesty for you."

Sadie winked at her then continued on. "We'll dress you like me and you'll sashay out of here. No one will know that I'm still up here. I'll give you a good head start and then I'll get ready for the party and leave, looking nothing like the blond bombshell who arrived earlier."

"Well, what's the worst that can happen?" Isabella asked with a shrug. "We get caught and Reynolds throws another fit. I'm sure Theron is too busy with his new fiancée to give a damn about my whereabouts."

"That's the spirit," Sadie crowed. "Let's do it!"

She was certifiably insane to have agreed to this. Isabella took a deep breath as the elevator stopped at the lobby level, flipped a long lock of the blond hair over her shoulder and waited for the doors to open.

The getup that Sadie had poured her into was many things. Modest wasn't one of them. And while Isabella didn't mind displaying her assets to her best advantage, this bordered on obscene.

The heels of her thigh-high boots clicked on the marble floor as she hurried for the exit. Her shorts were a slightly more expensive version of a denim Daisy Duke style, and they dipped low in front, showing her navel and more skin.

And her top. Not even a Dallas Cowboy cheerleader showed more cleavage.

But as Sadie said, no one would bother looking at her face. Not when so much else of her was on display.

She wobbled her way toward a waiting taxi and got in. As he pulled away, she supplied the address that Sadie had provided her. He didn't even blink an eye, and who could blame him with the way she was dressed? It amused her to think he might have assumed she was at the hotel for "business" purposes.

Nervousness tickled her stomach as they maneuvered through traffic. By the time the cab pulled up to the back entrance of the club, sweat beaded her forehead.

She sat for a moment staring out her window until the driver cleared his throat.

"Sorry," she muttered. She shoved the appropriate money over the seat and then got out. "Well, here we go," she said, as she tentatively walked to the door.

The hallway just inside the door was cloaked in darkness. A good thing. Even though Sadie had assured her that no one would notice the slight differences in the girls, this charade still made Isabella extremely nervous.

She was wearing so much makeup, that even her overbearing security team hadn't been able to tell it was her.

When she got to the door simply marked "girls," she eased inside. There was a flurry of activity, and no one paid her any mind. Another girl bumped into her as she walked past, and Isabella shied away, afraid of getting too close.

"Hey, Sadie," another girl called. "We weren't sure you were coming. You're up after Angel, so you better hurry and get ready."

Isabella's stomach dropped, and she swallowed back her panic. She could do this. No one knew it was her. While she wasn't the expert that Sadie was, she could still move well, and Sadie had spent the afternoon teaching her the necessary act.

She smiled and nodded in the girl's direction and took a spot at Sadie's dressing station to check her makeup and to make sure her wig was securely in place.

When she caught her reflection in the mirror, all that she could think was how sad her eyes looked. No matter how made-up her face was, how perfect the hair, the eyes told the story. And the story was that she'd lost the one man she'd hoped to spend the rest of her life with.

More to have something to do than any real need to repair her makeup, she slowly applied more lipstick, watching as her lips glistened blood red. Mechanically she brushed the mascara wand over her eyelashes, elongating her already dark lashes.

But still, her green eyes stared lifelessly back at her.

"Sadie, you're up in five," a male voice barked from the door. "Get a move on."

Isabella pushed herself jerkily from her chair and spared one last glance in the mirror. She looked scared to death.

Sucking in a deep, steadying breath, she adjusted her clothing, plumped up her breasts and headed for the door.

Theron stared out the window of Chrysander's penthouse, his mostly forgotten drink still in hand. Dusk was falling, and the lights of the city were coming alive, popping on the horizon.

He still wasn't sure his decision had been the correct one. He'd questioned himself repeatedly through the day, and yet, he could find no fault with the path he'd taken.

But now he had no idea what to do about Isabella.

He turned in irritation when his BlackBerry rang. It was sitting on the coffee table several feet away where he'd tossed it earlier. With a resigned sigh he walked over to pick it up.

Seeing Reynolds's name on the LCD immediately put him on edge. He hit the answer button and put the phone to his ear.

"Anetakis," he said shortly.

"Mr. Anetakis, this is Reynolds. We have a situation, sir."

Theron put his drink down with a thud. "What situation?" he demanded.

"Earlier this evening, Ms. Caplan gave us the slip. Again."

"What? And you allowed her to do this again?"

"I'm afraid it's worse, sir. I'll be happy to fill you in on the details later, but at the moment we're on our way to La Belle Femmes." He paused for a moment. "Are you familiar with it, sir?"

Theron's brow furrowed in concentration as he absorbed the information. "Isn't that a gentlemen's club? And why the hell are you going there?"

"Because that's where Ms. Caplan went," Reynolds said calmly. "I assumed you'd want to know."

"Damn right I want to know!" Theron exploded. "I'm on my way now, and don't think I won't want to know exactly how this went down."

He hurried toward the door, his finger on the button to call for his driver. By the time he made it to the lobby, the car was waiting in front of the building.

What in God's name was Isabella doing in a gentleman's club? What was she thinking? Was Marcus somehow responsible for this? Theron was going to kill him.

When his driver screeched up to the club entrance, Theron got out and saw Reynolds along with his two men hurrying toward him.

"Is she here?" Theron demanded.

"We just arrived," Reynolds explained. "We were about to go in to see."

Theron strode ahead of them to the door and was stopped by a large man wearing dark glasses.

"Your name, sir?" the man politely inquired.

"Theron Anetakis," he said impatiently. "Someone I know is in there. Someone who shouldn't be here."

"Unless you have a membership, I can't allow you inside."

Theron seethed with impatience and then he turned to Reynolds. "Take care of this. Pay the man whatever is necessary for membership and then rejoin me inside. I'm going in after Isabella."

"But sir, membership is not instant...."

Theron heard no more as he pushed by the man and went inside. He trusted that Reynolds and the others would be able to overcome whatever objections the club's security guard had to his presence.

The club was different than Theron was expecting. From the moment a gentlemen's club was mentioned, it conjured images of a seedy, back-alley environment where prostitution and drug use ran rampant. Here, though, it seemed the establishment catered to an upscale clientele.

The interior was clean, lavish even, reminding Theron of many high-roller areas of casinos. The waitresses, through scantily clad, weren't cheap-looking-tart material. The patrons were well-dressed, smoking expensive imported cigars and sipping only the finest brandy.

It was a place Isabella shouldn't even know existed.

Theron weaved around the tables, sharp-eyed, his brow creased in concentration as he took in every single woman. Toward the front of the room, more men were assembled in front of a curtained platform. Evidently a show was imminent.

He dismissed the men when he saw no women among them. Where the hell was Isabella and had Reynolds gotten his information correct?

He glanced toward the entrance and saw Reynolds and the two other security men rush in. Theron gestured curtly at them, and Reynolds wove his way through the tables to where Theron stood.

"Why do you think Isabella is here?" he demanded.

"I have it on good authority she is," Reynolds said grimly. "You're looking in the wrong—"

He was cut off when music began blaring behind Theron. He winced and turned around only to see the curtain rise and stage smoke slither sensuously up the long legs of a woman.

She wore thigh-high boots that only accentuated her slim legs and drew attention to her shapely behind. She began rocking in rhythm to the music, her hips swaying as her arms fell gracefully to her sides.

As the smoke cleared, she raised her arms and gripped the pole in front of her. But Theron's gaze was drawn to the tattoo in the small of her back.

He knew that tattoo. Knew it damn well. He should; he'd spent plenty of time fantasizing about it.

And then she turned, whirling around in a mass of blond hair—fake blond hair. He saw her eyes before she saw him. He saw the fear in her gaze, the wild panic as she surveyed the room full of men all eyeing her like a tasty treat.

Theron's blood boiled.

She looked up and locked gazes with him, her fear turning to utter shock as recognition flickered in her eyes.

Thirteen

Isabella blanched when she saw Theron who was clearly furious standing beyond the group of men all crowding the stage. He vibrated with rage, and his eyes flashed as he stared her down.

She had the sudden urge to cross her arms over her breasts and run for cover.

Before she could seriously contemplate doing just that, Theron stalked forward, closing in on the stage like a predator on the hunt.

He didn't stop at the edge, didn't call out to her to come down. He jumped onto the platform, and in one swift motion hauled her into his arms and threw her over his shoulder.

She gave a startled cry just as the music stopped and the place erupted in chaos. She raised her head to see Reynolds, Maxwell and Davison fend off the security guards trying to come to her aid.

Customers rose from their seats and viewed Theron with gaping mouths, but were too civilized to embroil themselves in the situation. It would probably ruin their thousand-dollar suits anyway.

The floor spun crazily as Theron leaped down. The force drove the breath from her, and she wiggled trying to get him to ease his grip.

He merely tightened his arm over the back of her legs as he strode for the exit. Then she heard him snarl, "Back off, she's mine."

And surprisingly, he walked through the door and into the night.

Still stunned, Isabella made no effort to free herself from his grasp, not that it would have done any good. His arm was like a steel band around her body, and he walked effortlessly, bearing her weight as if it were nothing.

He stopped at his car, and leaned down to thrust her through the opening into the interior. Immediately, he climbed in beside her and slammed the door.

"Imperial Park," he said curtly.

Laying at an odd angle on the seat, she attempted to straighten herself, but her legs bumped into him, and she pulled them hastily away which only made her position more precarious.

Damn the boots. She felt gawky and ungainly. A glance down made her gasp in dismay when she saw that her cleavage was precariously close to spilling from the suggestive top. She folded her arms over her chest and scooted back until her back hit the other door.

She opened her mouth to speak, but he silenced her with a glare.

"Not a word, Bella. Not one damn word," he said menacingly. Anger vibrated off him in waves. "I'll have a full explanation when we return to the hotel. Until then I don't want you to say anything."

She swallowed then gulped as she stared wordlessly at him.

Never had she seen him so…angry! He was usually so unbothered. Cool and collected. He was the epitome of order and calm.

The Theron she knew would never haul someone out of a public place nor would he snarl at a security guard twice his size.

She looked away, wrapping her arms a little tighter around herself.

"Here," he said gruffly as he shrugged out of his suit coat.

He held it out with one hand and pulled her forward as he settled it around her shoulders. She tugged at the lapels to bring it tighter around her, grateful that it at least covered her.

Several long minutes later, they pulled up to the hotel. Theron gave her a look that suggested she stay put, and she complied. He got out and walked around to her side and opened the door.

To her surprise, he reached in, drew his coat together so that not an inch of her flesh was displayed and then he simply plucked her out of the seat.

"Theron, I can walk," she protested.

"Silence," he ordered as he strode in the doors, ignoring the curious stares of passersby.

She frowned but settled wearily against his chest. He got into the elevator and stabbed at the button for her floor. Okay, she got that he was mad. Furious even. But he seemed to be taking it personally. Why wasn't he off somewhere with his new fiancée?

A fresh stab of pain soared through, taking her breath with it. She closed her eyes against the single truth that prevented her from having the man she loved. He belonged to someone else.

"Bella?"

His voice had changed, softened, and it reflected uncertainty. She pried open her eyes to see him regarding her with concern.

"Are you all right? Did something happen?" he demanded. "Did someone hurt you or threaten you?"

She shook her head, unable to speak past the lump in her throat. For a moment she could immerse herself in the fantasy that she did belong to him, that he cared about her in a deeper capacity than as a guardian, someone tasked to see to her welfare.

But it was a lie. It was all a lie.

"Then why?" he muttered.

The elevator opened, and with a shake of his head, he strode off and down to her room. Neither of them had a key, but then he didn't waste time trying to find one. He simply kicked loudly, instead of putting her down to knock. But who would open it? No one was there.

To her eternal surprise, and there had been many tonight, the door opened and a man who had security detail written all over him opened the door to admit Theron.

The surprises didn't end there. As soon as Theron walked in, a cry sounded from across the room.

"Bella! Are you all right?"

Isabella yanked her head left to see Sadie running across the room. Finally Theron let her down, and Sadie threw her arms around her.

"What are you doing here?" Isabella whispered. "Your party, Sadie. You weren't supposed to miss your party."

Sadie flushed guiltily. "The party doesn't matter. I should have never let you do this for me, Bella."

"In this we agree," Theron said stiffly. "It was irresponsible and dangerous. It's not a place that either of you should ever go into."

"But you missed your chance," Isabella said softly, ignoring Theron's outburst.

Sadie smiled sadly. "There'll be others. Besides, it wasn't worth the risk you took. I'm sorry."

"What happened?" Isabella asked in confusion. "Why are you still here and," she said, turning to face Theron, "how did he know where to find me?"

"Your security detail phoned me, as they should have," Theron said darkly.

Isabella turned back to Sadie. "How did they know?"

Sadie looked down and sighed. "When I left your room for the party, one of your guys immediately stopped me. They'd obviously seen you, posing as me, leave earlier and as we planned, never assumed it was you. However, they knew the real me hadn't entered your room, so they were suspicious. I had to tell them everything," she said uncomfortably. "They made me remain here while they went to get you." She glanced angrily at the man who was still standing by the door. "I had to endure a lecture from him the entire time you were gone."

"It's good that someone tried to talk sense into you," Theron bit out. He nodded toward the security man. "See that she gets home safely, and remain on watch to see that she doesn't go back to that club."

"But I work there!" Sadie exclaimed.

"Not any longer," Theron said with a growl. "I won't have Bella traipsing through some strip club because her friend works there."

"But—" Sadie sputtered even as she was escorted away by the security detail.

When the door closed behind them, Theron turned to glare at Isabella. He stepped forward, and she stepped back uneasily. His scowl became more ferocious as he reached to detain her.

"Now, Bella, I'll deal with you," he said in a soft, dangerous voice.

Theron's hands curled around her shoulders as he yanked Isabella to him. The coat she'd held so tightly around her fell to the floor, and her breasts thrust obscenely into his chest.

She couldn't bring herself to meet his gaze. If she did, he'd know. He'd immediately see everything she now wanted to hide. Things he hadn't been able to see before.

"Go get cleaned up," he said in a gruff voice. "I'll wait for you here."

Only too grateful to flee, she turned and headed for the bathroom. She grimaced when she caught a glimpse of herself in the mirror. Tawdry was a word that came to mind. Garish.

Sad.

She washed the heavy makeup from her face and tore the wig from her head. Then she unpinned her own hair and ran her fingers through it to tame it. A long, hot bath was extremely tempting, but not when Theron waited outside, likely growing more impatient by the moment.

She stripped out of the boots and clothes, tossing them aside. Then she realized she hadn't brought in something to change into. With a shrug, she made a grab for the bathrobe hanging on the back of the door and wrapped it securely around her.

Then she padded back out to the sitting room in bare feet, hands thrust into the pockets of the robe. Theron waited, standing by the window that overlooked the avenue below.

When he heard her, he turned, his eyes still flashing with unsettled intensity.

"Why are you here, Theron?" she asked, finally regaining her composure.

He closed the distance between them, once again curling his fingers over her shoulders. "You dare to ask that as if I have no right? As if you didn't just do something incredibly stupid? Do you have any idea what I thought when I heard where you'd gone? The fear I felt? Or the shock upon seeing you on that stage, half naked for all those men to leer at? Tell me, Bella, what would you have done if someone other than me had rushed that stage? What if he had put his hands on you? Forced you to go with him?"

She blinked at his ferocity and the absolute anger tightening his features. Any number of explanations circled her frazzled mind, but she didn't think he'd be interested in any of them. So she kept quiet.

Theron ran a hand through his hair in a gesture of frustration before locking gazes with her once more.

"Did Marcus know you were doing this?"

Isabella bobbed her head backward in surprise. "Marcus? Why would he need to know anything I was doing?"

"I would hope he was more protective of what was his—or what he had staked claim on anyway," Theron growled.

She blinked in confusion. "You're not making any sense. Marcus has nothing to do with anything. He's a friend. I don't feel the need to apprise him of my comings and goings."

Theron snorted. "*A friend?* Is that what they're calling them these days?" he asked, throwing her mocking words about kissing back at her.

"What are you insinuating, Theron?" she asked as she folded her arms over her chest.

"I was here, Bella. Last night. I came up...to see about you," he added uncomfortably.

"So?"

"And Marcus answered your door in only a bathrobe," he snapped.

Isabella's mouth fell open. "And from this, you assume I'm sleeping with him?"

"Are you saying you did not?" Theron challenged.

"I'm saying it's none of your damn business," she huffed.

A long silence fell between them as they stared at one another. Oh, she would have loved to have told him yes, that she'd slept with Marcus, but really, what was the point? He was engaged to Alannis, and she had no desire to make herself look promiscuous. He did still have control over her inheritance until she married someone else.

"I didn't sleep with him," she said tightly. "We were caught in the rain and he came up so that dry clothing could be brought to him. He changed into a robe, and I stayed in the tub until he was dressed. We ate room service and then he left."

There was a flicker of relief in Theron's eyes. Why? What could it possibly matter to him? And then he shook his head.

"Why do you insist on driving me utterly crazy?" he murmured. "Is it not enough that I spend my time thinking of you? Remembering the feel of your mouth beneath mine?"

He moved in closer, his breath hot against her face. Unconsciously, she licked her lips nervously as he moved and tilted his head in a dance around her mouth.

"You shouldn't…kiss me," she whispered.

"You've never had an objection before," he muttered just before his mouth closed hot over hers.

Fourteen

Isabella's knees wobbled, and she clutched frantically at Theron's shoulders to keep from sliding down his body. He caught her tightly against him as his lips plundered hers.

This kiss…was different. She moaned softly, a sound of surrender? Honestly, she didn't care. Maybe it was a sound of need. Or want.

He took her. There was no other word for it. He took possession of her mouth as if he owned it, as if he had exclusive rights to her mouth and refused to share it. Ever.

Her body melted against his, and she loved the hardness of his chest, his thighs, shivered as his hands roamed up her body to her neck. He cupped her nape, holding her so that she couldn't escape him. As if she wanted to.

She was a willing captive. This…this was what she'd dreamed about. Fantasized. Wanted so much. So desperately.

"I want to make love to you, Bella," he said with breathless urgency, his lips barely separating from hers. "I've fought it. *Theos,* but I've fought, but if I don't have you, I'm going to go mad."

"Yes," she whispered. "I want you so much, Theron."

His hands fumbled with the tie at her robe, his lips never leaving her mouth. It was as though he couldn't bear to stop kissing her. He devoured her even as he yanked her robe open.

And then his hands pressed against her naked skin, and she moaned and trembled, going completely weak against him.

"Soft, so soft and beautiful. Like silk," he murmured as his palms caressed her sides, moving up until he cupped her breasts.

Finally, he moved from her mouth, his lips brushing over her jaw and to her ear and then lower, down her neck. He nipped then sucked at the tender skin, eliciting shiver after shiver.

His mouth continued downward, and she caught her breath as he sank to his knees in front of her. He snaked his arms inside her robe and wrapped them around her waist, pulling her downward so that her knees bent.

His mouth was precariously close to her breasts, so much so that his breath beaded and puckered her nipples into tight knots. And then he slid his mouth over one, rolling his tongue gently over the peak.

Her robe fell to the floor at her feet, and she was naked in his arms. He sucked at her breast, his dark head flush against her body. How erotic it looked, this proud, strong man, on his knees, his arms wrapped tight around her—as though he'd never let go.

Before she allowed herself to become too entrenched in *that* fantasy, he released her nipple, and she groaned her protest.

He glanced up, his eyes glowing in the lamplight. "You're beautiful, Bella," he said in a low husky voice that was passion-laced.

His grip loosened just enough that he could rise to his feet, his shirt scraping along her bare skin. She reached out with her fingers to snag at his buttons, wanting them gone and to feel his bare skin against hers.

But he collected her hands in his and held them tightly together. "Oh, no, Bella *mou*. This is my seduction. And I intend to seduce you thoroughly."

He swung her into his arms and walked slowly to the bedroom, his gaze locked with hers. She was afraid to speak. Afraid that he would hastily back away if the spell was broken.

He laid her on the bed then straightened to his full height over her. She felt strangely vulnerable beneath his intense gaze. Shy and a little uncertain.

Her hands crept upward in an attempt to shield herself.

"Do not hide such beauty from me," he whispered.

Emboldened by the obvious approval in his eyes, she let her hands fall away. Lust flared over his face as his hands went to the buttons of his shirt. Halfway down, he lost patience and ripped the remaining buttons. He shrugged out of the sleeves and then tore impatiently at his pants.

She sucked in her breath and held it when his boxers, with his pants, slipped down and his turgid manhood came into view. Then it stuttered out, a silent staccato in the quiet as he moved closer.

He spread her knees and fit his body to hers, settling between her thighs as he came down onto the bed. Hot, silken and yet rough in a heady, masculine way, his skin clung to hers, burning her, making her move restlessly underneath him.

They kissed again, and she wrapped her arms around his neck, prolonging the mating of their tongues. Soft and wet, clinging and dueling, a precursor to the dance their bodies would yet perform.

"I've never felt so out of control," he admitted. "So restless and out of my skin. You make me crazy, Bella. I have to have you."

"Yes."

The softly whispered surrender slid from swollen lips. His

mouth skated downward to her neck and then over the slope of her shoulder.

He moved, lowering his body so that his lips found her breasts. She stared up at the ceiling, the intricate painting blurring as pleasure overtook her. For several long seconds, he lazily tongued the rigid peaks, and then he blazed a wet trail with his tongue down her midline to her belly.

He toyed with her belly ring for the briefest of seconds before traveling even lower.

She tensed when his mouth found her soft femininity, the very essence and core of her womanhood. Helplessly she arched into him, seeking more of his bold tongue. He chuckled and gave her another soft nuzzle.

"Please, Theron," she begged. "Take me."

"I want you to be ready for me, Bella *mou*," he said as he trailed one finger over her damp flesh.

"Take me," she said again as she looked down and met his gaze. "I'm yours."

Her words seemed to push him beyond his control. He slid up her body, spreading her legs and fitting himself to her in one deft movement. One moment he was probing, the next he slid inside her, breaking through the slight resistance as though it were nothing.

For a moment she went rigid with shock, only a twinge of pain, but more than that a sense of such fullness that it overwhelmed her. Her eyes flew open, and her hands went reflexively to his shoulders to push him away.

Theron stared at her in confusion even as his hips moved, and he thrust forward again. She relaxed beneath him, letting her hands glide over his shoulders and to his neck. Pleasure, sweet and yearning, bloomed, spreading like fire in the wind.

His lips found hers again in a gesture of reassurance, molding sweetly to hers, suddenly gentle and tender.

"Move with me, *agape mou*," he urged. "Wrap your legs around me. Yes, that's it."

Her skin came alive, crawling and edgy with need. Theron planted his elbows on either side of her head and held his body off her enough that she didn't bear the full brunt of his weight as he moved between her legs.

Breathing became hard. She panted against his lips as their mouths met again.

"Come with me," he whispered.

Helpless to do anything but follow the winding pleasure building so earnestly, she cried out as he stiffened above her. He gathered her softly against him, crushing her to his hardness. Murmured words fell against her ears, some she understood, some slipping away.

And then he collapsed, pressing his warm body to hers. For several long seconds, their ragged breathing was the only sound that filled the room.

Then he raised his head to stare down at her. He kissed her lightly then shifted, easing his body from hers. "I'll be right back."

She watched lazily from the bed while he strode nude to the bathroom and returned a moment later with a washcloth.

"Did I hurt you?" he asked in a low voice.

She sat up and reached for the cloth, but he held it out of her reach and then brushed it gently over her skin to clean her.

"No, you didn't hurt me," she returned quietly.

"Why didn't you tell me?"

There was no recrimination, no accusation in his voice.

"I wasn't entirely certain you'd believe me."

"And so you let me ravage you when you should have been handled gently? Made love to and cherished?"

There was genuine regret on his face. Not that he'd made love to her, if she had to guess, but for what he considered his rough treatment of her.

She reached out and touched his face, enjoying the feel of the slight stubble on his jaw. "You didn't hurt me, Theron. It was perfect."

He dropped the cloth on the floor and then framed her face in his hands. "No, it wasn't perfect, but I can make it that way."

He lowered his mouth to hers, kissing her with a tenderness that made her chest ache. Desire fluttered deep within, awakening and unfolding, reaching out.

He took his time, lavishing kisses and caresses over every inch of her body. He murmured endearments and praise, each one landing in a distant region of her heart that she'd reserved only for him.

She soaked up each touch, each word like parched earth starved for water.

And when he cupped her to him, sliding carefully into her wanting body, she knew she'd never loved him more than she did at this moment. For so long she'd waited to have him like this. Focused on her, seeing her, touching her and loving her as she loved him.

This time he urged her to completion before taking his own, and only when she quivered with the last vestiges of her orgasm did he sink deeply within her and hold himself so tightly that she could feel the tension rippling through his body.

He dropped his forehead to hers, their lips just an inch apart as he dragged in deep breaths. She tilted her chin upward so that her nose brushed against his, and then their lips met in a sweet kiss that she felt to her soul.

"Better?" he murmured.

She smiled. "Better."

Theron woke to a sweet female form wrapped tightly around his body. As he opened his eyes and blew a tendril of dark hair from across his lips, he realized that Isabella was more draped across him than wrapped exactly.

Her breasts were pressed to his chest, and one arm was thrown across his body possessively. Her limbs were tangled with his, and she slept soundly, her soft even breathing filling his ears.

Reality was swift to come, and with it, the weight of what he'd done. It wasn't unexpected, this guilt and resignation. He could blame it on passion, lust—a whole host of things—but he knew the truth.

He'd wanted her and he'd taken her, and he'd certainly known what he was about in the heat of the moment. Not once in his thirty-two years had he ever lost all conscious thought when making love, and he wasn't likely to start now.

He hadn't even used a condom, and for the life of him he couldn't dredge up a plausible excuse for his stupidity. It wasn't even that he didn't have one on him at the time. He lived his life in a state of preparedness, and he always had not one, but two condoms in his wallet.

And yet he hadn't stopped to get one, hadn't protected her, and worse, it had been a conscious decision. There was no one to blame in this whole mess but himself, and he damn well knew it.

Carefully, he extricated himself from her warm body. He tensed when she gave a soft little sigh, but then she snuggled back into the covers and settled down once more.

He strode to the bathroom to shower, aware that there would be consequences for his choices. Already he was mentally preparing and making plans. Through it all, there was an odd sense of peace instead of pained resignation.

Still, he dreaded all he had to do. And say.

Wrapping a towel around his waist, he walked out of the bathroom and recovered the clothing he'd worn yesterday. Thankfully he always kept several changes of clothing at his office. That would be his first stop.

As he was pulling on his pants, Isabella stirred, her long hair sliding over her body as she turned and reached out her hand as though seeking him. His body tightened, and arousal hummed through his veins, a soft whisper that grew louder as he stared down at her.

She opened her eyes sleepily, blinking when she saw him. He reached down and touched her cheek, smoothing a stray strand of her hair from her skin.

"There are things I have to take care of, Bella. Important things."

He bent and kissed her softly on the hair, and then without another word, turned and walked out of the bedroom.

Isabella stood beside the bed, wrapped in just the sheet, the ends clutched tightly in her hands. She glanced down at the discarded washcloth, at the evidence of her lost virginity, and felt an odd stirring deep in her chest.

Where had Theron gone? And would he be back? Or was she just the temptation that finally became too much, and he was rushing back to Alannis to make amends?

She closed her eyes and let her chin fall to her chest. She didn't want to be the other woman. She didn't like how it felt, didn't want to be responsible for someone else's sorrow. But why should she place another's over her own?

Feeling quiet sadness settle into her heart, she went into the bathroom to draw a hot bath. Part of her ached—a delicious ache—and she couldn't help but close her eyes and remember every touch, every kiss and caress, the feel of his body sliding over hers.

She soaked until the water grew tepid, and finally, shivering, she rose from the tub and wrapped herself in a towel.

There was a listlessness to her she was unused to. There was too much unknown, unresolved, and she worried that it would remain so.

Growing disgusted with her lethargy, she forced herself to dress. She refused to sit in her hotel room holding her breath like a lovesick fool, waiting for a man who might never return.

First she'd eat and then she'd head to her apartment. Her new furniture had been delivered, and Theron had arranged someone to stock all the necessities. She would go over and make a list of anything else she needed, and then maybe it was time to start thinking about what she was going to do with the rest of her life.

When she opened the door, she immediately came face-to-face with an unsmiling Reynolds. She tried to smile, but failed miserably. Then she sighed. "You might as well come in so I can apologize properly. Then you can accompany me to the hotel restaurant, and then we can go to my new apartment."

Reynolds actually smiled in return as he stepped inside. "*Now,* Ms. Caplan, you're getting the hang of how things are supposed to be done. You make my job a lot easier when I know where you're going and you aren't running off at every turn."

She made a face. "I truly am sorry I've been so much trouble. I think you'll find me a lot more accommodating from now on."

His amusement vanished, and he sobered as he studied her with questioning eyes. "I hope nothing has happened to upset you."

For a moment she said nothing. And then with a halfhearted smile, she gestured toward the door. "Let's go eat. I'm starving."

Theron settled wearily into the chair behind his desk and picked up the phone. Yet again, it would be the middle of the night in Greece, but he needed to have this conversation with Chrysander now so that he could go forward with his plans.

"*Nai,*" Chrysander barked in a sleepy tone.

"I've done a terrible thing," Theron said.

"Theron?" Chrysander asked in a more alert tone. "What the devil are you doing calling at this hour. Again. And what terrible thing are you talking about? Are you in jail?"

Theron had to laugh at that. "No, I'm not in jail."

"Then what is wrong?"

Theron rubbed his hand across his face. "I seduced Isabella."

There was a long pause. "I'm not sure I heard that correctly," Chrysander finally said. Then Theron heard him speak to Marley. "No, *agape mou,* nothing is wrong. Go back to sleep. It's just Theron." Then he came back to Theron. "Give me a moment to take this call in my office. Marley has been up all night with the baby."

Theron waited patiently as he heard shuffling in the background and even a sound like Chrysander kissing Marley. A few moments later, Chrysander's voice bled back over the line.

"Now tell me you didn't do what I think you said you did," Chrysander said dryly.

"I can't do that. It's worse, though."

"Worse than you seducing a young woman under your care? I fail to see how it can get any worse."

"She was a virgin, and I didn't use protection."

Theron cringed even as he said it. It was a conversation that made him sound sixteen years old confessing his sins to his father.

Chrysander cursed and blew out his breath. "Damn it, Theron, what in the world were you thinking? Okay, scratch that. You obviously weren't thinking. That much is established. But what about Alannis? Were you not just telling me and Piers that you were marrying her? What were you doing in bed with Isabella? And *Theos,* without protection. Are you stupid?"

"And you were so careful with Marley?" Theron said defensively.

"I was in a relationship with Marley," Chrysander growled. "I was not engaged to another woman, nor was she someone under my direct care. Theron, this goes beyond stupid."

"I'm not engaged to another woman," Theron said quietly. "I didn't ask her to marry me."

Another stunned silence ensued.

"You better back up and tell me the entire story," Chrysander said wearily. "It's obvious that you've got a huge mess on your hands. Start with the part where you didn't ask Alannis to marry you."

"I couldn't do it," Theron said with a sigh. "I arranged the night, had a party, the ring, the confetti—"

"Confetti? Who the hell has confetti for a marriage proposal?" Chrysander demanded, a thread of amusement in his voice.

"It added to the festive mood," Theron defended. "Everything was there. The moment was there...and I couldn't do it. I had my hand on the ring, the woman staring up at me, and then I let go of the box, and asked her to dance instead. We spent the evening celebrating her visit to New York instead of our impending nuptials."

"So how did this lead to you taking Isabella's virginity? Without protection," he added dryly.

"I've admitted my stupidity. There's no reason to keep beating me over the head with it," Theron said irritably. "It happened after I hauled her out of the strip club."

"You *what?*" Chrysander broke into laughter. "Theron, this is sounding more absurd all the time. Do I even want to know why someone you were supposed to be watching over was in a strip club?"

"It's not important. What's important is that afterward, I seduced Isabella. We slept together. Without protection. She was a virgin. That covers it."

"Yes, I'd say it does," Chrysander said.

There was another long silence and then Chrysander spoke again. "She was under our care. Our father agreed that the Anetakis family would always care for her should something happen to her father. You're going to have to marry her, Theron."

Adrenaline surged in Theron's veins. "I don't *have* to marry her, Chrysander. I'm *going* to marry her."

Fifteen

Isabella shoved aside the heavy curtains draped over the large window facing the street. Her apartment was on the top floor, larger by half than the apartments on the lower levels, and it had a wonderful view of a small park across the street.

There was no shortage of joggers, people out walking dogs, and children supervised by their nannies or mothers. It was a small mecca in the middle of a crowded city where someone could go and enjoy a short escape.

Could she live here knowing the man she loved was close by, married to someone else? On the surface it sounded absurd. In a city this size, she could go an entire lifetime without running into Theron. Except…except he controlled her inheritance and contact would be inevitable.

She sighed. She really did like the apartment, but she wasn't sure she could remain here.

The sound of her door opening didn't alarm her. Reynolds

had been left waiting when she'd only said she'd be a minute. He probably lost patience and was coming to collect her.

Footsteps sounded behind her, and yet she still couldn't tear her gaze away from the scene below. Maybe it was the normalcy of it all—the promise of an ordered existence where agonizing emotions such as love and jealousy or despair didn't dictate her every breath.

Firm hands took hold of her shoulders, skimming upward, eliciting a small gasp from her.

"Bella, *pethi mou,* are you all right? What are you doing here?"

She spun around in surprise and stared up at Theron's worried eyes.

"I went back to your suite and you were gone. I'm beginning to wonder if my life is going to be a study in never finding you where you're supposed to be."

There was a hint of amusement in his voice, but she was puzzled by his words. They made no sense.

"When I called Reynolds and he said you were here, I came right over. But Bella, there is no need of your apartment any longer," he said calmly.

She held up a hand to his chest, almost afraid to touch him. Her head was spinning a mile a minute, but she needed to understand what he was saying, or what he wasn't saying.

"I came to see if it was ready for me to move in," she said simply.

He captured her hand in his and held it in place over his heart. "You won't be needing this apartment, *pethi mou.*"

With his other hand, he dipped into his pocket and drew out a small square box. She stared suspiciously at it as he flipped the lid off and let it fall to the floor. Maneuvering still with the one hand, he turned it over and shook out the velvet jeweler's box. With a few more flips of his fingers, it came open, and a brilliant, sparkling diamond caught the light from the window and flashed in her eyes.

She watched in complete astonishment as he picked up her hand and slid the ring onto her third finger.

"We'll be married as soon as possible," he said matter-of-factly.

She shook her head, sure that she must still be in bed back in her suite—dreaming. "I don't understand," she stammered.

"We must marry," he said again, only this time the emphasis was on the *must*. "You were a virgin…and you could be pregnant," he finished softly. "I didn't think…that is I didn't use protection. For this I am sorry."

No, she wasn't dreaming. In her dreams, her marriage proposal had always been somewhat more romantic. But then she was getting precisely what she wanted. It was hard to argue with that, no matter the motivation behind the proposal.

"Okay," she said quietly.

Relief flashed in his eyes. Had he expected her to argue? Maybe play the martyr and give him a weeping, tragic refusal because he didn't love her?

He pulled her into his arms, but instead of kissing her, he hugged her tightly. "We should go back to your suite. We have arrangements to make. Unless you'd prefer my penthouse? I'm afraid I'm no more settled in this city than you are, but we'll remedy that. We can buy a house. Wherever you like."

She wedged an arm between them and levered herself away. "What about Alannis?"

There was quiet between them finally, and his expression sobered. "She and Sophia are flying back to Greece tomorrow."

Isabella tried to disguise the flinch. She didn't want to think of Alannis's heartbreak or her mother's disappointment. Neither woman had been anything but kind to her. And now she was the femme fatale. It wasn't a very good feeling.

She nodded, not wanting to delve too deeply into Alannis. She was a subject better left alone.

The sparkle of the diamond in the sun drew her gaze back to the gorgeous ring adorning her finger. And then she allowed some of the joy to shine on her like the sun beaming through the window.

With a tentative smile, she looked back up at Theron. "You really want to marry me? Okay, scratch that. Bad question. I'm sure you don't really want to marry me. But you don't have to. Just so you know. I mean the whole idea of putting a ring on my finger just because I was a virgin and we didn't use protection—well, it's archaic. Nobody does that anymore. I mean even if I turned out pregnant, there's nothing to say we'd have to be married—"

He silenced her with his mouth, pressing his lips to hers in a deep, lustful kiss. For several long seconds, all that she heard was the soft smooching sounds of their lips. She went positively boneless.

Finally he pulled away, his eyes glittering. He may not *want* to marry her, but she knew his eyes didn't lie. He wanted *her,* and he definitely desired her. It was a start.

"Now if we're through talking nonsense, let's return to the hotel," he said huskily.

He didn't look any different. Isabella watched Theron from across the sitting room of her suite as he went through a myriad of phone calls. First he'd talked to the person she'd rented the apartment from. Then a few business calls had interceded. Now he was back to talking to God-knew-who about flights and planes, and she wasn't sure what else. Her head was spinning.

Maybe she'd expected him to look…well, she didn't know. Engaged? But then he'd been engaged for several days. Just not to her.

A knock at the door interrupted her moody dissertation on Theron's phone calls. Reynolds, who had been going over plans with Theron, strode to the door and opened it.

Isabella couldn't see who it was with the way Reynolds held the door, but a moment after opening it, he stepped back and glanced over at her.

"Sadie Tilton to see you."

Isabella made a quick motion with her hand for him to let her in. Sadie popped her head around the door, her eyes filled with caution. They lightened as soon as she saw Isabella and she hurried over to where Isabella sat on the couch.

"What's going on?" Sadie hissed. "You sounded so weird when you called."

Isabella didn't say anything but she raised her hand so that Sadie could see. A quick glance around her told her that Theron wasn't paying either of them any attention, so involved was he on the phone.

"Oh my God!" Sadie exclaimed as she pounced on Isabella's hand. "He proposed?"

"Shh, he's on the phone," Isabella murmured. "And yes, well, sorta. He didn't exactly ask. He informed me we were getting married."

Sadie frowned. "Are you happy about it?"

Isabella smiled. "I will be. He's all I've ever wanted."

"What did he say then? And what about Alannis?"

"Not much. Just that he'd taken my virginity, I could be pregnant and we needed to marry."

Sadie winced. "Are you sure you want to marry a guy for those reasons? I mean what about love? Or at least a legitimate reason that doesn't predate this century."

Isabella looked at her friend and sighed. "I can't very well make him fall in love with me if we aren't together, Sadie. Yes, ideally he would love me now, and we'd marry for all the usual reasons, but I have to take what opportunities

I'm given. He feels something for me. That much I know. Something that goes beyond simple lust. He just needs time. But if I don't marry him, he'll marry Alannis, and where does that get me?"

"You're right, you're right," Sadie said in a low voice. "I was just hoping for something more. You've dreamed about this for so long. I wanted it to be perfect for you."

Isabella squeezed Sadie's hand. "It will be perfect. Maybe not yet, but it will be. The day he says *I love you* will make everything leading up to it worth it."

Sadie smiled. "Now that that's all settled, I have to say thank you. You didn't have to do it, but at the same time, I'm so grateful."

Isabella looked at her in puzzlement. "What on earth are you talking about?"

"The apartment, the rent, the account. You know, so I don't have to go back to work at the club."

Isabella shook her head.

Sadie frowned. "You didn't arrange for my apartment to be paid up for the next year?"

"No-o-o...."

The both turned and looked at Theron at the same time.

"Then I don't suppose you also arranged my meeting with Howard," Sadie murmured.

"No, I had no idea," Isabella said softly.

"You've got yourself a good man, Bella. Not that I'm fooling myself by thinking he did it for any other reason than he didn't want you ever going into that place," she said with a grin.

"He is a good man," Isabella agreed as she stared across the room at Theron.

As if sensing her perusal, he lifted his gaze, the phone still held to his ear and looked back at her. His eyes smoldered with quiet intensity. Suddenly all Isabella wanted was for everyone to be gone from her room and for it to be only the two of them.

In his arms, she could forget a lot. Including that she wasn't the one he would have chosen as his wife.

"How about I have Reynolds see you home?" Isabella murmured to Sadie.

For a moment Sadie looked startled but then she followed Isabella's gaze toward Theron and grinned. Sadie leaned forward and hugged Isabella tightly.

"Just don't leave town without letting me know what's going on, okay?"

Isabella hugged her back. "I won't."

Isabella got up and walked over to where Reynolds stood. "You'll see her home?" she asked, though it wasn't a request.

Reynolds looked quickly over at Theron, who evidently heard Isabella because he nodded at Reynolds and made a go gesture with his hand.

Moments later, Isabella closed the door, and for the first time since he'd put his ring on her finger, they were alone. Well, almost. There was still the phone.

Slowly, she walked over to where Theron sat at the desk in front of the window. He looked up, his eyes darkening when she placed her hands on his knees and then straddled him, sliding up against his chest.

He tensed and tried to ward her off as he continued talking, something about figures, finances, hotel plans, blah blah. None of that interested her as much as the possibility of getting Theron naked.

She took the hand he held between them and guided it to her chest, sliding it just inside the neckline of her shirt. He curled his fingers into a fist, as if denying her.

Isabella only smiled and began unbuttoning his shirt from the top down. His voice became noticeably more strained, and he even broke off twice as he seemed to lose his train of thought.

If she were a good fiancée, she'd leave him alone, become invisible while he conducted business and reappear later, but she'd already proven she wasn't the best at suppressing her own wants. Not when it came to Theron.

As she parted the lapels, she leaned forward and pressed her lips to his bare chest. She felt his quick intake of breath, heard his strangled response to whoever it was he was talking to.

She'd give him two more minutes tops. If he resisted beyond then, she'd have to give him credit for being very strong indeed.

Ignoring his disapproving look, she slipped from his lap and went seeking lower, unfastening the button of his pants. Every muscle in his thighs locked and went rigid when her hand caressed his equally rigid erection.

One minute left. Hmm.

She lowered her head as she gently freed him from constraint. When her mouth touched him, she heard his garbled response to whatever the other person on the phone had asked, and then she heard the unmistakable sound of a phone meeting the wall.

She smiled even as he lurched upward, grabbing her under the arms and hauling her into his arms.

A torrent of Greek flew from his mouth as he strode for the bedroom.

"English, Theron," she said with a laugh.

"*Theos,* but what are you trying to do to me?" he demanded as he tossed her onto the bed. "I'll have to ban you from my offices if this is the sort of thing you'll do when I'm trying to conduct business."

She tried to suppress the grin as he tore off his shirt and pants and sent them flying.

"Undress," he said seductively.

She raised an eyebrow. "Isn't that your job?"

He fell forward, landing his hands on either side of her shoulders as he stared down at her. Then he reached for her hands and pulled them over her head, transferring her wrists into one hand so the other was free.

Then he began to unbutton her shirt. His movements were jerky and impatient as he ridded her of every stitch of clothing.

When he was finished, he let go of her hands. "Turn over," he said.

She looked up in confusion.

His fingers roamed down her nakedness even as he urged her over.

"Do as I say, *pethi mou*."

She shivered at the authority in his voice. Maybe she had started this whole thing, but it seemed he intended to finish it.

Carefully she rolled until her belly pressed against the mattress. She tucked her hands high, just over her head as she felt Theron lean down once more.

His fingers danced across the small of her back, and then she realized he was tracing her tattoo. She smiled.

"Do you like it?" she murmured.

"It's driven me crazy since the first day you walked into my office," he muttered. "I've had the most insane urge to throw you down and trace it with my tongue."

"There's nothing stopping you," she said lazily.

"Indeed not."

She jumped and closed her eyes when his warm tongue made contact with her skin. He emblazoned a damp trail over the small of her back and then he pressed a kiss right over her spine.

"The fairy is misleading. You should have had a devil tattooed on you."

She smiled again and rolled over, meeting his smoldering gaze. "And where do you propose this devil go?"

His lips curled into a half smile before he dipped his head and kissed the area right above the soft curls at the juncture of her legs. "Here," he murmured. "Where only I can enjoy it."

"Don't tease me, Theron," she whispered. "I want you so much."

"Then take me, Bella." He spread her legs and covered her

with his body. And suddenly he was inside her, deep and full. "Take all of me," he said hoarsely.

She wrapped arms and legs around him, holding him tight as he filled her again and again. His lips found hers, sweet and warm. She drank from him, took from him, and still she wanted more. She wanted everything he had to give.

This time they came together, an explosion she felt to her very depths. As his body settled comfortably over hers, she sighed in utter contentment.

After a moment he rolled to the side and gathered her in his arms.

"Where did you learn such wickedness, Bella *mou?*" he asked as she snuggled into the crook of his arm and he stroked his fingers over her shoulder.

She rose up, positioning her elbow underneath so she could look at him. "What do you mean?"

"You were a virgin and yet you seduced me as thoroughly as someone with much more experience."

She laughed. "Theron, tell me you aren't one of these men who thinks the presence of a hymen equals complete ignorance on the woman's part."

But then given his antiquated views on honor, and the fact that he was marrying her over that thing called a hymen, perhaps it wasn't such a stretch to believe he thought she should be ignorant of sex.

He looked uncomfortable as he grappled with his answer. "I suppose I thought it unlikely that someone with no experience would be so…"

"Good?" she asked cheekily.

He gave her a look that suggested he wasn't amused by her teasing.

"I never said I wasn't experienced," she said lightly.

He tensed and raised his head to stare at her. "What do you mean by this? Who do you have experience with?"

She laid a hand on his chest. "Now, Theron, stop with the testosterone surge. You're the only man I've ever made love with. Experience can be gained without participation you know."

"As long as you don't ever decide to participate with another man," he said gruffly. "I will teach you everything you need to know."

She grinned. "And maybe as we've previously discussed, there are things I'll teach you, as well."

He yanked her to him, and she landed with a soft thud, her lips a breath away from his.

"Is this so? Well then, Bella *mou,* by all means teach me. I think you'll find me a willing pupil."

Sixteen

Theron reached across the seat and buckled Isabella's belt. She roused sleepily and looked questioningly at him.

"We'll be landing soon," he said. "Then we'll take a helicopter to the island."

She yawned and nodded, trying to knock some of the sleep fog from her mind. "I'm looking forward to meeting Piers, well officially. I've seen him but just once and we didn't speak," she said as she shifted in her seat. "Though it's been so long since I've seen Chrysander, it will be like meeting him for the first time all over again. What's he like?" she asked.

He raised one eyebrow. "What's who like, *pethi mou?*"

"Piers," she said a little grumpily. "You know, the one I just said I hadn't met."

He smiled. "You're not at your best when you first awaken."

She yawned again and just frowned.

"To answer your question, Piers is…well, he's Piers,"

Theron said with a shrug. "He travels the most of any of us now that Chrysander has settled on the island. He's flying in from Rio de Janeiro right now where he's overseeing the building of our new hotel."

"Married or otherwise attached?"

Theron laughed. "Not Piers. He has an aversion to becoming entangled with any female for more than the length of a casual affair."

"Did your mother mistreat him?" Isabella asked dryly.

Theron shook his head. "You, Bella *mou,* have quite a smart wit about you. I'm going to have to think of ways to keep that mouth of yours occupied."

"And Marley?" she asked as the plane began its descent. Already she could see tiny twinkling lights from the ground. "What's she like? I admit, I find it hard to imagine a woman who could so easily subdue a man like Chrysander. He always seemed so…hard."

"It wasn't easy," Theron said, his expression growing serious. "They went through a lot together. Chrysander is lucky to have her."

"So you like her?" Isabella prompted.

Theron nodded. "I like her very much. She's good for him. Softens him just enough."

"She sounds…nice."

"You have nothing to worry about," he soothed. "You'll like them, and they'll like you."

She managed a stiff smile. What she really wanted to ask is whether they'd liked Alannis more. How would they feel about the fact he was marrying someone else? She didn't know how it worked in Theron's family, but would they have expected him to marry Alannis for business reasons?

Theron's hand found hers just a moment before the plane touched down. She was content to let her fingers remain entwined with his as they taxied. A few minutes later, they were disembarking the plane, and Theron was urging her toward a waiting helicopter.

"If I had thought, I would have arranged for us to stay on the mainland overnight so that you could see the beauty of the island from the air in daytime," Theron said as they boarded.

"I'll see it on the way back, right?" she said with a smile as Theron settled beside her.

He nodded as the engines whirred too loudly for conversation any longer.

The ride across the inky darkness was a little disconcerting, and then Theron pointed to a flash of light in the distance. She strained forward, leaning over him as they drew closer to the source of the light.

A few moments later, the helicopter lowered onto the well-lit helipad, and the pilot gestured to Theron when it was safe to get out.

Theron opened the door and ducked out, then reached back to help Isabella from the seat. His hand over her back, urging her low, he hurried across the concrete landing area toward the lighted gardens leading to the house.

As they approached the entryway, a man stepped from the door. Even from a distance, Isabella recognized him as Chrysander. He smiled, and she relaxed, even managing a smile in return.

"Isabella, how you've grown, even since your graduation," he said as he enfolded her in a hug.

"Thanks for making me feel like a girl who just shed braces and training bras," she said dryly as she pulled away.

Chrysander stared at her in obvious surprise and then burst into laughter. "My apologies. You're far from that as Theron has no doubt found out."

She couldn't prevent the flush that worked its way up her cheeks.

"Why don't you stop trying to find things to say and let us

through," Theron said balefully. "Before we have to extricate both feet from your mouth."

Chrysander chuckled and gestured for them to pass. "Marley is waiting in the living room. She's anxious to meet you, Isabella."

He moved past her and Theron to call out in Greek to the man collecting her and Theron's luggage from the helicopter.

Theron took her arm and they walked inside. The house was absolutely beautiful, and she couldn't wait to see it in full light. And the beach. She could smell the salt air and even hear the waves crashing in the distance, but she wanted to see it and dig her toes into the sand.

A small, dark-haired woman who was bouncing a blanket-wrapped bundle in her arms was standing in the living room next to the couch. Isabella offered a tentative smile when she looked up.

"Theron!" she exclaimed as she walked in their direction.

Theron smiled broadly and caught her and the baby up in his arms. "How are my favorite sister and my nephew?"

"I'm your only sister," she said.

"Marley, I'd like you to meet Isabella, my fiancée," he said as he turned to Isabella.

Marley smiled, her blue eyes flashing in welcome. "I'm very happy to meet you, Isabella."

"Please, call me Bella," she offered. "And I'm very glad to meet you, as well."

"Has Piers arrived?" Theron asked with a frown as he surveyed the room.

"He's coming," Marley said. "He left to go change when we heard the helicopter. We've held a late dinner for you and Isabella."

Just then a tall, dark-haired man entered the room. He was easily the tallest of the three brothers, a little slighter than Chrysander but a bit more broad in the shoulders than Theron.

Where Theron and Chrysander had golden-brown eyes, Piers's were dark, nearly black. His skin tone was darker as well, as though he spent a great deal of time in the sun.

His expression was bland as he looked at Theron. "There you are." He glanced over at Isabella. "And this must be the bride-to-be?"

"One of the many it would appear," Isabella said, refusing to dodge the inevitable awkwardness of the situation.

Piers's eyebrows drew together at her bluntness then he cocked one and offered what Isabella suspected was as close to a smile as he got. "I like her, Theron. She has spirit."

Theron didn't look disquieted by her outburst, but then he seemed resigned to her mouth, as he'd put it.

Chrysander moved to his wife's side and put an arm around her. "Want me to put him down so that we can eat?"

"If he'll go down," Marley said wearily. "Colic," she said with a grimace as she handed the baby to Chrysander. "We've been up with him for the last two weeks. I just hope you can sleep through it."

Chrysander brushed his lips across her forehead. "Don't worry, *agape mou*. I'll sit with him until he settles. You go eat and then I want you to get some rest."

Isabella's heart melted at the look of love in Chrysander's eyes. She wanted that. Wanted it badly. It was all she could do not to sigh as Marley smiled back at him, her eyes glowing. The look of a woman who knew she was loved.

Then Marley looked at Isabella, and she cocked her head to the side as if studying her. Isabella quickly looked away, hoping she hadn't betrayed herself in that moment. It was bad enough that she knew the truth about her engagement. She had no wish for anyone else to know she had schemed her way into Theron's life.

"Come, let's go into the dining room," Marley said.

Dinner was laid-back with casual conversation. Marley

asked general questions about Isabella, her likes and interests. Piers remained quiet, his eyes following the conversation as he ate, and more than once, Isabella found him staring at her as if he were peeling back the layers of her skin.

It was a relief when Chrysander rejoined them and the conversation shifted to business. Even Piers shed his reserve and entered the fray as they argued and debated.

Marley caught Isabella's gaze, rolled her eyes and then motioned for Isabella to follow her from the table. The men didn't even notice when both women slipped away.

"Would you like to take a walk down to the beach?" Marley asked. "It's so beautiful by moonlight, and it's been awhile since Dimitri has settled down before two in the morning."

Isabella smiled. "I'd love it. I can't wait to see everything in daylight. It's beautiful just from what I can see."

They stepped through the sliding glass doors, and Marley led her down a stone walkway. The sounds of the ocean grew louder and then the pathway gave way to sand. Marley stopped and shed her shoes and urged Isabella to do the same.

"Oh, it's gorgeous," Isabella breathed when they walked closer to the water.

The sky was clear and littered with stars, carelessly strewn across the sky like someone playing jacks. The moon was high overhead, shimmering and reflecting off the dark waters.

"This is my favorite place in the world," Marley said softly. "It's amazing, like my own little corner of paradise."

"I don't think I've ever seen anything so beautiful."

Isabella walked to the edge of the wet sand and waited for another wave to roll in. Then she stepped into the foaming surf, loving the tickle of water over her toes.

"I told you we would find them here," Chrysander said in an amused voice. "My wife is forever escaping to her beach."

Isabella turned to see Theron and Chrysander standing,

hands stuffed into their pants as they watched the two women. She couldn't discern their expressions in the darkness.

"Come, Bella," Theron said. "Let's leave the two love-birds. You must be tired from our long trip."

Marley smiled at Isabella as she walked past on her way to Theron. He held his hand out to her as she neared, and she slid her fingers into his.

He brought them to his lips and pressed a gentle kiss against her knuckles. Isabella relaxed for the first time. It would be easy if Theron acted as though he wanted to marry her, almost as though he felt something beyond lust and desire. And maybe he did. Did he? Could he love her?

She let him pull her back onto the stone walkway toward the house.

"They seem so in love," she said when she and Theron stepped inside the door.

Theron nodded. "They have quite a story. I'll tell it to you sometime. Right now, however, I'm only wanting a bed and a soft pillow."

She laughed softly and ran her hand up his arm. "There are parts of my anatomy that make for a good pillow."

His lips firmed for just a moment, and he glanced up at her, his expression indecipherable. "I think it would be best if we kept separate bedrooms here."

She recoiled, her head drawing away in confusion. "I don't understand. Why wouldn't we share a bedroom? We're engaged."

He pulled her into his arms. "Yes, we are, *pethi mou*. And as such, I'd show you the respect you're due by not flaunting our sexual relationship in front of my brother and his wife. It's enough that he knows I took your virginity, but I won't draw anymore undue attention to you."

Hurt and humiliation hit her hard in the chest. "He knows? You told him?"

Theron blinked in surprise. "It is my shame to bear, Isabella. Not yours."

She closed her eyes and looked away. So Chrysander, and by default, Marley, did know that Theron was only marrying her out of some outdated sense of honor.

"I'll go up to my room then," she said quietly. "I assume my stuff will be there. I can find my way."

"Bella," he called as she started for the stairs.

She turned and stared bravely at him, determined not to show any emotion.

"I didn't do this to hurt you."

She smiled. A tremulous, hesitant smile, but she pulled it off. "I know, Theron. I know."

Then she turned and headed up the stairs in search of her room.

Seventeen

Isabella stared up at the ceiling, her hands behind her head. Sleep had eluded her, as she'd slept for most of the flight over. She'd opened her window before going to bed, and the sounds of the waves lured her.

A look at the bedside clock told her she'd lain awake for hours. With a resigned sigh, she tossed aside the covers and swung her legs over the side of the bed. If she were quiet, she could walk down to the beach and watch the sun rise. It wasn't as if she was ever going to sleep. She was too tightly wound. Too restless.

The air was warm coming in the window, so she dressed in a pair of shorts and T-shirt. Not bothering with sandals, she slipped out of her room into the darkened hallway and crept down the stairs.

The house was quiet and cloaked in darkness as she made her way through the living room. She stepped onto the patio and breathed in the warm, salty air. Briefly closing her eyes, she let the breeze blow her hair from her face, and then she stepped onto the stone path leading to the sand.

The skies were already starting to lighten to the east, the horizon going pale lavender as the morning star shone bright, a single diamond against velvet.

The water was calm, lapping gently onto the shore, spreading foam in its wake. She walked down the beach, letting the waves rush over her feet as the world went gold around her.

A distance from the house, she saw a large piece of driftwood. Marley's seat, Chrysander had called it laughingly. She settled gingerly on the aged wood and stared at the beautiful scene before her. Truly she'd never experienced anything like it.

Unsure of just how long she sat there, basking in the dawn, she picked herself up and headed back toward the house. Sand covered her feet and she paused at the entryway to the stone path cutting through the garden to clean it off.

Voices carried from a short distance away, and she smiled. Theron was up. She could hear his soft laughter. Marley too and apparently Chrysander.

She started up the staggered steps when she heard her name. A surge of excitement hit her. Were they discussing the wedding? She took another step forward but faltered with Theron's next words.

He sounded…resigned. What was it he said? She glanced quickly over the hedge lining the walkway to the stone retaining wall surrounding the patio. There was a lattice wall that afforded the patio privacy and was covered with leafy greenery.

She strained to hear the conversation and then making a quick decision, she hiked her leg over the hedge and hurried to the retaining wall where she hunkered just below the breakfast area where the others were gathered.

As she listened to Theron's low voice explain the entire story to his brother and Marley, she turned so her back pressed against stone and slowly she slid until she sat with knees hunched to her chest.

Hearing her teasing and blatant flirtation from the mouth of someone else made it sound harsher, less earnest than it had been. She listened as he outlined his confusion over his desire for her and his desire to make Alannis his wife.

She put her head down on her arms. She wanted to close her ears, but she couldn't. This was the hard truth, and she'd done all that he said. Her only comfort was that he made it seem as though she hadn't done it purposely, as if she hadn't planned to seduce him. No, he still blamed himself for that.

And then the statement that hit her square in the gut, stealing her breath—and her hope.

"I wanted...I wanted what you and Marley have found," Theron admitted to Chrysander. "I wanted a wife and children—a family, a life with a woman I cared about. I had it all mapped out. Marriage to Alannis, a comfortable life. It all flew out the window so fast that my head is still spinning."

No longer able to stand the pain his words caused, she vaulted up, staggering down the slight incline. She landed on one of the smaller walkways that circled the gardens and nearly ran headlong into Piers.

He gripped her arms to steady her and stared down with piercing eyes.

"I'm reminded of the saying that eavesdroppers rarely hear good of themselves," Piers said.

"No," she said in a small voice. "It would appear they don't."

Something that might have been compassion softened his expression. She turned pleading eyes up to meet his gaze. "Don't tell him I heard. You already know everything. Everyone knows. There's no reason to make Theron feel any worse."

"And you?" Piers asked. "What about you, Bella?"

"It would appear I have a lot to fix," she said quietly.

She shook herself from his hands and hurried through the

garden around to the back entrance. She stopped at the door and stared for a long moment at the helipad. Then she walked inside, making sure she wasn't seen as she mounted the stairs.

When she got to her room, she closed the door and leaned heavily against it even as a tear slid down her cheek.

Theron didn't love her. He couldn't. Because he loved Alannis. And because of Isabella, his chance of finding the happiness he wanted was ruined. Taken away by her selfishness and single-minded pursuit of *her* wants and *her* needs.

She took a long hard look at herself, and she didn't like what she saw very much.

Loving someone shouldn't hurt so much, shouldn't be so destructive. Was she nothing more than a spoiled rich girl unwilling to accept that she couldn't have what she most wanted?

And then in a moment of sudden clarity, of anguish and realization, she knew that she had to let Theron go. She wasn't what he wanted. Alannis was. Isabella didn't even want to know the hurt and disappointment that the other girl had endured. What had Theron told her? That he'd been unfaithful?

Theron was bearing the brunt of Isabella's actions—the dishonor. When the blame was solely hers.

He isn't yours to keep.

The single thought echoed and simmered through her mind. And she knew it was true, no matter how much it hurt, how much it made her heart ache and pulse.

She bowed her head, allowing the tears to slither down her cheeks, falling to the floor beneath her. For a moment she let herself cry and then she raised her head, determined to regain her composure. She had to figure a way out of this mess.

First of all, she couldn't let Theron know that she'd overheard his conversation. He would feel hugely guilty. He'd want to do the right thing—according to him.

But this time—this time *she* was going to do the right thing. Wiping at her face with the back of her hand, she went to her bags and dug for her handbag. Sophia had given her a card with her address and telephone number, had invited her to visit her in Greece whenever she resumed her plans to travel to Europe. Never mind that those plans had revolved around Theron and had been abandoned when Theron had relocated to New York.

Next she needed to locate a helicopter service, preferably one that wasn't on Chrysander's payroll. Not exactly easy when she was on an island, in a country where she didn't speak the language.

Hopefully Chrysander had internet in his office, or a directory, or something….

And then she had to talk to Theron.

The worst part is that she had to pretend that she'd never heard what Theron said. She had to smile and act as if nothing was wrong. As if her heart weren't breaking.

Isabella checked her watch as Marley cleared the dishes away after the light lunch she'd served on the patio. Isabella deserved an Oscar award, surely, because she'd smiled and laughed, responded when appropriate. Even as she cracked and broke on the inside.

Piers had watched her, his gaze finding her often, probing and assessing. When the eating was finally finished, it was all Isabella could do not to sigh in relief. Now she had a little time to talk to Theron before the helicopter would arrive to pick her up.

"Theron," she said as he stood from the table. "Could I speak to you? Alone?" she added with an apologetic look in the others' direction.

Piers's brow furrowed, and he gave her an inquisitive look as he stood. She avoided his scrutiny.

"Of course, *pethi mou*. Why don't we go for a walk on the beach?" Theron suggested.

She avoided his hand when he extended it, and instead, she

brushed past him and to the walkway. He followed her down to the water, and this time, the water failed to soothe her. It mocked her with its false serenity.

The sheer beauty of the brilliant blue, stretching outward seeking the distant skyline, taunted her. Below the surface, there were ugly things. Things that never saw the light, that never disturbed the pristine surface that sparkled in the sun.

When she stopped, her feet sinking into the sand, Theron's hands closed over her shoulders.

"What's the matter, Bella *mou?*" he asked in his deep timbre. "You seem sad today."

She turned in his arms, finally finding the courage to face him. "There are things I need to tell you, Theron."

His expression sobered. "What things?"

She broke away and took a step down the beach before turning again. "The whole reason I planned to travel to London this summer was because I thought you would be there."

Confusion clouded his eyes, and he started to open his mouth. She silenced him quickly with an outstretched hand. "Please, don't say anything. Let me finish. There's a lot I need to say, and I won't be able to finish if you start asking questions."

He hesitated and then nodded.

"When I arrived in New York and learned that you would be remaining there permanently, I changed my plans on the fly, opting to rent an apartment I didn't really want and invented a host of other reasons to throw me into contact with you."

Her hands closed over her arms, and she rubbed up and down despite the heat that prickled over her skin.

"I knew you planned to propose to Alannis. I knew you'd planned your life with another woman. I was determined to try and seduce you away from her."

He sucked in his breath and opened his mouth again, but she stared at him so hauntingly that he quieted again. Only the glitter in his eyes gave the impression of what he must be thinking.

"I pursued you relentlessly. I'd even planned to crash your engagement party but arrived too late. That was the reason that Marcus was in my room. He'd followed me home in the rain when I took off on foot to try and stop your proposal."

His lips thinned, and he turned his face away to stare at the ocean.

"I thought I'd lost you, but then you came to the strip club, and then we made love in my suite. The next day you told me we had to be married, and I knew that you felt you'd dishonored me. I knew you didn't love me, but I was determined to have the chance to make you love me, so I said yes. I let you say all those things. Because in the end I'd have the one thing I wanted most. You."

She found his gaze again even as tears glided down her cheeks. "You see, Theron, I've loved you since I was a little girl. I thought it was infatuation, that it would go away, but each time I saw you, my love grew until I knew I had to try. I couldn't just live my life standing on the outside of my dream, never giving us a chance."

She took in a deep steadying breath, her quiet sobs shaking her shoulders. "But I was wrong. And I'm sorry. I ruined things for you and Alannis."

Quiet lay between them. Theron stood stock-still, his hands shoved into his pockets.

"You don't love me," she said in a remarkably steady voice.

She hadn't intended it to be a question, but it felt like a plea from the depths of her soul. And then he turned to face her again and her hopes shriveled and died. There were a host of things reflected in those golden eyes. Confusion, anger, but not love. Never love.

Quickly, before he could react, she stepped forward and leaned up to kiss him on the cheek. "I hope someday you can forgive me."

She slid her ring off her finger then slipped her hand inside his. Without another word, she turned and ran back up the path to the house.

"Bella! Bella!" Theron shouted after her.

She brushed past Chrysander at the top of the pathway, ignoring his hands as they reached out to steady her.

"Isabella!" he called.

She swallowed the sob caught in her throat and ran inside. The helicopter would be here soon. Her bag was where she left it, at the doorway leading out the back of the house, past the pool and to the helipad.

She grabbed it and after a look back at the house, she hurried out to wait on the helicopter.

Eighteen

Theron stared at the ring resting in his palm then at Isabella's retreating back. He simply couldn't comprehend everything she'd admitted. It sounded too far-fetched.

Had she really loved him for so long? It didn't seem possible.

He watched as Chrysander slowly walked down the path toward him. He came to a stop a few feet in front of Theron.

"Trouble?" he asked.

"You could say that," Theron murmured, still trying to come to grips with all she'd told him.

"She seemed pretty upset," Chrysander said.

Theron closed his fist around the ring. "She gave me my ring back."

Chrysander arched an eyebrow in surprise. "Did she say why? It's easy for anyone with half a brain to see she's crazy about you."

Theron cocked his head then shook it. "She just told me the craziest story. I don't even know what to make of it."

"Care to share?"

Theron opened his hand to see the ring still lying there. It looked all wrong. It should be on Isabella's finger. She should be glowing with happiness, not staring at him with tearstained cheeks.

"She said she's been in love with me since she was a girl," Theron said slowly. "And that her trip to New York was because I was there." He looked up at his brother. "She said the entire reason she planned to go to London was because she thought I'd be there."

Chrysander smiled. "Sounds like a determined girl."

Theron nodded. "That's not all. She seduced *me*."

This time Chrysander laughed. "Now this I have to hear."

Theron quickly told Chrysander everything that had happened since the day Isabella had walked into his office, now armed with the knowledge of what she'd really been doing. It all seemed so much clearer now. The sultry teasing, the apartment hunting, the shopping.

Chrysander remained silent for a moment. "So, are you angry?" he finally asked.

Theron gave him a strange look. "Angry?"

"You wanted to marry Alannis. Isabella prevented that."

Theron shook his head. "Isabella didn't prevent that, Chrysander. I did. I didn't propose, and Isabella was nowhere near me when that happened."

"Okay, so what are you then?"

"Flattered? Overwhelmed? Completely and utterly gobsmacked?"

Chrysander grinned. "That about covers it."

"My God, Chrysander. She's so gorgeous. She lights up the entire room when she walks in. She makes me crazy. Absolutely and completely crazy. She could have any man she wanted. And she wants *me*."

"Enough to drive you to your knees, isn't it? Finding the love of a good woman. They can certainly tie you in knots."

"I love her," Theron whispered. "All this time, I've been so focused on wanting a wife and children, wanting to settle down with the picture-perfect family, and perfection has been staring me in the face all along."

Chrysander smiled. "Why are you telling me all this? It would seem you have a very upset young lady who seems determined to do what's best for you, whether you like it or not."

Theron frowned and clenched his fist around the ring. "Fool-headed, stubborn…" He shook his head and stalked up the pathway, Chrysander falling in behind him.

They were halfway to the house when Chrysander stopped. Theron turned around to see him frown.

"You hear that?" Chrysander asked.

Theron strained to hear. In the distance, he heard the unmistakable sound of an approaching helicopter. "Did you call for the helicopter?"

Chrysander shook his head. "One wasn't scheduled until Piers's departure tomorrow."

Both men hurried up the pathway then cut left to circle the gardens to take the shorter route to the helipad. Even before the helipad came into view, they saw the chopper descend.

"That's not one of ours," Chrysander said grimly.

Chrysander broke into a run, and Theron followed. If Chrysander was worried then so was Theron. But when they rounded the corner and he saw Isabella standing as the helicopter door opened, his blood froze.

"Isabella!" Theron shouted.

She didn't even turn around. She wouldn't have heard him over the roar of the blades.

Chrysander waved frantically to the pilot, and Theron raced ahead of him, trying to reach Isabella in time. He watched helplessly as the door closed behind her, and then, as he reached the edge of the concrete, the helicopter lifted off.

The draft blew his hair and clothing, but he stood, waving his arms in an effort to gain her attention. The helicopter rose higher and then headed in the direction of the mainland.

Chrysander cursed as Theron stood there frozen.

"I've got to find out where she's going," Theron said as he turned back to the house.

Ahead, Marley and Piers came out the back door, Marley in the protective arm of Piers.

"What's going on?" Piers shouted.

Theron strode past him and Marley while Chrysander hung back. He tore up the stairs and into Isabella's room only to find her things gone. There was no note, no hint of where she'd gone.

He ran back down, finding the others in the living room. Chrysander was on the phone trying to track down the pilot service and figure out a way to hold Isabella when she landed.

Piers approached him, a grim expression on his face.

"There's something you should know."

Theron looked sharply at him. "What?"

"This morning, Isabella was on the beach early. I found her on the other side of the patio, visibly upset by something she'd overheard in your conversation with Chrysander and Marley. She begged me not to say anything. She said she didn't want you to feel any worse."

Theron closed his eyes as he remembered waxing on about what he wanted. When what he wanted had been in front of his nose all along.

"I'm a damn fool," he muttered.

"No arguments here," Piers said with a wry smile. "The question is, what are you going to do to get her back?"

Isabella hadn't considered the repercussions of landing a helicopter on the estate of what appeared to be an extremely wealthy, Greek family. As soon as they settled on the ground, they were surrounded by a dozen security guards. All carrying guns.

So maybe this wasn't her best idea.

The door was wrenched open, and she found herself staring into the grim face of one of the gunmen. He barked out something in Greek, and Isabella stared helplessly back at him.

"I only speak English," she said.

"What do you want? Why are you here?" he asked in heavily accented English.

She took a deep breath and tried not to stare at the muzzle of the gun which was precariously close to her nose.

"I'm here to see Alannis Gianopolous. It's important."

"Your name," he demanded.

"Isabella Caplan."

He lifted a small wire and released a torrent of Greek into what she assumed was a microphone. A few moments later, he lowered the gun and took a step backward.

"This way please, Ms. Caplan."

He even reached a hand in to help her down. A few moments later, he escorted her inside the palatial estate that was situated on a cliff overlooking the ocean. In any other circumstance, she would have spared a moment of envy for such a gorgeous place.

"Isabella, my dear!" Sophia exclaimed as soon as Isabella was inside. She took hold of Isabella and kissed her on either cheek. "What on earth are you doing here? And where is Theron?"

Isabella looked down for a moment and then back up at the older woman. "I need to speak with Alannis. It's very important."

Sophia frowned slightly, concern filling her eyes. "Of course. Is everything all right?"

Isabella offered her a shaky smile. "No, but it will be."

"Wait here. I'll get Alannis for you," Sophia said.

Isabella walked to the huge glass window that overlooked the steep drop-off to the ocean. Alannis even lived in a perfect spot. Close to Chrysander and Marley. They could all be one big, happy family after Alannis married Theron.

"Isabella?" Alannis's soft voice filled the room.

Isabella turned to see the other girl staring at her, clear confusion written in her dark eyes.

"Mama said you wanted to see me."

Isabella gathered her courage and crossed the room to stand in front of Alannis.

"I came to apologize and to right a wrong."

Alannis frowned harder. "I don't understand."

Isabella took a deep breath. "I set out to break up you and Theron. I knew he wanted to marry you, but I've been in love with him forever, and I wanted him. I never stopped to think about what he wanted or that I was hurting two people in the process. You and him."

"But—" Alannis began.

"He wants to marry you," Isabella continued on, cutting her off. "You're who he wants. Go to him, Alannis. The helicopter is waiting to take you to the island. He'll be glad to see you. I've ended things with him. I gave him back his ring. Make sure he gives you a different one. You deserve a fresh start. One not tainted by me. Make him do it right, with all the romance and fuss you deserve."

Tears filled Isabella's eyes again. "I'm sorry I hurt you," she said. "I hope you'll be happy."

She turned to walk back out of the house.

"Isabella, wait," Alannis called. "You don't understand."

All Isabella understood is that if she didn't get out soon, she was going to come completely unraveled. She just prayed the taxi would be waiting as she'd arranged.

"Please show me out," she choked out to the security

guard who'd escorted her inside. "I have a taxi waiting out front."

As soon as the guard opened the front door, Isabella hurried down the drive toward the wrought iron gate. They opened automatically as she neared, and to her relief, a taxi waited outside on the street.

"The airport," she said as she climbed in. As she pulled away, she saw Alannis waving to her to stop. Isabella ignored her, turning away.

No one had ever told her doing the right thing would hurt so much.

"How long can it possibly take for the damn pilot to get out here?" Theron demanded as he ran his hand through his hair for the tenth time in an hour.

Frustration beat at him. He was stuck here on the island until Chrysander's pilot could come out. Now, finally, he was supposedly on his way.

Chrysander put down the phone and turned to Theron. "Isabella's pilot took her to the Gianopolous estate."

Theron stared at him in utter confusion. "Why on earth would she have gone to see Alannis? I had no idea she even knew where she lived."

"She's trying to make things right," Marley said softly. "First with you and now with Alannis."

He dug for his phone to retrieve Alannis's number. If he could reach Alannis before Isabella left then he could have her detained until he could go after her himself.

Chrysander handed Theron his phone, and Theron hastily punched in the numbers. A few seconds later, Sophia answered the phone.

"Sophia, thank goodness. Has Isabella been by there? What? She left in a taxi?" Sophia filled him in on where

Bella was headed then he hung up and turned to Chrysander. "Now where is your damn pilot?"

It had been impossible for Isabella to purchase a ticket leaving the country anytime soon. All the outgoing flights for the next few hours were booked. In the end, she'd gone to the charter service counter, plunked down her credit card, which she hoped was as platinum as the name stated, and hired a private jet to fly her to London.

At least she was on board now, waiting as the jet was fueled and was placed in the queue for takeoff. Exhaustion seeped into her bones. Not sleeping the night before coupled with the emotionally draining day had taken it all out of her.

She leaned her head back against the seat and closed her eyes. She heard shuffling in the distance and assumed it was the pilot, but then warm lips pressed gently to hers, and her eyes flew open.

Theron drew away, cupping her face in his hands as she stared at him in astonishment. He looked…well, he looked bedraggled. His clothing was dusty and rumpled, his hair was in disarray, and his golden eyes burned with feverish intensity.

Before she could say anything, he kissed her again, this time foregoing the gentleness of before. He dragged her to him, kissing her until she was left completely and utterly breathless.

Then he pulled away and uttered a command in Greek directed at the cockpit. To her increasing shock, the plane began to move. With Theron in it.

"Theron, wait," she protested. "This plane is going to London. You can't just leave here. What about Alannis? And your family?"

He pulled her out of her seat, maneuvered to the couch, then pulled her down onto his lap.

"Shouldn't we be in our seatbelts for takeoff?" she asked dumbly, still unable to comprehend that he was here.

"I'll catch you if there is any unexpected turbulence," he said silkily. "Now that you can't run anywhere and I have you all to myself, you'll have to listen to every word I'm about to say."

Her eyes rounded, and her mouth fell open. He traced her lips with his finger then pulled her down to replace his finger with his mouth.

"Foolish, impetuous, beautiful, frustrating woman," he murmured. "If you think you're going to get rid of me after you've hooked me and reeled me in, then you have another think coming, Bella *mou*."

Hope stuttered and made a soft pitter-patter in her chest. She stared at him unsure of what to say. So many things raced through her mind that she was absolutely speechless.

Then he rotated, sliding her off his lap and onto the seat next to him. He got to the floor on one knee and took her hand in his.

"I love you, my beautiful Isabella. I adore you. I can't imagine my life without you. Will you marry me and make me the happiest man alive?"

He slid the ring that she'd given him back on her finger. Then he leaned down and kissed her knuckle.

"This was never another woman's ring, *pethi mou*. I never gave Alannis a ring, and the one I intended for her was replaced by this one. I chose it for you. I never asked her to marry me. I was yours from the day you walked into my office. You turned my world upside down, and it's never been set to rights."

"You didn't propose?" she croaked around the swell of tears knotting her throat.

He looked back at her solemnly. "I would have never made love to you belonging to another woman. I intended to propose the night of the party. I had the ring. The moment was arranged. But all I could see was you. All I wanted was you. The morning after we made love, I went to see Alannis. I told her that I was going to marry you."

Isabella's face fell. Theron smiled and touched her cheek. "How tenderhearted you are, *agape mou*. Alannis isn't in love with me and is in fact, quite anxious for me to find you and put this ring back on your finger."

"She's not? You're not? In love with her, I mean?"

She closed her eyes and shook her head, sure she had to be dreaming.

"I'm in love with *you,*" he said softly. "Only you."

"But I heard what you told Chrysander, about you wanting what he and Marley had, a family, a wife. I don't fit into that anywhere," she said bitterly.

"What I want is you," he said simply. "Everything that I ever wanted, what I was so restless for and hoping to find was staring me in the face. I think I knew it that first day you came into my office. I saw that tattoo and it drove me crazy. I wanted to strip every piece of your clothing off so I could see more of it. But I had already started things rolling with Alannis. I fought my attraction to you because I was supposed to be acting as your guardian, not trying to think of ways to get you out of your clothing."

She raised a shaking hand to his face and cupped her palm to his cheek. He closed his eyes and leaned into her touch. Then he turned so he could press his lips to her fingers.

"Marry me, Bella."

"You want to marry me even if I don't want children right away?" she challenged.

"I have a feeling you'll keep me far too busy to think of children anytime soon," he said with an amused smile. He leaned in and kissed her again, his lips melting warm and sweet over hers. "We have all the time in the world, my precious love. Just promise me that we'll have it together."

She was sure that her smile lit up the entire universe as she stared back at him in awe.

"I love you, too," she whispered. "So much."

He sobered for a moment as he cupped her face lovingly. His expression serious, he said in a quiet voice, "You could already be pregnant. Will it upset you very much if you are?"

She grinned, her heart lightening with every breath. "I'm not pregnant."

"Oh, then you've already…it's that time of the…"

"No," she said with a slight laugh. "I'm on birth control."

His brows came together in confusion and then he glared at her, but there was no heat in his scowl. "You little minx."

"Are you angry that I didn't tell you when you informed me before that we were to be married?" she asked a little nervously.

"If you can forgive my dimwitted actions and the fact that I didn't give you the most romantic proposal before, then I can forgive you for effectively capturing me, hook, line and sinker."

"Yes," she said as she threw her arms around him.

He laughed. "Yes, what, *pethi mou?*"

"Yes, I'll marry you. I love you so much."

He stood and swept her into his arms. She blinked in surprise when she realized that she'd completely missed their takeoff.

"Now, if that's settled, why don't you and I go join the mile high club," he said wickedly.

She smiled as he carried her into the small bedroom in the back of the plane, her heart overflowing with sweet, unending joy.

And as they came together in body and soul, they whispered their love again and again.

Epilogue

The bride—and the groom—showed up to their wedding bare-footed. Theron stood on the beach of Anetakis Island waiting next to the priest as Chrysander escorted Isabella to him.

She was dressed in a bikini top, and a floral sarong floated delicately down her legs. Her toenails—which Theron had painted himself in a night full of decadence—shone a bright pink. An ankle bracelet caught the sun and shimmered above her foot, and Theron knew that it was his name engraved in the small silver band.

His gaze traveled upward to the diamond teardrop belly ring that he too had purchased and delighted in putting on her. But what took his breath away was her radiant smile. Just for him.

She was so beautiful she made his chest ache.

Piers stood to Theron's left, having flown in again for the wedding. Alannis and Sophia both were standing on the bride's side next to Marley.

There was a festive air, and everyone wore broad smiles. He could even detect the glimmer of tears in the women's eyes.

And then he reached out and took Isabella's hand, pulling her to him. It didn't matter that the vows weren't spoken, or that the priest cleared his throat cautiously. He simply had to kiss her.

Their lips met in a heated rush, soft against hard, sweet against salt. When he finally pulled away to allow the priest to officiate, tears shone in Isabella's eyes.

There was an odd catch in Theron's throat as he recited his vows. The words carried on the breeze, firm and clear.

Finally they were pronounced man and wife, and she became his.

There was much dancing on the beach, and later they moved to the gardens. Sophia and Alannis took great delight in teaching both Marley and Isabella traditional Greek dances while the men looked on, their smiles indulgent.

Later the helicopter came and whisked Theron and Isabella away to the bridal suite he'd arranged, a cottage on a cliff overlooking the sea.

He carried her to bed, where she whispered she had one last wedding gift for him.

Intrigued, he reared back as she untied the sarong and pulled it from underneath her.

"Do you remember telling me I should get another tattoo?" she asked with a mischievous glint.

His brow furrowed. "You didn't. Bella, tell me you didn't go to some tattoo parlor alone and undergo pain to get another tattoo."

"I didn't go alone. Marley went with me."

"And does Chrysander know this?" Theron asked incredulously.

Isabella laughed. "He might have had a thing or two to say when he barged in after us."

Theron muttered in Greek as he shook his head.

She hooked her thumbs in her bikini bottom and slowly, sensuously worked it down. There just above the juncture of her legs, right in the center, a straight line down from her belly ring, was an angel holding a pitchfork.

Theron couldn't contain his chuckle. Then he leaned down and brushed his lips across the design. "My own little demon angel," he said as he worked downward with his mouth.

* * * * *

THE TYCOON'S
SECRET AFFAIR

BY
MAYA BANKS

To Dee, who loved Piers from the start

One

Jewel paused just outside the perimeter of the outdoor bar and stared over the sand-covered floor to the blazing torches lining the walkway down to the beach.

Music played softly, a perfect accompaniment to the clear, star-strung night. In the distance, the waves rolled in harmony with the sultry melody. Soft jazz. Her favorite.

It was pure chance that had directed her to this tiny island paradise. A vacated seat on a plane, a bargain ticket price and only five minutes to decide. And here she was. A new place, a vow to take a few days for herself.

Not being completely impulsive, the first thing she'd done when she'd arrived was to find a new temporary job, and as luck would have it, had learned that the owner of the opulent Anetakis hotel was going to be in temporary residence here and needed an assistant. Four weeks. A perfect amount of time to spend in paradise before she moved on.

The opportunity had almost been too good to be true. Along with a generous salary, she'd also been given a room at the hotel. It had the makings of a marvelous vacation.

"Are you going out or are you going to spend such a lovely night indoors?"

The vaguely accented male voice brushed across her ears, eliciting a trail of chill bumps down her spine. She turned and was forced to look up for the source of the huskily spoken words.

When she met his eyes, she felt the impact clear to her toes. Her belly clenched, and for a moment it was hard to breathe.

The man wasn't just gorgeous. There were plenty of gorgeous men in the world, and she'd met her share. This one was…powerful. A predator in a sea of sheep. His eyes bore into hers with an intensity that almost frightened her.

There was interest. Clear interest. She wasn't a fool, nor did she indulge in silly games of false modesty.

She stared back, unable to wrest herself from the force of his gaze. Black. His eyes were as black as night. His hair was as dark, and his skin gleamed golden brown in the soft light of the torches. Firelight cast a sheen to his eyes, shiny onyx, glittering and proud.

His jawline was firm, set, a strong tilt that denoted his arrogance, a quality she was attracted to in men. For a long moment he returned her frank appraisal, and then his lips curved upward into a slight smile.

"A woman of few words I see."

She shook herself and mentally scolded her tongue for knotting up so badly.

"I was deciding on whether to go out or not."

He lifted one imperious brow, a gesture that seemed more challenging than questioning.

"But I can't buy you a drink if you remain inside."

She cocked her head to the side, allowing a tiny smile to relax the tension bubbling inside her. She wasn't a stranger to sexual attraction, but she couldn't remember the last time a man had affected her so strongly right off the bat.

Awareness sizzled between them, almost as if a fuse had been lit the moment he'd spoken. Would she accept the unspoken invitation in his eyes? Oh, she knew he'd asked to buy her a drink, but that wasn't all he wanted. The question was whether she was bold enough to reach out and take the offer.

What could a single night hurt? She was extremely choosy in her partners. She hadn't taken a lover in two years. She just hadn't been interested until this dark-eyed stranger with his sensual smile and mocking arrogance came along. Oh yes, she wanted him. So much so that she vibrated with it.

"Are you here on holiday?" she asked as she peered up at him from underneath her lashes.

Again his lips quirked into a half smile. "In a manner of speaking."

Relief scurried through her belly. No, one night wouldn't hurt. He'd leave and go back to his world. Eventually she'd move on, and their paths would never cross again.

Tonight…tonight she was lonely, a feeling she didn't often indulge in, even if she spent the majority of her time in isolation.

"I'd like a drink," she said by way of agreement.

Something predatory sparked in his eyes. A glow that

was gone almost as soon as it burst to life. His hand came up and cupped her elbow, his fingers splaying possessively over her skin.

She closed her eyes for a brief moment, enjoying the electric sensation that sizzled through her body the moment he touched her.

He led her from the protective awning of the hotel into the night air. Around them the warm glow of torches danced in time with the sweet sounds of jazz. The breeze coming off the water blew through her hair, and she inhaled deeply, enjoying the salt tang.

"Dance with me before we have that drink," he murmured close to her ear.

Without waiting for her consent, he pulled her into his arms, his hips meeting hers as he cupped her body close.

They fit seamlessly, her flush against him, melting and flowing until she wasn't sure where she ended and he began.

His cheek rested against the side of her head as his arms encircled her. Protective. Strong. She reached up, sliding her arms over his shoulders until they wrapped around his neck.

"You're beautiful."

His words flowed like warm honey over jaded ears. It wasn't the most original line, but that was just it. Coming from him, it didn't sound like a line, but rather an honest assessment, a sincere compliment, one that maybe he'd ordinarily be unwilling to give.

"So are you," she whispered.

He chuckled, and his laughter vibrated over her sensitive skin. "Me beautiful? I'm unsure of whether to be flattered or offended."

She snorted. "I know for a fact I'm not the only woman to have ever called you beautiful."

"Do you now?"

His hands skimmed over her back, finding the flesh bared by the backless scoop of her dress. She sucked in her breath as his fingers burned her flesh.

"You feel it too," he murmured.

She didn't pretend not to know what he meant. The chemistry between them was combustible. Never before had she experienced anything like this, not that she'd tell him that.

Instead she nodded her agreement.

"Are we going to do anything about it?"

She leaned back and tilted her head to meet his eyes. "I'd like to think we are."

"Direct. I like that in a woman."

"I like that in a man."

Amusement softened the intensity of his gaze, but she saw something else in his expression. Desire. He wanted her as badly as she wanted him.

"We could have that drink in my room."

She sucked in her breath. Even though she knew what he wanted, the invitation still hit her squarely in the stomach. Her breasts tightened against his chest, and arousal bloomed deep.

"I'm not..." For the first time, she sounded unsure, hesitant. Not at all the decisive woman she knew herself to be.

"You're not what?" he prompted.

"Protected," she said, her voice nearly drowning in the sounds around them.

He tucked a finger underneath her chin and forced her to once again meet his seeking gaze. "I'll take care of you."

The firm promise wrapped around her more securely than his arms. For a moment she indulged in the fantasy of what it would be like to have a man such as this take care of her for the rest of her life. Then she shook her head. Such foolish notions shouldn't disrupt the fantasy of this one night.

She rose up on tiptoe, her lips a breath away from his. "What's your room number?"

"I'll take you up myself."

She shook her head, and he frowned.

"I'll meet you there."

His eyes narrowed for a moment as if he wasn't sure whether to believe her or not. Then without warning, he slid a hand around her neck and curled his fingers around her nape. He pulled her to him, pressing his lips to hers.

She went liquid against him, her body sliding bonelessly downward. He hauled her against him with his free arm, anchoring her tight to prevent her fall.

He licked over her lips, pressing, demanding her to open. With a breathless gasp, she surrendered, parting her mouth so his tongue could slide inward.

Hot, moist open-mouthed kisses. He stole her breath and returned it. His teeth scraped at her lip then captured it and tugged relentlessly. Unwilling to remain a passive participant, she fired back, sucking at his tongue.

His groan echoed over her ears. Her sigh spilled into his mouth.

He finally pulled away, his breaths coming in ragged heaves. His eyes flashed dangerously, sending a shiver over her flesh.

Then he shoved a keycard into her hand. "Top floor. Suite eleven. Hurry."

With that he turned and stalked back into the hotel, his stride eating up the floor.

She stared after him, her body humming and her mind

in a million different pieces. She was completely shattered by what she'd just experienced.

"I must be insane. He'll eat me alive."

A low hum of heady desire buzzed through her veins. She could only hope she was right.

She turned on shaking legs and walked slowly into the hotel. It wasn't that she was being deliberately coy by putting her mystery man off. Mystery man… She didn't even know his name, but she'd agreed to have sex with him.

Then again, it had a certain appeal, this air of mystery. A night of fantasy. No names. No expectations. No entanglements or emotional involvement. No one would get hurt. It was, in fact, perfect.

No, she wasn't being cute. But if she was going to go through with this, it would be on her own terms. Her dark-eyed lover wouldn't have complete control of the situation.

With more calm than she felt, she went up to her room. Once there, she surveyed her reflection in the bathroom mirror. Her hair was slightly mussed and her lips swollen. Passion. She looked as if she'd had an encounter with the very essence of passion.

The sultry temptress staring back at her wasn't a woman she recognized, but she decided she liked this new person. She looked beautiful and confident, and excitement sparked her eyes at the thought of what waited for her in suite eleven.

After a lifetime of loneliness, of being alone, the idea of spending the night in a lover's arms was so appealing that it was all she could do not to hurry out to the elevator.

Instead she forced herself to take steadying breaths. She stared at herself until the wildness faded from her eyes and coolness replaced it. Then she smoothed her long blond hair away from her face.

Satisfied that she had herself under control, she walked out of the bathroom to sit on the bed. She'd wait fifteen to twenty minutes before she headed up. No need to seem too eager.

Two

Piers prowled his suite, unaccustomed to the edginess that consumed him ever since he'd parted ways with the blond bombshell downstairs. He stopped his restless pacing and poured a drink from the crystal decanter on the bar, but he didn't drink it. Instead he stared at the amber liquid then glanced at his watch for the third time.

Would she come?

He cursed his eagerness. He felt like an errant teenager sneaking out of the house to meet a girlfriend. His reaction to the woman couldn't be explained except in terms of lust and desire.

He wanted her. Had wanted her from the moment he spotted her staring longingly through the open doorway of the hotel. He'd been mesmerized by the picture she portrayed. Long and sleek with slender legs, a narrow waist and high, firm breasts. Her hair fell like silk over her shoulders and down her back and his fingers itched to dive into the tresses and wrap them around his knuckles while he devoured her plump lips.

Even now his groin ached uncomfortably. Never had he reacted so strongly to a woman, and it bothered him even as the idea of taking her to bed fired his senses.

A soft knock at his door thrust him to attention, and he hurried across to open it. She stood there, delightfully shy, her ocean eyes a strange mixture of emerald and sapphire.

"I know you gave me a key," she said in a low voice, "but it seemed rude to just barge in."

He found his voice, though his mouth had gone dry as soon as she spoke. He reached for her hand, and she placed it trustingly in his. "I'm glad you came," he said huskily as he pulled her forward.

Instead of leading her farther inside, he wrapped his arms around her, molding her to the contours of his body. She trembled softly against him, and he could feel her heart fluttering like the beat of hummingbird wings.

Unable to resist the temptation, he lowered his mouth to hers, wanting to taste her again. Just once. But when their lips met, he forgot all about his intention to sample.

She responded hotly, her arms sliding around his body. Her hands burned into his skin, through the material of his shirt as if it wasn't there. His impatience grew. He wanted her naked. Wanted him to be naked so he could feel her skin on his.

Thoughts of taking it slow, of seducing her in measured steps flew out the window as he drank deeply of her sweetness. He wasn't sure who was seducing whom, and at this moment, it didn't matter.

His lips scorched a path down the side of her neck as his fingers tugged impatiently at the fastenings of her dress.

Smooth, creamy skin revealed itself, and his mouth was drawn relentlessly to the bare expanse as her dress fell away.

She moaned softly and shivered as his tongue trailed over the curve of her shoulder. He pushed at the dress, and it fell to the floor leaving her in only a dainty scrap of lacy underwear.

All his breath left him as he looked down at the full round globes of her breasts. Her nipples puckered and strained as if begging for his attention. The tips were velvet under his seeking fingers. He toyed with one and then the other before cupping one breast in his palm and lowering his head to press a kiss just above the peach areola.

Her breath caught and held, and she tensed as his tongue lazily traced downward to suck the nipple into his mouth.

Her taste exploded in his mouth. Sweet. Delicate like a flower. So feminine. Perfect. His senses reeled, and he pulled away for a moment to recoup his control. *Theos* but she drove him mad. He reacted to her like a man making love to his first woman.

Already his manhood strained at his pants, and he was dangerously close to flinging her on the bed and stroking into her liquid heat.

Finesse. He must take it slower. He wouldn't allow her such power over him. He would make her as crazy as she made him, and then and only then would he take her.

Jewel grabbed his shoulders as her knees buckled. She needn't have worried. He swept her into his arms and carried her toward the bedroom just beyond the sitting area of the suite.

He laid her on the bed then stood back and began to hastily strip out of his clothing. There was something incredibly sexy about a man standing over her as he undressed. His eyes burned into her, heating her skin even from a distance.

First his shirt fell away revealing smooth, muscled shoulders, a rugged chest and narrow waist with enough of a six-pack to suggest he wasn't an idle businessman. Hair dotted the hollow of his chest, spreading just to his flat nipples. It was thicker at his midline, trailing lower to his navel, tapering to a faint smattering just above the waist of his pants.

She stared hungrily at him as he unfastened his trousers. He didn't waste time or tease unnecessarily. He shoved them down his legs, taking his boxers with him. His erection sprang free from a dark nest of hair. Her eyes widened at the way it strained upward, toward his taut belly. He was hugely aroused.

Her question must have shone on her face. He crawled onto the bed, straddling her hips with his knees. "Was there any doubt that I wanted you, *yineka mou?*"

She smiled up at him. "No."

"Rest assured, I want you very much," he said huskily. He lowered his head until his mouth found hers in a heated rush.

Her entire body arched to meet him, wanting the contact, the warmth and passion he offered. It had been so long since she'd purposely sought out the company of another person, and this man assaulted her senses. He flooded her with a longing that unsettled her.

He pushed her arms over her head until she was helpless beneath him. He didn't just kiss her, he devoured her. There wasn't an inch of her skin that didn't feel the velvet brush of his lips.

Her gasp echoed across the room when he licked and

suckled each breast in turn. His tongue left a damp trail down her midline as he licked down to the shallow indention of her navel. There wasn't a single muscle that wasn't quivering in sharp anticipation.

His hands followed, his palms running the length of her body, tracing each curve, each indention on thcy settled on her hips. He tucked his thumbs underneath the thin string holding her underwear in place, and then he pressed his mouth to her soft mound still covered by transparent lace.

She cried out softly, unnerved by the electric sensation of his mouth over her most intimate place, and yet he hadn't even made contact with her flesh.

His hands caressed their way down her legs, dragging the underwear with it. At her knees, he simply ripped impatiently, rending the material in two. He quickly discarded it and returned impatient fingers to her thighs.

Carefully, he spread her, and she began to shake in earnest.

"Don't be afraid," he murmured. "I'll take care of you. Trust me tonight. You're so beautiful. I want to give you the sweetest pleasure."

"Yes. Please, yes," she begged.

He kissed the inside of her knee. With a brush of his lips, he moved higher, kissing the inside of her thigh, and then finally brushing over the curls guarding her most sensitive regions.

With a gentle finger, he parted her. "Give me your pleasure, *yineka mou*. Only to me." And then his mouth touched her. She bucked upward with a wild cry as his tongue delved deep. It was too much. It had been too long. Never had she reacted so strongly to a man.

"So responsive. So wild. I can't wait to have you."

He rolled away, and she gave a sharp protest until she saw he was only putting on a condom. Then he was back, spreading her thighs, stroking her to make sure she was ready for him.

"Take me. Make me yours," she pleaded.

He closed his eyes, his fingers tight at her hips. He spread her wide and surged into her with one hard thrust.

Her shocked gasp spilled from her lips. Her fingers tightened at his shoulders, and she lay still, simply absorbing the rugged sensation of having him inside her.

His eyes flew open. "Did I hurt you?" he demanded harshly, the strain evident on his face as he held himself in check.

She touched his cheek, trying to soften the lines. His eyes glittered dangerously, and she realized just how close he was to the edge of his control. In that moment, she relished her power, and she wanted to taunt the beast. She wanted to experience the wildness she could see lurking beyond the iron facade.

"No," she said softly. "You didn't hurt me. I want you so much. Take me now. Don't hold back."

To emphasize her request, she dug her nails into his shoulders then lifted her hips in a move that lodged him deeper inside her.

He made one last effort to hold back, but she wouldn't allow it. Wrapping her legs tightly around his waist, she arched into him, reaching for him, pulling him closer. She wanted him. She *needed* him.

He dropped down, surrendering with a growl. He gathered her close, fastening his lips to the vulnerable skin of her neck as his body took over. Harder and faster, his power overwhelmed her. There was a delicious mix of erotic pain and sensual bliss. Heaven. It wasn't something she'd ever experienced before. It was like riding a hurricane.

"Let go," he rasped in her ear. "You first."

She complied without argument, surrendering completely to his will. Her orgasm flashed, terrifying and thrilling all at the same time. She spun wildly out of control, her cries mixing with his.

Then he was moving faster, and harder, driving into her with savage intensity. His lips fused to hers almost in a desperate attempt to staunch his own sounds, but they escaped, harsh and masculine.

Then he stilled inside her, his hips trembling uncontrollably against hers. He smoothed his hands, now gentle, over her face, through her hair and then he gathered her close, murmuring words she didn't understand against her ear.

When his weight grew too heavy, he shifted to the side, pulling her into his arms. He slipped from the warm grasp of her body then rolled away from her for a moment to discard the condom.

She waited with breathless anticipation. Would he want her to leave now or would he want her to spend the night? She was too sated and boneless to even think about getting up, but neither did she want any awkward situations.

He answered her unspoken dilemma by pulling her back into his arms and tucking her head underneath his chin. A few moments later, his soft breathing blew through her hair. He had fallen asleep.

Cautiously so as not to awaken him, she curled her arm around his waist and snuggled deeper into his embrace. Her cheek rested against the hair-roughened skin of his chest, and she inhaled deeply, filling her nostrils with his male scent.

For the space of a stolen moment she felt safe. Accepted. Even cherished. It was silly if she dwelled on it, but tonight she wouldn't. Tonight she just wanted to belong to someone and not to feel so alone in the world.

Even in sleep, he seemed to sense her disquiet. His arms tightened around her, bringing her even closer to his warmth. She smiled and gave in to the sleepy pleasure seeping into her bones.

Piers awoke unsure of the time, a rarity for him. He usually woke every morning before dawn, his mind alert and ready to take on the day's tasks. Today however sleep clouded his brain, and uncharacteristic laziness permeated his muscles. Something soft and feminine stirred his senses, and he woke enough to realize that she was still in his arms.

Instead of rolling away, of distancing himself immediately, he remained there, breathing in her scent. He should get up and shower, make it clear the interlude was over, but he hung on, unwilling to send her away just yet.

She stirred when his hands smoothed over her back, down to her shapely buttocks and over the curve of her hip. He had to have her again. One more time. Even as warning bells clanged in his mind, he was turning her, sliding over her as he reached to the nightstand for another condom.

As her eyes fluttered sleepily, he slid inside her, slower this time, with more patience and care than he'd taken her the night before. He didn't want to chance hurting her, and if he was honest, he wanted to savor this last encounter.

"Good morning," she murmured in a husky voice that sent a shudder over his body.

He thrust deeper then leaned down to capture her mouth. "Good morning."

She yawned and stretched like a cat, wrapping her arms

around his neck to pull him down again when he drew away. Sleek and beautiful, she matched his movements, rocking gently against him.

If last night had been the storm, this was a calm rain afterward. Gentle and extremely satisfying.

He tugged her hair from her face, unable to resist kissing her again and again. He couldn't get enough of her. The thought that he didn't want her to go rose in his mind. Before it could take root, he tamped it back down, determined not to get caught in an emotional trap.

He'd existed for too long without such entanglements, and he'd be damned if he allowed it to happen again.

She enveloped him in her tight grasp, her sweet depths clinging to him as he withdrew and thrust forward. He set an easy pace, one that would prolong their pleasure.

And when he could no longer delay the surge of exquisite pleasure, he pushed them both over the edge, leaving them gasping for breath and shaking in each other's arms.

For a long moment he lay there, still sheathed deeply inside her, his face buried in her sweet-smelling hair.

Then reality encroached. It was morning. Their night together was over, and it was best to end things now before things had a chance to get messy.

He rolled away abruptly, getting up from the bed and reaching for his pants.

"I'm going to take a shower," he said shortly when she did nothing more than watch him from her perch in his bed, her eyes probing him with a wary light.

She nodded, and he disappeared into the bathroom, his relief not as great as his regret. And when he returned a mere ten minutes later, he found her gone from his bed, from his hotel room. From his life.

Yes, she'd understood well the rules of the game.

Maybe too well. For a moment he'd allowed himself to wish that maybe, just maybe she'd still be lying there. Warm and sated from his lovemaking. Belonging to him.

Three

Jewel stood outside the third floor offices of the Anetakis Hotel and smoothed a hand through her hair for the third time. It was a bad nervous habit and one destined to bring down more tendrils from the elegant knot she'd fashioned.

Instead she placed her palms over her skirt and removed nonexistent wrinkles as she waited admittance into Piers Anetakis's office.

She knew she looked cool and professional, a look she strove hard for. The woman who'd let loose with such abandon two nights before no longer existed. In her place was an unreadable face devoid of any emotion.

Still, despite her best efforts, thoughts of her lover drifted erotically through her mind. She'd left while he was in the shower, but she'd hoped to run into him again. A chance meeting. Maybe it would lead to another night even though she'd sworn it would only be one.

It was just as well. He was probably already gone back to wherever it was he lived. She'd move on herself in a few more weeks, armed with enough money to sustain her travels.

At times, she wondered what it would be like to settle in one place, to have all the comforts of home, but such an idea was alien to her. She'd learned long ago that a home wasn't in the cards for her.

She glanced down at her watch. Two minutes past eight. She was to have been summoned at eight. Apparently promptness wasn't one of Mr. Anetakis's strong points.

She clutched her briefcase to her and stared out the window to the waves crashing in the distance. The sea lost some of its romance in the daylight. It was still beautiful and striking, but at night under the flicker of torches and the glow of the moon, it took on a life of its own.

Her mouth twisted ruefully. She was still thinking of her dark-eyed lover. He was hard to forget, and she knew she'd be thinking of him for a long time to come.

Behind her the door opened, and an older woman stuck her head out and smiled at Jewel. "Miss Henley, Mr. Anetakis will see you now."

Jewel pasted a bright smile on her face and marched in behind the woman. Across the room Mr. Anetakis stood with his back to them, a cell phone stuck to his ear. When he heard them come in, he turned and Jewel halted. Her mouth flew open, and her eyes widened in shock.

To his credit, Mr. Anetakis merely raised an eyebrow in recognition, and then he closed his phone and nodded to the other lady.

"You can leave us now, Margery. Miss Henley and I have a lot to discuss."

Jewel swallowed nervously as Margery quietly left the room and shut the door behind her. Her fingers curled around

her briefcase, and she held it almost like a shield as Mr.
Anetakis stared holes through her. God, how this must look.

"You have to know I had no idea who you were," she
said in a shaky voice before he could speak.

"Indeed," he said calmly. "I could see the shock when
I turned around. Still, it makes things a bit awkward,
wouldn't you say?"

"There's no reason things should be awkward," she
said crisply. She moved forward, holding an outstretched
hand. "Hello, Mr. Anetakis. I'm Jewel Henley, your new
assistant. I trust we'll work well together."

His lips twisted into a sardonic smile. Before he could
reply, his phone rang again.

"Excuse me, Miss Henley," he said in a cool voice.
Then he picked up his cell phone.

He wasn't speaking English, but it was obvious the phone
call wasn't to his liking. He frowned and then outright
scowled. He barked a few words into the receiver before
muttering something unintelligible and snapping it closed.

"My apologies. There is something I must attend to at
once. You can see Margery in her office, and she'll get
you…set up."

Jewel nodded as he strode out the door. As soon as the
door shut, all her breath left her in a whoosh that left her
sagging. Of all the rotten luck. And to think she'd hoped
they'd run into each other again so they could have a repeat
performance.

On wobbly knees she went to find Margery and then
prayed that she'd get through the next four weeks without
losing her composure.

Piers got out of the helicopter and strode toward the car
waiting to pick him up. As they drove toward the airport

where his private jet awaited, he snapped open his phone and placed the call that he'd been deliberating over since he left his office.

His human resources manager for the island hotel picked up on the second ring.

"What can I do for you, Mr. Anetakis?" he asked once Piers had identified himself.

"Jewel Henley," he bit out.

"Your new assistant?"

"Get rid of her."

"Pardon? Is there a problem?"

"Just get rid of her. I want her gone by the time I return." He took a deep breath. "Transfer her, promote her or pay her for the entirety of her contract, but get rid of her. She can't work under me. I have a strict policy about personal involvement with my employees, and let's just say she and I have history."

He waited for a moment and when he didn't hear anything, he said, "hello?" He cursed. The connection had been cut. Oh well, he didn't require a response. He just wanted action.

Even if he hadn't already been extremely distrustful of situations that seemed too coincidental, his brother's assistant had sold valuable company plans to their competitor. After that debacle, they'd all assumed very strict requirements for the people working closest to them. They could ill afford another Roslyn.

Still, his chest tightened as the car stopped outside his plane, and he got out to board. He wasn't so much in denial that he could refute that the night had been more than just a casual one-night stand. Which was all the more reason to cut ties now. He wouldn't give up any power, no matter how subtle, to a woman ever again.

* * *

Jewel sat in Margery's chair behind her desk filling out a mountain of paperwork while Margery puttered around in the background making phone calls and grumbling at the printer when it didn't spit out the appropriate documents.

She'd spent the morning on pins and needles, waiting for Piers to return so they could at least try and air things out and get it behind them. The old saying about an elephant in the room was appropriate, only Jewel felt like there was an entire herd.

At lunch, she went down to the small café and nibbled on a sandwich while watching the seagulls dive-bomb tourists who had bread to feed them. If Margery let her on the company computer this afternoon, she'd e-mail Kirk and let him know she'd arrived on the island and would be staying a few weeks.

He was her only friend, but they rarely saw each other. He was forever taking assignments to far-flung places, and she was equally determined to travel her own way. It amused her that they were essentially lost souls who wandered from place to place. Neither had a home, and maybe that was why they understood each other.

An occasional e-mail, sometimes a phone call, and every once in a while they crossed paths on their travels. Those were good times. It was nice to connect to another person even if it was only for a few hours. He was as close to a brother or family member as she'd ever imagined having.

After finishing her sandwich, she tossed the wrapper and walked back to the employee elevator. Would Piers be back? A flutter abounded in her stomach, but she swallowed back her nervousness and forged ahead. It wouldn't do to let him know she was put off by their unintentional relationship. If he could be cool about it then so could she.

When she walked back into Margery's office, Margery looked up, a grim expression on her face. "Mr. Patterson wants to see you immediately."

Jewel's brow crinkled. Maybe it was more personnel stuff to sign. Lord knows she'd had enough paperwork this morning to choke a horse. With a resigned sigh, she turned and left Margery's office and went several doors down to the human resource manager's cubicle.

He looked up when she tapped on the frame of his open door.

"Miss Henley, come in. Have a seat please."

She settled down in front of him and waited expectantly. He cleared his throat and tugged at his collar in an uncomfortable motion. Then he leveled a stare at her.

"When you hired on, it was with the condition that it was a temporary position. You were to be Mr. Anetakis's assistant for the duration of his stay here."

"Yes." They'd been through all of this and she was impatient to get on with it.

"I'm sorry to say that he no longer requires an assistant. He's had a change of plans. As such, your services are no longer required."

She stared, stunned, for a long moment. "Excuse me?"

"Your employment here is terminated effective immediately."

She stood, her legs trembling, her fingers curled into tight fists. "That bastard. What a complete and utter bastard!"

"Security will escort you to your room and wait while you collect your things," he continued as if she hadn't let loose with her tirade.

"You can tell Mr. Anetakis that he is the lowest form of pond scum. Verbatim, Mr. Patterson. Make sure he gets my message. He's a gutless piece of chicken shit, and I hope he chokes on his damn cowardice."

With that she turned and stormed out of his office, slamming the door as hard as she could. The sound reverberated down the hallway, and a few people stuck their heads out of their cubicles as she stalked past.

Unbelievable. He hadn't even had the courage to fire her himself. He let his personnel director handle it while he ran for the hills. What a crock.

Two security guards fell into step beside her when she neared the elevator. It pissed her off that she was being treated like a common criminal.

She rode the elevator with them in stiff silence. They walked behind her to her door and positioned themselves on either side of the frame while she went in. How long would they give her before bursting in? The thought amused her even as rage crawled over her in waves.

Shedding her uncomfortable heels, she sank onto the bed like a deflated balloon. Damn the man. She had enough money to get off the island, but little else. Certainly no money to plan her next venture. She'd spent what she had to get here and taken the good-paying job to restock her resources. With the money earned in this job, she would have been able to travel, albeit economically, for the next six months without worrying about finances.

Now she faced the only choice available to her if she wanted a roof over her head. Going back home to San Francisco and the apartment that belonged to Kirk was her only option.

It had been an agreement between them. If she ever needed a place to stay, she was to go there. The utilities were taken care of each month and the pantry was stocked with staples.

She didn't even have a way to contact him other than e-mail, and sometimes he went weeks without checking it. She just hoped he hadn't planned one of his rare trips home at the same time she'd be there.

Her fingers dug into her temples, and she closed her eyes. She could look for work here on the island, but she'd already exhausted most of her possibilities when this job had landed in her lap. Nothing else paid nearly as well, and now she had no desire to stay where she might actually run into Piers Anetakis. The worm.

San Francisco was it, she admitted with forlorn acceptance. Hopefully she could land a job, save up some money. Having a rent-free place to stay would be helpful but she hated to take advantage of Kirk's generosity.

"Damn you, Piers Anetakis," she whispered. He'd managed to turn the most beautiful night of her life into something tawdry and hateful.

With a resigned shake of her head, she knew there was little point in feeling sorry for herself. There was nothing to do but pick up and go on and hopefully learn a lesson in the process.

Four

Five months later...

Piers descended the steps of his private jet and strode across the paved runway to the waiting car. The damp, chilly San Francisco air was a far cry from the warm, tropical air he was used to. He hadn't taken the time to pack appropriate clothing, and the thin silk shirt and light suit coat didn't offer much in the way of protection from the pervading chill.

The driver had already been instructed as to Piers's destination, so he sat back as the car rolled away from the airport toward the hospital where Jewel was being treated.

What had happened to her? It must be serious if she'd broken down and phoned him after he hadn't been able to uncover her whereabouts for five months. Guilt was a strong motivator, and yet his efforts had come to naught.

No matter. He now knew where she was. He'd see to it

that she had the best care and settle an amount on her to compensate her loss of employment, and then maybe he could get her out of his head.

When they finally rolled up to the hospital, Piers wasted no time hurrying in. At the help desk he was given Jewel's room number, and he rode the elevator to the appropriate floor.

At her door, he found it slightly ajar and issued a soft knock. Not hearing any summons, he pushed the door open and quietly walked in.

She was barely more than a rumpled pile of sheets on the bed, her head propped haphazardly on her pillow. Her eyelashes rested on her cheeks, and her soft, even breathing signaled her sleep.

Even in rest, she looked worried, her face drawn, her brow wrinkled. Her fingers were clutched bloodlessly at the sheet gathered at her chest. And yet she was as beautiful as he remembered, and unfortunately for him, he'd been haunted by her beauty for the last five months.

He removed his suit coat and tossed it over the chair beside her bed and then settled himself down to sit and wait for her to wake. The slight movement alerted her, and her eyes flew open.

Shock registered as soon as she saw him. Her eyes widened in what looked to be panic. Her hands moved immediately to her stomach in a protective gesture he'd be blind to miss.

Then he saw what it was she was protecting. There was an unmistakable swell, a taut mound that shielded a baby!

"You're pregnant!"

Her eyes narrowed. "Well, you needn't sound so accusing. I hardly got that way by myself."

For a moment he was too stunned to realize her implication, and then when it came, it trickled like ice down his spine. Old memories came back in a wave, and hot anger quickly melted away the cold in his veins.

"Are you saying it's mine?" he demanded. Already his mind was moving in a whir. He wouldn't be trapped again by a conniving woman.

"She," Jewel corrected. "At least refer to your daughter as a human being."

Damn her. She knew that by personalizing the vague entity she shielded that he'd be inhuman not to react.

"A daughter?"

Against his will, his voice softened, and he found himself examining her belly closer. He impatiently brushed aside her cupped hands and then snatched his own hand back when her belly rippled and jumped beneath his fingers.

"*Theos!* Is that her?"

Jewel smiled and nodded. "She's active this morning."

Piers shook his head in an attempt to brush away the spell. A daughter. Suddenly he envisioned a tiny little girl, a replica of Jewel but with his dark eyes. Damn her for making him dream again.

His expression hardened, and he once again focused his attention on Jewel. "Is she mine?"

Jewel met his steady gaze and nodded.

He swore softly. "We used protection. *I* used protection."

She shrugged. "She's yours."

"You expect me to accept that? Just like that?"

She struggled to sit up against her pillows, her fingers clenched into tight balls at her sides. "I haven't slept with another man in two years. She's yours."

He wasn't the gullible fool he'd been so many years ago. "Then you won't object to paternity testing."

She closed her eyes wearily and sank back into the covers. Hurt flickered in her eyes when she reopened them, but she shook her head. "No, Piers. I have nothing to hide."

"What is wrong with you? Why are you here in the hospital?" he asked, finally coming around to the matter at hand. He'd been completely blindsided by the discovery that the child she was pregnant with was…could be his.

"I've been ill," she said in a tired voice. "Elevated blood pressure. Fatigue. My doctor said my job had a lot to do with it, and he wants me to quit. He says I *must* quit, that I don't have a choice."

"What the devil have you been doing?" he demanded.

She lifted one shoulder. "Waitressing. It was all I could find on such short notice. I needed the money before I could move somewhere else. Somewhere warmer. Somewhere I could make more money. It's very expensive here in San Francisco."

"Then why did you come here from the island? You could have gone anywhere."

She cast him a bitter glance. "I have an apartment here. One that is paid for. After I was fired, I had little choice in where to go. I had to have a place to sleep. I intended to save enough money and then go somewhere else."

He flinched as guilt consumed him. Damn, but this was a mess. Not only had he had her fired, but he'd sent a pregnant woman into a bad situation.

"Look, Jewel, about your firing…"

She held up a hand, her expression fierce. "I don't want to discuss it. You're a coward and a bastard of the first order. I wouldn't have *ever* spoken to you again if our daughter didn't need you, if *I* didn't need your help."

"That's just it. I never intended for you to be fired," he said patiently.

She glared at him. "That's hardly comforting given that I *was* fired and that I *was* escorted out of your hotel."

He sighed. Now wasn't the time to try and reason with her. She was growing more upset by the minute. If she chose to believe the worst in him, and it was obvious she did, he was hardly going to change five months worth of anger and resentment in five minutes.

"So what is it that you need from me?" he asked. "I'll help in any way I can."

She stared at him, suspicion burning brightly in her ocean eyes. Maybe he was wrong to want his daughter to have his eyes. No, she should definitely have Jewel's eyes. Dark-haired like him, but with her mother's sea-green eyes. Or were they blue? He could never tell from one moment to the next.

Then her shoulders sank, and she closed her eyes. "My physician won't discharge me until he's certain I have someone to care for me."

She said the latter with a measure of distaste, as if it pained her to be dependent on anyone.

"I'll be on bed rest until my surgery."

Piers sat forward. "Surgery? Why do you need surgery? I thought you said you were only ill. Blood pressure." He knew enough about that from his sister-in-law's pregnancy to know that the prescribed treatment for stress or elevated blood pressure was merely rest and to be off one's feet. "You can't have surgery while you're pregnant. What about the baby?"

She stared back at him patiently. "That's just it. When they did a sonogram to check on the baby, they found a large cyst on one of my ovaries. Instead of shrinking, as a lot of cysts do during the course of the pregnancy, this one has gotten larger, and now it's pressing on the uterus. They have no choice but to remove it so that it won't interfere with the pregnancy or possibly even harm the baby."

Piers cursed. "This operation, is it dangerous? Will it harm the baby?"

"The doctor doesn't think so, but it has to be done soon."

He cursed again, though he didn't allow the words past his lips. He didn't want to be ensnared in another situation where he stood to lose everything. Once a fool, but never again. This time things would be done on his terms.

"You're going to marry me," he announced baldly.

Five

"You're out of your mind," Jewel burst out.

Piers's eyes narrowed. "I'd hardly say my speaking of marriage constitutes an unsound mind."

"Crazy. Certifiable."

He bristled and let out an irritated growl. "I am not crazy."

"You're serious!"

She stared at him with a mixture of stupefaction and horror.

His breath escaped in a long sound of exasperation.

Her mouth fell open. "For the love of God. You think I'd *marry* you?"

"There's no reason to sound so appalled."

"Appalled," she muttered. "That about covers my reaction. Look, Piers. I need your help. Your support. But I don't need marriage. Not to you. Never to you."

"Well if you want my support, you're damn well going to have to marry me for it," he growled.

"Get out," she bit off. She held a trembling hand up to point to the door, but Piers caught it and curled his fingers around hers. He brought it to the edge of the bed and gently stroked the inside of her wrist.

"I shouldn't have said that. You made me angry. If you're pregnant with my child, of course you'll have my support, Jewel. I'll do everything I can to provide for you and our daughter."

Astounded by his abrupt turnaround, she could only stare at him, her tongue flapping to try and come up with something, anything to say. How could he still affect her this way after all he'd done?

"Then you'll say no more about marriage?"

His lips tightened. "I didn't promise that. I have every intention of marrying you as quickly as possible and definitely before this surgery."

"But—"

He held up his hand, and to her utter annoyance, her mouth shut, cutting off her protest.

"You are having a dangerous surgery. You have no family, no one to be with you, to make decisions if the worst should happen."

A cold trickle of dread swept down her spine. How did he know anything about her family? Had he had her investigated? Her stomach rolled as nausea welled. She couldn't bear for anyone to know of her past. As far as she was concerned it didn't exist. She didn't exist.

"There has to be another way," she said faintly. Already the strain of him being here, of standing up against this hard man, was wearing on her.

It must have been obvious, because his expression

softened noticeably. "I'm not here to fight with you. We have a lot to work out and not much time. I need to speak with your doctor and have you transferred to a better facility. I'll want a specialist to take over your care. He can give us a second opinion on whether this surgery is the best solution with you pregnant. I'll see to the arrangements for our wedding."

"Stop right there," she said as fury worked its way up her spine until her neck was stiff and locked. "You won't come barging in here, taking over my life and making decisions for me. I'm not some brainless idiot who needs you to rush in and save the day. I've spoken to the doctors. I'm well aware of what needs to be done, and I will make the decision as to what is best for me and my daughter. If that bothers you, then you can take yourself right back to your island and leave me the hell alone."

He held up a placating hand. "Don't upset yourself, Jewel. I'm sorry if I've offended you. Taking over is what I do. You asked for my help, and I'm here to offer it, and yet now you don't seem to want it."

"I want your help without conditions."

For a long moment they stared at each other, neither backing down as the challenge was laid.

"And I'm afraid that I'm unwilling to just sit back and not have a say."

"You're not even convinced this is your child," she threw out.

He nodded. "That's true. I'd be a fool to blindly accept your word. We hardly know each other. How do I know you didn't set the entire thing up? Regardless, I'm willing to help. I have much to make up for. For now I'm willing to go with the assumption that you're carrying my daughter. I want us to marry before you have any further medical treatment."

"But that's just insane," she protested.

He continued on as if she hadn't spoken. "I'll have an agreement drawn up to protect both our interests. If it turns out you've lied and the child is not mine, the marriage will immediately be terminated. I'll provide a settlement for you and your daughter, and we'll go our separate ways."

She didn't miss the way he said "your daughter," the way he purposely distanced himself from the equation. If she lied. She almost shook her head. She would have had to have jumped directly from his bed into another man's for the timing to be such that the baby could be someone else's. What he must think of her. Hardly a basis for marriage.

"And if she is yours?" she asked softly.

"Then we remain married."

She was already shaking her head. "No. I don't want to marry you. You can't want this either."

"I won't argue about this, Jewel. You will marry me and you'll do it immediately. Think about what's best for your daughter. The longer we spend arguing, the longer you and the baby are at risk."

"You really are blackmailing me," she said in disbelief.

"Think what you want," he offered with a casual shrug.

"She is your child," she said fiercely. "You get those damn tests done, but she's yours."

Piers nodded. "I'm willing to concede that she could be mine. I wouldn't have offered marriage if I didn't think the possibility existed."

"And yet you don't want to wait for those results before you tie us together?"

"How strangely you put it," he said with mild amusement. "Our agreement will allow for any possibility. As

I've said, if it turns out you've lied to me, our marriage will end immediately. I'm prepared to be generous in spite of the lie, but it will be on my terms. And if, as you said, that she is my daughter, then the best course is for us to be married and provide a stable home for her."

"With two parents who can barely tolerate one another."

He raised one eyebrow. "I wouldn't go that far. I'd say we got on quite well together that night in my hotel room."

A deep flush worked its way over her cheeks. "Lust is no substitute for love, trust and commitment."

"And who is to say those things won't follow?"

She stared at him in astonishment.

"Give it a chance, Jewel. Who is to say what the future holds for us. For now, it isn't wise to dwell on things that might not even be an issue. We have your surgery to contend with and of course the results of the paternity test."

"Of course. Silly me to consider the cornerstones of marriage when in fact we're considering getting married."

"There is no need to be so sarcastic. Now, if we're finished, I suggest you get some rest. There are many things to be done, and the sooner I arrange everything, the sooner you can be at ease."

"I haven't said I'll marry you," she said evenly.

"No, and I'm waiting for your answer."

Frustration beat at her temples. How infuriating was this man. Arrogant. Convinced of getting his way each and every time. And yet, the jerk was right on all counts. She needed him. Their daughter needed him.

Sadness crept over her, and she lay back, closing her eyes. She felt disgustingly weepy. This was so far removed from the way she'd dreamed things might be one day. In her more sane moments, she'd accepted the fact that she'd probably never marry, never have someone she could absolutely trust. Trust just wasn't in her makeup. And yet, it hadn't stopped her fanciful daydreams of a strong, loving man. Someone who wouldn't abuse her trust. Someone who would love her unconditionally.

"It won't be as bad as that," Piers said gently as he took her hand in his once more.

She opened her eyes to see him staring intently at her.

"All right, Piers. I'll marry you," she said wearily. "But I'll have conditions of my own."

"I'll provide a lawyer to represent your interests. He can look over my part of the agreement and advise you accordingly."

How sterile and cold it all sounded. More like a hostile business takeover than a marriage. A delicate shiver skirted up her spine and prickled her nape. There was no doubt that she was making a mistake. Perhaps the biggest mistake of her life. But for her child, she'd do this. She'd do anything. From the moment she discovered she was pregnant, her child became everything to her. She wouldn't lose her daughter. If she had to marry the devil himself, she'd grit her teeth and bear it.

"How about I choose the lawyer and have him bill you," she offered sweetly.

To her surprise he chuckled. "Don't trust me? I suppose you have no reason to. Of course. Choose your lawyer and have him send me the bill."

Her eyes narrowed. He was positively magnanimous, but then he could afford to be now that he'd won.

"Is there anything you need? Anything you'd like me to bring you?"

She hesitated for a moment. "Food."

"Food? They don't feed you here?"

"Really good food," she said hopefully. "I'm starving."

He smiled, and she felt the jolt all the way to her toes. Damn the man for looking so disgustingly appealing. She didn't want to be attracted to him anymore. Her hand smoothed over her belly in another silent apology. She didn't regret a single thing about their night of passion, but it didn't mean she wanted to dwell on it forever.

"I will see what I can do about getting you some really good food. Now, get some rest. I'll be back after a while."

As if she would rest now that he'd arrived and turned her life upside down.

Then he surprised her by leaning down and brushing his lips across her forehead in a surprisingly tender gesture. She held her breath, enjoying the brief contact. As he drew away, his fingers trailed down her cheek.

"I don't want you to worry about anything. Just rest and get well and take good care of your...our daughter."

He seemed to struggle with the last as if he was making a concession to her claim, and yet, he looked grim. Maybe he had no wish for children. Tough. He now had a daughter, and he might as well get used to the idea.

He gave her one last look and then turned to walk briskly from the hospital room. When the door shut behind him, Jewel let out her breath in a long whoosh.

Married.

She couldn't imagine being married to such a hard man. She'd had enough hard people in her life. Emotionless, cold individuals with no heart, no love. And now she was consigned to a marriage that would be a replica of her childhood.

Her hands rubbed and massaged her swollen belly. "It will never be like that for you, sweetie. I love you so much already, and there'll never be a day you won't know it. I swear. No matter what happens with your daddy, you'll always have me."

Six

"I've done a terrible thing," Piers said when his brother, Chrysander, muttered an unintelligible greeting in Greek.

Chrysander sighed, and Piers could hear him sit up in bed and fight the covers for a moment.

"Why is it becoming commonplace for my younger brothers to call me in the middle of the night with those exact words?"

"Theron messed up lately?" Piers asked in amusement.

"Not since he seduced a woman under his protection," Chrysander said dryly.

"Ahh, you mean Bella. Why do I imagine that it was she who did the seducing?"

"You're straying from the topic. What is this terrible thing you've done, and how much is it going to cost?"

"Maybe nothing. Maybe everything," Piers said quietly.

A curse escaped Chrysander's lips, and then Piers heard him say something to Marley in the background.

"Don't worry Marley over this," Piers said. "I'm sorry to have disturbed her sleep."

"It's too late for that," Chrysander growled. "Just give me a moment to go into my office."

Piers waited, drumming his fingers on the desk in his hotel room. Finally Chrysander came back on the line.

"Now tell me what's wrong."

Just like Chrysander to get to the point.

"I had an affair—a brief affair, a one-night stand really."

"So?" Chrysander asked impatiently. "This isn't new for you."

"She was my new assistant."

Chrysander cursed again.

"I didn't know she was my assistant until she showed up for work. I had her fired."

Chrysander groaned. "How much is she suing us for?"

"Let me finish." This time it was Piers who was impatient. "I didn't intend to fire her at all. I asked my human resources manager to transfer her, or promote her or pay her for her entire contracted term, but he only heard the get rid of her part and fired her. She disappeared before I could remedy the situation, and I wasn't able to locate her. Until now."

"Okay, so what's the problem?"

"She's in the hospital. She's ill, she needs a surgery…and she's pregnant."

Dead silence greeted his announcement.

"*Theos,*" Chrysander breathed. "Piers, you can't let this happen again. Last time—"

"I know," Piers said irritably. The last thing he needed was a recap of that disaster from his brother. It was bad enough he'd been made a complete fool of, but his brothers had witnessed the entire debacle.

"Are you certain the child is yours?"

"No. I've asked for paternity testing."

"Good."

"There's something else you should know," Piers said. "I'm going to marry her. Soon, as in the next few days."

"What? Have you lost your mind?"

"Funny, that's what she asked me."

"I'm glad one of you has sense then," Chrysander said heatedly. "Why on earth would you marry this woman when you don't even know if the child is yours?"

"It's amazing how the tables have turned," Piers said mildly.

"Don't even start. I heard the same thing from Theron when he was so set on marrying Alannis. Never mind that I was right about what a disaster that would be. You two warning me about Marley was an entirely different situation, and you know it. You don't have a relationship with this woman. You slept with her one night, and now she claims to be pregnant with your child, and you're going to marry her? Just like that?"

"She needs my help. I'm not stupid. I'm having our lawyer draw up an ironclad agreement that provides stipulations for the possibility that the child isn't mine. For now, with her surgery looming, it's best that we marry. This way I can make decisions for her care and that of the child's. If it does turn out to be my daughter, how would I feel if I had sat back and done nothing while I waited for the proof?"

"Daughter?"

"Yes. Apparently Jewel is pregnant with a girl."

Despite his doubts and his heavy suspicions, he couldn't help but smile at the image of a little girl with big eyes and a sweet smile.

"Jewel. What's her last name?"

"Oh no you don't, big brother. There's no need to get all protective and have her background dug up. I can handle this myself. You just concern yourself with your wife and my nephew."

"I don't want you hurt again," Chrysander said quietly.

And there it was. No matter how much he wanted to avoid the past, it was always there, hanging like a dark cloud. Unbidden, the image of another child, a sweet baby boy, dark-haired with a cherubic smile and chubby little legs, came painfully to mind. Eric. Not many days had gone by that Piers hadn't thought of him in some form or fashion, but not until now had such pain accompanied the memories.

"This time, I'm going to make sure that my interests are better protected," Piers said coldly. "I was a fool then."

Chrysander sighed. "You were young, Piers."

"It was no excuse."

"Call me if you need me. Marley and I would like to come to your wedding. It will be better if family is there."

"There's no need."

"There is every need," Chrysander said, interrupting him. "Let me know the details, and we'll fly out."

Piers's hand gripped the phone tighter. It was nice to have such unconditional support. And then he realized the irony. He hadn't exactly offered Jewel his unconditional support. He'd strong-armed her and taken advantage of her situation.

"All right. I'll call when I have the arrangements made."

"Be sure and let Theron know as well. He and Bella will want to be there."

Piers sighed. "Yes big brother."

Chrysander chuckled. "This is a small thing I ask. It's not as if you've ever listened to me before."

"Give Marley my love."

"I will—and Piers? Be careful. I don't like the sound of this at all."

Piers hung up the phone. He should call Theron, but he couldn't bring himself to face another inquisition. Especially now that Theron had joined the ranks of the deliriously happy. He'd be appalled that Piers was going to marry a woman he barely knew, a woman who might well be lying to him.

Instead he phoned his lawyer and outlined his situation. Then he arranged a security detail for Jewel. He and his brothers took no chances with those close to them after what had happened to Chrysander's wife, Marley. Next he called to see when Jewel's doctor would next be making his rounds. He intended to be there so he'd know exactly what was going on.

Lastly, he called a local restaurant and arranged for a full-course dinner to be prepared for pickup in an hour.

Jewel was ready to fidget right out of the bed. She'd only gotten up to use the bathroom, and now she'd decided she'd had enough. The doctor was releasing her tomorrow now that someone had shown up to take *care* of her. She had to work to keep the snort of derision from rising in her throat.

She could do without Piers Anetakis's brand of caring.

The thin hospital gown offered little in the way of modesty, and so after showering, she dressed in a pair of loose-fitting sweats and a maternity shirt. She toweled her hair as dry as she could and left it loose so it would finish drying.

She had settled in the small recliner to the side of her bed when the door opened, and Piers strode in carrying two large take-out bags.

She sat forward nervously as his gaze swept over her. Then his eyes narrowed, and he set the bags down on the bed.

"You should not have showered until I was here."

Her mouth fell open in shock. "What?"

"You could have fallen. You should have waited for me to help or at least called for the nurse."

"How do you know I didn't call for one of the nurses?"

He stared inquisitively at her, his eyes mocking. "Did you?"

"It's none of your business," she muttered.

"If you're pregnant with my child, it's every bit of my business."

"Look Piers, we need to get something straight right now. Me being pregnant with your child does not give you any rights over me whatsoever. I won't allow you to waltz in and take over my life."

Even as the sharp protest left her lips, she realized how stupid she sounded. That's precisely what he had done so far. Taken over. What else explained the reason for this marriage he proposed?

She bit her lip and looked away, her hand automatically moving to her belly in a soothing motion.

Piers began taking food out of the bags as if she'd said nothing at all. The smells wafted through her nostrils, and her stomach growled. Heavenly.

She raised an eyebrow. She wouldn't have thought he'd give much thought to what she could or couldn't have.

"Thank you, I'm starving."

He prepared a plate and handed it to her along with utensils. Then he fixed a plate for himself and settled on the edge of the bed.

"I can get back into the bed so you have a place to sit," she offered.

He shook his head. "You look comfortable. I'm fine."

They ate in silence, though she knew he watched her. She refused to acknowledge his perusal, though, and concentrated on the delicious food instead.

When she couldn't eat another bite, she sighed and put down her fork.

"That was wonderful, thank you."

He took the plate and set it on the counter along the wall. "Would you like to get back into bed now?"

She shook her head. "I've had enough bed to last a lifetime."

"But shouldn't you be in bed with your feet up?" he persisted.

"I'm doing well. The doctor wants me on moderated bed rest until my surgery. That means I can get up and move around. He just doesn't want me on my feet for long periods of time."

"And this job you had, you were on your feet all the time?" he asked with a frown.

"I was waitressing. It was necessary."

"You should have phoned me the minute you knew you were pregnant," he said fiercely.

Her expression turned murderous. "You had me fired. You told me quite plainly that you wanted nothing further to do with me. Why on earth would I be calling you? I wouldn't have called you now if I hadn't needed you so badly."

"Then I suppose I'll have to be grateful you needed me."

"I don't need you," she amended. "Our daughter does."

"You need me, Jewel. I have a lot to make up for, and I plan to do just that. We can talk about your firing when you aren't in the hospital and you're feeling better."

"About that," she began.

He raised an eyebrow. "Yes?"

"The doctor is releasing me in the morning."

"Yes, I know. I spoke to him before I came back to your room."

Her fingers curled into tight fists, but she kept the frustration from her expression. Or at least she tried.

"I don't need you hovering over me at every moment. You can drop me off at my apartment—"

Before she got any further he shook his head resolutely, his expression implacable.

"I've arranged for the rental of a house until your surgery. I'll take you there of course. I've hired a nurse to see to your needs—"

It was her turn to break in, her head shaking so stiffly that her neck hurt.

"No. Absolutely not. I won't have some nurse hired to babysit me. It's ridiculous. I'm not an invalid. I have to stay off my feet. Fine, I can do that without a nurse."

"Why must you be so difficult?" he asked mildly. "I'm only doing what is best for your health."

"If you want to hire someone, hire a cook," she muttered. "I'm terrible at it."

Amusement curved his hard mouth into a smile. It was amazing what a difference it made in his face. He looked almost boyish. She stared at him in astonishment.

"A cook can be arranged. I, of course, wish to see that my daughter and her mother are well fed. Does this mean you aren't going to fight moving in with me?"

She made a sound of protest, but it quickly died. She'd walked right into that one. With a long suffering sigh, she uttered a simple, "No."

"See, that wasn't so hard, now was it?"

"You can quit the gloating. It's not very attractive on you."

His grin broadened. The amazing thing was, it made him look quite charming. *Dangerous, Jewel. He's dangerous. Don't fall for that charm.*

"I'm going to take you home with me, Jewel," he said patiently. "There's little point in arguing. All the arrangements have been made. Tomorrow I hope to see to the wedding arrangements. Understandably, concerns for your health came before our marriage, but once I have you settled in, I'll see to the necessary plans."

The beginnings of a headache thrummed at her temples. Was this what her life was going to be like? Him calling all the shots and her meekly following along? Not if she could help it. Right now, she was tired, worried and more than a little stressed, and as weak as it made her feel to hand everything over to him, it also felt good to relinquish her problems. Even if it was just for a little while.

"Does your head hurt you?" he asked.

She drew her hand away, unaware until now that she'd been rubbing her forehead. "Stress," she said in a shaky voice. "It's been a long couple of weeks. I'm tired."

What an idiot she was, outlining her weaknesses in stark detail. As if he hadn't already honed in on her disadvantages.

To her surprise, he didn't make any sharp or sarcastic remarks. He took her hands gently in his, and lowered them to her lap. Then he carefully helped her up.

Too stunned to do more than gape at him, she cooperated without complaint. He stepped behind her and sank down onto the seat, pulling her down onto his lap.

She landed with a jolt of awareness that five long months hadn't diminished in the least. There was still potent chemistry between them, much to her dismay.

His warmth wrapped around her, soothing her despite her rioting emotions. She was almost in complete panic when his fingers dug into her hair and began massaging her scalp.

A soft moan of surrender escaped her. Bliss. Sheer, unadulterated bliss. His strong fingers worked to her forehead and then her temples.

Bonelessly she melted further into his chest. He stiffened slightly and then relaxed as he continued his ministrations. For several long minutes, neither spoke, and only the sound of her soft breathing could be heard.

"Better?" he asked softly.

She nodded, unable to form coherent words. She was floating on a cloud of sheer delight.

"You are worrying yourself too much, *yineka mou*. The stress is not good for you or the baby. Everything will be all right. You have my word on it."

The statement was intended to comfort her, and she did appreciate his effort. But for some reason, his vow sounded ominous to her ears. Almost like this was a turning point in her life where nothing would ever be the same. Like she was giving up control, not just for the short term.

Of course things are changing irrevocably, you idiot. You're pregnant and getting married. How much more change could you possibly make?

Still, she tried to draw some comfort in the serious promise in his voice. He didn't trust her. She didn't think he even particularly liked her, but he desired her, that much was obvious. And she desired him. It wasn't enough. Not even close, but it was all they had.

Not exactly a prime start to a marriage.

Seven

Jewel tilted her head so she could see out the window as Piers pulled through the gates of a sprawling estate covered in lush green landscaping and well manicured shrubbery. The house came into view when they topped the hill, and her eyes widened in appreciation. Despite the size of the grounds, the house was what she'd deem modest in comparison.

Still it was gorgeous. Two stories with dormers and ivy clinging to the front. He'd said he rented the place. Who knew such places were for rent?

He parked in front of the garage that was adjacent to the main house. Behind them, the car carrying her newly assigned security detail pulled in. Before she could get out, one of the guards appeared and opened her door. He hovered protectively, shielding her…from what? Only when Piers reached for her hand, did the guard step away.

"I'm not helpless, you know," she said dryly when he tucked her against his side. But she would have been lying if she denied that having his help thrilled her in an inexplicable way. His body was warm and solid against hers. Strong. The idea that she wasn't alone nearly brought her to her knees.

"I know this," he said in his brusque accent. "But you've only just gotten out of the hospital, and you're carrying a child. If at any time you need help, it is certainly now."

She relaxed against him, refusing to spoil their first moments home with senseless, petty arguments.

Home. The word struck her in the chest, and even as she thought it, she shook her head in mute denial. She had no home.

"Is there something wrong?" he asked as they stopped at the door.

Embarrassed over her emotional display, she uttered a low denial.

He opened the door, and they stepped into the expansive foyer. Beyond was an elegant double staircase curving toward the top where a hallway connected the two sides of the house.

"Come into the living room, and I'll see to your things."

She allowed him to lead her to a comfortable leather couch that afforded a view of the patio through triple French doors. It would be a perfect breakfast spot, she thought with longing. The morning sun would shine perfectly on the garden table.

What would it be like to have a home like this? Filled with laughter and children. And then it occurred to her that it was entirely possible that part of that dream would come true.

She looked down at the gentle mound covered by her

thin shirt and slowly smoothed her hand over it. The baby kicked, and Jewel smiled.

She wanted to give her daughter all the things she'd never had, the things she longed for. Love, acceptance. A stable home.

Would Piers provide those things? Everything but love. Could Jewel love her baby enough to compensate for a father who didn't want her or her mother?

Damn if she hadn't done what she'd sworn never to do.

Piers traipsed inside the living room, hauling her two suitcases with him.

"I'll take these upstairs, and then I'll be down to make us some lunch. Is there anything you need in the meantime?"

Unnerved by his consideration, she shook her head. "I'm fine."

"Good, then I'll be right back."

She heard him rattle up the stairs, and she returned her perusal moodily to the outside. No longer content to look from afar, she got up and walked to the glass doors. She pressed her hand to the panes as she gazed over the magnificently rendered gardens.

It was extremely beautiful, but it almost looked sterile, as if no one ever touched it, or even breathed on it for that matter. It seemed…artificial. Not a living, breathing entity. Not like the ocean. It was always alive, rolling, sometimes peaceful and serene and at other times angry and forbidding.

A hand slipped over her shoulder, and she jumped. As she turned, she saw that Piers stood behind her, his expression mild and unthreatening.

"Sorry if I startled you. I called from across the room, but you didn't hear me obviously."

She offered a half smile, suddenly nervous in his presence.

"It's beautiful isn't it?"

"Yes, it is," she agreed. "I prefer the ocean, though. It's more…untamed."

"You find these gardens tame?"

"Mmm-hmm."

"I suppose I can see your point. Would you like to eat now? I had something dropped by before we arrived. It will only take a few minutes to warm everything up."

She turned sideways to face him. "Could we eat outside? It's a beautiful day."

"If you wish. Why don't you go on outside. I'll bring out the food in a moment."

His footsteps retreated across the wooden floors. When he was gone, she slipped out of the French doors and onto the stone patio.

The coolness caused her to shiver, but it was a beautiful day, one of the few where nothing marred the blue sky, and she didn't want to waste it by returning indoors.

She settled into one of the chairs to wait for Piers. It seemed odd to have this arrogant man waiting on her. He was clearly used to having the tables turned and being served.

The doors opened, and Piers elbowed his way out carrying two trays. He was a man of continuing surprises. He'd shown up at the hospital in time for her release, wearing a pair of faded jeans and a casual polo shirt, a far cry from the expensive designer clothing she knew he usually wore. He looked almost approachable. No less desirable, but definitely less threatening. In a more cynical moment, she wondered if he'd done it on purpose to lull her into a false sense of security.

He set a tray in front of her then placed his own across the table before taking a seat. She picked up her fork but made the mistake of looking over at him before she began to eat. He was staring intently at her, his food untouched.

"We have a lot to talk about, Jewel. After you eat, I plan to have the conversation we should have had a long time ago."

He sounded ominous, and a prickle of unease swept over her. What was left for them to discuss? He'd demanded she marry him, and she'd agreed. He'd demanded she move in with him, and she'd agreed. Quite frankly her acquiescence was starting to irritate the hell out of her.

They ate in silence, though she knew he watched her. The heat of his stare blazed over her skin, but she refused to acknowledge his perusal. He already had enough power over her.

When she'd finished, she put her fork down, and still refusing to look at him, she turned her gaze back to the gardens.

"Ignoring me won't help."

Finally she turned, sure she must look guilty. Now she felt childish for being so obvious, but the man made her nervous.

"We need to clear the air on a few matters. Mainly your firing."

She stiffened and clenched her fingers into small fists. "I'd just as soon not discuss it. No good can come of it, and I *am* supposed to keep my stress level down."

"I never intended to have you fired, Jewel. It was a despicable thing to have happened to you, and I accept full blame."

"Well who the hell else's fault would it be?" she demanded.

"It wasn't what I intended," he said again.

"Whether you intended it or not, it's what happened. Mighty coincidental that I got the sack as soon as you found out who I was, wouldn't you say?"

Piers blew out his breath, and his gaze narrowed. "You aren't going to make this easy, are you?"

She leaned back, this time giving him the full intensity of her stare. "Why should it be easy for you? It wasn't easy for me. I had no money left, no job. I came here because it was the only place I had to stay, and waitressing was the only quick job I could land. Then I started getting sick." She stopped and shook her head. She wasn't going to get into it with him.

"You're right. I'm sorry."

He looked and sounded sincere. Enough so that her next question slipped out before she could think better of it.

"If I wasn't supposed to be fired, how exactly did I end up sacked and escorted out of the hotel?"

Piers winced and dragged a hand through his hair. "As I said, it's completely my fault. I told my human resources manager to reassign you, or promote you or even to pay you for the term of your contract but I'm afraid the first words out of my mouth were to get rid of you. The rest, unfortunately, he didn't hear because the connection was severed. By the time I returned to the hotel and discovered the misunderstanding, you were gone. I had no luck tracing your whereabouts. In fact, I'd given up ever hearing from you again until you called."

She stared at him in disbelief. First, she couldn't believe he'd actually admitted his wrongdoing. Second, she couldn't fathom him looking for her afterward. It sounded suspiciously like he genuinely regretted what had happened.

"I don't get it," she said with genuine confusion. "Why couldn't we have just been adults about it? Why was it so important to you to get rid of me? I realize it wasn't an ideal situation, but it was an honest mistake. Neither of us knew who the other was or God knows I wouldn't have gone to bed with you that night."

"Then I guess it's a good thing you didn't know who I was," he said softly.

She looked down at her belly. "Yes, I don't regret it now at all."

"Did you then?"

He didn't look offended, only genuinely curious. He'd been honest with her so far, so she couldn't be anything other than completely honest with him.

"No. I didn't regret our night together."

He seemed satisfied with her answer. "To answer your question, it wasn't personal. What I mean is that it's not as if it was something you did. I have a strict policy about allowing anyone to work closely with me who has had any sort of a personal relationship with me. It's a necessary rule, unfortunately."

She raised an eyebrow. "You say that as if you were once burned."

"In a manner of speaking. My brother's personal assistant was enamored with him, but she was also selling company secrets and framed my sister-in-law."

"Sounds like a soap opera," Jewel muttered.

He chuckled. "It seemed like one at the time."

"You could have simply told me. You owed me that much given the fact we had spent the night together," she said, pinning him with the force of her gaze. "If you'd been up front with me, none of this would have happened. There would have been no misunderstanding."

"You're right. I'm afraid the shock of finding out who you were made my judgment particularly bad. I'm sorry."

His quietly spoken apology softened some of her anger. If she was honest, she still held resentment for the easy way he'd summarily dismissed her from his life. Not that she'd expected undying love and commitment, but hadn't the night meant something? Even enough to rate a personal dismissal instead of the job being handed off to a stooge?

Still, if this marriage was to be anything short of difficult and laced with animosity, she knew he had to let go of some of that resentment. Be the bigger person and all that jazz. Funny how taking the high road was never particularly fun.

"I accept your apology."

Surprise flickered in his dark eyes. "Do you really, I wonder?"

"I didn't say you were my best friend," she said dryly. "Merely that I'd accepted your apology. It seems the thing to do in light of our impending nuptials."

Amusement replaced the surprise. "I have a feeling we're going to get along just fine together, *yineka mou*." His gaze dropped to her stomach. "That is if you're telling me the truth."

For a moment, pain shadowed his eyes, and she wondered what sort of hell occurred in his past that would make him so distrustful. It went beyond mistrust. He didn't *want* to be the father of her child. He wanted her to be a liar and a deceiver. It was as if he knew how to handle those. But a woman telling him the truth? That was the aberration.

She must be insane to walk into this type of situation. There was every way for her to lose and no way to win.

"It does me little good to tell you that you're the father when you're determined not to believe me," she said evenly. "We'll have the paternity tests done and then you'll know."

"Yes. Indeed we'll know," he said softly.

"If you'll excuse me, I need to go dig out my laptop," she said as she rose from her seat. "I need to send an e-mail."

"And I have arrangements to make for our wedding."

She nodded because if she tried to say anything, she'd

choke. Not looking back at him, she hurried to the doors and went inside. Piers hadn't told her which bedroom was hers, but she'd find it easily enough.

She hit the stairs, and after going into three rooms on the upper level, she found her bags lying on the bed.

She unpacked her clothing first and put everything away before settling back onto the bed with her laptop. She checked her e-mail, but didn't see anything from Kirk. Not that she expected to. Sometimes they went months with no communication depending on his assignment and whether she was in a place she could e-mail him. Still, she felt like she owed him an explanation, and so she spilled the entire sordid tale in an e-mail that took her half an hour to compose.

When she was done, she was worn out and feeling more than a little foolish. There was no advice Kirk could offer, but she felt better for unloading some of her worries. He'd know better than anyone her fears of marriage and commitment.

Leaving her laptop open, she leaned back on the soft pillows to stare up at the ceiling. Contemplating her future had never been quite so terrifying as it was now.

Piers walked up the stairs toward Jewel's room. She'd been sequestered for two hours now. Surely that was enough time to have completed her personal business.

He stopped at her door and knocked softly, but he heard no answer from within. Concerned, he pushed open the door and stepped inside.

Jewel was curled on her side, her head buried in the down pillows. Sound asleep. She looked exhausted.

Her laptop was precariously close to the edge of the bed, and he hurried over to retrieve it before it fell. When

he placed it on the dresser, the screen came back up and
he saw that a new e-mail message was highlighted by the
cursor. It was from someone named Kirk.

With a frown, he scrolled down the preview screen to
read the short message.

Jewel,
  I'm on my way home. Don't do anything until I get
there. Okay? Just hang tight. I'll be there as soon as I
can hop a flight.
Kirk

Piers stiffened. Hell would freeze over before he'd
allow this man to interfere in his and Jewel's relationship.
She'd agreed to marry him, and marry him she would. He
didn't question why it was suddenly so important that the
wedding take place, but he'd be damned if he let another
man call the shots.

With no hesitation, he clicked on the delete button and
then followed it to the trash bin to permanently delete it
from her computer. Afterward, he pulled her e-mail back
up and then replaced the laptop on her bed, making sure it
was far enough from the edge so that it wouldn't topple over.

For a long moment, he stood by her bed and stared
down at her sleeping face. Drawn to the pensive expression, even in rest, he touched a few strands of her blond
hair, smoothing them from her cheek.

What demons existed in her life? She didn't trust him.
Not that he blamed her, but it went beyond anger or a sense
of betrayal. She wore shadows like most women wore
make-up. Somewhere, some way, someone had hurt her
badly. They had that in common.

As much as he'd like to swear never to hurt her and to

protect her from those who would, he knew that if she'd lied to him about the child, that he'd crush her without a second thought.

Eight

Jewel studied the unsmiling face of the man she'd chosen to represent her interests and wondered if any lawyer had a sense of humor or if they were all cold, calculating sharks.

But then she supposed when it came to her future and that of her child, she wanted the biggest, baddest shark in the ocean.

"The agreement is pretty straightforward, Miss Henley. It is in essence a prenuptial agreement which states that Mr. Anetakis's assets remain his in the event of a divorce and that yours remain yours."

Jewel snorted in amusement. What assets? She didn't have a damn thing, and Piers knew it.

"What else?" she asked impatiently. With a man like Piers, nothing could be as simple as it appeared. There were strings, hidden provisions. She just had to find them. "I want a complete explanation, line by line."

"Very well."

He shoved his glasses on and picked up the sheaf of papers as he took his seat again.

"Mr. Anetakis will provide a settlement for you regardless of the paternity of the child you carry. If DNA testing proves the child his, then he will retain custody of the child in the event of a divorce."

Her mouth fell open. "What?" She made a grab for the paper her lawyer held, scanning the document until she found the clause he referred to.

"He's out of his damn mind. There is no way in hell I'll sign anything that gives up custody of my child."

"I can strike the clause, but it's possible he won't agree."

She leaned forward, her breath hissing through her teeth. "I don't give a damn what he agrees to. I won't sign it unless this so-called clause is removed in its entirety."

Furious, she stood and snatched the paper back as the lawyer reached for it. "Never mind. I'll see to it myself."

She stormed out of the lawyer's office into the waiting room where Piers sat. He was sitting on the far side, his laptop open and his cell phone to his ear. When he looked up and saw her, he slowly closed the laptop.

"Is there a problem?"

"You bet there is," she said behind gritted teeth.

She thrust the offending piece of paper at him, pointing to the custody clause.

"If you think I'm signing anything that gives away custody of my child, you're an idiot. Over my dead body will I ever be separated from my child. As far as I'm concerned, you can take this…this prenuptial agreement and stick it where the sun doesn't shine."

He raised one dark eyebrow and stared back at her in silence.

"You don't seriously think that I would give up custody of *my* child, do you? If indeed it turns out I am the father."

She threw up her hands in exasperation. "You just don't miss a chance to take your potshots at me. I'm well aware of the fact that you don't believe this child is yours. Believe me, I get it. Reminding me at every opportunity just serves to further piss me off. And haven't you ever heard of a thing called joint custody? You know, that thing called compromise, where the parents consider what's best for the child and agree to give her equal time with her parents?"

"If the child is mine, I don't intend to see her on a part-time basis, nor do I intend I should have to work around your schedule. I can certainly provide more for her than you can. I'm sure she'd be much better off with me."

She curled her fingers into a tight fist, crumpling the document as rage surged through her veins like acid.

"You sanctimonious bastard. Where do you get off suggesting that my child would be better off with you? Because you have more money? Well big whoop. Money can't buy love, or security. It can't buy smiles or happiness. All the things a child needs most. Quite frankly, the fact that you think she would be so much better off with you tells me you don't have the first clue about children or love. How could you? I doubt you've ever loved anyone in your life."

Her chest heaved, and the paper was now a crumpled, soggy scrap in her hand. She started to hurl it at his feet, but he quickly rose and gripped her wrist, preventing her action. His eyes smoldered with rage, the first sign of real emotion she'd seen in him.

"You assume far too much," he said icily.

She wrenched her hand free and took a step backward.

"I won't sign it, Piers. As far as I'm concerned this marriage doesn't need to take place. There is no amount of desperation that would make me sign away my rights to my child."

He studied her for a long moment, his face as immovable as stone. "All right," he finally said. "I'll have my lawyer strike the clause. I'll call him now and he can courier over a new agreement."

"I'd wait," she said stiffly. "I'm not finished with my stipulations yet. I'll let you know when we're done."

She turned and stalked back into the lawyer's office, only to find him standing in the doorway, amusement carved on his face when she'd sworn he couldn't possibly have a sense of humor.

"What are you looking at?" she growled.

He sobered, although his eyes still had a suspicious gleam. "Shall we get on to your additions to the agreement?"

Three hours later, the final contract had been couriered from Piers's lawyer's office, and she and Piers read over and signed it together.

Jewel had insisted on an ironclad agreement that stated they would share custody of their child but that she was the primary custodian. She could tell Piers wasn't entirely happy with the wording, but she'd been resolute in her refusal to sign anything less.

"Clearly you've never learned the art of negotiation," Piers said dryly as they left the lawyer's office.

"Some things aren't negotiable. Some things *shouldn't* be negotiable. My child isn't a bargaining chip. She never will be," she said fiercely.

He held up his hands in mock surrender. "All I ask is that you see my side of the equation. As determined as you are to retain custody of your child, I am equally deter-mined not to let go of mine."

Something in his expression caused her to soften, some of her anger fleeing and leaving her oddly deflated. For a moment, she could swear he seemed afraid and a little vulnerable.

"I do see your point," she said quietly. "But I won't apologize for reacting as I did. It was a sneaky, under-handed thing to do."

"I apologize then. It was not my intention to upset you so. I was simply seeking to keep my child where she belongs."

"Maybe what we should be doing is working to prevent a divorce in the first place," she said tightly. "If we manage to make this marriage a success as you have suggested, then we won't have to worry about custody battles."

He nodded and opened the car door for her. She settled in but he stood there for a long moment, his hand on the door. "You're right. The solution is to make sure it never comes down to a divorce."

He quietly closed her door and strode around to his side. He slid in beside her and started the engine.

"Now that the unpleasantness is out of the way, we should move on to the more enjoyable aspects of planning a wedding."

Thus began an afternoon of shopping that made her head spin. Their first stop was at a jeweler. When they were shown a tray of stunning diamond engagement rings, she made the mistake of asking the price. Piers clearly wasn't happy with her question, but the jeweler answered her with ease. It was all she could do to scrape her jaw off the floor.

She shook her head, putting her hands out as she backed away from the counter. Piers caught her around the waist and pulled her back with tender amusement.

"Don't disappoint me. As a woman it's supposed to be ingrained for you to want to pick the biggest, most expensive ring in the shop."

"Indeed," the shop owner said solemnly.

"It's not good form to ask the price anyway," Piers continued. "Just pick the one you want and pretend there are no price tags."

"Your fiancé is a very wise man," the man behind the counter said. Laughter shone in the merchant's eyes, and Jewel relaxed at their teasing.

Trying not to think about the fact that what one ring cost could feed an entire third world nation, she went about studying each setting. After trying on no less than a dozen, she found the perfect ring.

It was a simple pear-shaped diamond, flawless as far as her untrained eye could tell. On either side was a small cluster of tiny diamonds.

"Your lady has exquisite taste."

"Yes, she does. Is this the one you want, *yineka mou?*" Piers asked.

She nodded, ignoring the sick feeling in her stomach. "I don't want to know how much it cost."

Piers laughed. "If it will make you feel better, I'll match the cost of the ring with a donation to the charity of your choice."

"Now you're making fun of me."

"Not at all. It's nice to know my new wife won't break me inside of a year."

He was trying hard to keep from laughing, and she leveled a glare at him. She marveled at the ease in which he flipped his credit card to the cashier, as if he were paying for a drink instead of a ring that costs thousands upon thousands of dollars.

He slid the ring on her finger and curled her hand until it made a fist. "Leave it on. It's yours now."

She glanced down, unable to keep from admiring it. It *was* a gorgeous ring.

"Now that the ring is out of the way, we should move onto other things like a dress and any other clothing you might need."

"Wow, a man who likes to shop. However have you existed as a single man this long?" she teased.

His expression became shuttered, and she mentally sighed at having once again said the wrong thing at the wrong time.

Determined to salvage the rest of the day despite its rocky start, she tucked her hand into his arm as they left the jeweler.

"I'm starving. Can we eat before we attack the rest of the shopping?"

"Of course. What would you like to eat?"

"I'd love a big, nasty steak," she said wistfully.

He laughed. "Then by all means, let's go kill a cow or two."

Nine

The fact that Jewel hid in her room didn't make her a coward exactly. It just made her reserved and cautious. Downstairs, Piers greeted his family who had flown in for the wedding. She still couldn't understand why. It wasn't as if this was a festive occasion, the uniting of kindred souls and all that gunk that surrounded marriage ceremonies.

All she knew about the rest of the Anetakis clan was that Piers had two older brothers, and both were recently married, and at least one child had been added. Hers would be the second.

And from all Piers had told her, his brothers were disgustingly in love.

She closed her eyes in recognition that she was green with envy, and she dreaded having to meet these disgustingly happy people.

They'd know it wasn't all hearts and roses between her and Piers. For that matter, she was sure Piers had told them the entire truth and that they were marrying because of a one-night stand and a faulty condom.

She stared back at her reflection in the mirror and tried to erase the glum look from her face. The dress she'd chosen for the occasion was a simple white sheath with spaghetti straps. The material gathered gently at her breasts, molding to her shape then falling over her belly where it strained and then hung loose down her legs.

She'd debated on whether to put her hair up or leave it down, but Piers had seemed to delight in her hair the night they met and so in a moment of sheer vanity, she brushed it until it shone and let it hang over her shoulders.

And now she procrastinated like the coward she was, knowing everyone was downstairs waiting for her.

Still bereft of the courage needed to walk down those stairs, she walked to her window to look down over the gardens. The sky was overcast and light fog had descended over the grounds. A perfect fit to her melancholy mood.

For how long she stood, she wasn't sure. A warm hand slid over her bare shoulder, but she didn't turn. She knew it was Piers.

Then something cool slithered around her neck, and she did turn her head.

"Be still a moment," he said as he reached under her hair to fasten a necklace at her nape. "My wedding gift to you. There are earrings to match, but I honestly couldn't remember if your ears were pierced or not."

She put a hand to the necklace and then hastened to the mirror so she could see. A gasp of surprise escaped when she saw the exquisite diamond arrangement.

"Piers, it's too much."

He smiled over her shoulder. "My sisters-in-law inform me that a husband can never do too much for his wife."

She smiled back. "They sound like smart women."

"There, that wasn't so bad was it?"

Her brow crinkled. "What?"

"Smiling."

Her eyes flashed in guilty awareness. He held out the box with the earrings, and she gazed in wonder at the large stones twinkling back at her.

"Are your ears pierced?"

She nodded. "I seldom wear earrings, but they are pierced."

"Then I hope you'll wear these today."

She took them and quickly fastened them in her ears. When her gaze returned to his, she found him watching her intently.

"Speaking of my sisters-in-law, they're anxious to meet you."

"And not your brothers?" she asked.

"They are a bit more reserved in their welcome. They worry for me. I'm afraid it's a family tradition to try and ruin the nuptials of the others," he said dryly.

She didn't know whether to laugh or feel dismay. Finally laughter won out. "Well at least you're honest. For that I'm grateful. It will keep me from making a fool of myself in their presence."

He shrugged. "You have nothing to be reserved about. You are to be my wife and that fact affords you the respect you are due. Theron is the soft touch in the family anyway. You'll have him eating out of your hand in no time."

She couldn't imagine anyone related to Piers being a soft touch.

"Are you ready?" he asked as he slipped his hands over

her shoulders. He squeezed reassuringly as if sensing her deep unease. "We have just enough time for you to be introduced to my family before the minister is due to arrive for the ceremony."

Inhaling deeply, she nodded. He took her hand firmly in his and led her out of the bedroom and down the stairs. As they neared the bottom, she heard the murmur of voices in the living room.

Butterflies scuttled around her stomach, and the baby kicked, perhaps in protest of her mother's unease.

When they rounded the corner, Jewel took in the people assembled in the living room with a bit of awe. The two men were obviously Piers's brothers. There was remarkable resemblance. Both were tall and dark-haired, but their eyes were lighter than Piers's, a golden hue while Piers's were nearly black.

The two women standing next to his brothers were as different as night and day. Before she could continue her silent perusal, they looked up and saw her.

The brothers gave her guarded looks while the two women smiled welcomingly. She was grateful for that at least.

"Come, I'll introduce you," Piers murmured.

They closed the distance, stopping a few feet from the two couples.

"Jewel, this is my oldest brother Chrysander and his wife Marley. Their son, Dimitri is with his nanny for the day."

Jewel offered a tremulous smile. "I'm happy to meet you."

Marley smiled, her blue eyes twinkling with friendliness. "We're happy to meet you too, Jewel. Welcome to the family. I hope you'll be happy. When are you due?"

Jewel blinked and then returned her smile. "I'm a little over five months along."

"Hello, Jewel," Chrysander said in his deep voice.

She swallowed and nodded her greeting to Piers's oldest brother. Intimidating. How could anyone stand to be around the three of the Anetakis brothers at the same time?

Piers turned to the other couple. "This is my brother Theron and his wife, Bella." Piers's entire expression softened into a fond smile when he touched Bella's arm. She smiled mischievously back at Piers and then looked up at Jewel.

"We're both happy to meet you, Jewel," Bella said. She nudged Theron with her elbow. "Aren't we, Theron?"

"Of course, Bella *mou*," he said in a teasing tone. It was as if all attempt to maintain a serious air went out the window when he looked at his wife. Then he turned his attention to Jewel. "Welcome to our family. I'm not sure whether to offer my congratulations or my condolences on marrying my brother."

Jewel smiled at his attempt at humor, and Piers snorted.

"If you're quite through insulting me, I'll offer everyone a drink to celebrate the occasion. The minister should be here at any moment to perform the ceremony."

The others watched her curiously as Piers left her side to collect a chilled bottle of champagne. He passed glasses to everyone and then popped the cork.

When he came to her, he handed her a glass of mineral water instead. She was touched by his thoughtfulness and smiled her thanks.

Chrysander cleared his throat, and Marley slipped her arm into his. "Our best wishes for a long and…happy marriage," he added after a slight pause.

They raised their glasses in a toast, and for a moment, Jewel wished, oh how she wished that it was all real, and that this was her family and that she and Piers were in love and expecting their first child with all the joy of a happily married couple.

She dreamed of Christmas celebrations, birthdays and get-togethers just for the heck of it and a loud rambunctious family, loyal to a fault.

Tears pricked her eyelids as she bade goodbye to that dream and embraced her reality. She hastily gulped her water in an effort to regain control of her emotions.

Piers stood at her side and bent his head low to her ear. "What is it, *yineka mou?* What has upset you?"

"I'm fine," she said, pasting on a bright smile.

The doorbell rang, and she jumped.

His fingers cupped her elbow, and he rubbed a thumb across her skin in a soothing manner. "It's just the minister here to marry us. I'll go let him in."

She almost asked him not to go, but how silly was she to be worried about being left alone with his relatives? She chanced a glance at the two couples, standing so close, so lovingly together, and her heart ached all over again.

"Between you and Marley, Theron is going to get all the wrong ideas," Bella said to Jewel.

"And how is this?" Theron demanded.

"All these babies and pregnant women," she said mischievously. "I fully expect Theron to start hinting about knocking me up just any day now."

Jewel laughed, charmed by Bella's easy humor and how relaxed she was around everyone. Clearly she wasn't worried about her place in this family. No one seemed to mind her outrageous statement in the least.

Marley tried to stifle her laughter while Chrysander just groaned. Theron's eyes took on a sensual light that almost made Jewel feel like a voyeur.

"Oh no, Bella *mou*. We have much practicing to do before we get you pregnant."

"See, Jewel, it's not so hard to train the Anetakis men," she said cheekily. "Marley has whipped Chrysander into admirable shape, while I have turned Theron to my way of thinking. I can't imagine you being any less successful with Piers."

"Theron, keep your woman quiet," Chrysander said mildly. "She's inciting discontent among the female ranks."

Marley elbowed him sharply, but her eyes were alight with amusement and love.

Piers walked back in with an elderly man, their heads turned in conversation. When the minister saw Jewel, he smiled and went forward, his hands outstretched.

"You must be the bride to be. You look lovely, my dear. Are you ready for the ceremony to begin?"

She swallowed and nodded, though her legs were trembling.

The minister introduced himself to the others, and after a few moments of polite conversation, Piers motioned that he was ready to begin.

It was all quite awkward, at least for Jewel. The rest acted as if this was the sort of ceremony they attended every day. Piers and Jewel stood in front of the minister while each couple flanked them.

Her throat tightened as she listened to Piers promise to love, honor and cherish her all the days of his life and until death do they part. And then it struck her square in the face that she wanted him to love her. Why? Did that mean she loved him? No, she didn't. She couldn't. She didn't know how to love any more than she knew how to be loved. But it didn't stop the yearning inside.

When the ceremony concluded, Piers brushed a per-functory kiss across her lips and then stepped back to receive his brothers' somewhat muted congratulations.

Chrysander insisted on taking them all out to eat after-ward, and a limousine took all three couples into the heart of the city to an upscale restaurant that boasted delicious seafood.

She was hungry, but the idea that she was now married effectively put a damper on her appetite. She picked and pushed at her food until finally Piers took notice.

He picked up her hand, and the band he'd placed on her finger just hours before gleamed behind the diamond en-gagement ring in the low light.

"Are you ready to return home?" he whispered so the others wouldn't hear. "I can send them on at any time."

"They're your family," she protested. "I've no wish to cut short your visit."

He laughed. "You're very thoughtful, *yineka mou,* but I see them often, and if there is ever a time I can send them away, surely my wedding day is one of them? They would understand—having had their wedding nights not too long ago."

She froze as his meaning became clear. Surely he wasn't thinking that…no, he couldn't, could he? He'd been present when her doctor said there was no reason she couldn't indulge in lovemaking, but she'd assumed that Piers had taken it as the doctor thinking they were in a normal relationship. Did this mean he wanted to make love to her? To actually consummate the marriage?

His hand covered hers, idly stroking the tops of her fingers as he turned to the others and told them that he and Jewel were ready to go.

There were hugs, polite kisses and teasing good-byes.

Piers hugged each of his sisters-in-law, and she could tell that he regarded them with great affection. It was quite a change to the way he looked at her with so much distrust in those dark eyes.

And then they were on their way. Piers had left the limousine to the others and called for a car to pick them up. The ride home was quiet, and finally, unable to stand the tension, she turned her head in the darkness of the backseat only to see him staring at her, those dark eyes nearly invisible.

"What is bothering you, *yineka mou?*"

"Are you expecting a wedding night?" she blurted.

White teeth flashed as he smiled. It was a decidedly predatory smile, and it sent shivers down her spine.

"But of course. You're my wife now. A wedding night usually does follow a wedding, does it not?"

"I…I just wasn't sure, I mean this isn't a real marriage, and I didn't think you wanted much to do with me."

"Oh, I intend for it to be very real," he said softly. "Just as I intend for you to spend tonight and every night in my bed."

Ten

All she had to do was say no. It wasn't as if Piers would force her. Jewel stepped from the car, her hand in Piers's as he pulled her to his side. A shiver overtook her when the night chill brushed her skin, and she unconsciously moved closer to his warmth.

The question was, did she want to tell him no? And what purpose would it serve except to make him further distrust her and her motives?

As soon as the thought materialized, she clenched her teeth in anger. If the only reason she could muster to go to bed with him was so that he'd trust her more then she needed a serious reality check, not to mention she needed a few more brain cells.

Admit it, you want him.

And there it was. She did. The one night they'd shared burned brightly in her memory. She was married to him, and she wanted him to love her. She wanted him to trust her, and neither could happen if she maintained the distance between them.

Determined to embrace her marriage without being a martyr, she slipped her fingers tighter through Piers's and hurried alongside him into the house.

"I know today was hard for you, *yineka mou.* I hope it wasn't too taxing for you and the baby."

Had he changed his mind about making love to her? It sounded like he was offering an out. Or was he simply giving her the choice?

"I'm perfectly all right," she said softly as they stepped into the foyer.

He turned, putting his hands gently on her upper arms. "Are you?"

She stared back, knowing what he was really asking. Slowly she nodded, her senses firing in rapid succession.

"Be sure, Jewel. Be very sure."

Again she nodded, and before she could say or do anything else, he pulled her to him and covered her mouth hotly with his.

He swallowed her breath, took every bit of air and left her gasping for more. How was it he made her so weak? She sagged against him, clutching desperately at his shirt.

His tongue invaded her mouth, sliding sensuously over her lips and inside, tasting her and giving her his taste.

"Sweet," he murmured. "So sweet. I want you, *yineka mou.* Say you want me too. Let me take you upstairs. I want to make love to you again."

"Yes. Please, yes." She gasped when he swung her into his arms. "Piers no, I'm too heavy."

"Do you doubt my strength?" he asked in amusement as he mounted the stairs.

"I'm huge," she said in exasperation.

"You're beautiful."

He carried her through the doorway to the master bedroom and laid her carefully on the bed. With gentle fingers he slipped the thin straps over her shoulders and let them fall. He tugged farther until the dress eased over her sensitive breasts, the material scraping lightly at her nipples.

Farther and farther, it inched over her belly, then to her hips and finally down her legs. When it swirled around her ankles, he pulled it free and dropped it on the floor.

Sharp tingles raced up her legs when he rasped his palms back up to her hips where he tucked his thumbs underneath the lace of her panties. Then he lowered his mouth and pressed a kiss to her taut belly as he slid the underwear down and then free. Her legs parted in exquisite anticipation as his mouth traveled lower and lower still.

Cupping her behind, he gently spread her wider, and his tongue found her in a heated rush. She arched off the bed, twisting wildly as pleasure consumed her.

His mouth found her again and again, gentle and worshipping. It was hard to breathe, hard to think, hard to do anything but feel. Her orgasm built, and every muscle in her body tightened in response. Just when she knew she couldn't bear it any longer, he pulled away, and she whimpered in protest.

"Shhh." He murmured to her again in Greek, raining soft words over her skin as he moved up her body. How had he gotten his clothes off without her noticing?

Flesh against flesh, smooth, comforting, a balm to her reeling senses. His mouth closed around one taut nipple, sucking and tugging. One hand cupped her rounded middle, his fingers splayed possessively over their child.

It was the first movement he'd made to actually acknowledge her presence, and she wondered if he even knew what he was doing.

"Open your legs for me, *yineka mou*. Welcome me inside."

She could barely make herself respond. She shook and quivered as he settled between her thighs, his shaft nudging impatiently.

And then he was inside her in one smooth thrust.

She cried out and gripped his shoulders, her nails digging deep.

"That's it. Hold on to me. I've got you."

Their lips fused, their tongues tangling wildly as their bodies met and retreated. Pressure built until she simply couldn't bear it any longer. Her release exploded with the force of a hurricane.

He followed, surging into her, over and over, his husky groan filling her ears as he poured himself into her.

She closed her eyes, allowing sweet fuzzy bliss to encompass her, and when she gained awareness, it was to Piers's arms wrapped tightly around her, her body tucked into his side.

His lips moved through her hair as his hand went to cup her backside in a possessive gesture. She melted bonelessly into him and sighed in contentment. The wispy hairs on his chest tickled her nose and whispered across her lips, but she didn't move. She felt safe. More than that, she felt loved.

Jewel awoke the next morning to Piers sitting on the side of the bed holding a tray with breakfast and a single long-stemmed rose. He had only a pair of silk pajama bottoms on, and her gaze was drawn to his muscled chest, a chest she'd slept on for most of the night.

"Good morning," he said. "Are you hungry?"

"Starved," she admitted as she sat up in bed.

Then she realized she was still nude, and she yanked at the sheet, a hot flush surging up her neck and to her cheeks.

Piers caught her hand, stopping the sheet from its upward climb. "Don't be shy with me. I've seen and tasted every inch of your sweet body."

She slowly uncurled her fingers and relaxed her tense shoulders. He leaned in and kissed her long and slow, his lips exploring hers. This fantasy he spun allured her, drew her in and surrounded her in its firm grip.

A night of making love, breakfast in bed, tender kisses and gentle words.

If only it were all real.

Was he playing with her? Toying with her emotions? How could he act with such caring when he thought she was a liar and a manipulator?

"I'd give a lot of pennies for your thoughts right now."

She blinked and looked up to see him staring intently at her. No, he didn't really want to know what she was thinking. It would put the frown he so often wore right back on his face, and right now, she enjoyed the odd tenderness in the dark depths of his gaze.

"I'm thinking this is a nice way to wake up," she said with a smile.

He rubbed his thumb over her bottom lip and then trailed his fingers over her cheek, pushing back the wayward strands of her hair.

"Eat your breakfast. Your appointment is in two hours."

An appointment she'd forgotten in the aftermath of her wedding. She was scheduled for a sonogram as part of her pre-op workup. Afterward, she'd have more blood drawn and talk to the scheduling clerk about when she would be admitted to the hospital.

He placed the tray over her legs then handed her the utensils. "I'm going to go shower and shave. I have a few calls to make, and then I'll drive you to your appointment."

She glanced at his lean jaw, shadowed by the night's growth. Unable to resist, she lifted fingers to touch the hard edge of his chin and brushed the tips over the rough surface. His eyes closed as he leaned into her palm.

"Thank you."

He pulled away. "You're welcome. I'll leave you to eat now."

She watched as he walked away, his long stride eating up the floor. Despite the fact she had a delicious meal in front of her, her thoughts were of Piers in the shower, water sluicing over his muscled body. If she were daring, she'd go join him, but she had to admit, she had reservations about approaching him. So far, she'd allowed him to make the moves. It gave her an opportunity to study him and to figure out more about this man who'd upended her life.

Again she looked down at the sparkling diamond on her third finger. The weight was odd. She hadn't grown used to it yet, but she was fascinated by the sight and also by the meaning. In many ways it was a stamp of possession. She belonged to someone.

Realizing she'd spent too much time daydreaming, she hurriedly ate. After showering and dressing, she ventured downstairs where she found Piers in his study on the phone.

When he looked up and saw her standing at the door, he held up one finger to signal he'd be just a minute and then turned back to the phone.

Not wanting to intrude, she retreated back to the living

room to wait. He wasn't long. He was tucking his phone into his pocket when he strode into the living room.

"I've arranged for a chef for the time we're here. He'll arrive this afternoon in time to prepare tonight's dinner."

"You didn't really need to do that. I was only teasing."

"On the contrary. It was an excellent idea. You certainly don't need to be on your feet cooking, and if it was left to me, I'm afraid you'd grow tired of my limited culinary repertoire."

"You're shamelessly spoiling me," she protested, though it sounded weak even to her.

He half-smiled, something flickering in his eyes. It was that same look he always seemed to wear around her. "That's the idea." He looked down at his watch. "Are you ready? We ought to leave now in case traffic is bad."

She nodded and rose from her perch on the couch.

When they arrived for her appointment, Piers surprised her by staying at her side every step of the way. She'd imagined that he might sit in the waiting room, but he went back and listened with concentration to everything the nurse and the doctor had to say.

When it came time for her sonogram, Piers was like a child in a candy store. He studied each image, and one time he almost touched the screen.

"Is that her?" he asked as he pointed to one tiny fist.

The sonogram tech smiled. "She's sucking her thumb. Here's her chin," he said, tracing a small curve on the screen. "Here's her fist. She's got her thumb in her mouth."

Tears simmered in Jewel's eyes as she stared in awe at her child. "She's beautiful."

Piers turned to her, his voice husky and oddly emotional. "Yes, she is *yineka mou*. Very beautiful like her mother."

"What about the cyst?" Jewel asked anxiously. "Has it gotten smaller?"

"Unfortunately no. I'll have to compare the measurements to the last we recorded, but I think it's grown a little larger."

Jewel's face fell, and she closed her eyes. Somehow she'd hoped for a small miracle. That maybe the cyst would shrink so she wouldn't have to undergo surgery. She didn't want to risk anything that would harm her baby.

Piers found her hand and squeezed reassuringly. "We'll speak with the doctor and all will be well."

She clung to him, basking in his confidence. She needed it desperately because hers was flagging.

The sonogram tech rolled the portable machine out of her room, and she and Piers waited in anxious silence. He seemed far too calm, but then what did she expect? He didn't want this child. Didn't even believe it was his.

But he's here.

That meant something, didn't it?

The silence was disturbed when the doctor came back in, his expression pensive as he studied her chart.

"Miss Henley, it's good to see you again."

Piers cleared his throat. "It's Mrs. Anetakis now. I'm her husband, Piers." He thrust out his hand to shake the doctor's, and Jewel blinked as she watched Piers take control of the situation.

He and the doctor spoke of her condition and upcoming surgery as if she weren't in the room. At first she listened in befuddlement, and then anger stirred. This was her health, her child.

"I will decide when the surgery is to be scheduled," she said fiercely.

Piers touched her once on the knee. "Of course, *yineka*

mou. I am merely trying to understand all that is at stake here."

She flushed, sure she sounded petty and difficult, but she could literally feel the threads of her life slipping away, becoming permanently tangled in his.

"It should be done soon, Mrs. Anetakis," the doctor said. "I've consulted with a colleague of mine who will be assisting. It's a delicate surgery to be sure, but we feel confident of its success."

"And my baby?" she whispered.

He offered a soothing smile. "Your child will be fine."

"All right."

As they prepared to leave, the nurse gave Jewel instructions for when to report to the hospital. The entire thing scared her to death. Before she'd been able to put it out of her mind, but now it was there, staring her in the face.

"Come," Piers said quietly. He guided her toward his car and settled her inside.

For the first several miles, they drove in complete silence. Jewel stared out at the passing scenery, her mind occupied with the coming surgery.

"Tell me something. If you could live anywhere, anywhere at all, where would it be?"

Startled by the unexpected question, she turned to look at him. "The beach, I suppose." She smiled suddenly. "I've always dreamed of one of those big houses that overlooks the beach from a cliff." Her eyes closed as she imagined the sound of the waves crashing on the rocks. "A patio to watch the sun set in the evenings. What about you?"

His eyes never left the road, but she could feel him tense slightly.

"I've never given it much thought."

"Where did you live before? I mean before all this?"

A sardonic smile quirked his lip. "I don't have a permanent residence. I travel often and when I'm not away on business, I choose one of my hotels and I stay there."

"Your life sounds a lot like mine."

He cocked his head to the side and glanced at her for a moment. "How so?"

She shrugged. "No home."

He frowned as though he'd never had such a thought. And then his lips twisted ruefully. "I suppose you're right. Indeed I have many residences but no home. Perhaps you can solve that for me, *yineka mou.*"

They pulled into the long drive to the house, but it wasn't until they came to a stop in the circle drive that Jewel saw the car parked in front of them. Was Piers expecting more company?

Then her gaze traveled to the front entrance and to the man sitting on the steps by the door.

"Kirk!"

As soon as the car stopped, she flew out and ran toward her friend.

Kirk rose when he saw her, a deep scowl on his face. But he caught her as she ran into his arms and hugged her fiercely.

"What the devil is going on, Jewel?" he demanded.

"I think that should be what I'm asking," Piers said coolly.

Jewel turned to see Piers staring at them, his eyes steely.

"Piers, this is a good friend of mine, Kirk. Kirk, this is Piers…my husband."

Kirk swore. "Damn it, Jewel, I told you to wait until I got here."

She swung back around to Kirk. "What are you talking about?"

"I e-mailed you after you e-mailed me telling me your

situation and that you were marrying this guy." He made an angry sweeping motion toward Piers.

"But I didn't get any e-mail. I swear. I had no idea if you'd even get mine."

Piers stepped to Jewel's side and wrapped an arm around her. He held her so tightly that she couldn't move.

"And did you rush all this way to offer us your congratulations?" Piers asked smoothly. "I'm sorry to say you missed the ceremony."

Kirk frowned even harder. "I'd like to talk to Jewel alone. I'm not leaving here until she convinces me that this is what she wants."

"Anything you have to say in front of my *wife,* can be said in front of me."

"Piers, stop," she said sharply. "Kirk is a very dear friend, and I owe him an explanation." She pried herself away from Piers and laid her hand on Kirk's arm. "Have you eaten anything?"

Kirk shook his head. "I hopped a flight and came straight here."

"Come in then. We can go out on the patio to eat, and we can talk."

She could have broken a stone on Piers's face. Without a word, he turned and stalked away, disappearing into the house.

"Nice guy," Kirk muttered.

Jewel sighed. "Come on in. I'll get us something to eat."

Eleven

Piers stood in the living room, sipping his drink and staring broodingly to the terrace where Jewel sat entertaining her guest.

Just who was this Kirk to her? Was he the father of her child? Had he left her high and dry and now had a change of heart? For all he knew, the two of them could be taking him on the ride of his life.

His eyes narrowed when he saw Jewel smile and then laugh at something Kirk had said. Then they both stood and Kirk drew her into his arms, hugging her tightly.

Piers's fingers curled into tight fists at his side. Then, before they returned inside, he walked away, determined not to give her the satisfaction of rising to her bait.

He was halfway across the room when he realized what he was doing. Running. That made him more furious than the thought of her making a fool of him. No woman was going to force him into retreat.

He turned to face them when the French doors opened. His gaze swept coldly over Kirk and then Jewel. She answered him with a frown, her eyes reproachful.

"Everything cleared up?" he asked mildly.

"Not really," Kirk said in a tight voice. "I've offered my assistance to Jewel so that her only alternative isn't marriage to you."

"How kind, only it's too late. She's my wife."

"Divorces are easy enough to get."

"I suppose they are, providing I was willing. I'm not."

"Stop it, both of you," Jewel demanded. "Kirk, please. I appreciate your help more than you know, but Piers is right. It's too late. We're married, and I want to make the best of it."

Kirk's expression softened as he looked at Jewel. "If you need anything at all, get in touch with me. It might take me a few days to get to you, but I'll be there, okay?"

Jewel smiled and hugged him tightly. "Thank you, Kirk. I appreciate everything you've done and for letting me stay in the apartment."

So it was Kirk's apartment and not Jewel's. She obviously hadn't been exaggerating when she said she had no money and no place to stay.

Guilt crowded into his mind again at the idea of her alone and in desperate need of help.

Kirk kissed her forehead and then pulled away. "If you're sure there isn't anything I can do, I'm going to head back to the airport and see if I can hop a flight today. If I'm lucky, I can be back on location in a day and a half."

"I'm just sorry you made the trip for nothing. If I'd gotten your e-mail, I would have told you not to bother coming."

Piers fought to maintain a neutral expression. Deleting the e-mail had backfired on him. If she was telling the truth.

She walked Kirk to the door, and they both disappeared outside. A few minutes later, Piers heard the car drive away and then Jewel came back inside, her expression stormy.

"What the hell was all that about?" she demanded.

He raised an eyebrow at the force of her anger. She was bristling from head to toe and her eyes shot ocean-colored daggers at him.

"Funny, I should be asking you that question."

"What are you talking about? Kirk is a good friend of mine. The only friend I have. If you have a problem with that, you can take a hike."

"So fiercely loyal," he murmured. "I wonder, though, if that loyalty extends to me?"

"Cut the crap, Piers. If you want a fight, let's fight, but I don't have time for little psychological games."

"Is that what we're doing? Fighting? It's a little soon for our first marital spat, wouldn't you say?"

"Go to hell."

With that, she turned and stomped up the stairs. A few seconds later, the door to her bedroom slammed with enough force to shake the house.

So she had a temper. He'd purposely baited her for no other reason than his anger over his apparent jealousy. The woman had him tied in knots, and he didn't like that one little bit.

If this Kirk was so hot to trot to come to Jewel's aid, where had he been when she really needed him? If he was the father of her child, had he deserted them both and was now only back because he had competition? Or was this an elaborate hoax for them both to con him out of a fortune? He must have played right into Jewel's hands when he offered her a generous settlement if the child turned out not to be his and they divorced. It was probably her plan all along.

But then the entire scheme hinged on him granting her a divorce. He smiled coldly. He couldn't wait to inform her that there would *be* no divorce.

Dinner was quiet and strained. Jewel was still furious over the way Piers had acted toward Kirk, and Piers's face was cast in stone. He ate as though nothing had occurred between them at all, and that made her even angrier. How were they supposed to have an argument when he didn't cooperate?

Dessert was served, and as much as she wanted to enjoy the decadent chocolate tart, it tasted like sawdust.

"I've been thinking," Piers said. He spoke coldly, with no warmth or inflection in his voice.

She didn't answer and continued to concentrate on dissecting her dessert.

"I no longer feel that divorce is an option."

Shocked, she dropped her fork, and winced at the loud clatter. "What? You believe that the baby is yours now? Before we get the results?"

He raised an eyebrow in a manner meant to make her feel inferior and at a disadvantage. It was mocking, almost as if he were laughing at her.

"I'm not a fool, Jewel. You'd do well to remember that."

"Then why this nonsense about a divorce? The child is yours, but you've never been inclined to believe that. Why on earth would you suggest there be no divorce until you're sure?"

"Maybe I'm just letting you know that your plan won't work. I won't grant a divorce, regardless of whether the child is mine."

He seemed to be studying her, waiting for a reaction. What kind of reaction? What was he thinking now?

And then it hit her like a ton of bricks. Her mouth fell open in disgust.

"You think this is a scheme to extort money from you. You think that Kirk is the father, and that I'm some whore sleeping with both of you."

She hadn't imagined that anyone had the power to hurt her anymore. Long ago, she'd developed impenetrable armor against the kind of pain other humans inflicted. Despite it all, hurt overwhelmed her. She felt betrayed even though she never imagined she had his loyalty.

With shaking legs, she clumsily got out of her chair, shoving it backward with more force than was necessary. She was determined not to break down in front of him. Before she escaped the room, she turned one last time to him.

"Who did this to you, Piers? Who made you into a bastard who won't trust anyone, and how long will it take you to figure out that I'm not her?"

She hurried away, no longer able to stand his brooding gaze.

Instead of retreating upstairs, she let herself out the French doors and ventured into the gardens. A chill chased away the flush of anger, and she gathered her arms close to her as she walked down a spiraling pathway deeper into the heart of the greenery.

Old-fashioned street lamps lit most of the paths. Finally she found a round, stone table with a circular bench. It was the perfect place to sit and enjoy the night air.

What had she done? She rubbed her stomach absently, thinking about her daughter and the future. A future that didn't seem quite as bright as it had before. Piers was being vengeful over a perceived wrong she hadn't dealt him, and so he'd decided, as if she had no choice or say in the matter, that there wouldn't be a divorce.

Oh, she knew according to his stipulations that there would never be a divorce because she knew the child was his. Only he seemed convinced otherwise.

What kind of life had she consigned herself and her child to? Would Piers's attitude soften toward their daughter when he learned the truth? And what about Jewel? Would she forever be relegated to just being the woman who gave birth to his daughter or would he soften toward her as well?

"You shouldn't be out here alone."

She whirled around, her anger surging back when she saw Piers standing there, hands shoved insolently into his pockets.

"I'm hardly alone, am I? No doubt there are countless security men surrounding me."

He nodded as he walked closer. "Yes, but you shouldn't take such a risk just because I have a security detail."

"Tell me, Piers, will your security detail protect me from you?" she asked mockingly.

"Interesting choice of words. I feel as though I'm the one in need of protecting."

She turned away, her shoulders shaking. "I want out, Piers. Immediately."

She heard his swift intake of breath and his hiss of anger.

"I've just told you I won't grant you a divorce."

"At this point, I couldn't care less. It isn't as if I ever intend to marry again. I just want to be away from you. Keep your damn settlement. I don't want anything from you. Just my freedom. I'll leave immediately."

She lurched forward, taking the spiraling pathway that

would lead her back to the house, but Piers was beside her in an instant, his hand tight around her arm.

"You can't go anywhere at this hour, Jewel. Be sensible."

"Sensible?" She laughed. "Now you tell me to be sensible. I should have been sensible the moment you walked back into my life and took it over."

"Stay until morning. You won't have to concern yourself with me asserting my husbandly rights."

"And you'll let me go?" she asked incredulously.

"If you still want to, then yes."

She studied him in the dark, and shook her head at the emotionless set to his face. Did he feel anything ever? Did he have a soul or had he given it away long ago?

"All right then. I'll leave first thing in the morning. Now if you'll excuse me, I'd like to go to bed."

Piers watched her go, his chest tight with something that felt remarkably like panic. Of all the reactions he might have expected, this wasn't one of them. When confronted with her deception, he'd expected tears, recriminations, even pleas to help her anyway. He hadn't expected her to tell him to go to hell and leave. Where was the profit in that?

Now he was stuck with thinking of a way to persuade her to stay. Until he figured out this puzzle, he needed her where he could find her at all times. For the first time, a surge of excitement tingled his nape. Could it be that she was really pregnant with his child? That this time, he had rights where the child was concerned?

If so, there was no way he would let Jewel walk out of his life.

Twelve

Unable to sleep, Jewel spent her time packing her clothing. She hadn't even unpacked everything yet, so the task didn't take her long. The rest of her time was spent sitting on the bed, her hands braced on the mattress as she silently stewed.

Why had she married Piers? It was a stupid decision, and yes, she'd been desperate, but not so desperate that she had called Kirk. No, she'd called *Piers* and then allowed him to take over and demand she marry him.

Face it. You're a hopeless dreamer.

All of the things she supposedly no longer believed in had guided her every step for the last five months. Was it any wonder she'd royally screwed up?

At two in the morning, she was lying in bed, in the dark, staring toward the window at the full moon spilling through the panes. She'd just closed her eyes and considered that she might finally fall asleep when sharp pain lanced through her side, stealing her breath with its intensity.

She drew her knees up in automatic defense, and another tearing pain ripped through her abdomen. She couldn't breathe, couldn't think, couldn't even process what she needed to do.

When the agony let up, she rolled toward the edge of the bed. Fear was as strong as the pain now. Fear for her child. Was she losing her baby?

Tears blurred her vision as she groped for a handhold. Her feet dangled above the floor when pain assaulted her again. She fell the rest of the way, landing with a thump on her side. She lay there, gasping for air, tears rolling down her cheeks as wave upon wave of pain shredded her insides.

Piers, she had to get to Piers.

She pushed her palm down on the surface of the floor, trying to lever herself up. The pain was unrelenting now. Nausea rolled through her stomach, swelling in her throat until she gagged.

She clamped her mouth shut and took deep breaths through her nose.

"Piers!"

It sounded weak, and her door was closed.

"Piers!" she said louder, and collapsed again when pain slashed through her side again.

Oh God, he wasn't coming. He probably couldn't hear her, and she couldn't get up.

Tears slipped faster down her cheeks, and she moaned helplessly as the tearing sensation overwhelmed her.

Then she heard the door fly open. The light flipped on, and footsteps thumped across the floor.

"Jewel! What's wrong? Is it the baby?"

Piers knelt beside her, his hands flying across her body and her stomach. He started to turn her, and she cried out in pain.

"Tell me what's wrong, *yineka mou*. Tell me how to help you," he said desperately.

"Hurt," she gasped out. "I hurt so much."

"Where?"

"My side, my stomach. Low—around my pelvis. God, I don't know. It hurts everywhere."

"Shhh, I'll take care of you," he said soothingly. "It'll be all right. I promise."

He gathered her in his arms and lifted her up.

"Will you be all right if I lay you on the bed for a moment? I need to get dressed, and then I'll drive you to the hospital."

She nodded against his chest, unable to form even a simple word.

He strode into his bedroom and settled her on the same bed they'd made love in the night before. His scent surrounded her, and oddly, offered her comfort.

It seemed to take him forever to dress, but finally he was back, pulling her to him. He hurried down the stairs and outside into the chilly night.

"I'm going to put you in the backseat so you can lie down," he murmured. "I'll have you at the hospital quickly. Try to hold on, *yineka mou*."

She curled into a ball as soon he put her down and clenched her fingers into tight fists to combat the urge to scream.

Not the baby. Please don't let it be the baby.

She barely registered the car stopping or Piers picking her up again. There were voices around her, a prick in her arm, the cold sheets of a bed, bright lights and then a strange man peering down into her eyes.

"Mrs. Anetakis, can you hear me?"

She nodded and tried to speak. Piers squeezed her hand—how long had he been there holding it?

"The cyst on your ovary has caused your tube to torque. I've called in your obstetrician. He wants us to prep you for surgery."

A low whimper erupted from her throat. Piers moved closer to her, smoothing his free hand through her hair in a comforting gesture.

"It will be all right, *yineka mou*. The doctor has assured me that you will receive the best care. Our baby will be just fine."

Our baby, she thought drowsily. Had he said our baby or was she imagining it? She couldn't quite get her thoughts together. The pain had diminished and she felt like she was floating on a light cloud.

"What did you do to me?" she asked.

She heard a light chuckle from the nurse at her head.

"Just something to make you more comfortable. We'll be wheeling you in to surgery in just a moment."

"Piers?"

"I'm here, *yineka mou*." Again his hand stroked her hair, and she turned into his palm, her eyes fighting to stay open.

"You said our baby. You believe she's yours?"

There was a hesitation, and she blinked harder to keep him in focus. There were worry lines crowding his forehead. Was he concerned for the baby?

"Yes, she is mine," he said huskily. "She's our daughter, and you'll take good care of her during the surgery, I'm sure. Rest now and don't try to speak. Let the medicine take the pain way."

She gripped his hand tightly, afraid that if she let go, he'd leave. The bed going into motion startled her, and she pulled his hand closer.

"Don't go."

"I'm not going anywhere," he said soothingly.

His lips brushed across her forehead, and she relaxed, closing her eyes and allowing the pain to leave her.

The voices dimmed around her. Then Piers kissed her again and told her softly that he would be waiting for her. Why? Where was he going? She wanted to ask but couldn't muster the energy to do anything more than lie there.

The bed rolled again and suddenly she was in a frigid room. She was lifted and transferred to a much harder surface, and it was cold. A cheerful voice sounded in her ear and asked her to count backward from ten.

She opened her mouth to comply but nothing came out. She even managed to open her eyes, but by the time she mentally made it to eight, everything went black.

Piers paced the confines of the surgery waiting room like a caged lion, edgy and impatient. He checked his watch again only to find that three minutes had passed since the last time he'd checked it. Damn it, how long would it take? Why weren't they telling him anything?

"Piers, how is she?"

Piers looked up to see Theron striding into the waiting room, his hair rumpled as if he'd rolled out of bed and onto the plane. But then he had. Piers felt guilty for dragging his brother out of bed in the middle of the night, but he was grateful to have him here.

Piers briefly embraced his brother and the two sat down.

"I don't know yet. They took her in a few hours ago, but I haven't heard anything since."

"What happened? Is the baby all right?"

"The cyst on her ovary caused a tubal torsion. She was in unspeakable pain so they took her to surgery to remove the cyst and probably the tube as well. She was scheduled for surgery in a week's time anyway so this just moved up the timeline."

"And the baby?"

"There are...risks, but they've assured me they'll do everything they can to prevent anything from happening to the baby."

"How long has she been in surgery?"

"Four hours," Piers said bleakly. "What could be taking so long?"

"You'll hear something soon," Theron said comfortingly. "Have you called Chrysander?"

Piers shook his head. "There was no need. It would take him too long to get off the island and come here. By the time he did, it would all be over with."

"Still, you should call him. He'd want to know, he and Marley both."

"I'll call them when I know how she is."

The two brothers sat in the waiting room. After a while Theron left and returned with coffee for the both of them. Piers sipped the lukewarm brew, not really tasting it.

"You're different, you know."

Piers looked up in surprise. "What are you talking about?"

"You seem more settled...more content even. I noticed it in your eyes when we were here for the wedding."

"As opposed to what?" he asked mockingly.

"As opposed to the way you've existed ever since Joanna screwed you over and left with Eric."

Piers flinched. No one ever mentioned Eric to his face. He was sure his family probably said a lot behind his back, but never when he was around. The pain was still too fresh.

"Don't ruin your chance at happiness, Piers. This is your chance to have it all."

"Or lose it all again. Maybe I already have."

"What do you mean?"

Piers took another gulp of the coffee and put the cup aside.

"She was going to leave me in the morning. Her bags were already packed when I found her on the floor in terrible pain."

"Want to talk about it?" Theron asked carefully. "I've been accused of being dense once or twice by a certain woman in my life."

"You seem so sure it's me who is the problem," Piers said dryly.

"You're a man, and men are always in the wrong. Haven't you learned anything yet?"

The corner of Piers's mouth lifted in a smile. Then he sobered. "I was an ass."

"Yes, well, it won't be the last time. It seems an inherent part of our genetic makeup."

"A male friend of hers showed up yesterday to come to her rescue. I didn't take it very well."

"No one can blame you for that. It's part of being territorial."

Piers snorted. "Next you'll be telling me that we're all cavemen stomping around and marking our territory like dogs."

"Quite an image you've conjured there, little brother. I imagine that's precisely what we do, just not in the literal sense."

Theron glanced sideways at Piers.

"So she was going to leave you because you didn't appreciate her male friend showing up?"

"I might have accused him of fathering her child and the two of them of running a scam to extort money from me."

Theron winced. "Damn, when you decide to pull off the gloves, you go for the full monty."

"As I said, I was an ass. I was angry. I told her that I wouldn't grant her a divorce, and she told me to take my settlement and go to hell."

"Doesn't sound much like a woman after your money does it?"

He'd thought the same thing himself.

"I want to trust her, Theron."

"And that frightens you."

And there it was in a nutshell. Funny how his brother cut so quickly to the heart of the matter. Yes, he wanted to trust her, but he was afraid, and it infuriated him.

"I don't want to ever allow a woman that much power over me again."

Theron sighed and put his hand on Piers's shoulder. "I understand, really I do. But you can't shut yourself away from the world for the rest of your life just because you got hurt once."

"Hurt?" Piers made a derisive sound. "I wish it was only hurt. She took from me what I loved most in the world. Somehow that goes beyond simple hurt."

"Still, as cliché as it sounds, life goes on. I want you to be happy, Piers. Chrysander and I worry about you. You can't go on traveling from one hotel to another your entire life. At some point you need to settle down and start a family. Jewel has given you that opportunity. Perhaps you should make the most of it. Give her a chance."

"Mr. Anetakis."

Both men yanked their heads up as a nurse appeared in the waiting room.

"Mrs. Anetakis is out of surgery. You can visit her in recovery for a moment if you like."

Piers shot up and hurried over to the nurse. "Is she all right? The baby?"

The nurse smiled. "Mother and baby are fine. The surgery went well. The doctor will stop in to talk to you in recovery before she's taken to a room. She's going to be very groggy, but you can talk to her for a moment if you like."

"I'll wait here," Theron said. "You go ahead."

"Thank you," Piers said sincerely. Then he turned to follow the nurse to see Jewel.

Thirteen

Her pain was different. It wasn't as agonizingly sharp as before. Instead it had settled to a dull ache, not as deep as it had been, but on the surface. Jewel tried to shift and gasped when it felt as though her belly had been ripped in two.

"Careful, *yineka mou.* You mustn't try to move. Tell me what it is you need, and I will help you."

Piers. She opened her eyes,, squinting as the light speared her eyeballs. She quickly shut them again and cautiously opened them a slit as she tried to bring him into focus.

And then she remembered.

"The baby," she whispered. She reached her hands out in panic, feeling for her belly then gasping as more pain crashed through her system.

Piers took her hands and pulled them gently away from her belly.

"The baby is fine, as are you. See?" He carefully levered one of her hands to the swell of her belly but wouldn't allow her to exert any pressure.

She looked down at the unfamiliar feel of bulky bandages, but the swell was still evident. Tears flooded her eyes as her insides caved in relief.

"I was so afraid. I can't lose her, Piers. She's everything to me."

He cupped her cheek and rubbed his thumb over the damp trail underneath her eye. "Your surgery was a success. The doctor says the baby is doing well. They've been monitoring you for contractions." He gestured toward a machine at the side of her bed. "See? You can see and hear her heartbeat."

She turned her head and tuned into the soft *whop whop whop* sound that echoed in the still room.

"It's really her?"

Piers smiled. "Yes, our daughter is making her presence known."

She caught her breath as suddenly she remembered the scene just before they'd taken her to surgery. At first she thought surely she'd imagined it, but no, here again he was staking his claim. Why had he changed his mind?

"Thank you for getting me here so quickly," she said in a low voice. "I was so afraid I wouldn't be able to get to you."

He sobered as he gazed intently at her, his dark eyes seeming to absorb her. "You wouldn't have suffered for as long as you did if I had been there with you. From now on, you'll sleep in my room in my bed so if anything like this happens again, I'll know immediately. I don't like to think what could have happened if I hadn't heard you call out."

She processed his statement, blinking the cloudiness

from her mind. Everything was so fuzzy, and he confused her more than ever. It was as if their argument had never happened, as though he hadn't accused her of trying to pawn off another man's child on him.

"There will be plenty of time to talk later," he chided gently. "You're worn out and in pain. You need rest. I'll be here when you wake up. You can ask the questions I see burning in your eyes then."

She shook her head and winced when the movement caused a ripple of pain through her belly. "No, I have to know now. You said—implied—some terrible things, Piers. I won't stay with a man who thinks so little of me, not even for my daughter. Kirk is willing to help me get back on my feet. I should have called him in the first place."

"But you didn't," he said mildly. "You called me, as you should have. I think it best if we leave Kirk out of the equation."

She started to protest but he held a finger over her lips.

"Shhh, don't upset yourself. I owe you an apology, *yineka mou.* I'm sure it won't be the last I ever have to offer you. I would appreciate your patience with me. I'm not an easy man. I realize this. I should not have implied what I did. From this day forward, we go on as a family. You're having my child. We owe it to her to be a solid parental unit, not one where I continually upset you and cause you such stress. If you'll give me another chance, I'll prove to you that our marriage will work."

She stared at him in absolute stupefaction. His sincerity was etched on his face. His eyes burned with it. There was no arrogance to his voice, just simple regret.

Something inside her chest, perilously close to her heart, unfurled and loosened. Forgotten for a brief moment was the pain that throbbed in her abdomen and the fuzziness caused by the pain medication. Warmth, blessed and sweet, hummed through her veins. Hope. It had been so long since she'd felt such a thing that she hadn't identified it at first. For the first time, she had hope.

He drew her hand to his mouth and pressed a soft kiss inside her palm. "Do you forgive me? Will you give me another chance to make things right?"

"Yes, of course," she whispered, her voice so shaky that her words came out in barely a croak.

"And you'll stay? There'll be no more talk of leaving?"

She shook her head, too choked to say anything more.

"You won't regret it, *yineka mou,*" he said gravely. "We can make this work. We can do this."

She smiled and then grimaced as pain radiated from the center of her body. Piers leaned forward, directing her attention to the small device lying beside her on the bed. He picked it up and pressed it into her palm.

"This is for pain. You press the button here, and it injects a small amount of medication into your IV. You can press it every ten minutes if you have the need."

He depressed the button himself, and a split second later, she felt the slight burn as it entered her vein. The relief was almost instantaneous.

"Thank you."

"I will take care of you and our baby," he said solemnly. "I don't want you to worry about a thing except to get better."

She smiled up at him, her eyelids fluttering sleepily.

"Tired," she said in a half murmur.

"Then sleep. I'll be right here."

She turned toward his voice, and when he started to move his hand from hers, she curled her fingers around his, keeping them laced. He relaxed and tightened his grip on her hand.

"When am I getting outta here?" she mumbled as she fought the veil of sleep.

He chuckled lightly. "There's no hurry. You'll leave when the doctor feels it's safe for you to do so. In the meantime enjoy everyone fussing over you."

"Just you," she muttered just before she surrendered to the dark.

"Are you sure everything is prepared?" Piers said into his mobile phone as he entered Jewel's room.

Jewel looked up and smiled and Piers held up one finger to signal he would be finished shortly.

"Good. Very good. I owe you one, and I have no doubt that you'll collect."

He snapped his phone shut and hastened to Jewel's side. He bent down and brushed his lips across hers in greeting.

"How are my girls today?"

"Your daughter is very active, which is a blessing and a curse."

Piers gave her a sympathetic look. "Do her movements aggravate your incision?"

She grimaced. "I think she's playing target practice. She's has uncanny accuracy for kicking that precise spot."

"I'm sorry. I know it must be painful for you."

"The alternative doesn't bear thinking about, so I'm grateful for her movements."

"Has the doctor been by to see you yet?"

"He came by while you were out. He said if all goes well today and I have no further contractions, that I can be released tomorrow. I'm to be on strict bed rest for a week and then I can get up and around as long as I don't overdo it."

"And I will see to it that you obey his instructions to the letter."

She was careful not to laugh, but she grinned in amusement. "Why do I get the feeling you're going to enjoy my convalescence?"

He gave her an innocent look. "Why would you think such a thing?"

"Because you're a man used to bossing people around and having them obey you implicitly," she said darkly.

"You say this as if it was a bad thing."

This time she did chuckle and promptly groaned when her belly protested. Piers gave her a disapproving frown, and she rolled her eyes.

The past several days had been good considering she was stuck in a hospital bed. After the first day, the nurse had come in to help her get up, and Jewel had spent fifteen minutes trying to argue that there was no need for her to get up when every movement nearly split her in two. It was the threat of a catheter that finally gave her the motivation to endure sitting up and standing.

Piers had been wonderful. The brooding man who'd so insolently told her there would be no divorce had seemingly disappeared, and was replaced by someone who saw to her every need. She had to admit that he was trying very hard to put their past disagreements behind them.

A light knock sounded at the door, and to her surprise, Piers's brothers and their wives crowded into her room. She must have looked as mortified as she felt because Piers squeezed her hand.

"Don't worry, *yineka mou*. You look beautiful. They won't stay long enough to tire you. I'll see to it."

He was lying through his teeth, but she loved him for it.

The thought hit her between the eyes and was more painful than the stapled incision in her belly. Love? Dear God, she'd fallen in love with him.

She tried to smile, but what she wanted to do was crawl into a deep, dark hole. How could she have allowed herself to fall in love with him—with any man? Apparently she hadn't had enough hurt in her life. No, she obviously wanted to pile on more pain and disappointment.

It was all well and fine to want to be loved, but to offer her love on a silver platter? She was just asking for rejection.

"Jewel? Have we come at a bad time?" Marley asked quietly.

Jewel blinked and saw that the two couples were standing at the foot of her bed, studying her intently.

"No. No, of course not. I'm sorry. I'm still a bit muddled. It's probably all the pain medication they've funneled through me."

Beside her Piers frowned, and she just hoped he'd remain quiet about the fact she hadn't had pain medication in three days. The doctor hadn't wanted her to be on any narcotic for an extended period of time. It was too risky for the baby.

She smiled brightly at Bella and Marley and opted to keep her gaze away from Chrysander and Theron. They intimidated the hell out of her, and she wasn't in the habit of giving up that kind of advantage to anyone.

"How are you feeling?" Bella asked as she moved forward.

She perched on the side of Jewel's bed and flipped her long dark hair over her shoulder.

"Has Piers been bullying you? Marley and I can take him outside and rough him up for you."

Jewel smiled and swallowed to keep from laughing.

"Don't make her laugh," Piers growled. "It hurts her too much. Besides, I have you and Marley wrapped around my finger, remember?"

Chrysander let out a loud guffaw. "Don't let him fool you, Jewel. All either woman has to do is look at this idiot brother of mine, and he gives them whatever they want, much to mine and Theron's dismay."

"As if you both don't spoil them shamelessly," Piers said dryly.

"That may be true, but a woman can never have too many men at her disposal," Marley said cheekily.

"There is only one man at your disposal, *agape mou,*" Chrysander growled. "And you would do well to remember that."

Jewel watched the interaction between the three brothers and Bella and Marley, and for the first time, she didn't feel like an outsider. The horrible feeling of intense longing didn't hit her like it did the first time she'd met them. This time she felt more of an equal, as if she belonged in this intimate circle of family members.

"You must be feeling better," Bella said from her perch on the bed. "You're smiling so beautifully. You look quite radiant for someone who has just undergone surgery."

"It's the pregnancy," Theron said slyly. "A woman never looks more beautiful than when she is pregnant."

"Nice try," Bella said dryly. "Your flattery will get you nowhere. And if you start lusting after pregnant women, I'll make it so you'll never be able to father children."

Jewel couldn't help but laugh when Theron all but paled. She put her hand over her belly and groaned, but even amidst the pain, it felt so good to laugh. She felt lighter than she had in a long time.

"Are you all right?" Piers asked quietly.

She waved him off. "I'm fine. Truly." Then she turned to Bella. "Why do I get the feeling this is an ongoing battle between you and Theron?"

Bella grinned. "If Theron had his way, I'd have already popped out a veritable brood of children, but I'm too young, and we have so much to do together before I think of having babies. I'll eventually give in and fill his nursery, but until then I live to torment him."

Jewel studied Theron's face as Bella spoke. His eyes shone with love for his wife, and she knew that he didn't exert any real pressure. It was obviously a long-standing joke between them.

"Besides, Marley has taken it upon herself to provide enough Anetakis children for both of us," Bella added with a smirk.

Piers eyebrows shot up. "Marley?"

Marley blushed while Chrysander smiled smugly and wrapped his arm around her waist. It was a possessive gesture not lost on Jewel.

"You're pregnant again?" Piers demanded.

"In seven months she'll give me the daughter I want," Chrysander said arrogantly.

"And if it's another son?" Marley challenged.

Chrysander looked down at her, passion blazing in his eyes. "Then we'll simply try again until we get it right."

Marley and Bella both laughed, and Jewel joined them, holding her belly all the while.

What a marvelous family. A family that she was now a part of. It was simply too much to take in.

"We should probably go now," Chrysander said as he

studied Jewel. "You look as though you're in pain, and we don't want to tire you out. We simply wanted to come by to check in on you and to let you know that if there is anything you need, anything at all, just let us know. You're family now."

She stared back at him, tears in her eyes. "Please, don't go. You're not bothering me a bit. I've so enjoyed having you all."

"Tell me," Bella said, leaning forward to capture Jewel's attention. "Are they letting you have real food yet? I'm simply dying for some pizza. Theron thinks it's barbaric, and so I'm shamelessly using you as an excuse to get some really greasy, cheesy pizza."

"You call that real food?" Theron asked in mock horror.

"Oh I'd love pizza," Jewel said with real longing. "Double pepperoni and extra cheese. Oh, and light sauce if no one objects."

"Tell you what," Bella said. "We'll order one our way and let the rest fend for themselves. What you suggested sounds positively divine."

Jewel looked hopefully at Piers who sighed in resignation.

"What man can possibly say no to a woman when she looks at him that way?"

Both Theron and Chrysander laughed.

Chrysander clapped Piers on the back. "Now you're learning, little brother. Now you're learning."

Fourteen

"I have a surprise in mind," Piers said as he wheeled her out of the hospital's front entrance. "It will take a while to execute, so what I want you to do is relax and try to rest as much as possible."

A flutter of excitement bubbled in her stomach. She felt like a kid at Christmas. For someone who'd never gotten accustomed to any sort of surprise, she was fast finding she liked them very much. Or at least the anticipation of having one.

Piers's security detail stood outside the limousine awaiting their arrival. One opened the back door, and Piers scooped Jewel up from the wheelchair and carefully placed her in the seat, taking extra care not to jostle her. Then he walked around to the other side while all but one of his security team slipped into a car parked behind the limousine. The last man got into the front with the driver.

"Where are we going?" she asked curiously when they went the opposite direction of the house she and Piers had been staying in.

"The airport."

She raised her eyebrows. "Where are we going?"

Familiar excitement lit her veins. She loved to travel for the excitement of going to a new place, meeting new people and experiencing different cultures. Only this time she wasn't going alone, and that thrilled her more than she would have thought possible.

He smiled and reached over to take her hand. "If I told you, it would spoil the surprise."

"But my clothes, my things. I haven't packed."

"All taken care of," he said smoothly. "This is why I hire a staff."

"Did you pack my chef?" she asked mournfully. "He made the most delicious food."

Piers chuckled. "I assure you, you won't go hungry."

A while later they pulled up next to a small jet parked on a private airstrip. Piers waited while his security got out and boarded the plane. Then he walked around to her side and picked her up.

"I'll take her if you like, Mr. Anetakis," Yves offered. He was the only one who Jewel knew by name. The rest were a mystery to her, but then Yves seemed more of a personal bodyguard for Piers while the rest operated on the perimeter.

Piers shook his head. "Thank you Yves, but I'll take Mrs. Anetakis to the plane."

Each step he took was in careful consideration of her comfort. When he reached the steps to the plane, he ducked down and walked inside.

Never before had she seen the inside of a private jet, and

if she'd been expecting a smaller version of a regular
airliner, she was mistaken. There were seats in the front
covered in soft, supple leather that looked incredibly luxurious and comfortable. Beyond them was a sitting area
with a recliner and a couch along with a coffee table, television and a mini bar.

Piers followed the direction of her gaze. "After we take
off, I'll show you the rest. There's a bedroom in the back
of the plane that you can lie down in. There's also a small
kitchenette, so if you want anything, you've only to let the
flight attendant know."

Her eyes widened. "Flight attendant? You have one for
the plane?"

"Of course. She travels with the pilot. They're a
husband and wife team. It's an arrangement that suits them
well. Now, would you like a window or an aisle seat?"

"Window," she said.

He carefully settled her in place and then took the seat
next to her. Before fastening his seat belt, he reached over
and gingerly buckled hers into place, leaving it loose
around her belly.

The flight attendant walked up with a smile and greeted
Piers. Then she turned her smile on Jewel. "I'm very happy
to meet you, Mrs. Anetakis. If there is anything I can get
you during the flight, don't hesitate to ask. We'll be cleared
for take off shortly. Would you like something to drink
while you wait?"

Jewel shook her head. "No thank you. I'm fine for
now."

Minutes later, they taxied down the runway and took
off. Jewel leaned her head on Piers's shoulder and
snuggled into his warmth. As curious as she was to see
the rest of the plane, getting up and moving hurt too much.

She was perfectly content to remain here for the duration of the flight.

"You're still not going to tell me where we are?" Jewel asked several hours later as their car wound its way along a curving highway.

Piers smiled. "Patience, *yineka mou.* I think you'll find it's well worth the wait."

She sighed and relaxed in her seat. Wherever they were, it was beautiful and unspoiled. She'd lay odds it was in the Caribbean or some similar tropical place. Were they going to one of his hotels?

They stopped at a security gate where Piers punched in a code. Huge iron gates swung slowly open, and they continued up the drive.

Lush greenery abounded. It was like driving into a private paradise. Flowers, plants, fountains and even a mini waterfall cascaded over rocks in the distance.

And then she saw the house. Her mouth fell open at the sight of the stunning cottage, well if you could call something so huge a cottage. But despite its size, it had the look of a cozy, stone cottage. It looked positively homey.

"Is this where we're staying for the time being?" she asked when the car pulled to a stop beside another large fountain with flowers floating serenely in the pool surrounding it.

"This is your house, *yineka mou.* It now belongs to us."

She was struck positively speechless.

"But the best is yet to come," he said.

She watched him walk around the front of the car and wondered how on earth it could get any better?

He helped her from the car and motioned his security men who were standing several feet away. They quickly disappeared while Piers put a strong arm around her waist and urged her toward a walkway leading around the house.

And then she heard it. The distant sounds of waves crashing. She inhaled deeply, catching the salty air in her nostrils.

"Oh Piers," she breathed.

They topped a small rise between a section of gardens and the wooden deck jutting from the house over a sharp cliff. She looked out and all she could see was a great expanse of ocean. Brilliant blue, so stunning it almost hurt her eyes to look at. It sparkled like a million sapphires.

The walkway continued, smooth in places and at other areas it became a series of steps leading down to the beach. The house was situated on the cliff in a secluded cove between two outcroppings. It afforded them a small stretch of sandy beach, completely private.

It was the most magnificent view she could have imagined. And it was theirs.

"I don't know what to say," she whispered. "This is my dream, Piers. I can't believe this is ours."

"It's yours, *yineka mou.* My wedding gift to you. I have it on good authority it comes equipped with a full staff, including a certain chef you've grown extraordinarily fond of."

She threw her arms around him, ignoring the painful jolt to her incision. "Thank you. It's so wonderful, Piers. I don't know how I'll ever be able to thank you."

"By taking good care of yourself and my daughter," he said seriously. "I don't want you taking the pathway down to the beach unless I'm with you."

"I promise," she said joyfully. Right now she'd promise him the moon.

"Come inside. Dinner has been held for us. We'll eat on the terrace and watch the sun go down."

She went eagerly, anxious to see the inside of the house. He gave her a quick tour of the downstairs before they walked onto the deck in the back. Their places had been set, and she eased into her chair to wait for the food.

"It's so gorgeous," she said in awe. She was completely and utterly overwhelmed by the knowledge that she lived here now, that this place was hers. It was all simply too good to be true.

"I'm glad you like it. I was afraid I wouldn't have everything in place before you were released from the hospital."

"You didn't already own it?"

"I had my representatives looking for just the perfect place the day you told me where you'd like to live more than anywhere else. When they found this place, I knew it was perfect. The sale isn't quite final, but I convinced the owner to allow us to take possession of it until all the paperwork can be finished."

She was unable to keep the wide smile from forming on her face. "That's the most wonderful thing anyone has ever done for me."

He put his hand over hers, his palm warm and soothing. "Tell me, *yineka mou*. Has anyone ever done a wonderful thing for you? I get the impression yours has not been an easy life."

She stiffened and tried to withdraw her hand, but he wouldn't allow it. His grip tightened around her fingers, but his touch stayed soothing the entire time.

"What is it you won't tell me?" he asked quietly. "Surely there should be no secrets between a man and his wife."

She turned away to stare at the ocean, the breeze blowing across her cheeks and drying the invisible tears she shed.

"It's nothing so dramatic," she said matter of factly. "My parents died when I was very young. I barely remember them, and even now I wonder if the people I remember aren't just one of the many foster families I was shuttled through."

"You had no relatives to take care of you?"

She shook her head. "None that would, anyway."

A young woman came out then carrying a tray of food, and Jewel sighed in relief. She didn't miss Piers's frown, which told her the conversation wasn't closed, just delayed.

Still, nothing good would come of her rehashing the past.

They ate in companionable silence. Jewel enjoyed the sounds and smells of the ocean and found herself more relaxed than she'd been in longer than she could remember.

As the sun dipped lower on the horizon, the sky faded to soft hues of pink and purple with threads of gold spreading from the disappearing sun. The ocean shimmered in the distance, reflecting the brilliance of the sunset.

She hadn't realized she'd long since stopped eating, so entranced by the view was she. Only when the maid returned to collect the dinner plates, did Jewel break from her reverie.

"You look tired, *yineka mou,*" Piers said gently. "I think I should take you upstairs so you can get ready for bed."

She yawned and then chuckled at how easily she'd given herself away. "Bed sounds really good right now. Does the bedroom have windows we can open? I'd love to be able to hear the ocean."

"I think you'll find the view from our bedroom magnificent, and we can certainly open the windows if that is your wish."

He helped her to her feet and they returned inside. They took the stairs slowly, and she bit her lip when the upward movement put awkward pressure around the area of her incision. Her entire belly felt bruised and tender.

When they entered the master bedroom, she let out a sound of pure delight. The entire back wall that faced the ocean was glassed in from floor to ceiling. She left Piers's side to peer over the water, her palms pressed to the cool glass.

Her throat suspiciously tight, she turned to face Piers. "This has been the most wonderful day. Thank you so much."

"I'm glad you approve," he said huskily.

She returned her attention to the view, watching as the last bits of the orange glow from the sun disappeared into the sea.

"What about your work? Your hotels?"

He came to stand beside her, studying the ocean with her.

"Most of my work can be handled from here. I have a phone, my computer and a fax machine. There will be times I need to travel. Up to now, I've always done the bulk of the traveling, but I find myself unwilling to continue on that track. Either my brothers will have to help shoulder the load or we'll hire someone to do most of the traveling."

"You won't miss it?" she asked lightly.

"A few months ago I would have said yes, very much, but now I find myself more reluctant to be away from my wife and our child."

Warmth spread through her chest. How like a family

they sounded. She wasn't entirely certain what had caused him to change his tune, but she had no desire to question it. She only hoped it lasted.

Fifteen

For the next several days, Jewel rested and recovered under the watchful eye of Piers and the staff he'd hired. It seemed odd at first to have other people in the house, but they blended so seamlessly into the background that Jewel quickly became accustomed to their presence.

Piers even had a physician come to the house to check her incision and remove the staples so she wouldn't have to make the trip into town.

In short, she was spoiled and pampered endlessly, and she was fast becoming bored out of her mind. She was positively dying to explore her surroundings. A trip down to the beach was foremost on her wish list, but she also wanted to go beyond the grounds of their estate and see the rest of the island.

According to Piers, the island was small and not yet discovered by the many tourists that flocked to the Caribbean.

Fishing was the main source of industry for the locals. There were plans to build an elaborate resort, an exclusive playground for the wealthy where no expense would be spared and guests would be lavished with personal attention.

The goal was to keep the island as private and as unspoiled as possible while still providing an influx of capital for the locals.

Jewel broached the subject of a trip down to the beach over breakfast, the day after the doctor had removed her staples and pronounced her fit.

Piers frowned for a moment. "I'm not sure you should be descending the stairs this soon after your surgery, *yineka mou.*"

"But I'll have you to hang on to," she cajoled. "Please, Piers. I'm about to go stir-crazy. I've watched from a distance for so long, I'm beginning to feel like I'm viewing postcards."

He smiled. "I find I can deny you nothing. All right. After breakfast we'll go down to the beach. I'll have the cook prepare a picnic lunch."

She bounced on her seat like an excited child. "Thank you. I can't wait to see it!"

"Be sure and wear some comfortable shoes. I don't want you slipping on the steps."

She smiled at his solicitousness. How perfect things were right now. Gone was the feeling that at any moment her world could come crashing down around her. If only…if only he'd open up to her.

For days she'd argued with herself, vacillated from having the courage to ask and having it disappear. The other problem was that if she managed to get him to talk to her about his past then she'd be forced to speak of her own.

Soon, she promised herself. But not this morning. Nothing was going to ruin their outing to the beach.

Picnic basket in one hand, his other firmly wrapped around hers, Piers made his way down the steps carved into the face of the cliff. With each downward movement, the sounds of the ocean got louder and Jewel became more excited.

When their feet finally hit the sand, Jewel stopped and looked up at the impressive rocky cliffs looming over and around them, isolating their stretch of beach from the rest of the world.

"It's like we're in our own little world," she said in awe.

Piers smiled. "No one can see you except by boat, and I have it on good authority the locals don't fish this end of the island."

"Conjures up all sorts of naughty possibilities, doesn't it?"

His eyes glittered in response. "You can be sure once you are well that I'll be all too willing to indulge in some of those possibilities."

She laughed and kicked off her shoes, digging her toes into the warm sand. Unable to resist the lure of the foaming waves, she hurried toward the water's edge, anxious to feel the water swirling around her ankles.

The cascading water met her and rushed over her feet. She threw out her arms to embrace the breeze and smiled in absolute delight as her hair billowed behind her. Closing her eyes, she inhaled deep and wished she could stop time, right here in this perfect moment.

"You look like a sea nymph," Piers said. "More beautiful than a woman should be allowed to look."

She turned to see him standing beside her, his pants rolled up to his knees, his feet bare.

"Is it safe to swim here?"

He nodded.

"We'll have to do it sometime."

"You look happy, *yineka mou*. Have I made you so?"

The vulnerability that flashed in his dark eyes made her catch her breath. This strong, arrogant man was as human as the next person. Not questioning the wisdom of doing so, she flung herself into his arms, wrapping hers around his neck.

"You're so good to me, Piers. You do make me so very happy."

Tentatively, he returned her embrace and as she pulled her head away to look at him, their eyes met. Their lips were but an inch apart, and she licked hers nervously, in anticipation of what she knew was about to happen.

Instead of waiting on him, she pulled him close, fitting her mouth to his. He seemed willing to let her dictate the pace, and she explored his mouth thoroughly, learning every nuance, his taste, feeling the warmth of his tongue.

His fingers were a soft whisper against her neck. They delved farther into her hair, holding her closer as she deepened the kiss. The salt from the ocean danced on their tongues, mixing with the heady sweetness of their passion.

Finally she pulled away, gazing up at him through half-lidded eyes. "And do I make you happy?" she asked huskily.

He ran his thumb over her cheekbone, stroking to the corner of her mouth. "You make me very happy."

She smiled brilliantly at him then grabbed his hand and tugged him farther down the beach. "Come on! Let's explore."

Indulgently, he allowed to her to pull him along. They covered every inch of the beach from cliff to cliff. By the time they returned to where the picnic basket lay, she was starving.

"Help me with the blanket," she said as she unfurled the brightly colored quilt. Laughing, she fought with the billowing material as it refused to cooperate.

"Here, let me."

Piers wrestled the blanket to the sand and piled their shoes at each corner to hold it down.

"Now hurry and sit before it flies away again," he said.

She gingerly eased down and dragged the basket into the middle of the quilt. Piers sat beside her and they began divvying up the food.

The sun shone bright above them, and the sand glistened like tiny jewels, scattered to the water's edge. She sighed and turned her face up into the warmth.

"You look very content, *yineka mou.* Like a cat sunning herself."

"Haven't you ever wished that a single moment could last forever?"

He became pensive as though he were giving her question serious consideration. "No, I can't say I have, but if I were given to such flights of fancy, then today would be one such time."

She smiled. "It is perfect, isn't it?"

"Yes. It is."

They finished eating, and Jewel lay back on the blanket, enjoying the sounds and smells of the ocean. The warmth of the sun's rays lulled her to sleep, and before she knew it, she was being shaken awake.

"It's time to return to the house, *yineka mou.* The sun will be setting soon."

She yawned and blinked lazily as his face came into view. She smiled up at him and held up her hand so he could help her.

Together they collected the remnants of their lunch,

and Piers packed them and the blanket into the basket. He reached for her hand when they arrived at the bottom of the steps, and she slipped her fingers into his.

Tonight. Tonight she'd broach the subject of his past, and for the first time, she wouldn't avoid hers. She wanted to know his secrets, the source of the pain she saw lurking in the depths of those shuttered eyes.

Would he share those secrets or would he block her out? And should she press him on something that clearly he had no wish to discuss?

True to his word, after the night Piers had found Jewel on the floor of her bedroom writhing in pain, she'd slept each night in his bed. In deference to her incision, he spooned against her back, and she enjoyed the warmth and security his muscled body offered.

Most nights she wondered if they'd resume their love-making after the tenderness left her abdomen. Tonight, however, she lay there, cuddled against his chest, gathering her courage to broach the subject of his past.

"Piers?"

"Mmm-hmm."

Carefully she started to turn over to face him.

"Will you tell me who hurt you so badly?"

He went still, and she wished the lamp was on so she could gauge his reaction.

"Who made you so distrustful of women?" she continued on. "And why is it that you don't want this to be your child."

He put a finger on her lips. "That's where you're wrong, *yineka mou*. I want her to be mine very much."

Jewel cocked her head to the side. "But you seem so convinced that she isn't."

He turned on his back to stare up at the ceiling. She tentatively cuddled into the crook of his arm and laid her head on his shoulder. When he didn't resist, she relaxed, allowing her fingers to trail through the hairs on his chest.

"Ten years ago I met and fell in love with a woman. Joanna. I was young and stupid and convinced I had the world by the tail."

"Don't we all at that age," she said with a slight smile.

He chuckled. "I suppose you're right. Anyway, she became pregnant, and so we married right away."

Jewel winced at the similarities but remained quiet as he continued.

"She gave birth to a boy. We named him Eric. I adored him. I was as happy as a man can be. I had a beautiful wife who seemed devoted to me. I had a son. What more could I ask for?"

Jewel's mouth turned down unhappily. She could only imagine what he'd say next.

"And then one day I came home to find her packing. Eric was two years old. I remember him crying the entire time I tried to reason with Joanna. I couldn't understand why she was leaving. There hadn't seemed to be any problems. I had no warning.

"Finally, when I told her that she could leave but there was no way in hell I'd let my son go, she told me that he wasn't my child."

Jewel sucked in her breath. "And you believed her?"

A derisive sound escaped his lips. "No, I didn't believe her. But to make a long story short, her lover who she was involved with when she and I met had devised the perfect plan to milk me for all they could. Several months and a paternity test later, it was proved that Eric wasn't my son. Joanna took him and a great deal of my money, and I haven't seen either since."

"Oh Piers, I'm so sorry," she whispered. "How horrible of her to allow you to fall in love with a child you thought was yours and then to yank him so cruelly away. How could she do that to either of you?"

Piers trailed his fingers up and down her bare arm.

"I have nightmares sometimes. I hear Eric calling to me, asking why I won't help him, why I left *him*. All I can remember is the day they left, and how Eric screamed and cried, how he stretched his arms out trying to get to me, and all I could do was watch her walk away with my son. It's a sight I'll never get out of my mind."

"You miss him."

"He was my entire world for those two years," he said simply. "I realize now that I didn't love Joanna. I was infatuated with her, but I did love Eric."

Jewel rose up and cupped his cheek in her palm as she lowered her mouth to his. Then she drew his hand down to her swollen belly where their daughter bumped and turned between them.

"She's yours, Piers. Yours and mine."

"I know, *yineka mou*. I know."

Sixteen

"Piers looks more at ease than I've ever seen him," Marley said to Jewel as the two stood on the patio overlooking the ocean.

Jewel turned to the other woman and smiled. "Really? I hope I can take credit for it."

Bella laughed as she took another sip of her wine. "Of course the credit is yours. I'd swear the man is in love."

Jewel bit her lip and turned away. She wanted Piers to love her, but he'd never said the words. She wasn't sure he was capable of offering his love to another woman after what had happened with Joanna.

"Your house is beautiful, Jewel," Marley said. "I just wish it wasn't so far away from Greece."

"Or New York," Bella said dryly. "You think Piers planned it this way?"

Jewel grinned. "But we have jets at our disposal, don't we?"

"Hmm, you're right," Marley said thoughtfully. "The world shrinks quite a bit when airplanes are involved. No reason we couldn't all meet in New York for some shopping. Theron is a soft touch, and he'd no doubt accommodate us."

Bella glared over at Marley. "Just because he isn't an ape swinging from tree to tree and beating his chest while muttering stuff like 'you my woman' doesn't mean he's a softy."

"She's very protective and possessive when it comes to Theron," Marley said with a roll of her eyes. "All I meant was that of the three brothers, Theron would be the most accommodating when it comes to us wanting to get together. Chrysander and Piers would spend a month planning the security team."

Bella nodded. "You're right about that."

Jewel looked at the two women in question. "Piers mentioned what had happened to Marley when I asked him why the need for all the security people. Has nothing been resolved yet?"

Marley sighed unhappily. "As a matter of fact, we think the men who kidnapped me have been arrested. Chrysander got the call yesterday but we didn't want to ruin our time here. When we leave, we're flying back to New York with Bella and Theron so that I can identify the suspects."

Bella threaded her arm around Marley's waist and squeezed. "I'm so sorry, Marley. What rotten timing for you when you've been so ill with the new baby."

Marley smoothed a hand over her still flat stomach. "Chrysander is worried it will be too much, and he's still feeling so guilty. He hates that I have to do this."

Jewel touched her hand in a comforting gesture. "Still, what a relief to know that they've been apprehended. I can only imagine the fear you've been living in."

"And the inconvenience it's caused you and Bella," Marley added. "I know that Theron and Piers have taken extra precautions because of the potential threat to anyone close to them. Maybe we can all relax a little now."

Bella held up her glass in a toast. "To freedom and relaxation."

Jewel held up her glass of water as did Marley and the women clinked the crystal.

"I'm so glad you're all here," Jewel said.

Bella looped her arm through Jewel's. "We're grateful you've made Piers so happy. He's been so…hard."

Marley nodded. "It took him a long time to accept me. Of course now he'd do just about anything if I needed him, but it wasn't like that in the beginning."

Jewel sobered. "Marley, do you think you could pull Chrysander to the side for me? There is something I'd like to discuss with him, something I'd prefer Piers not to know right now."

Marley lifted a brow. "Okay, I can do that, but you should know that Bella and I are insatiably nosy, and you'll have to fill us in first."

Jewel laughed and squeezed Marley's hand with her free one. "I'll tell you after Chrysander. That way you two don't try to talk me out of it."

"Uh-oh," Bella said with a groan. "I don't like the sound of that."

"I'm too curious to try and dissuade her," Marley said. "If you'll stay out here Jewel, Bella and I will make sure Piers is occupied while you talk to Chrysander."

"Thank you."

The two women disappeared indoors leaving Jewel to gaze out over the sea. She was so absorbed by the view, that she didn't hear Chrysander when he came out.

"Marley tells me you'd like to speak with me."

Startled, she made a quick turn, and swallowed as she stared back at Piers's older brother. He raised a brow in surprise.

"Do I frighten you, Jewel?"

"Oh no, of course not...okay, yes, you do," she admitted.

"It is certainly not my intention," he said formally. "Now tell me, what can I do for you?"

She twisted her fingers nervously in front of her. This was probably a stupid idea, and Chrysander would probably tell her she was out of her mind. He might even be angry that she intended to pry into Piers's past.

"Piers told me about Joanna...and Eric."

Chrysander's eyes grew cold.

"I know how hurt he was by what happened."

Chrysander sighed and moved closer to Jewel. "He was devastated, Jewel. Hurt is a very tame word for what he went through. He loved Eric, considered him a son for two years. Can you imagine thinking a child is yours for that long? And then having him snatched away?"

She swallowed and lowered her gaze. "No, I can't imagine. It would devastate me too."

"Perhaps you can understand now that he's told you about them."

She looked up again, braving Chrysander's stare. "That's just it. I want your help."

Chrysander's brows came together in confusion. "My help? With what?"

"Finding Eric."

"No. Absolutely not. I won't allow Piers to go through that all over again."

Jewel put her hand over Chrysander's when he turned to go back inside.

"Please. Hear me out. Part of the problem was that Piers never got to say good-bye. He never got any closure. His wound is still raw and bleeding. He's still grieving for that two-year-old he lost. His only memory of Eric is of the day she left with him, how Eric screamed and cried for him. Maybe if he could see him now it would help to ease some of that pain. I can only imagine that he's wondered over the years if Eric is happy, if he's well, if he's needed anything. If he saw that Eric wasn't hurting, maybe it would go a long way to healing the awful pain Piers feels."

"You would do this?" Chrysander asked. "You would willingly bring a child back into his life that he loved? Risk contact with a woman he once loved just to make him happy again?"

"Yes," she said huskily. "I would do anything to ease his hurt."

Chrysander studied her for a long moment. "You love my brother very much."

She closed her eyes and turned away. "Yes," she whispered. "I do."

"All right, Jewel. I will help you."

She grabbed his hand. "Thank you."

"I just hope when this is all over that my brother is still speaking to me," he said wryly.

She shook her head vigorously. "I'll tell him you had nothing to do with it. I'll take sole responsibility."

"My brother is a lucky man, I think."

"I just hope he thinks so," she said wistfully.

"Give him time. I have no doubt he'll figure it out."

Chrysander leaned forward and kissed her forehead. "I'll do some digging and let you know what I come up with."

Bella slipped out through the glass doors. "I'm afraid

we've held him off for as long as possible. I hope you're done, because Theron and Piers are convinced we're plotting some evil."

Chrysander chuckled. "Bella, I have no doubt that where you're concerned, it's absolutely true. I haven't forgotten that you dragged my wife into a tattoo parlor not so many months ago."

Jewel burst out laughing. "A tattoo parlor? You have to tell me about this, Bella. Did Chrysander have a heart attack?"

"He might have bellowed a bit loudly just before he dragged us out," Bella said with an innocent grin.

Jewel wrapped an arm around Bella in a show of loyalty.

"Just what we needed around here. Another woman to cause trouble," Chrysander said with a mock groan.

The door opened, and this time Marley came out with Theron and Piers on her heels. Both men wore expressions of suspicion as they surveyed Chrysander laughing with Bella and Jewel.

"Whatever he's said, don't believe a word," Theron said as he dragged Bella back against his side.

"Why do I gain the impression that my family is plotting against me?" Piers murmured as he went to stand at Jewel's side.

She wrapped her arms around him, hugging him close. Then she leaned up to brush her lips across his jaw. "You're being paranoid. Chrysander was just divulging all your family secrets."

Both Theron and Piers donned expressions of horror. Chrysander held up his hands. "Don't worry. I've told them nothing you'll be sorry for later."

"You mean there is dirt they'd be sorry for?" Bella asked. "Do tell. Theron always acts as if I'm the trouble-maker in the family."

Jewel relaxed against Piers and enjoyed the laughing and teasing that went on between the others. She already liked Bella and Marley so much, and she was beginning to lose her uneasiness around Theron and Chrysander. To their credit, both men had seemingly accepted her presence in Piers's life.

Piers's hand went to her belly as it often did, rubbing lightly over the swell. She wasn't even sure he realized what he was doing, but it made her heart ache with love for him.

She was beginning to realize that for all his coldness and aloofness that he was a man of great passion. When he loved, he did so with everything he had. How fortunate both her and her child would be to have his love and devotion. She would never have to worry about being alone or of being accepted again.

"Are you ready for dinner, *yineka mou?*" he murmured close to her ear. "I have it on good authority that the chef has prepared all your favorites tonight."

"Hmmm, I think I could get used to being so spoiled," she said with a sigh.

"You're easily satisfied," he teased.

"I just want you," she said seriously.

Fire blazed in his eyes, and his grip tightened around her midsection.

"Don't tempt me so or I'll forget we have guests and take you upstairs to bed."

"And this would be bad why? Your brothers all have wives. Surely they'd understand."

He laughed and kissed her on the nose. "You're bad for my control, *yineka mou.* Come, let's go eat. I'll carry you up to bed later."

Seventeen

"Mrs. Anetakis, there is a call for you."

Jewel looked up to see the maid holding the cordless phone out to her. She took it and smiled her thanks at the younger woman. After she'd retreated, Jewel put the phone to her ear.

"Hello?"

"Jewel, this is Chrysander. I have some information for you about Eric. I'm glad you asked me to look into this. The news is not good."

Jewel frowned and got up from her seat at the breakfast table on the terrace. She ducked back inside so she could better hear over the distant roar of the ocean.

"What's wrong?"

"I found him. He's in foster care. He was made a ward of the state of Florida two years ago. He's been through six homes in that time."

"Oh no. No, no, no," she whispered. Her fingers curled tightly around the phone as she battled tears. This would destroy Piers.

"Jewel, are you all right?"

She swallowed the knot in her throat. Memories that she'd spent her life suppressing boiled to the surface.

"I'm okay," she said shakily. "Thank you for doing this, Chrysander. I'd appreciate it if you could e-mail me all the information you have. I want to thoroughly investigate this before I tell Piers."

"I understand. I'll send it over as soon as we get off the phone. And Jewel, if you need any further help from me, let me know."

"Thanks, Chrysander. How is Marley doing?"

Chrysander sighed. "It's been difficult for her. She's already ill with the pregnancy, and the stress of having to identify the kidnappers and give more statements is getting to her."

"I'm sorry," she offered softly. "Will you be much longer in New York? Will she have to remain there for the trial?"

"Not if I can help it," he said fiercely. "The District Attorney has offered a plea bargain. If they accept it, then they'll forego a trial, and Marley will be finished with this nightmare."

"Give her my love, please."

"I will. Let me know if there is anything else I can do."

"I will, Chrysander."

She hung up the phone and then went to find her laptop. A few minutes later, she received Chrysander's e-mail. She frowned as she read through the details. A few phone calls would have to be made, but she couldn't wait to tell Piers what she'd discovered. There was no need for

Eric to be in foster care when he had a family all too willing to take him in.

Piers sank into his chair behind his desk and looked ruefully at the piles of mail in front of him. Never before had he been so lax when it came to work matters. He had Jewel to thank for his inattention lately.

His e-mails were in the hundreds, his voice mail had reached capacity, and he hadn't opened mail in several days. His brothers would give him hell, but they'd also be happy to know that work wasn't his life any longer.

With a sigh, he powered up his computer so he could sift through the backlog of e-mails. Then he reached for his phone and turned on the speaker so he could weed through voice mails. Most were routine reports from various construction projects. A few minor emergencies from panicked hotel managers, and one offer to buy the new hotel in Rio de Janeiro. That one made him smile. There weren't many corporations that could afford one of the Anetakis's hotels. They spared no expense.

As soon as the voice mails were squared away, he dialed Chrysander's number. He wanted to check in on Marley and find out the results of their trip to New York to identify her kidnappers.

When he received no answer, he called Theron instead. They spent several minutes talking about business. Theron brought him up to speed on Chrysander and Marley and then conversation drifted back to business.

As he chatted, he idly sorted through the envelopes piled on his desk. When he got to one addressed to him from the laboratory that had performed the paternity test, he froze.

"I'll speak to you later, Theron. Give Bella my love."

He hung up and stared at the envelope in front of him. A smile eased his face as he fingered the seal. Here would be the proof of his paternity. In black and white, irrefutable proof that he was a father.

Last time it had gone the other way, and he'd lost everything that mattered most to him. This time…this time it would be perfect. He had a daughter on the way. His child.

Mine.

The surge of possessiveness that rocketed through his body took him by surprise.

He tossed the envelope aside. There was no need to open it. He knew what it would say. His trust in Jewel also surprised him, but he realized he did indeed have faith in her. He trusted her not to betray him.

After sorting through a few more envelopes he glanced back over at the letter. He should open it and revel in the feeling. Then he could go find Jewel and make mad, passionate love to her.

The idea made him tighten with need.

He felt like celebrating. Maybe he'd take Jewel on a trip to Paris. She loved to travel, and her doctor had pronounced her fully recovered from her surgery. To be on the safe side, he could schedule a check-up and a sonogram. Then they could take the private jet. They could make love in Paris and then maybe go on to Venice. Take the honeymoon they hadn't been able to take when they'd gotten married.

He picked up the envelope again, smiling as he turned it over. He only hesitated a moment before tearing it open and unfolding the letter within.

He scanned the contents, the perfunctory remarks thanking him for his business, and finally he got to the bottom where the results were posted.

And he froze.

He read it again, sure that he'd missed something. But no, there it was in black and white.

He wasn't the father.

Icy rage flooded his veins, burning, billowing until he thought he would explode. Again. It had happened again, only this time it was different. So very different.

What had she hoped to accomplish? Would she, like Joanna, wait for him to form an attachment to the child before leaving? Use the child as a bargaining tool?

Was Kirk the father or was he yet another man she dangled from her fingertips like a windup toy?

Older and wiser? He wanted to puke at his stupidity. In his arrogance, he'd imagined that he'd never be deceived as he'd been in the past, but what had he done to prevent it?

He looked down at the offending document again. His hands were shaking too much to keep it still. Damn her. Damn her to hell.

She'd wormed her way into his life, into his family's lives. His sisters-in-law loved her, and his brothers had accepted her. Because of him. Because he'd brought her into their unsuspecting midst.

Never had he felt so sick. He wished he'd never opened the damn thing.

What a fool he'd been. What a fool he'd always be. All this time wasted on building a relationship that was based on lies and treachery. He'd bought the house of her dreams, done everything in his power to make her happy.

And worse, he'd bought into the fantasy as well. He'd begun to believe that they could be a family. That he'd been gifted another chance at a wife and child. That he'd finally been given hope.

He stared bleakly at the paper in his hand. The worst part was he had to have played right into her hands by offering her a settlement regardless of her child's paternity. She won either way. And him? He'd lost everything.

Jewel clutched the printouts to her chest and hurried to Piers's office. She knew it would hurt him to find out Eric's fate and that Joanna had abandoned him two years ago, but the most important thing was getting Eric out of his current situation.

Nausea rose in her throat at the thought of the young boy in so many foster homes. Had he harbored the same hopes she had when she was a little girl, only to be disappointed over and over?

She didn't knock but burst through the door, breathless from her pace. She stopped abruptly when she saw Piers sitting at his desk, a document crumpled in his hand, his expression so horrible that she nearly forgot why she'd come.

"Piers?"

He turned his cold gaze to her, and she shivered as a chill washed up her spine.

She took a step forward. "Is everything all right?"

He rose slowly with calculated precision. "Tell me, Jewel. How did you think you would get away with it? Or did you just want to prolong the truth until you had me completely wrapped around your finger?"

Her heart sank. How had he found out about Eric? Why was he so angry?

"I was on my way to tell you now. I thought you'd want to know."

He laughed but the sound was anything but joyous. It skittered abrasively over her skin, and she shrank away from his obvious anger. Rage. That was the word for it. He vibrated with it.

"Oh yes, Jewel. I wanted to know. Preferably when this whole charade began. Did you enjoy hearing me spill my guts about Joanna and the deception she perpetrated? Did it give you satisfaction to know that yours was even more sound?"

She shook her head in confusion. What was he talking about?

"I don't understand. Why are you so angry? And at me? I didn't do this, Piers."

He gaped incredulously at her. "You didn't lie to me? You didn't try to foist another man's child off on me? You amaze me, Jewel. How you manage to sound the victim. The only victim here is me and the poor child you're pregnant with."

Hurt crashed over her, making her fold inward in a familiar defense mechanism she'd perfected over the years.

"You hate me," she whispered.

"Are you suggesting that I could love someone like you?" he sneered.

He thrust the paper forward. "Here is the truth, Jewel. The truth you never saw fit to give me. The truth I deserved."

She took the paper with a shaking hand, tears obscuring her vision. It took her three times to make sense of the words and when she realized what it said, she went surprisingly numb.

"This is wrong," she said in a low voice.

Piers snorted. "You'd still keep up the pretense? It's over, Jewel. These tests don't lie. It states with absolute certainty that there is no chance I could be the father of your child."

She stared up at him, tears trickling down her cheeks. He was cold. So cold. Hard. And unforgiving.

"You've waited for me to fall," she choked out. "You've been waiting for this since the day I called you. It's the only outcome that was acceptable to you. You weren't going to be satisfied until you proved I was no better than Joanna."

"You have quite a flair for dramatics."

She scrubbed angrily at her tears, furious that she'd allowed him to make her cry. "The results are wrong, Piers. This is your child. *She* is your child."

Something flickered in his eyes at her vehemence, but then he blinked, and it was gone, replaced with ice.

There would be no convincing him. He'd already tried and convicted her. She had some pride. She wouldn't beg. She wouldn't humiliate herself. She'd never allow him to know how shattered she was by his rejection. Or how much she loved him.

She lifted her chin and forced herself to stare evenly at him, steeling herself until she could no longer feel the shards of pain that pelted her.

"Someday you'll regret this," she said quietly. "One day you'll wake up and realize that you threw away something precious. I hope, for your sake, you don't take too long and that one day you can find the happiness you're so determined to deny yourself and others around you."

She turned stiffly, her heart breaking under the weight of her pain. She gripped the papers she'd intended to show Piers and held them close to her chest as she walked away. He made no effort to stop her, and she knew he wouldn't. He'd stay here, holed up in his refuge until she'd gone.

Methodically she took the stairs to the master bedroom. She got out a suitcase and began putting her clothing inside.

"Mrs. Anetakis, is there something you need?"

Jewel turned to see the maid standing in the doorway wearing a perplexed look.

"Could you arrange for a car to take me into town?" Jewel asked. "I'll be ready in fifteen minutes."

"Of course."

Jewel turned back to her packing, willing herself not to break down into more tears. She would survive this. She had survived worse.

When she had packed everything she thought she'd need, she smoothed out the papers that had all the information about Eric. No matter that she and Piers were no longer together, she couldn't allow that child to remain in the system, unwanted and tossed from family to family.

She closed her eyes and sighed. This would be so much easier with the money and power of the Anetakis name. Slowly she opened her eyes again and frowned. She may not have the money but she did have the name. Yes, Piers had provided a settlement for her in the case of a divorce, but who knows how long it would take to lay hands on it. She needed money now. Eric couldn't wait.

She went to her dresser and pulled out the diamond necklace and earrings Piers had given her on her wedding day. With one fingertip, she stroked the brilliant stones, remembering the way he'd fastened the necklace at her nape.

Between her engagement ring and the necklace and earrings, she should be able to raise enough cash to rent a place in Miami. But she'd need enough money to remain solvent until she would collect her settlement from Piers.

"Mrs. Anetakis, the car is ready for you."

Jewel closed her suitcase and smiled her thanks. She looked one more time around the room she'd shared with Piers and then walked down the stairs behind the maid.

When she was settled into the car, she directed the

driver to take her to the airstrip. She didn't have time to call for Piers's jet, though she didn't have any qualms about using it. She had no desire to be stuck here in this place for any longer than necessary. She'd take the first flight off the island, and go to New York to see Bella and Marley and pray that they'd help her save Eric.

Eighteen

"Jewel, what on earth are you doing here?" Bella asked as she all but dragged Jewel inside the doorway. "Does Piers know you're here? Did he come with you?"

Jewel swallowed the knot in her throat. Damn if she was going to get all weepy again.

Marley appeared behind Bella, her face soft with sympathy.

"What happened?" Marley asked.

Despite her resolve, Jewel burst into tears. Bella and Marley flanked her, each wrapping an arm around her as they guided her into Bella's living room.

"Are Chrysander and Theron here?" she managed to ask around her sobs.

"No, and they won't be back for a while," Bella said soothingly. "Now sit down before you fall over. You look dead on your feet."

Jewel perched on the edge of the couch while the other women took a seat on either side of her.

"What has that idiot brother-in-law of mine done?" Marley asked grimly.

Jewel tried to smile through her tears at Marley's show of loyalty. "I'm afraid he'd say it was what I'd done to him."

Bella snorted. "With that man, I'd hardly believe that. Besides, it's easy to see that you're crazy in love with him."

Jewel buried her face in her hands. "That's just it. He believes the absolute worst of me."

Marley put a hand on her shoulder and squeezed. "Tell us what happened."

With little reluctance, Jewel spilled the entire sorry tale from start to finish, including the part about Joanna and Eric and the paternity results.

"What an idiot," Bella said scornfully. "Did he even call the laboratory to double-check the results? Did he question them at all? Clearly there was some mix-up at the lab."

Jewel gave her a watery smile. "Thank you for believing in me. But the thing is, he got what he was waiting for. He's been waiting since the start for me to fall off the pedestal, so to speak. He hasn't been able to believe in a woman since Joanna."

"So what are you going to do?" Marley asked. "You're in love with him."

"But he doesn't love me. Moreover, he doesn't want to love me. I can't live with someone who distrusts me as much as he distrusts me."

"What about Eric?" Bella questioned. "Surely you won't leave him in his current situation."

"No," Jewel said fiercely. "And that's why I've come. I need your help."

Marley put her hand on Jewel's. "Anything."

"I pawned the jewelry that Piers gave me. It's enough to rent a small place in Miami so I can set up a permanent residence. But I'll need enough money socked away that the state will see me as a stable, financially able parent for Eric. I won't get a settlement from Piers until the divorce, and I have no idea how long that will take."

Bella grinned. "The lovely thing about having my own money, is that I don't need to rely on the Anetakis billions. No offense, Marley."

"None taken," Marley said dryly.

"I have some cash on hand that I can give you, and I'll wire you more funds so that you can rent something a little better than a 'small place' in Miami. If small is good, then bigger is better, right?"

Jewel squeezed both women's hands. "Thank you so much. I was so worried that you'd hate me, that you'd believe that I'd deceived Piers."

Marley sighed. "I have a feeling that Piers is going to wake up one day and realize he's made the worst mistake of his life. I almost wish I was there to see it."

"Don't feel so bad, Jewel," Bella said soothingly. "I'm afraid all of the Anetakis men are rather dense when it comes to love."

"So true," Marley agreed.

"You'll keep us posted on how things go with Eric? I'd love to meet him," Bella said.

"Of course I will."

"Do you have travel arrangements for your trip to Miami?" Marley asked.

Jewel shook her head. "Not yet. I've barely had time to breathe. I came straight here from the island."

Bella stood, her expression one of take charge. "First things first. We're going to go have a nice girly lunch followed by an afternoon of complete pampering at the spa. God knows you pregnant women need it. Then we're going to arrange for a private jet to fly Jewel to Miami, and I'll have a driver waiting there to pick her up and take her wherever she needs to go. Piers may be a dumb ass, but you're still family."

Jewel burst into tears again, and Bella groaned.

"Is it any wonder I have no desire to procreate? Pregnancy turns women into hormonal messes."

Marley dabbed quickly at her eyes, and Jewel burst out laughing. Marley joined her, giggling through her tears and finally Bella joined them as well.

"Okay, enough sniffling. Let's get out of here before the men return. I'll leave them a note telling them I've taken Marley off for an afternoon of debauchery. They won't be the least bit surprised," Bella said with a grin.

"Promise me you'll both visit me in Miami," Jewel said fiercely. "I'll miss you both terribly. I've always wanted a family—sisters—and I couldn't ask for better sisters than you two."

"Oh, I'll visit," Marley promised. "I'll blame it all on Bella. It's my standard excuse and keeps me out of trouble with Chrysander. Theron loves her so much that he's frighteningly indulgent with her."

"You're both very lucky," Jewel said wistfully.

Marley gave her a stricken look. "I'm so sorry, Jewel. That was incredibly thoughtless of me."

"Blame it on the pregnancy," Bella said. "Surely having a parasite inside you sucking all your brain cells has to negatively impact you sooner or later."

Marley and Jewel both cracked up.

"You're so delightfully irreverent," Jewel teased. "It's no wonder Theron loves you so."

"Come on, let's go, let's go. My man radar tells me the menfolk will be home soon. The more distance we put between here and where we're going, the less likely they'll be able to track us down."

They linked arms and headed out the door only to be stopped by Reynolds, Theron's head of security.

Bella sighed and cast a baleful look in the man's direction. "Can we count on you for a little discretion or will you break your neck reporting to Theron?"

Reynolds cleared his throat. "That will depend on where you think you're going."

Marley pressed forward. "What we have here, sir, is a damsel in distress. A very pregnant damsel in distress. She is in sore need of a day at the spa. You know, where we do all those frightening girly things that scare the devil out of men."

Reynolds swallowed and paled slightly. "Well as long as it's that and not a more inappropriate place."

Bella glared at him as she walked by him to the car. "You're never going to let me live down that strip club are you?"

"Strip club?" Jewel asked. "This I've got to hear."

"And I'll tell you all about it once we're wrapped in mud from head to toe," Bella said as they got into the car.

Bella leaned forward as Reynolds got into the front seat. "There's one more thing, Reynolds. This is top secret stuff. You didn't see Jewel, don't know who she is, never saw her in your life, *capiche?*"

Reynolds nodded solemnly. "Who?"

Bella smiled in satisfaction and leaned back in the seat once more.

"He's really an okay guy when he doesn't have a corncob wedged up his arse."

"I heard that," Reynolds commented.

Bella grinned and winked at the other two women.

"Okay girls, a day at the spa it is. Then we'll get Jewel to the airport and on her way to Miami."

Piers stared broodingly into the surf, hands shoved into the pockets of his trousers—pants that he hadn't changed out of in three days. He looked and felt like he'd been on a monthlong bender. He hadn't showered or shaved. The staff avoided him like the plague, and when he did come into contact with them, they all glared at him with disapproving eyes. As if he'd been the one to drive her away.

And he had, in a way. He hadn't made it easy for her to stay. No, he hadn't asked her to leave in so many words, but what woman would stay with a man who'd been so cruel, so derisive?

He closed his eyes and inhaled the sea air that Jewel so loved. She loved the ocean like he loved her. Passionately.

Love was supposed to be without barriers or conditions. He'd never offered that to Jewel. He hadn't even offered his unconditional support. No, he'd demanded and she'd given. He'd taken and she'd offered.

What a bastard he was.

How was she supposed to have ever been able to tell him the truth when he made it impossible for her to do so? He'd all but told her that he'd toss her out without thought if he found out she'd lied.

And the truth was he didn't care.

He'd realized it the moment he'd found her gone. He didn't care if the baby was his biological child or not. Jewel was married to him, which meant both belonged to him. He would be the baby's father because it was what Jewel wanted. It was what *he* wanted.

He hadn't loved Eric any less even knowing that he wasn't his biological child. He already loved his daughter, and nothing would change that. He'd ruined his chance at having a family. A wife and a daughter. All because he'd been so sure Jewel was another Joanna.

Jewel was right. He'd been waiting for her to fail, for her to give him the ammunition he needed to destroy her because it beat him being destroyed a second time. She was right about another thing, and it hadn't taken him long to realize it. He'd destroyed something very precious.

"I love you, *yineka mou*," he whispered. "I don't deserve your love, but I can give you mine. I can try to make up for the many wrongs I have done to you. Please forgive me."

Just saying the words he'd vowed never to give another woman freed something buried deep in his soul. He breathed deeply, as past hurts fell away, carried on the wind further out to sea. He'd allowed himself to be ruled by bitterness and anger for too long. It was time to let go and embrace his future with Jewel.

He turned and strode back to the stone steps leading up to the house. He began barking orders as soon as he stepped inside. At first he was met by cold resistance, until the staff figured out what it was he was doing. Then there was a flurry of activity as everyone stumbled over themselves to provide him what information they could.

"I called a car for her to drive her into town," one of the maids offered.

When the driver was summoned, he said he'd driven her to the small airport and carried her single bag inside.

Frustrated, Piers took the car to the airport to question the ticket agent, but not even the Anetakis name was able to yield him any results. No one would tell him what if any flight Jewel took—or to where.

Kirk.

The name shot back through his memory. Of course. She had often gone back to Kirk's apartment when she needed a place to stay. Surely that's where she would go. She seemed to trust this fellow, and there was genuine affection and concern between them.

He looked down in disgust. He couldn't go anywhere looking as he did right now. He'd likely be arrested for vagrancy.

On his way back to the house, he phoned his pilot and instructed him to be fueled and ready to depart within the hour.

He was going to find Jewel and bring her and their child back where they belonged. Home.

Nineteen

Piers stood outside the San Francisco apartment and knocked. A few moments later, the door opened, but it wasn't Jewel who stared back at him. It was Kirk.

"Is Jewel here?" Piers asked stiffly.

Kirk's eyes narrowed. "Why would she be here? Why isn't she with you?"

Piers closed his eyes. "I had hoped she'd come here. Do you have any idea where else she might go?" It galled him to ask for this man's help, but to find Jewel, he'd do anything.

"You better come in and tell me what the hell is going on," Kirk said.

Piers followed him inside and the two sat down in the living room.

"Spill it," Kirk said.

"I said some terrible things to her," Piers admitted. "I wasn't thinking straight. I was angry and I lashed out."

"About?"

Knowing he needed this man's help, Piers poured out the entire story from start to finish. Maybe if he seemed remorseful enough, Kirk wouldn't think he was a total bastard and give him any information he had on Jewel.

"You are a first-class jerk, aren't you? Jewel wouldn't lie about something like that. Did she ever tell you about her childhood? I'm guessing not or you wouldn't have shoveled that horse manure at her."

"What are you talking about?"

Kirk made a sound of disgust. "From the time her parents died when she was barely older than a toddler, she was shuttled from one foster family to another. The first few were merely temporaries as the state tried to place her in a more permanent environment. The first was a real gem of a family. The oldest son tried to abuse her. She told her case-worker, who thankfully believed her. So she was placed in another home, this time with another foster child, a girl about her age. What Jewel didn't know was that the family never had any intention of taking both girls. They took two so they could choose. And it wasn't Jewel they chose. So she lost a family she'd grown to trust and a sister she loved."

"*Theos,*" Piers said through tight lips.

"Things started looking up when a couple who couldn't have children decided they wanted to adopt Jewel. She went to live with them. The adoption was nearly final when the mother discovered she was pregnant. After years of infertility, she'd stopped trying and now she was suddenly pregnant. They couldn't afford more than one child, and you can imagine which one they chose. Once again, Jewel was rejected."

Piers closed his eyes. Just as he'd rejected her and her baby.

"After that, she didn't believe in happy endings any longer. You might say she grew up fast. She went through the motions of the system until she was old enough to be out on her own. Since then she's moved around constantly, never settling in one place, never forging ties with people. Never having a home. She simply doesn't believe she deserves one."

Kirk stared hard at Piers. "You've taken the one thing from her guaranteed to hurt her the most. *If* you find her, don't expect her to welcome you back with open arms."

Piers stared back at the other man, his stomach churning. "If she contacts you will you let me know immediately? She's pregnant and alone. I need to find her so I can make this right."

Kirk studied him for a long moment before finally nodding. Piers handed him his card.

"Call me day or night. It doesn't matter."

Kirk nodded and Piers rose to leave.

"Where will you go now?" Kirk asked when he saw Piers to the door.

"To New York to see my brothers. Something I should have done already," Piers said grimly.

Piers knocked on his brother's door and waited with dread for it to open. He didn't like facing his brothers with his mistakes, and he liked asking for their help even less, but if it would get Jewel back, he'd do anything.

"Piers? What the devil are you doing here? Why didn't you call to let us know you were coming? And where's Jewel?"

Piers looked up, wincing at the barrage of questions coming from Theron.

"Can I come in?"

Theron stepped to the side. "Of course. We were just about to sit down for dinner. I have to say, you look awful."

"Thanks," Piers said dryly.

They walked into the formal dining room, and Chrysander, Marley and Bella all looked up. Only Chrysander seemed surprised. The two women were more subdued.

Chrysander's sharp gaze found him. "What's happened?" he asked bluntly.

"Jewel left me," he said bleakly.

Theron and Chrysander both began talking at once while the women merely exchanged glances and remained silent.

"That doesn't make sense," Chrysander said. "Not after she spent all that time—"

Marley cut him off with a sharp elbow to his gut. Then she frowned at him and shook her head. Chrysander gave her a curious look but remained silent.

Bella stood, her hands on her hips. "Why did she leave you, Piers?"

Her voice was deceptively soft. It reminded Piers of the reason men feared women so much to begin with.

"Bella, perhaps Piers would prefer not to tell us such private things," Theron suggested.

Marley raised an eyebrow. "He's here isn't he? He obviously wants our help. We deserve to know if he deserves it or not."

Piers winced. "If you want to know the truth, no, I don't deserve your help, but I'm asking for it anyway."

"Why?" Bella demanded.

Piers looked at both women. "Because I love her, and I made a terrible mistake."

"So you called the stupid lab and they figured out it was all a mistake then?" Marley said furiously.

Chrysander and Theron turned to Marley and Bella.

Marley flushed and cast an apologetic look at Bella, who merely shrugged.

"I haven't called the lab. I don't care about the bloody results. I love her and our child. I don't give a rat's ass who the biological father is. She's my daughter, and I don't plan to give her or Jewel up."

"Why do I get the impression that we're the only two without the faintest clue what the devil is going on?" Theron said to Chrysander.

"No, but I bet our lovely wives could fill us in," Chrysander said as he rounded on Bella and Marley.

Both women crossed their arms over their chests and pressed their lips together.

Frustration beat at Piers's temples. He walked past his brothers to stand in front of Marley and Bella.

"Please, if you know where she is, tell me. I have to make this right with her. I love her."

Marley sighed and glanced over at Bella.

"I might have helped her get a place in Miami," Bella hedged.

Chrysander's eyebrows went up. "But isn't that where…"

Marley shot him another furious glance.

"Where in Miami?" Piers said, ignoring the exchange between Marley and Chrysander.

"If you go down there and upset her again, I'll personally sic every member of Theron's security team on you," Bella threatened.

"Just tell me, Bella. Please. I need to see her again. I need to make sure she and the baby are all right."

"When I spoke to her yesterday, they were just fine," Marley said casually.

"It would appear that you and Bella have been very busy women," Chrysander said darkly.

Marley sniffed. "If things were left to you men, the world would be a disaster."

"I think we've been insulted," Theron said dryly.

Bella thrust the piece of paper she'd been writing on toward Piers. "Here's her address. She trusted me, Piers. Don't screw this up."

Piers hugged her quickly and kissed her on the cheek. "Thank you. I'll bring her back for a visit as soon as I can."

Jewel smoothed her hand over Eric's hair as he slept and smiled at how peaceful and innocent he looked. Tucking his blanket around him, she turned to tiptoe from his bedroom.

Once in the kitchen, she prepared a cup of decaf tea and sipped the soothing, warm brew.

Her arrival in Miami couldn't have come at a better time. Eric had been taken from his previous home and was awaiting placement along with several hundred other children. It had taken several days to complete the paperwork, have the home study and background checks, but Eric was finally hers.

At first he'd been silent and restrained. No doubt he thought his placement with her was as temporary as all his other ones. She didn't try to persuade him any differently. It would take time to win his trust.

The important thing was that he had a home now. Thanks to Bella's generosity, they both had a home.

After checking on Eric one last time, she went into the living room and settled into her favorite chair. Nights were difficult, when all was silent. She missed Piers and the easy companionship they'd developed.

She had nearly dozed off in her chair when the doorbell rang. She got up quickly so it wouldn't disturb Eric and went to look out the peephole. No one knew her here, and she was wary of anyone knocking on her door. Surely Social Services wouldn't pay a surprise visit at this time of night.

What she saw shocked her to the core.

Piers. Outside her door, looking worried and a little haggard.

With fumbling fingers, she unlocked the deadbolt and opened the door a crack.

"Jewel, thank God," he said. "Please, can I come in?"

Her grip tightened on the door as she stared through the crack. Anger, pain—so much pain—surged through her veins. What could he possibly have to say to her that hadn't already been said?

She steeled herself, opened the door just enough that she could see him and he could see her.

"I won't ask how you found me. It isn't important."

He started to interrupt, holding up one hand in a plea, but she shook her head.

"No, you've said enough. I let you say all those things, and I took it, but I don't have to now. This is my home. You have no rights here. I want you to leave."

Something that looked suspiciously like panic spasmed in his eyes.

"Jewel, I know I don't deserve even a moment of your time. I said and did unforgivable things. I wouldn't blame you if you never spoke to me again. But *please,* I'm begging you. Let me in. Let me explain. Let me make things right between us."

The sheer desperation in his voice unsettled her. She wavered on the brink of indecision, her anger warring with the desire to relent and let him through the door. He stared at her with tortured eyes and slowly, she stepped back and opened the door wider.

He was inside in an instant. He gathered her in his arms and buried his face in her hair.

"I'm sorry. I'm so sorry, *yineka mou.*"

He kissed her temple, then her cheek and then clumsily found her lips. He kissed her with such emotion that it staggered her.

"Please forgive me," he whispered. "I love you. I want you and our baby to come home."

She pulled away, holding onto his arms for support. "You believe she's yours?" She couldn't keep the bitterness or suspicion from her voice.

"I don't care who the biological father is. She's mine. Just as you are mine. We're a family. I'll be a good father, I swear it. I love her already, and I want us to be a family, Jewel. Please say you'll give me another chance. I'll never give you any reason to leave me again."

He gathered her hands in his, holding them so tightly that she was sure her fingers were bloodless.

"I love you, Jewel. I was wrong. So wrong. I don't deserve another chance, but I'm asking—no *begging*—for one because there's nothing I want more than for you and our daughter to come home."

She stood there, mouth wide open, trying to process everything he flung at her. He loved her. He still didn't think he was the father. He didn't *care* if he wasn't the father. He wanted her and the baby back.

Her throat swelled, and her nose stung as tears gathered in her eyes. How difficult must this have been for him, to come all this way, thinking that the baby wasn't his, but wanting them anyway, accepting them anyway.

She should be angry, but the results had confirmed his worst fears, and yet it didn't matter.

He'd humbled himself in front of her, made himself as

vulnerable as a man could make himself. She had only to look at the sincerity burning like twin flames in his eyes to know that he spoke the truth.

He loved her.

"You love me?"

She needed to hear it again. Wanted it so desperately.

"I love you so much, *yineka mou*."

She shook her head. "What does that mean, anyway?"

"What does what mean?"

"Yineka mou."

He smiled. "It means my woman."

"But you called me that the first night we made love."

He nodded. "You were mine even then. I think I fell in love with you that very night."

Tears welled in her eyes, and she swallowed back the sob that clawed its way up her throat.

"Oh Piers. I love you so much."

She threw herself back into his arms, holding onto him as tightly as she could. He held her just as firmly, his hands stroking her hair. Then his palm slid down to cup her belly.

He trembled against her, his big body shaking with emotion. When he spoke, there was a betraying crack that told her how close he was to breaking.

"How is our child?"

She closed her eyes as tears slipped from the corners. Then she reached down to hold on to his wrist as she stepped away.

"She's yours, Piers. I swear it to you. I haven't slept with another man. Only you. Please tell me you believe me. I know what the tests said, but they were *wrong*."

He stared back at her, hope lighting his eyes. He swallowed and then swallowed again. "I believe you, *yineka mou*."

She closed her eyes and hugged him again, burying her face in his strong chest.

"I'm sorry for hurting you, Jewel. I won't do so again, you have my word."

"There is something I must tell you," she said quietly.

He stiffened against her and slowly drew away, his eyes flashing vulnerability.

"You should sit down."

"Just tell me. There is nothing we can't work out."

She smiled. "I hope you won't be angry at what I've done."

"We can fix it. Whatever it is. Together, *yineka mou.*"

She took his hands in hers as they sat on the couch. "I came to Miami to find Eric."

He went completely still. "Why?"

"I thought you needed closure. I thought if you could see him happy and well adjusted that you could carry that memory instead of the one where he screamed and cried as his mother took him away."

"And did you find him?"

There was anticipation in his voice that told her how eager he was to know of Eric's well-being.

"Yes, I found him," she said softly.

Her grip tightened around his hands.

"Joanna abandoned him two years ago."

"What?"

Anger exploded from him in a volatile wave. He bolted from the couch, his hands clenched into fists at his sides.

"Why didn't she bring him to me? She knew I loved him. She knew I'd take him in."

Jewel shook her head sadly. "I don't know, Piers. He was taken into foster care and has been there for the last two years."

"This must be rectified. I won't allow him to remain in foster care. Not like you were, *yineka mou*. I won't allow your pain to be his."

She stood beside him, touching his arm. "How did you know about me?"

Piers looked at her with such pain in his eyes. "Kirk told me when I went to San Francisco looking for you. *Theos, Jewel.* I am so shamed by the way I treated you."

"Piers, Eric is here," she said gently.

His mouth dropped open in shock. "Here?"

She nodded. "He's asleep in his bedroom. You see, I couldn't allow him to remain in foster care either. I knew how much he meant to you, and I know how painful my childhood was. I searched for Eric before we split up. It was why I came to your office that day. I was going to tell you that I'd found him and that he was in foster care. I thought we could both fly to Miami to get him."

He closed his eyes and let out a groan. "Instead, I drove you away, and you came here yourself to take care of him."

"He's here, and he very much needs a mother and a father."

"You would do this? You would take in a child that is not your own?" he asked.

"Isn't that what you plan to do? What you planned to do when you thought our daughter was not your own?"

He gathered her close in his arms, his body trembling against hers. "I love you, *yineka mou*. So much. Never leave me again. Not even if I deserve it."

She laughed lightly. "I won't. Next time, I'll stay and fight, which is what I should have done this time. You won't get rid of me so easily again."

"Good," he said gruffly. "Now let's go see our son."

Epilogue

"She's the most beautiful girl in the world," Piers said proudly as he held up six-week-old Mary Catherine for his brothers to admire.

"You can only say that because Marley is having another boy," Chrysander pointed out.

"Listen to them," Bella said in disgust. "Why is it that babies turn men's minds to mush?"

"I thought that was good sex," Marley said mischievously.

"Well, that too," Jewel said with a laugh.

Eric stood with the Anetakis men, looking absurdly proud of his little sister. Jewel's heart never failed to swell when she saw the love between father and son.

Eric's adoption had become final just two weeks before Mary Catherine had been born. A week later, Piers had received a frantic phone call from the laboratory that had performed the paternity test. They had, indeed, made a mistake and mixed up his results with someone else's. Piers had been horrified all over again over the fact that he'd blasted Jewel, but she reminded him that he'd taken her word on faith long before he knew the results were in fact in error. That was enough for her.

Bella had been quick to point out that all they'd needed to do was wait for Mary Catherine to be born because no one in their right mind would ever deny that she was an Anetakis through and through.

She was dark haired and dark eyed, and blessed with the olive complexion of her father. She was for all practical purposes a miniature Piers.

Jewel looked around at her family, all gathered at her home on the cliff overlooking the sea. There was so much happiness here. It was hard to believe at times that it was all hers. That she had a family. That she belonged. She and Piers had both been drifters for so long, but somehow they'd found their way to one another and had at long last found what mattered the most. A home.

"I'd like to propose a toast," Chrysander said as he raised his glass. "To the Anetakis wives. I've no doubt they'll keep us on our toes well into our old age, and I plan to enjoy every minute of it."

"Here, here," Theron said as he raised his own.

Piers turned to smile at Jewel, and she rose to stand by his side as they both looked down at the bundle in his arms. She put out her arm, and Eric snuggled against her side.

"I'd also like to propose a toast," Jewel said. "To Bella. May she give Theron a house full of girls all as beautiful and as sassy as she is."

"Bite your tongue," Bella said, but her eyes twinkled merrily.

Theron put his arm around his wife. "God help me if that is true. One Bella is all this world needs."

"I'd like to propose a toast to love and friendship," Marley said. She pulled Jewel and Bella away from their husbands and linked her arms around them both.

Jewel and Bella squeezed back.

"To love and friendship," they both echoed.

* * * * *

MILLS & BOON®

Want to get more from Mills & Boon?

Here's what's available to you if you join the exclusive **Mills & Boon eBook Club** today:

✦ *Convenience – choose your books each month*
✦ *Exclusive – receive your books a month before anywhere else*
✦ *Flexibility – change your subscription at any time*
✦ *Variety – gain access to eBook-only series*
✦ *Value – subscriptions from just £1.99 a month*

So visit **www.millsandboon.co.uk/esubs** today to be a part of this exclusive eBook Club!

MILLS & BOON®
By Request

RELIVE THE ROMANCE WITH THE BEST OF THE BEST

A sneak peek at next month's titles...

In stores from 20th March 2015:

- **One Wild Night** – Kimberly Lang, Natalie Anderson and Heidi Rice

- **Claimed by the Millionaire** – Katherine Garbera, Michelle Celmer and Metsy Hingle

In stores from 3rd April 2015:

- **His Temporary Cinderella** – Jessica Hart, Cara Colter and Christine Rimmer

- **His Secret Baby** – Marie Ferrarella, Carla Cassidy and Cindy Dees

---